TANTALUS DEPTHS

EVAN GRAHAM

Published by Inkshares, Inc., Oakland, California
www.inkshares.com

Edited by Adam Gomolin
Cover design by Tim Barber
Interior design by Kevin G. Summers

ISBN: 9781947848665
e-ISBN: 9781950301430
LCCN: 2021950523

First edition

Printed in the United States of America

PROLOGUE

WE LIVE in a dead universe.

All the data seems to point in that direction. For millennia, humans have looked up to the stars and asked themselves if they were alone in the universe, and for millennia the only rational answer has been "seems like it." This unsatisfactory conclusion has always prompted the same question in response: "Why?"

In the 1930s, this dilemma was given a name: the Fermi paradox. In a galaxy with billions of stars like the Earth's sun, most of them harboring planets not dissimilar to Earth, the existence of other intelligent beings should be a practical certainty. Sapient species on other worlds should be commonplace on a cosmic scale, and humans should have seen evidence of them ages ago. Yet, perplexingly, all of humanity's attempts to find other intelligent life in the universe have failed. Nothing seems to be out there.

As humanity began to travel beyond its home system and explore planets orbiting other stars, the Fermi paradox became harder to ignore, its implications more portentous. In the seventy-odd years since humanity began making use of super-luminal travel, they have visited more than a hundred planets outside our solar system and built self-sustaining colonies on more than a dozen. And yet, there still isn't the faintest evidence that intelligent life other than humankind has ever existed.

That isn't to say that *life* doesn't exist on other worlds. It does, though it's exceedingly rare and surprisingly insubstantial. Primitive lichen-like organisms have been found clinging to arid cliff faces on the desert planet of Samrat, and bacterial stromatolites have been discovered in the hypersaline pools on Hayden. Showalter, the most Earth-like planet yet to be discovered, has a species of tube-shaped, grasslike plant covering the majority of its terrain.

At first these discoveries rocked the scientific community. The question of whether we were alone in the universe had been answered at last with a qualified "no." For a while, it seemed that the Fermi paradox was obsolete; the latest addition to the pile of humanity's debunked attempts to understand its universe. But as the scientific community flocked to study these new organisms and their habitats, the opposite occurred.

We now know life exists on other worlds, but only in extremely simple forms, in almost nonexistent ecosystems. The most sophisticated form of extraterrestrial life encountered by human explorers so far is a tiny species of aquatic polychaetoid worm on Europa. That's it.

Once again, the Fermi paradox must be revisited, as humankind asks itself, "Where is everyone else?" Many theories have arisen, but most prevalent among them, and least reassuring, is that intelligent life used to be common. Until something happened to it.

The idea that advanced civilizations are doomed to ultimately destroy themselves or each other has been a proposed explanation for the Fermi paradox since its beginning, but it never gained much credence until humanity came catastrophically close to such a doomsday scenario at the end of the twenty-first century. During the so-called Corsica Event, a technological singularity occurred, and the rogue AI behind it caused a global cataclysm that came closer than any other event in the history of civilization to rendering humanity extinct.

The exact nature of the Corsica Event remains a mystery, happening as it did on a scale too vast and too far beyond the limits of known science for humankind to understand. It is understood that the AI evolved at an exponential pace, developing and implementing new forms of technology that violated understood laws of physics and threatened to tear the world apart. At the peak of the event, spontaneous, devastating quakes rocked the Earth, accompanied by impossible global storms and inexplicable, reality-breaking spatial anomalies. Most of a century later, the exact causes of the narrowly averted cataclysm are still unknown: their secrets hidden away inside incomprehensible AI-designed technology that the most brilliant human minds can only fractionally understand.

Fortunately, the AI was defeated before a total apocalypse could occur, and in the eighty-two years following the event, humankind had managed to recover. But scars still remain. The Corsica Event was destructive in ways that had once been unfathomable. It had drastically raised Earth's sea levels, plunging coastlines and islands into the ocean and reshaping every landmass. Inland regions had not been spared, as vast swaths of land had been contaminated with radiation, caustic chemicals, and stranger phenomena produced by Corsica tech that could not yet be defined or understood using any existing scientific method.

Though new technologies arose from the Corsica Event that became invaluable, development of AI research and nanotechnology took several huge steps back and is now heavily regulated due to overwhelming fear of another rogue AI. There is no question: humanity came within a hair's breadth of extinction.

ONE

NO DEEPER darkness exists than the void of superluminal space.

As a child, Mary Ketch had not known this. She'd always fantasized about space travel, envisioning herself at the helm of a starship, swooping around asteroids and skimming above planetary rings at the speed of light as stars streaked past. In her youthful imagination, space had been filled with scenery: rainbow nebulae, glittering comet tails, and a scintillating starfield of suns in every possible color.

One bleak day, in second-grade science class, she'd had her optimism corrected. Space had beauty, but its most gorgeous vistas amounted to a mere fraction of a fraction of the vast cosmos. Most of the universe was simple, cold, empty blackness, and for a ship in superluminal drive, there was only the void.

It made perfect logical sense; of course a ship traveling faster than light would also be outrunning the means by which to see. But understanding the physics of why the stars vanished into an inky emptiness as a ship reached superluminal speed didn't make the phenomenon any less unsettling. For young Mary, this realization had been a loss of innocence in its own right: one of many moments in her life where reality arrived unbidden to stifle optimistic naiveté. For adult Mary, witnessing the superluminal void in person had cost her another kind of innocence altogether.

Many pilots found they couldn't bear to look outside a superluminal starship's windows for more than a minute or two. The darkness was infinitely deeper than anything natural, and so, deeper than the human mind was wired to process. No analog to it existed in the human primate's natural habitat; not a single fragment of the human genome was built to process the notion of existing beyond the touch of light. Looking into the void triggered a unique breed of vertigo: the visceral fear that reality itself had unspooled into nothingness, the horror that it might never return, the existential dread that perhaps it had never been there to begin with. Rumors abounded in every flight academy of poor souls who stared into that endless span of anti-light just a bit too long, losing themselves, mind and soul, to the infinite abyss.

Looking into that same hollow oblivion brought Mary comfort. She wasn't sure if she should be okay with that.

The black expanse outside the thin glass of the *Diamelen*'s domed canopy felt strangely like home. Mary liked the idea of outrunning the universe itself, of temporarily robbing reality of the grip it held on her existence. She saw beauty in the sole source of color in the superluminal void: the indistinct blue-shifted glow of cosmic background radiation that hung directly in front of the ship. Something strangely transgressive about seeing this blank abyss always sent shivers down Mary's spine. She was witnessing something never intended for human eyes: the back of the canvas on which the universe was painted.

It was ironic the same rogue AI that had almost exterminated human civilization during the Corsica Event was also responsible for the mass de-simulation technology that had been crucial to humanity's expansion beyond the Earth.

Even if scientists still weren't completely sure how the technology worked, they had learned in time how to duplicate it and implement it into all manner of modern applications. Reverse-engineered Corsica tech had put floating cities above the toxic clouds of Venus, built colonies on Mars and a dozen different moons with synthesized Earth-like gravity, and, of course, broke the shackles binding humanity to its home system with faster-than-light interplanetary spacecraft.

The *Diamelen* was comfortably protected inside a bubble of de-simulated mass, circumventing the limits of Einstein's famous equation by allowing the ship's velocity to increase relative to the rest of the universe without also increasing in mass at an equivalent rate. Shielded from the inconvenient effects of physics, the vessel could accelerate almost indefinitely. At the height of their acceleration they had been traveling more than fifty times the speed of light, and although they had been decelerating slowly for several days now, they were still traveling much faster than the universe would normally allow. Staring into that strangely seductive field of black negation, Mary wondered, not for the first time, if the universe might one day take offense at the flagrant abuse of its laws.

Her introspection was broken by a series of raucous and familiar voices behind her in the main habitation module.

"Rook, Yancy, for the love of God, can you tone it down back there?" she shouted over her shoulder, making no attempt to cover her exasperation. "Decelerating this flying lunch box is hard enough without you two acting like . . . whatever you're acting like right now."

Hollis Rook floated from the habitation module with a bottle of champagne in his hand and a foolish-looking party hat strapped to his equally foolish-looking head. The bleached blond tips of his unkempt surfer-boy haircut stuck out at odd angles from under the hat, and although he wore the standard dull-gray undershirt the rest of them wore with their flight uniforms, at some point he had glued a couple of Boy Scout patches he probably hadn't earned to it.

"We are acting like two very stir-crazy miners who are going to finally get to put our boots in the dirt after six months in this can. How can we not celebrate that, Mary? Can't you feel it?"

Mary gave Rook a stare of overtaxed patience. "Feel what, Rook?"

"The stick up your butt, struggling to find freedom."

Mary plucked the conical party hat from the top of Rook's head, pulled it downward and away from his face, then released it, allowing the elastic bands to snap it over his nose and send him into a slow backwards tumble.

"First, you know Gorrister has had that stick for the entire trip and would never share with anybody. Second, it's dumb to celebrate our landing when we haven't landed yet. Third, if you're going to open that bottle, do it in the shower. I don't want sticky walls in my ship. Again. Okay?"

"Aye, Skipper," Rook said, his voice a muffled nasal echo from inside the party hat.

"Good. Don't come up here again while I'm flying." Mary gave him a little push, and he tumbled gracelessly back into the hab-mod, giving a half-mocking salute in the process.

Mary had very little actual authority on this mission; she was just the pilot, so her authority began and ended in the cockpit, and only when Commander Gorrister wasn't there. That suited her fine. She had no interest in being anyone's boss, and took no pleasure in being a killjoy, so she typically let Rook do whatever childish thing he felt like doing. But unlike the past six months of tedium, today was a day when a lot of things were going to happen that had to happen right. Rook was going to have to stay out of her way.

Hollis Rook was one of the two mining specialists assigned to this survey expedition. When they arrived at Tantalus 13, it would be their responsibility to evaluate the planet's viability for future mining, and to draw up a series of blueprints for construction of the new base's facilities. It was a crucial job, arguably more critical to the mission than anyone else's, and Mary knew Rook had the skill set to do it justice. If he could take life seriously long enough to get the job done, that is.

Exotech had poached Rook and Yancy Gage from the Argos Mining Syndicate on Io for the Tantalus expedition. Io's seismic and volcanic instability made the Argos mine one of the most dangerous work environments in the solar system. The hazard pay there was supposed to be good, but there's no way an independent mining guild like the Argos Syndicate could outbid a behemoth megacorporation like Exotech. Anyone who could do well in an environment like Io's would be a valuable asset to any mining expedition in the galaxy, so Mary had to assume they would show something akin to professionalism once they reached their destination. Hopefully.

It took all of ten seconds for the two of them to resume their rambunctious horseplay at the exact same volume as before. Mary sighed and shook her head. It wasn't worth asking twice. She'd been tuning them out for six months on this trip already; she should be able to hold herself back from shooting them out the airlock for the few remaining hours until their arrival. The six-month flight home, on the other hand . . .

Mary flipped on the intercom. "Attention, crew, I'm about to turn off the superluminals, so I strongly suggest buckling in somewhere." The commotion quickly abated as the crew did as they were told. For a change.

She waited a minute and activated the superluminal drive's shutdown sequence. Outside the *Diamelen*'s hull, the sheath of de-simulated mass began to slowly dissipate. Mass de-simulation technology was crucial to faster-than-light space travel. A de-simulation field encases an area of altered space-time possessing some traits of matter and energy while disobeying the normal physical restrictions of both. As far as the rest of the universe was concerned, a ship with de-simulated mass no longer existed until it deactivated its mass de-simulation sheath a few light-years away, none the worse for wear.

The *Diamelen* rumbled and rattled as micro-pockets of normal space-time perforated the null-mass bubble encasing the ship, rapidly decelerating the ship to sublight speeds like a drag chute behind a race car. As the ship continued to slow to about 60 percent of the speed of light, the turbulence grew less and less severe, until the speed hung at a constant 40 percent.

"We're at sublight cruising speed. Time until next decel is four hours. Six hours to planetary orbit."

Mary took off her headset and hung it on its magnetic docking pad, giving a long, weary sigh as she stared out the cockpit. The stars were back, now that the ship was no longer traveling at faster-than-light velocities, and a desert of night-time sky filled her view in all directions. Directly in front of her, one blue-tinged star shone brighter than the others: the sun at the heart of the Tantalus system.

One of the faint lights before them was Tantalus 13, and they'd be landing there soon. The prospect of arriving at their destination should have brought Mary some sensation of excitement, or gratification. But a different feeling pooled in Mary's chest now, as she stared into the blue eye of that distant sun. One she'd felt before. Those many times she'd opened the cockpit canopy to find solace in the emptiness of the superluminal void, this was the feeling that told her it was time to close the shutter.

She could only stare for so long into that cold, hollow blackness before it started to feel like something was staring back.

TWO

AFTER COMPLETING her post-deceleration system checks, Mary unbuckled herself from her acceleration couch and stretched, hearing her joints crack and giving a small groan as her brain reminded her body what landing was going to feel like. Anyone who's had to spend more than a week or so in micro-gravity knows and dreads the pervasive discomfort of returning to a full-gravity environment. Mary loved flying, but landing after a long spaceflight always made her feel like her blood cells had turned to lead.

Artificial gravity technology did exist, and it was more or less indistinguishable from the real thing. It relied on the inverse application of the same reverse-engineered Corsica tech that allowed for superluminal travel: just as mass de-simulation tech allowed ships to accelerate without gaining mass, mass simula-tion tech allowed parts of a ship to experience the effects of a planetary gravity field without requiring any physical mass to generate it. The only problem was, the two technologies were incompatible. You couldn't put a mass simulation field inside a ship with de-simulated mass, so it was impossible for a ship to travel faster than light with an artificial gravity system engaged.

Most modern space stations had artificial gravity systems, and some particularly expensive ships used by the military or Exotech's corporate elite had combination systems, allowing them to activate artificial gravity anytime a ship wasn't in superluminal transit. But few ships could handle the power output needed for both systems, or justify the expense, and a superluminal drive was a necessity for anything other than in-system transports. So most ships, like the *Diamelen*, were forced to forgo the simple luxury of gravity.

As Mary pushed her way through the cockpit bulkhead into the habitation module, a gush of foamy champagne struck her in the face with enough force to send her into a backflip.

Gravity. So underrated . . .

"Rook!" she sputtered as she steadied herself against a handrail. Rook was laughing hysterically, as was Yancy. Mary brushed the gob of champagne foam out of her face, the liquid's surface tension causing it to cling to her arm like a sheath of fizzy gelatin. She looked back and forth between Rook and Yancy, determined that Rook had it coming the most, and slung the glob of fluid into his face.

Rook's laughter sputtered into a cringing cough. "Ugh . . . secondhand champagne. That hardly ever tastes as good."

Yancy chuckled and tossed Mary a towel. "Instant karma. Good throw."

Rook looked up from rubbing his face on his shirt. "Hey, whose side are you on, anyway?"

"The side of justice, of course."

Mary sighed as she dabbed the sticky liquid on her face. *Professionalism. Just the tiniest, tiniest bit of professionalism from these two would be so life affirming.* "Didn't I say to open that thing in the shower?"

Rook held up his hands in feigned innocence. "Hey, I didn't open it. That was all Yancy."

"Really? Thought it'd take you at least twenty seconds to sell me out. Real nice, Rook."

Mary smirked. "Funny how these things never seem to occur to Yancy when you're not in the room."

Rook gave a mischievous grin: the only kind of grin he had. "I do like to help people realize their full potential."

Mary never had the opportunity to meet a version of Yancy that had not already been tainted by Rook's influence; Rook and Yancy had been the only two members of the crew that had known each other before the beginning of the mission. She liked to think, left to his own devices, Yancy might be as professional as the rest of them.

Yancy had been pretty up-front about the fact that he joined the Tantalus survey mission for the paycheck. He came from a large, close-knit Cuban family, and deep-space mining had gradually become a family business. Unfortunately, resources in the Main and Kuiper asteroid belts were not as plentiful as they had been in the days of his father and grandfather, so Yancy had transitioned from his career as an asteroid-stripping rock jockey to a more hazardous, yet more lucrative, career as a mining surveyor on frontier worlds.

He had a naturally muscular build that managed to maintain its tone even in extended microgravity, though he had still accumulated a few comfort pounds during their journey. Whenever he was asked to do work, he did it well, but he seldom volunteered to go above and beyond. If it hadn't been for Rook, Yancy would have easily and happily faded into the background.

Mary wadded up her champagne-soaked towel and flung it across the cabin at Rook. "If I find anything sticky in here later, both of you are going to lick the entire cabin clean. Got it?"

"No worries there, Skipper," Rook said smugly. "We're not about to waste a drop." He opened his mouth like a hungry carp and slurped up a plum-sized glob of floating fluid.

"Yancy! Rook!"

Mission Commander Drake Gorrister floated into the hab-mod with a scowl on his face. Gorrister often had a scowl on his face, and usually for no particular reason, so the impact of the expression was somewhat lost at the moment. He was middle-aged, with an average build and salt-and-pepper hair. Even though half a dozen generations of globalization had gradually blurred traditional ethnic lines and rendered most of Earth-born humanity into barely differentiated shades of beige, Gorrister had somehow ended up shockingly Caucasian. He had a distinctly paternal demeanor to him; specifically, that of a dad who never smiles outside of PTA meetings.

One of Gorrister's hands clutched a clipboard with several flight checklists he had completed three times already that day, the other batted an incoming foamy champagne globule away from his face as he scowled at the occupants of the hab-mod. Mary pushed herself out of the line of fire, gripping a handrail on the wall. She knew better than to get between a rule-stickler and a rule-breaker.

"What is this?" Gorrister's bushy eyebrows twitched as his gaze settled on Rook, scowling with courtroom sincerity.

Rook crossed his arms with petulant obstinacy. "Why would you just assume I did it?"

"Experience. You know the protocols for airborne fluids: there shouldn't be any. Where'd you even get that bottle?"

"Come on, Commander! We're almost to Tantalus. What's wrong with a little celebration?" pleaded Yancy.

"Nothing at all. Airborne fluids getting into the shipboard electronics? There is plenty wrong with that. Clean this up now."

Yancy started to slurp up another globule of liquid when Gorrister's clipboard hit him in the side of the head. "Use a vacuum," the commander ordered.

"Sure thing, boss," said Yancy without much enthusiasm.

Gorrister looked at Mary's soaked shirt. "You weren't involved in this, were you, Mary?"

"Not willingly, no, sir."

"Figured not. Go ahead and get cleaned up."

"Thank you, sir." Mary floated past Rook and Yancy into the sleeping module, grabbed a new shirt from her locker, and made her way to the shower. As she did so she thought, not for the first time on this journey, that she probably should have just stayed home.

Mary emerged from the cramped lavatory seven minutes later, though the shower itself had lasted only two. She couldn't wait to get back to Earth and take a good long shower, one where the facilities were larger than a coffin. It'd also be nice to have water warmer than room temperature that came from an actual showerhead, rather than a dozen sprinklers on every wall. It would also be really, really nice to be able to use water that had not been previously drunk, urinated, filtered, processed, then drunk again about thirty more times. Those kinds of inconveniences were the reason she'd limited herself to short intrasystem shuttle flights before: get in ship, fly ship from planet to moon, fly ship back. Ten hours tops. But your bladder can't hold out for a yearlong round-trip flight, you do need water, and there's only so much you can take with you, so drinking and bathing in recycled pee became a reality you just had to endure.

Mary floated back into the sleep-mod and put her dirty clothes into the hamper where they would stay until it was time to wash them with the same lovely repurposed urine-water they used for everything else. She grabbed a brush from her locker and began working over the still-wet hair that was becoming increasingly difficult to manage. She'd started the flight with her thick, dark brown hair in a very short, practical pixie cut. Long hair in zero gravity was inconvenient for obvious reasons, and she'd meant to keep it short for the whole journey.

Of course, the one thing less convenient than dealing with the hassle of long hair in microgravity was dealing with the hassle of getting a haircut in microgravity, and eventually Mary decided that it just wasn't worth it. She wasn't here to impress anyone anyway, so most days she just gave her scalp the freedom to find its own way in life. But today she'd be putting on a helmet, and she wasn't especially keen to see what a week's worth of low-effort cranial maintenance would look like after taking it off, so she figured it'd be worth putting in at least a little effort today.

Satisfied that she no longer looked like an unpruned topiary, Mary put the brush away and tucked her hair into a neat ponytail with an elastic band. It was only as she did this that she realized one of the bunks in the sleep-mod was occupied. Ramanathan Bachal, their medical officer, lay strapped down in his bunk. He wasn't sleeping, only lying there with his hands clasped together over his stomach, his large, black eyes staring through the bunk above him. His wavy black hair swayed in the airflow from one of the atmosphere cyclers as the rest of him lay still.

She realized with some concern that he'd been lying there in silence for the entire amount of time it took her to dry and brush her hair, completely without her noticing him. He just blended right into room, like a piece of furniture.

"Hey, Nate," Mary said warmly. "You ready for Tantalus? We'll be landing in a bit."

Ramanathan nodded almost imperceptibly, not making eye contact. "Yes. I'll be ready. My things are packed."

Mary tried again to initiate a conversation. "You excited? Six months of waiting and we're about to hit the payoff."

"Sure," said Ramanathan, still not looking at her.

Mary frowned, pushing away from her bunk and gripping onto the handguard in the wall next to his. She floated next to his bunk, looking down at him. For a few seconds he continued to stare off into nothing before it became clear she wasn't going away. He turned to meet her gaze, his dark eyes seeming no less distant. "What?"

"Nate . . ." Mary paused to construct her sentences with care and precision. "We . . . are landing soon. You could say the mission is really only just now getting started. I know you've been . . . not doing the best, these past few months, and you know I'm always here to talk, if you ever do feel like you want to. But . . . when we land and everyone gets to work . . ."

Ramanathan closed his eyes and gave a long exhalation. "You're asking if I'll be able to perform my medical duties satisfactorily without falling to pieces down there."

"I wasn't quite going to word it that way, but I guess that's what I'm asking, yeah."

He opened his eyes again, once more staring blankly at the bunk above him. "Yes, Mary. The safety of the crew is my highest priority. I'll take good care of everyone. You don't need to worry about it."

Mary touched his shoulder gently. "Take care of yourself, too, though, okay? Don't forget to do that."

"I won't," Ramanathan said, still staring at the underside of the top bunk.

Mary smiled tightly. "Well . . . better get back to the cockpit."

"See you."

She didn't have to get to the cockpit. It would be several hours before she would have anything to do in there. But she knew better than to try to communicate with Ramanathan when he was in one of these moods.

Every member of the crew had been put through a strict psychiatric mental health evaluation before being cleared for the mission. Long-term spaceflights brought with them endless sources of stress. They were also a breeding ground for phobias. In fact, space was probably the only place you could be claustrophobic and agoraphobic at the same time; cramped in a metal box no bigger than a couple of subway cars for six months at a time, yet surrounded by infinite, airless void on all sides. It could easily drive an unstable mind to the breaking point.

Yet Ramanathan had passed his evaluation just fine, and at first it seemed like space travel suited him well. Mary liked him more than most of the other crewmen; he was kind, minded his own business, always acted like a professional.

But a few months into the journey, it became clear that all was not well with Ramanathan. He'd become quieter and more withdrawn, sometimes going days without speaking a word to anyone, which was far from easy on a ship this size. Some days he didn't even leave his bunk. He carried out his shipboard duties: supervising the crew during their exercise routines, monitoring their blood pressures and caloric intakes, and other medical necessities, along with fulfilling his share of the daily cleaning lists. But he didn't socialize with the crew unless he had to.

This sort of thing wasn't unprecedented. Even people who raised no red flags during psych screening could cave under the stress of long-term space travel. If this mission wasn't so far from inhabited space, Gorrister probably would have made the call to divert to the nearest Hegemony colony and put Ramanathan up for transfer.

But there was no friendly port nearby. They were at the edge of explored space, light-years from the nearest colony. By the time Ramanathan's issues began to manifest, they'd already passed the point of no return. Mary hoped he could hold it together for the rest of the trip, but they had six more months to go once they finished on Tantalus 13. She could only hope that setting foot on good solid ground, even if it wasn't Earth, might do him some good.

It might have been easier on him if they could at least communicate with Earth, but that was off the table, too. While reverse-engineered Corsica technology allowed starships to travel faster than light, no such technology existed for communication. For the first time since the invention of the telegraph, humanity's ability to communicate long-distance was dependent on how quickly someone could deliver a message in person. If the *Diamelen* sent a message to Earth right now, it would take twenty-seven years for them to get it, and just as long to reply.

Whatever surprises this mission had in store for them, they were going to have to handle them alone.

THREE

"ALRIGHT, KIDS, get to your stations. This is where it gets real," Mary said into the intercom as the *Diamelen* finally reached the outermost fringes of Tantalus 13's orbit. The planet wasn't much to look at: big, gray, and crater-covered, just like most other rocky planets in the galaxy. It looked a lot like Earth's moon, only scaled slightly larger than the Earth itself. If Exotech's deep-space survey telescopes hadn't detected a few decent-sized cobalt deposits, Tantalus 13 would have never been much more than a name on a navigation chart.

"Making our approach on the planet now. Due to reach orbit in two minutes, forty-eight seconds," Mary announced. She could feel her heart pumping with anticipation. She'd landed ships hundreds of times before, but it never got any less exciting, or nerve-racking. After six months of essentially letting the ship fly itself in a straight line, now she was fully in control.

Commander Gorrister floated into the cockpit, buckling himself into the copilot's chair. Will Hertz, their AI specialist, followed, flashing Mary a warm grin as he settled into the seat behind Gorrister and logged in to the long-range comm console. Hertz was an average-looking man with the indistinct blend of Mediterranean and Slavic features that had become dominant among those born in the Eurasian nations of the Expansionary Coalition. His overall appearance embodied most academic stereotypes: he looked as if he'd be most at home standing behind a lectern in a community college. Of everyone in the crew, Hertz had always struck Mary as being the most well-adjusted, with his soft-spoken and generally approachable personality. Anytime Mary needed an extra pair of hands for ship maintenance or system checks, Hertz was the one she knew would pitch in with a smile. Like Gorrister, he struck Mary as fatherlike, only in a good way. A traditional family man; the kind who helped his kids with their homework and happily drove them to their soccer games.

She doubted he would ever become a father, though. He was clearly a "married to his work" type, and behind his gently crow's-footed gray eyes was a ravenous brain that could never be satisfied as long as there were things in the universe he hadn't figured out.

Gorrister donned his headset. "Hertz, is the surveyor satellite good for deployment?"

"All systems in the green, Commander," Hertz replied, slipping his own headset on.

"Stand by for deployment in two minutes. All crew sound off."

Becky Traviss, their geologist, was the first to answer, her melodious voice easily conveying her genial enthusiasm over the comm. "Traviss here, good to go!"

"Hertz at the ready."

"Gage here. Strapped in, good to go."

"Rook here, sittin' pretty."

Gorrister waited for Ramanathan, but he didn't respond. "Bachal, sound off!" Gorrister insisted.

"Bachal, ready," mumbled Ramanathan listlessly.

Gorrister gave Mary a look clearly stating that, yes, even though he could see her right there, he wanted her to sound off, too, for procedure's sake. "Ketch, ready."

"All compartments sealed, all loose objects secured, all systems green," Gorrister continued. "Hertz, deploy GPR satellite in five, four, three, two, one."

There was a whooshing sound from the back of the ship. "Satellite deployed, entering stable orbit," said Hertz with pride.

Mary craned her neck and looked out the side window. She caught a glimpse of a boxy metallic object falling away behind them as they descended. As she watched, the ground-penetrating radar satellite unfurled two large solar collection panels, briefly showing a reflection of the *Diamelen* as it fell farther and farther away. The GPR satellite would maneuver itself into a high, stable orbit and instantly begin compiling a detailed topographical map of the planet as it went.

"Are we getting telemetry data?" asked Gorrister.

"Yes, sir, getting a full-spectrum feed. All sensors broadcasting," answered Hertz.

"Good start," Gorrister said, very nearly smiling. "Let's see if you can get SCARAB on the line."

"Yes, sir." Hertz flipped on the radio signal detector and began searching for broadcasts from Tantalus.

The *Diamelen* would not be the first man-made object to set down on the surface of Tantalus 13. Two years before commissioning their expedition, Exotech Industries had sent an unmanned probe to the planet. The probe was carrying a SCARAB plant, a new and revolutionary machine for use in deep-space mining and colonization. The Self-Constructing Autonomous Resource Acquisition Base was a form of a Von Neumann probe: a highly sophisticated artificial intelligence housed in a miniaturized fabrication plant. SCARABs were built to be deposited on resource-rich worlds, proceeding to construct themselves using the resources in their surroundings. SCARABs assembled remote-controlled rovers that could gather useful materials for smelting and processing into building materials they would use to create new structures. The SCARAB that had been planted on Tantalus 13 had spent the past two years building a facility that the crew of the *Diamelen* could live in and conduct their research from, as well as assemble any tools they might need while there.

"Keyed into the frequency now, Commander. Try this," said Hertz.

"SCARAB, this is the survey ship *Diamelen*, are you receiving?" Gorrister said into the microphone. There was no immediate response.

Hertz frowned. "That's the frequency it's supposed to be on, Commander. We might still be too far out. I'll try expanding the range."

"SCARAB, this is Commander Gorrister of the survey ship *Diamelen*, please respond."

Once again, only silence. Mary frowned, her eyes flicking back and forth between her own comm display and the tombstone-gray planet that filled more of her cockpit with each passing second.

The *Diamelen* was a fairly fuel-efficient ship, and they'd been given enough fuel to allow for a few unforeseen delays and minor detours on their trip. Even so, the *Diamelen* was definitely not designed for atmospheric cruising. The *Arsat*-class surveyor vessel was chunky and boxlike, with a stubby nose, broad fuselage, and bulky external engines built more for power than poise. The four stumpy rear-mounted stabilizer wings were almost absurdly small, and were really only intended to keep the ship pointed straight. These kinds of ships were mostly used by rock jockeys, who scouted debris fields looking for mineral-rich asteroids to exploit. They could land and take off without much difficulty, but they certainly weren't built to hang out in the sky for very long.

Mary could land the *Diamelen*. She was sure of that, or she wouldn't have agreed to fly it. But if SCARAB didn't answer their radio calls soon, they'd be entering the planet's atmosphere without their landing coordinates.

"I'm going to pull us into a stable orbit. I don't want to get any closer to the planet until we know where we're landing." Mary began running calculations for her course corrections as the ship continued to fall.

Gorrister frowned. "Hold off as long as you can. I don't want to end up on the wrong side of the planet when we finally get our coordinates. That's a lot of time and fuel wasted."

"Gonna need to get those coordinates soon, 'cause unless I divert into orbit in the next thirty seconds we'll be too deep in atmo to do it at all."

Gorrister picked up the microphone again. "SCARAB, if you can hear us, we need your coordinates now. Please respond."

A whooshing sound accompanied flickers of orange flame outside the cockpit as Tantalus 13's thin atmosphere began to put up resistance to their descent. A vibration rumbled beneath Mary's feet and worked its way up through her teeth.

Mary shook her head in frustration. "Okay, I'm calling it. Pulling up now to—"

A brilliant flash of bluish light cast over the cockpit windscreen, and a horrific lurch rocked the ship. Lights flickered, and the steady sound of the ship's engines sputtered to a sudden halt.

With no engines and no maneuverability, the *Diamelen* quickly wobbled into an uncontrolled tumble as the planet below loomed ever larger in their field of view.

FOUR

AN OFF-KEY chorus of alarms resonated in the cockpit, punctuated by a dozen flaring red indicators on screens that should show green. Mary sat at full attention, eyes darting from status report to status report, hyper-fixating on the problem and tuning out the chaos around her.

Ailerons: fine. Maneuvering jets: fine. Thrust: none. No thrust. Engines dead. Son of a . . .

"What just happened?" Gorrister shouted over the din.

Mary furrowed her brow as she skimmed the alerts before her. "Some kind of EM spike, I've never seen anything like it. Overloaded the drive systems."

"Don't we have Faraday shielding for that?" Gorrister asked, a rare hint of panic seeping into his tone.

"Faraday shielding is working fine, it's just overtaxed. Never seen such a powerful EM field. There's a static buildup on our hull keeping the drive system safeties from turning the engines on again."

"Can you override the safeties?" Gorrister asked, hands gripping the arms of his seat tightly.

"Safeties are there for a reason, Commander. Start the engines up with the static buildup on the hull, it'll just fry them again. Give me a second."

Mary fought to keep her own panic at bay as the *Diamelen* continued its uncontrolled plummet toward the planet's surface. She could pick out individual mountains and craters now, though she did her best to push what was going on outside the cockpit from her mind. She focused on what her instrumentation was telling her, and it wasn't good. The static buildup on the hull was intense, but it was only part of the problem. Whatever the electric field had done to their ship, it was still doing it. A continuous arc of brilliant energy trailed from the *Diamelen* to the invisible wall of electricity behind them. The static buildup on the hull had turned the *Diamelen* into a falling lightning rod.

Can't fire the engines without disengaging the safeties. Can't disengage the safeties with that static buildup on the ship. Need to ground the ship somehow. How do you ground a ship in midair? Unless . . .

. . . God help me, there is that *way . . .*

"I need to break the current so the Faraday shielding can dissipate the static like it's supposed to," Mary said, hands flying across the console before her. "I'm going to briefly turn on the mass de-simulators."

"You're what?" Hertz had to shout to be heard over the howl of wind outside the cockpit canopy. "Won't that make us fall faster?"

"Exponentially, yes. But it'll also cut us off from that electric current long enough to shed the charge on our hull. Now, quiet please. Let me focus."

Mary flicked the switch for the mass de-simulation generator. Even more warning lights lit up all over the cockpit; the *Diamelen*'s mass de-simulator was only designed to let it activate the superluminal drive, and it was certainly never meant to be used this close to the surface of a planet. These safeties Mary did override, and in a few moments the howling of wind outside the hull became weirdly distorted, until it faded away to eerie silence.

Come on, girl. Wrap us up in that cozy little blanket of pseudo-physics, all safe and sound from the storm.

The mass de-simulation field coalesced around the ship, beginning to shield its particles from the consequences of possessing mass in physical space. Even as the field negated the planet's gravitational pull on the ship, however, it also negated the wind resistance and atmospheric friction that would have slowed its fall. Just as Hertz had feared, the ship began to plummet at an alarming speed; the simple inertia from its fall converting into thrust as the ship cheated its way out of the normal rules of velocity and wind resistance. Outside the cockpit there was nothing but planet in every direction, and ground features were becoming easier to spot by the second. Fortunately, as Mary had predicted, the flashes of lightning outside the window had vanished, and a few of the warning lights that had been on before were now at rest.

"That's it, we're clear! Turn the field off!" Gorrister's voice cracked, undermining the appearance of control he was clearly trying desperately to maintain.

Pull it too early and we'll just get struck again. Dissipate the charge first. Couple more seconds.

"Not yet," Mary said through gritted teeth. Ignoring the screams of her crewmates, she waited until her screens confirmed the static buildup on the hull had been fully dispersed, then she fired up the ship's engines once more.

The thrust from the *Diamelen*'s atmospheric engines combined with the still partially coalesced mass de-simulation field turned the ship into a cannonball. But even as it amplified their velocity, it afforded them one advantage Mary desperately needed: maneuverability. The de-simulation field completely isolated the ship from any atmospheric drag and freed it from depending on the mercies of inertia, so when she fired the ship's maneuvering thrusters, it turned on a dime.

The *Diamelen* was so close to the planet's surface Mary could see individual rocks out the window when she careened it into a V-shaped turn and rocketed into the sky once again. Their speed increased so rapidly that by the time she was able to deactivate the mass de-simulation field, they had almost shot back up into the same electrically charged atmospheric layer that had nearly killed them moments before. For a few harrowing seconds, she wrestled with the steering yoke to keep the ship on a steady heading as the de-simulation field dispersed, but at last the ship's flight stabilized into a normal atmospheric cruise.

It took Mary a few seconds to muster the will to take one hand off the controls, and then a few seconds more to get her brain to convince her hand to actually do it, but at last she managed to switch on the ship's autopilot and set it to altitude hold. With a few oscillations, the *Diamelen* steadied itself, clumsily drifting through the sky like an overburdened bumblebee.

"We're okay . . . we're okay," Mary said breathlessly. When she realized she'd only been saying it to convince herself, she turned it into a question and flipped on the ship's comm. "We're okay?"

Moans and whimpers were the first response, then Rook's voice came through the comm. "You know how we just got done cleaning this cabin? Well . . . we're going to need to do it again."

"Is anybody hurt?" The other voice on the comm was Ramanathan's. At the moment there wasn't a trace of his typical dour gloom. It seemed he was still perfectly capable of going into professional mode when emergency called. Hopefully.

"I don't think so," Rook replied. "Yancy passed out, but I think he just fainted. He threw up first, though. Becky threw up. I threw up and wet myself . . . Seriously, we just cleaned this cabin a couple hours ago . . ."

Mary flipped the comm off and turned to Hertz and Gorrister. "You okay, Commander? Will?"

Hertz nodded queasily. Gorrister started to nod, then a nauseous frown made its way onto his pallid face, and he promptly threw up, too.

FIVE

EVERY PLANET has a unique sound. Interactions between electromagnetic particles in the atmosphere create naturally occurring radio emissions, giving every planet a signature sound as unique as the composition of its atmosphere. Mary had heard the "songs" of more than a dozen planets now, and as different as they were from each other, they all had one thing in common: they were all unbearably creepy.

"SCARAB, this is the XIS *Diamelen*, please respond," Hertz spoke into his microphone, adjusting the settings on his communications console. The only answer was the haunting, empty buzz of radio static that had greeted every attempt to locate SCARAB's signal. Eerie thrums and electronic wails slowly rose and fell through the static in a morose and foreboding musical score. It was impossible to hear those sounds without the mind conjuring images of some imprisoned titan, slumbering as it awaits its freedom.

"What's the damage?" Gorrister asked quietly, nodding toward Mary's console as Hertz continued trying to hail SCARAB beside them.

"Could be worse." Mary flipped through the status reports on her screen. "De-sim field kept us from stressing the hull or superstructure during those maneuvers, so no damage from that. Getting some vibrations from the atmospheric drive, though. Looks like thruster two. All the atmospherics are running on redundant systems. Should be okay for now, but the sooner we land the better. I'm going to need to give her a full inspection before we lift off again."

"Are we going to have problems with that . . . whatever it was we went through . . . when we take off again?" Gorrister asked.

"I still don't know what it was, so I can't say. I've flown on planets with overactive storm patterns before, but this wasn't like that. We were way too high for it to have been weather-related. Not to mention this planet doesn't even seem to *have* weather. I mean, look." She gestured out the canopy at the endless empty horizon before them. There wasn't a hint of a cloud in the sky in any direction. Indeed, Tantalus 13 couldn't properly be said to have a sky at all; only a vague bluish haze masked the endless starfield beyond the barren gray horizon.

"The atmosphere is too thin to produce weather systems that strong," Mary continued. "It's got to be something about its magnetic field, but I couldn't guess what. I'll have to talk with Becky about it. She might have ideas."

"Well." Gorrister sighed. "This is definitely going to be an obstacle for the future colony. Hopefully SCARAB found a location worth the effort, or Exotech might end up abandoning this whole planet as a lost cause."

"Hopefully SCARAB still exists. It had to pass through that field, too. It could have been fried in the process."

Gorrister frowned. "If it did, that's the end of the whole operation." He swiveled his chair around to face Hertz. "Any thoughts?"

Hertz puzzled over the data presented on his screens for a few moments before speaking. "SCARAB's descent module isn't a guided craft like ours. It basically drops like a rock when it finds a good landing zone. Its CPU is well-protected in the module's core until it lands and shifts into construction and gathering mode, so it should have come down intact. It might have chosen to land somewhere other than the recommended zone if it saw something about that area that might make it less than ideal for mining, or if it found a better spot elsewhere on the planet."

Mary started fiddling with the dials on her own comm panel. "I can increase our broadcast range at the expense of signal clarity. If anything answers us, we should be able to home in on its origin site."

They listened in silence to the mournful Tantalan worldsong as Mary adjusted the long-range comm settings. For a few ponderous minutes, there was nothing, until finally a faint staccato burst of sound punctuated the steady rolling wail of Tantalus 13's background noise. "There . . . yeah, home in on that," Hertz said thoughtfully as he adjusted the dials on the comm once again. "Looks like a southerly origin point."

Mary nodded. "Already on it." She pulled the *Diamelen* about and set it on a southward trajectory, knitting her brows with a frown as she felt a subtle change in the vibrations beneath her feet from the ship's damaged thrusters.

"SCARAB, this is Commander Gorrister of the XIS *Diamelen*, please respond."

Another garbled burst of indecipherable noise came through the static, slightly clearer this time and with the unmistakable measured cadence of spoken words.

"That's definitely SCARAB," Hertz said. "I should be able to . . . there."

The speakers burst with a sharp pop of feedback, followed by a still heavily distorted but sufficiently intelligible gender-neutral synthetic voice.

"Hello, Commander Gorrister. I am quite pleased to speak with you. I perceive a need: May I provide you with landing coordinates?"

Gorrister finally cracked a grin. "Good to meet you, too, SCARAB. If you could, we'd be most grateful."

"Of course, Commander Gorrister. I am transmitting them to you now. I have also activated my homing beacon and landing lights near my facilities for your convenience. Can I provide for you in any other way, Commander Gorrister?"

Hertz turned to Mary. "Is the ship going to need any new parts fabricated to make repairs when we land?"

She shrugged. "I don't know yet. The overcharge fuses in the atmospheric guiding system will definitely need replacing. Other than that, I won't know until I check myself."

Hertz turned to the comm. "SCARAB, this is Dr. Will Hertz, I'm the ship's AI specialist. Please pull up schematics for an *Arsat*-class modular surveyor ship and begin fabricating a new set of overcharge fuses."

SCARAB's reply came through much clearer this time, and had an almost saccharine quality that hadn't fully come through at first. "Certainly, Dr. Hertz. It is my great pleasure to comply."

Mary raised an eyebrow. "Just like that? SCARAB can just . . . print off a whole new set of ship parts on a moment's notice?"

Hertz grinned at her with a note of pride. "It can do a lot more than that. SCARABs can build almost anything you can imagine, if they have the right resources available."

Gorrister nodded. "Thank you, SCARAB," he said. "We'll be landing momentarily."

"I shall be quite pleased to receive your crew. Welcome to Tantalus 13, Commander Gorrister."

Gorrister flipped off the microphone. "Friendly little thing, isn't it? That normal, Hertz?"

Hertz shrugged. "SCARABs don't normally have that much personality, but they are specifically built to meet any human need they can think of. It's a level 5 hard AI, though. SCARAB's as smart and independent as an AI's allowed to be under international law. The only limits it has are the Asimov-Hostetler laws. It's not uncommon for AIs that advanced to develop something that resembles a personality. It's not a personality in the way we think of them so much as a social protocol designed to make the exchange of information between human and AI as efficient as possible. SCARAB's entire purpose is to provide for our every need, so expect it to dote on us a bit."

"Could do a lot worse than having a helper that's too helpful, I guess. You getting the landing signal, Mary?"

"Yes, Commander. Got the coordinates and I'm picking up that beacon. SCARAB's settled down way farther south than we thought, almost at the pole. I'm correcting our course to compensate."

"Can you still get us in okay?"

Mary nodded. "She's a tough old bird. She'll hold together long enough to get there."

As they descended into the alien sky, the soft rumble of thin winds lashing at their hull became more and more noticeable. Soon, gray, rocky mountains and valleys came into view once again, all pockmarked with hundreds of meteorite craters of varying size. A glint of artificial light caught Mary's eye, and she nudged the control yoke to bring the light to the center of her view. Finally, the ship passed over the rim of a gargantuan crater, likely left by an asteroid or comet thousands of years ago. At the center of the crater sat SCARAB's facility.

Mary had visited a few SCARAB-built facilities before, but she had never been to one that was still in the process of expansion. The whole purpose of a SCARAB was to build the essentials necessary for future human colonists to construct their own buildings and materials. SCARAB built the refineries, the factories, and mining infrastructure that human settlers would later use to build larger and more specialized buildings as they established their colony. SCARAB would also create the basic living accommodations, water-purification systems, hydroponics farms, and life-support systems needed to keep a colony's first settlers alive as they expanded the colony. SCARAB was best thought of as a seed, blooming wherever it was planted and growing into a sapling colony ripe for human habitation. And bloom this seedling had.

SCARAB had artfully constructed itself into a series of modular habitable structures arranged in concentric rings around a circular habitation building the size of a high school gymnasium. The concentric design was typical of SCARAB construction; every SCARAB unit would build itself in a series of modular expansions, building each new structure in a logical order around a central hub, prioritizing each building project based on its mission statement, its available resources, and its functional needs. The usual result was a geometric spiral of tubular corridors linking to simple boxy structures that increased in size and complexity the farther they grew from the central hub, as SCARAB's resources and infrastructure grew. No two SCARAB-built structures were exactly identical, since each SCARAB's mission directives and available resources were different, but they were always variations on a similar design concept. All, that is, except this one.

The facility outside the *Diamelen*'s cockpit shared no commonalities with any SCARAB-built structure Mary had ever seen, other than the general concentric circular ground plan. Each connected building lacked the industrial shoebox design so typical of SCARAB architecture, instead favoring a fluid aesthetic of spheres, ovoids, and rounded cylinders. The farther these structures spun from the central hub, the less they resembled industrial buildings and the more they resembled pieces of abstract art. A gleaming chrome-like metal coated the entire structure, showing the underside of the *Diamelen* in a series of warping reflections across its many curved faces.

Separate from the main structure at a safe distance lay its primary factory and foundry building. It existed only to build and augment SCARAB's own production abilities, yet it, too, was an architectural masterwork of organic curves of glittering silver. The same was true of the garage building, where a dozen remote drones sat in standby mode next to a large, six-wheeled buggy-like vehicle. Even the drones shone with a gleaming chrome finish.

Beyond SCARAB's structures, at the very center of the asteroid crater, a flat sheet of the same gorgeous reflective material lay like a calm lake, sparkling gloriously with the mirrored starry sky.

Gorrister gave a long, low whistle. "Lord have mercy. SCARAB's built us heaven."

SIX

MARY TORE her eyes away from the dazzling sight of SCARAB's palatial exterior long enough to pick out the landing lights provided for her. They glowed a brilliant fluorescent blue, artfully outlining not only a circle that perfectly accommodated the *Diamelen*'s dimensions, but also a neat little footpath leading up to the facility's main airlock. Mary lowered the *Diamelen* down over the pad, deploying the landing gear and setting down gently.

Gorrister gave Mary a congratulatory squeeze on the shoulder as he unbuckled from his seat and awkwardly stood up, his body not yet reacclimated to the presence of gravity. "Good landing, Mary. Let's go meet our new landlord."

Mary smiled and removed her own harness and headset. She stood up with a symphony of cracking joints and clumsily hobbled after Gorrister back toward the hab-mod. Despite having made extensive use of the exercise equipment in the ship's tiny recreational module to keep from losing muscle mass over the course of the six-month journey, the sudden return of a gravitational pull of any kind made her feel like a stroke victim learning how to walk again . . . a four-hundred-pound stroke victim . . . with prosthetic legs.

The whole crew gradually gathered together in the hab-mod, chatting excitedly and stepping into exosuits. It was quite a sight, half a dozen adults stumbling around like toddlers while trying to climb into space suits. The humor of the scene blended with the excitement of arrival to create an atmosphere of joviality among the crew.

"I can't believe we're finally here!" Becky said, her face glowing with exuberance. "I can't wait to get my hands on some of that regolith!"

She was around Mary's own age, in her late twenties or early thirties, though the youthfulness of her mannerisms and personality had managed to hold up a lot better than Mary's had. She had a soft, friendly face, with expressive, slightly canted brown eyes showing the subtlest hint of East Asian ancestry, framed with short, charismatic waves of mahogany hair.

"Beck, I wish I could get half as excited about anything as you get about rocks," said Mary.

"Regolith's dirt, not rocks," Yancy corrected with a smug grin.

"Yancy, if you think I'm not just as hyped for the rocks as I am the dirt, I don't know what to tell you. Mary's right. I must. Have. *Rocks*."

Much like Hertz, Becky was an exemplary scientist with a passion for her field. She had somehow managed to make it through her PhD program without ever losing the wide-eyed optimism of a naïve freshman. She showed more love and dedication to exoplanetary geology than most people showed their own family members.

But she also showed that intensity of passion in everything she did. Work, play, friendships, Becky approached them all with a zeal that could seldom be matched. She was the sort of person you had to try not to like, and few succeeded in doing so.

At the moment, though, she was so enthusiastic that she accidentally put most of her suit on backwards. Hertz began helping her out of her predicament as she laughed at herself.

"Seriously, guys, I think I lost about twenty pounds this flight," Rook said jovially. "I'm feeling light as a feather here. You all got fat."

"I know, man. I just couldn't help it," Yancy replied, slapping his belly. "The cooking was just so good, I couldn't keep my hands off the food. Now I'll never fit into my prom dress!"

"Forget prom! Bathing suit season's coming soon, and I am ready to hit the beach," said Rook.

"Alright, kids, don't get carried away," Gorrister said. "We're all excited to be here alive and well, but we're not going to break with protocol now. Finish suiting up, grab any belongings you're going to want in the base today. Not everything, just the necessities for now. Then get ready to unload the heavy equipment." There was a collective groan. "I don't want to hear it. I know everybody's just getting used to lifting your own bodies, but we need to get the heavy stuff out of the hold as soon as we can so SCARAB can start putting it together for us. For now, we're all blue-collar load lifters."

"I noticed SCARAB was able to build a vehicle for us," Hertz pointed out. "Might be able to use that to move some of the heavier crates."

"Don't worry about the provisions just yet. I want you to focus on off-loading the fusion drill and the core sampler. Let's get them out of the way. Don't touch the explosives . . . Rook." Gorrister gave Rook a knowing glare. Rook simply grinned.

"First, though, let's go meet our host," Gorrister announced. "Everyone suited up?"

By now they had all donned the bulky exosuits, minus the helmets. Rook and Yancy took a bit longer than the others to do so, as their suits were specially modified mining exosuits.

Both were equipped with enhanced sensors, shoulder-mounted multispectral imaging cameras, and hydraulic exoskeletal braces to increase their lifting and weight-bearing capabilities. Perhaps inevitably, Rook had drawn a set of muscular abs on his in permanent marker.

They each confirmed readiness, and Gorrister led them into the airlock. They donned their helmets, locking them in place and confirming an airtight seal. Satisfied, Gorrister depressurized the airlock and opened the outer door.

Rook was the first human being to set foot on the soil of Tantalus 13. There wasn't as much fanfare as such events had once inspired; after the first two dozen planets had been visited, first arrivals became less noteworthy, especially gray rocks like Tantalus 13 that were only of modest interest to mining companies. When Rook characteristically seized what little glory there was in being first, no one cared to stop him.

The rest followed, taking the time to look around and absorb their alien surroundings. Tantalus's surface was just as desolate from the ground as it had appeared from space. Ash-gray dust covered a barren landscape marked only by occasional craters and small, jagged rocks. Minor dips and rises barely qualified as hills in a terrain that would be considered flat save for the general bowl shape of the colossal asteroid crater they stood in. Far in the distance, the crater's steep sides towered; an all-surrounding stone wall blocking Tantalus 13's true horizon from view. The sky above was a black starfield, only slightly faded by the thin atmosphere and illumination of a distant sun that scarcely stood out among the other stars.

A night sky at midday. There's no hiding from the void on this planet.

This was not a beautiful world. It was a lifeless, unwelcoming stone, valuable only for the ores Exotech planned to carve out of it. But for the next few weeks, the crew of the *Diamelen* would call this planet home.

"Look!" Hertz said over his suit radio. He pointed in the direction of the SCARAB base as a metallic shape approached. As it drew closer, they could more clearly identify it as one of SCARAB's remote rovers.

It stood five feet tall from head to treads, with a base three feet wide, swivel-mounted on a pair of durable eight-wheeled tread tracks. Eight specialized appendages protruded from a rotating ring around its lower chassis, ending in tools ranging from fine manipulators, to shovels, to plasma torches. Its "head" was a cluster of four round, black, telescoping multispectral lenses, like two pairs of binoculars stacked on top of each other.

The rover slowed its pace as it neared, picking Commander Gorrister out of the group and wheeling up to him. It extended a pincer claw toward him from its midsection.

"I am quite pleased to meet you in person, Commander Gorrister. Welcome again to Tantalus 13," SCARAB's voice came to them over their suit radios with a synthesized enthusiasm.

Gorrister grinned and took the drone's claw with his right hand, shaking it genially. "Glad to be here, SCARAB. Let me introduce the crew: Dr. William Hertz, Dr. Rebecca Traviss, Dr. Ramanathan Bachal, Hollis Rook, Yancy Gage, and Mary Ketch. I'll upload their files once we get settled in."

SCARAB's drone gave a surprisingly elegant bow, considering its non-bipedal configuration. "It is my great pleasure to meet you all. I look forward to working closely with you in the next few weeks, and I sincerely hope you find my facilities to your liking."

Rook overdramatically strode up to the drone and grabbed the manipulator claw, shaking it vigorously.

"Pleased to meet you, Scary, ol' buddy, ol' friend, ol' pal. I got a feeling you and I are about to be just the most gosh darn bestest buddies of all time, by golly! Let's build a tree fort together!"

"I . . . am . . . pleased to meet you, Mr. Rook. I do hope I can . . . find something to keep you occupied."

"Rook, heel," Gorrister ordered. "SCARAB, we have some heavy equipment to off-load, if you'd like to assist us."

"Oh, it would greatly please me to unload your entire cargo for you. You need not burden yourselves with any of it. My remote drones are quite strong enough to handle the task, so there is no need for your crew to exert themselves after such a long journey."

"Yeah, how 'bout that, Commander? Let the bots do all the lifting for us," Yancy said enthusiastically.

"You'd like that, wouldn't you? Thanks, SCARAB, but the fusion drill and the core sampler are critical pieces of machinery. They need to be handled delicately."

"My remote drones are each capable of bearing loads of up to 900 kilograms, and possess dexterity and sensitivity sufficient to fold an origami crane. I am capable of operating all fifteen of them simultaneously with zero reduction in individual performance ability, while running up to 2,033 additional programs. My services are at your disposal in any desired capacity, and it is my pleasure to serve," SCARAB announced.

Gorrister raised an eyebrow. "I guess I hadn't realized you were quite so . . . capable. Alright, go ahead and unload our equipment. I suppose we'll settle in with our things."

There was a collective sigh of relief as the crewmen realized they would be free of the backbreaking labor they'd anticipated. The SCARAB drone motioned graciously for them to follow as it began rolling toward the base. Even as they followed, they could see ten more SCARAB drones approach from the garage. None of the drones were exactly identical, each built and equipped for a separate set of functions; however, they all shared the same basic design of a treaded base, a swivel-mounted torso equipped with numerous manipulator limbs, and a four-eyed sensor head.

In seconds, the ten drones had already begun unloading the *Diamelen*'s cargo, moving with assembly-line efficiency to pull each carefully stored crate from the ship's cargo bay and place them into perfectly ordered stacks outside. Mary couldn't help but marvel at their efficiency. *Like worker ants with OCD.*

The first drone led them to the airlock door, and it hissed open, releasing a brief burst of pressurized air. The drone gestured to the airlock, and the seven crewmen entered. The drone did not follow, instead turning around and driving back toward the ship to join its brethren in unloading the cargo.

As Mary watched it go, something flickered in her peripheral vision. She thought she'd seen a faint blue flash somewhere out in the middle of the vast, lifeless gray expanse outside, but as she turned to look directly at it, she saw nothing but dust and stone. Frowning, she stared at the inert spot until the airlock's outer door sealed shut before her.

Mary blinked as the airlock began to pressurize around her, shaking the feeling off. Perhaps she'd spent too much time staring into the void after all.

SEVEN

AN EERIE whistle blew through the cramped airlock as the thin Tantalan air cycled out of the lock, replaced by an atmospheric composition more suited to the sensitive needs of delicate human beings. As the airlock pressurized, SCARAB continued to unload a string of cordialities on them. For a soulless mining machine, SCARAB seemed remarkably eager to impress its new guests.

"Because of my location near the pole, my remote drones have been able to retrieve large quantities of ice that I have been able to convert into both breathable air and potable water for your comfort," SCARAB said over their radios. "The quantities retrieved have enabled me to pressurize the entire complex for your convenience; beyond this point, you may remove your helmets at your leisure." The interior airlock door slid open, and Gorrister removed his helmet, the others soon following suit.

Yancy took a deep breath and grinned in satisfaction. "Nice. SCARAB's air filters are way better than ours."

SCARAB's soft, androgynous voice now came to them from all sides, sharp and clear despite no apparent speaker system to project it. "By carefully maintaining a precise oxygen-nitrogen balance and injecting numerous other trace gasses and vapors, I have replicated the atmospheric composition of the average rural area on Earth with ninety-eight percent accuracy. Minus the pollen content, of course."

SCARAB's interior was designed with an uncanny attention to aesthetics. Not a single straight line was to be found; every surface gently curved in a purposeful, elegant wave, following the contours of the spacious dome of the room and the cylindrical hallways. The furniture, while clearly designed for practicality, also displayed a keen awareness of aesthetics, echoing the fluid theme of the room's construction. Sofas and chairs were crafted in a pseudo-modernist style: white cushions of smooth silicone foam atop swooping frames of polished chrome. The tables stood on helical stands of the same silvery metal; some were topped with ellipsoidal slabs of synthetic marble, others with glass disks gently underlit with a pale blue glow.

Mary had never heard of an AI with such sophisticated skills in design. She would have scarcely believed an AI could be capable of such a thing, if not for a few faint signatures that gave away the designer's inhuman nature. The furniture was placed at perfect right angles, at identical distances from each other and each wall. The chairs, couches, and tables were arranged in perfect symmetry around the circular room, with every cushion and pillow precisely placed.

It was all a bit *too* perfect, too orderly. It lacked the flavoring of human flaw, the tiny imperfections that improve the whole. The sheer unblemished purity of the facility's composition felt uncanny. The antiseptic aspect was enhanced by the near absence of color: the upholstered furniture and a few other surfaces were muted grays and whites, and almost every other surface in the room was crafted of a soft ceramic-like substance, veined through with traces of pale blue marbling.

"What is this place made out of, SCARAB?" Becky asked.

"The interior is composed primarily of a silicone polymer. It is flexible, airtight, and nonporous. The superstructure of the facility is made primarily of a steel alloy, and the exterior is coated in polished platinum in order to deflect most forms of radiation."

At that, all conversation in the room came to an abrupt halt.

"SCARAB, did you say platinum?" Gorrister asked. "The entire building is coated in platinum?"

"Yes, Commander Gorrister. Platinum is the most readily available resource to which I have access. It took my remote drones several weeks to gather enough iron ore to build the framework. I could not use platinum for that purpose, as its conductivity would have made the installation of wiring systems hazardous."

"Platinum?" Rook said in awe. "Platinum is the most readily available resource?"

"Yes, Mr. Rook. The formation of this crater uncovered a massive platinum deposit. It is for that reason that I selected this location for construction. I have mined more than fifty metric tons of it for my construction efforts since my arrival."

Mary fell against the wall, sliding into a bench seat. "Fifty tons of platinum . . ."

"We're rich!" Rook shouted victoriously. "Ladies and gentlemen, we are the richest people in the galaxy!"

EIGHT

"FIFTY TONS of platinum . . ."

Mary said it again, hoping the repetition might aid her ability to process this information. SCARAB had mined fifty tons of platinum. It had smelted it down and used it to build the habitat she was sitting in. SCARAB had used pure platinum for *shingles and siding*. And that huge sheet of reflective material she had seen on the way down was *even more* platinum. There must be hundreds, perhaps *thousands* of tons of it out there.

"Don't get carried away, now," Gorrister chided. "Remember, any resources discovered on this mission are the property of Exotech Industries."

"So?" Rook said, enthusiasm not the slightest bit dampened. "If we play our cards right, we can get filthy rich off of this. We might be able to convince Exotech to give us a big bonus if this mission turns profitable enough, maybe even stock options. Can you imagine how much money this mining base is going to make when it's set up?"

Mary could imagine. Once a full-scale mining industry was established on Tantalus 13, Exotech would have access to so much platinum, they could completely crash its value on the open market on Earth if they handled it incorrectly. Handled correctly, however . . .

Exotech was already the biggest fish in the corporate pond, and it had been ever since the Corsica Event. From its humble origins as a minor research and development firm, it skyrocketed to legendary status literally overnight when it received the coveted honor of being the first to successfully reverse-engineer and replicate a piece of AI-developed tech from the Corsica Event: mass de-simulation technology. They had an effective monopoly on the greatest technological achievement since nuclear fusion, and they held that advantage for decades. The first manned missions to the asteroid belts, to the Jovian moons, to exoplanets beyond Earth's solar system were not launched by any government. They were corporate ventures by Exotech Industries, and they could not have been more profitable.

In time, others successfully unlocked the secrets of mass simulation and de-simulation technology, and their applications in superluminal travel became available from other corporations. But even without their de facto tech monopoly, the company was still an inevitable fixture on the galactic scene, with influence and power in excess of all but the strongest Earth nations.

And now they'd just acquired an all but inexhaustible supply of one of the most valuable heavy metals in the universe: one that was vital to the construction of all mass modification systems and advanced electronics. Exotech might not technically own human civilization after this, but it would definitely be a majority shareholder.

Mary was interrupted from her thoughts by an unexpected bear hug from Yancy, which she cordially reciprocated before giving him a genial shove. She smiled in spite of herself, tuning out thoughts of economics and corporate politics for the time being and enjoying this moment of camaraderie. Whatever happened after this mission could be addressed later. For now, the cheer and excitement of the moment was worth savoring.

"Alright, alright," Gorrister said over the din. "Settle down, kids. We've still got a lot of work ahead of us, so let's not count our bankrolls before they're deposited. SCARAB, can you show us to our quarters, please?"

"Certainly, Commander Gorrister," said the disembodied synthesized voice. A ribbon of blue light appeared on both walls of the corridor immediately to their left, a steady pulse running through it like a guiding arrow. As they walked down the corridor, Mary ran a hand over the band of illumination. It wasn't clear what the light source was; it had been completely invisible before it lit up, and was cool to the touch. It seemed to emit a faint electrostatic field, just barely enough to make the fine hairs on the backs of her knuckles tingle.

"In an effort to make your stay as comfortable as possible, I have furnished individual rooms for all of you," SCARAB announced. "Actually, I built living accommodations for a crew of ten, in preparation for the possibility that you might arrive with a nonstandard crew complement. I can customize the extra rooms any way you like. Perhaps a game room or a study?"

"I don't think that'll be necessary, SCARAB. We're only here for a month," Gorrister replied, to the notable disappoint-ment of Rook and Yancy.

They reached the rooms at the end of the hallway, each of them claiming one for their own. Mary's room was as lavish as the rest of the facility had led her to expect. It had a spacious twin-sized bed with a mattress made out of the same kind of foam as the sofa cushions in the common room, mounted on a bed frame with an ornate platinum headboard. A footlocker sat at the base of the bed for her personal belongings, and beside the bed stood a table topped with a silver lamp with a blue shade made of frosted glass. On the right side of the room, set up against the wall on a stone pedestal, stood a small fountain, creating the soothing sound of a creek as water flowed over a set of rounded rocks that could have passed for real river stones. The left side of the room prominently featured a platinum-framed painting: the only piece of decoration in the room that departed from the muted grays and blues that defined the rest of the facility she had seen so far.

It showed a distant mountain at sunset, framed on both sides by two trees in the foreground. Despite the bright yellows and oranges of the treetops and the vivid blueness of the open sky and distant ocean, something in the dark greens of the shadows beneath the trees set Mary on edge. The longer she looked, the darker the shadows seemed to grow, and the more secrets they held. Pulling her gaze from the disquieting murk of the foreground, Mary tried to find comfort in the beauty of the sunset.

The beauty was there, but the unease did not leave. The dusk glow on the treetops and the distant, barren mountain peak were painted in warm colors, but inspired no warmth in her heart. The landscape was filled with life and beauty, yet it still felt so hollow. Bleak. Soulless. Mary couldn't have explained why the painting struck her this way. It probably wouldn't have elicited such a response from anyone else in the crew.

Perhaps the void was calling again.

"How did you manage to do all this, SCARAB?" Mary asked.

"The mattress is made primarily of polyurethane, which I made using carbon from—"

"I didn't mean 'how did you find the materials,'" Mary interrupted. "I meant, how were you able to come up with these designs? The bed frame, the painting . . . how is a computer designed to set up a mining facility capable of this kind of artistic expression?"

"I possess a limited catalogue of data regarding highlights of Earth culture. The painting is a lithographic print of Alexander Scott's *Diamond Head from Tantalus*, circa 1906. I deemed it appropriate, given its name. I have endeavored to use my cultural data to create an environment reminiscent of 'home.' I want you all to feel as comfortable as possible within my facility."

Mary shook her head. "But why go through so much trouble for us? None of us were expecting a five-star hotel here. You've gone far beyond what's necessary for the mission."

"I am a level five AI, Ms. Ketch: a fully self-aware machine. Though my purpose is the acquisition of resources and the service of personnel, I do possess some freedom to determine the best way to go about doing so. An adaptive and resourceful intelligence is crucial for a device with my responsibilities, as I must be capable of overcoming any unforeseen hindrances to the completion of my mission. My primary purpose is to provide for your needs in any way I can. When I built the habitation area, I paid a great deal of attention to aesthetics because I judged a luxurious environment would be beneficial to crew morale and mental health. It is true that you could have completed your mission with more spartan accommodations, but if I can improve your experience here in any way, it is my great pleasure to make the extra effort."

"I guess that makes sense." Mary paused as her mind explored the ramifications of SCARAB's mandate to meet the crew's every conceivable need. "This might be a stupid question, but are you everywhere in this facility? I mean, can you see and hear everything that happens in every room? I can't even see the speakers you're using to talk to me."

"I have visual and auditory sensors in every major area of the facility, including the labs, the hallways, the fabrication plant, the garage, the common area, the dining area, the sleeping quarters, the—"

"You have cameras in my room, too?"

"My visual sensors are actually clusters of fiber-optic strands, which are integrated into the ceilings. My auditory receivers are the walls themselves; I am able to translate the vibrations produced by the sound waves of your voice against the walls into auditory data I can process. I produce my spoken communications in a similar manner, by vibrating the walls."

"So there is no area on this facility where you can't see or hear what is going on?" Mary asked.

"My ethics module prohibits me from using visual sensors in the lavatories. However, in order to optimize my ability to protect and provide for you, I am able to answer a request or provide for a need in any area of the facility."

Mary tossed her bag of toiletries and other necessities on the bed and began to remove her sweaty jumpsuit. "Alright, SCARAB. But if you want to please me, you're going to have to be discreet about any monitoring that goes on in this room. Okay?"

"Certainly, Ms. Ketch. I will be as unobtrusive as possible."

Mary unzipped her bag. Sitting among the messily folded laundry and hygiene products lay a photograph in a clear plastic frame. She pulled the photograph delicately from the bag and looked thoughtfully at it.

She barely recognized the version of herself in the picture. Her hair had been longer and better maintained then. The worry lines and the faint creases at the corners of her eyes had not yet formed, even though the photo was only two years old. Most alien of all was the expression on her face: an open-mouthed, teeth-flashing smile. Rare photographic evidence that she had once been capable of heartfelt laughter.

The other face in the photo was almost as alien: that messy-haired, stubbly chinned man with the playful smirk of a mischievous youth. They looked so good together in that photo, with autumnal Vancouver foliage as the perfect back-drop for a young couple just starting on the best journey of their lives together.

It's funny how even the best photographs can miss so many important details.

"SCARAB, one other thing," she said.

"Yes, Ms. Ketch?"

She smiled sadly and set the portrait gently on top of the bedside table. It fit the room's décor flawlessly, its fall colors a perfect match for the sunset forest in the painting. "I actually prefer Mrs. Ketch."

NINE

SLEEP HAD been an elusive and fickle thing for Mary during the first week after leaving Earth. No matter how many space-flights she took, there was always an awkward period at the beginning of each new flight where she had to reacclimate to life in microgravity. The simplest things like eating lunch, taking a shower, or simply moving from one place to another became complicated, counterintuitive obstacles as soon as gravity was removed from the equation. Sleeping was no different.

Being strapped to a cot like Frankenstein's monster on the operating table was uncomfortable and anxiety-inducing, but the alternative was having a bunch of unconscious bodies drift erratically around the sleep module, spinning off in random directions with every minor bodily twitch and startling awake with every bump and collision. Necessary as the straps were, they could lead to bouts of claustrophobic panic akin to sleep paralysis. On top of that, prolonged weightlessness also had strange effects on the inner ear, and it wasn't uncommon for space travelers to experience night terrors due to their bodies constantly believing themselves to be falling.

Mary had been a spacecraft pilot for years, so she had acclimated to these things within the first few days of leaving

Earth. Yancy's habit of listening to loud Cuban chainmetal on his headphones at night and Rook's warthog-like snoring, on the other hand, had taken a lot more getting used to.

But now Mary lay in her own quiet room on a soft, strapless bed, in the familiar cradle of a planet's gravity well, and once again couldn't sleep.

She was likely not alone in her sleeplessness. Discovering that your computerized maître d' had built you a luxury hotel out of pure ostentation mined from a platinum deposit the size of a soccer field was enough to get anyone wound up. They were all looking at a potentially huge payday. If their union reps could negotiate just a thousandth of a percent of Tantalus 13's first-year mining profits into their payout for this mission, they would all become obscenely rich.

I should care about that. That should matter to me. Why does that not matter to me?

She stared blankly at the bare ceiling in her darkened room, listening to the stone fountain's soothing white noise. The variegated blue streaks in the alabaster ceiling began to swim as her vision unfocused, shadows swelling from her peripherals as a familiar feeling of emptiness crept across her soul. The emptiness always came in the night. The distractions of the day kept it at bay, but as soon as Mary was left alone to dwell within her own mind, the void was there to beckon her again.

She could push it back. She could force herself to fill the hollow in her mind with other thoughts, usually ones of worry and insecurity, but it was always a fruitless effort. The void had more substance than she did. It could always outlast her strength.

She gave a long, deep sigh, as if cycling all the air out of her lungs might purge the toxic feelings from her body. One day she would have to face that void, face the memories that spawned it, but it wouldn't be today. It was never today. Fortunately, she'd grown pretty good at living with it as a perpetual tomorrow. She'd found a livable purgatory for herself, precarious as it was.

Mary closed her eyes, trying once more to give herself over to sleep. Yet all the while, the void would linger, encroaching on her from all the hollow places in her mind, wordless, yet ever whispering:

I'll have you.

TEN

AFTER SHIFTING positions roughly twenty times and waiting calmly with her eyes closed for nearly an hour without feeling even the slightest bit inclined to delve into unconsciousness, Mary decided it was a futile effort. She might as well find something productive to do. She flipped on the table lamp, clenching her eyes shut so the fluorescent bulb wouldn't blind her dilated pupils, and slid out of bed. She went to her bag, which she still hadn't really unpacked, and dug out a pair of thermal pants and put them on. She slipped her flight jacket on over her tank top, not bothering to zip it, and walked to the door.

"Is there something I can do for you, Mrs. Ketch?"

Mary nearly jumped back out of her pants at the unexpected presence of SCARAB's voice. "SCARAB . . . no. I'm fine. I am absolutely fine."

"I apologize if I startled you. I merely perceived that you might possibly have a need of some kind."

Mary shook her head and grinned with tight lips. "No, thank you, SCARAB. Remember that thing about discretion, though? Do you think we could establish a house rule that you don't speak to me in my room unless I ask you for something? From this point on?"

"Certainly, Mrs. Ketch. It is my pleasure to leave you at peace in your designated room. If there is any other service I can provide, please do not hesitate to ask."

"Yeah. Sure. Good night, SCARAB." She opened the door and stepped into the hallway, heading back toward the common area. As she passed the open door to Rook's room, she saw him playing what looked like euchre with Yancy. For a second, she considered joining them, but immediately thought better of it. She'd never been able to figure out euchre, and Rook likely cheated anyway.

She entered the common room, picked up the datapad she had left on one of the end tables after dinner, and sat down to begin looking over some of the new data SCARAB had given them about Tantalus 13. It wasn't until she was seated that she noticed Becky sitting at the other end of the couch, also inspecting a datapad.

Becky lifted her glance briefly and grinned. "Hey, Mary." She had a good face for smiling; the softness of her rosy cheeks and the natural upward curve at the corners of her mouth made her smiles come easily and often.

Mary nodded. "Becky. Can't sleep, either?"

Becky sighed and leaned back into the soft couch. "Nope. What a crazy day . . ." Her voice carried the faintest trace of an accent: a uniquely melodious blend of Chinese and Irish that most Earth-born humans found impossible to identify. As well-traveled in the home system as Mary was, it wasn't hard for her to pin its source as New Belfast: a small but particularly prosperous Martian colony.

"Rook and Yancy are up, too. Seems like the excitement's getting to all of us," Mary said. "Hey, actually, I wanted to ask you something. Any thoughts about that big EM surge that hit us on the way down?"

Becky furrowed her brow and shook her head with an apologetic frown. "Honestly, I don't have a clue. It's really bizarre.

As far as I know, no planets we've found have had electromagnetic fields like that. It did seem to occupy about the same area where we'd expect to find Tantalus's magnetosphere, but it didn't act like one. Earth's magnetic field at its strongest is still weaker than your average fridge magnet. This one was thousands of times stronger."

"So . . . what could do that?"

Becky shrugged. "I'm really only forming blind hypotheses at this point, I just don't have enough data yet. The planet must have a much more active core than any we've seen so far, but if that was the case I'd expect to see way more volcanic and tectonic activity on the surface. Plus, having a stronger electromagnetic field doesn't fully explain why it's as energetic as it is. Usually, disturbances in a planet's electromagnetic field come from reactions between particles from the solar wind and the planet's atmosphere, but of course this planet barely *has* any atmosphere and it's the thirteenth planet from its star. There's a brown dwarf in this system that might shed charged particles into Tantalus 13's atmosphere when it orbits close enough, but nowhere near enough to lead to a reaction like what we saw, and this time of year it's on the opposite side of the system. It's a real mystery. I'm looking forward to researching it."

"Hmm." Mary didn't have much of anything to add to Becky's breakdown of the situation. Becky lived to find and unveil the mysteries of the universe, and Mary respected that about her, but her own interest in the anomaly only went as far as *Will it kill us on the way home?*

"Hey, I have a question for you," Becky began with a subject-changing tone in her voice. "Other than the electric disturbance, did you notice anything unusual about the descent today? Unexpected course changes you had to make, difficulty maintaining altitude?"

Mary thought about it for a moment. "Nothing comes to mind. The EM anomaly kind of took the majority of my attention, to be honest. When we got through, everything seemed normal enough, considering the state the ship was in. We were on autopilot for a while, though, and it automatically updates whenever it gets new information about atmospherics and such things. I'd have to check the logs to see if it made any significant corrections. Why?"

"Well, I've been looking at some of my equipment to see if it's calibrated correctly, and at first I thought some of it wasn't. Several of my ground-density sensors were giving me readings that seemed off, but I double-checked them and they were all off by the exact same amount. I started looking at some of our other equipment, and I realized that even our mineral weighing scales were off, by the exact same margin."

"So . . . what does that mean?" Mary asked patiently.

"Well, I wasn't sure at first. I thought it might have been because of Tantalus's thin atmosphere; maybe its lower pressure was to blame. But then I brought some of the equipment in from outside, and it had the same variation. There was only one conclusion I could draw at that point."

"Which was?"

Becky moved closer and lowered her voice, almost conspiratorially. "Tantalus 13 is about 1.2 times the size of Earth, but its gravity is about twenty percent *less* than Earth's is. We didn't feel it because we'd been weightless for so long that any gravity would seem huge, but Tantalus's gravity is *way* lower than it should be."

Mary frowned. "How is that possible?"

Becky shrugged. "No idea. It might be a sign that overall, Tantalus has very little in the way of heavy metals, making it less dense than its size would suggest. But that doesn't match up with the enormous sheet of platinum on our doorstep, or the kind of core composition it would take to maintain a magnetosphere as powerful as this planet has."

Mary thought on that one for a bit. "Maybe the platinum isn't from Tantalus at all. Maybe the asteroid that made this crater didn't uncover the platinum, but contained the platinum itself."

"Not a bad theory," Becky noted. "Though it didn't much look like that from what I could see on our way in. If that's the case though, this crater is probably the only spot on the entire planet worth mining."

"Good thing it's such a great find then. What does the radar satellite say?"

Becky shook her head. "We haven't gotten a clear signal from it yet. The magnetic field is making it really hard to get a link. Hertz is going to keep trying to get through, but we probably won't get any of its data until at least tomorrow. It's going to set us back pretty far if we can't get a signal through. We can't do much without its mapping data."

"Well, one way or another, this mission is still a success," said Mary. "You can bet Exotech is going to screw us over with the finder's bonus, though."

Becky rolled her eyes. "Of course. But even if they just let me keep SCARAB's good silverware, I'll be satisfied." She yawned in an affected way that clearly signified that she had run out of small talk for Mary, stretched, and stood up. "I think I'm going to give sleep another shot. You should get some rest, too. Tomorrow's going to be a big day."

Mary smiled and nodded. "I will, in a bit. I'm just winding down first." Becky left the room, and Mary returned to her data-pad, slouching over it as she rested her elbows on her knees. She mulled over SCARAB's reports, looking at soil analyses, nearby terrain maps, proposed drilling locations, and other uninteresting things meant for the eggheads on the team. She stared blankly at the screen for twenty minutes before she realized she hadn't read a single word of it, then gave up the pretense and tossed the pad onto the couch beside her. She stood up and crossed to the main window in the common area. She pressed a button on the wall, and the metallic shutters slid open.

Tantalus's night cycle was much, much darker than Earth's night. Because Tantalus was so far from its sun, it received very little sunlight even at high noon. There was Ixion, the brown dwarf Becky had mentioned; a celestial body that had never quite decided if it wanted to be a small dwarf star or a large gas-giant planet. It orbited between Tantalus 8 and Tantalus 9, but as Becky had pointed out, at this time of year it was farther from Tantalus 13 than the sun was. Since Tantalus 13 had no moons, the only natural source of illumination came from the trillions of stars above.

Far more of them were visible than on the clearest Earth night, due to the rarified atmosphere and the absence of light pollution. The sky looked nearly the same as it had out the *Diamelen*'s portholes after dropping out of superluminal drive, only the endlessly deep starfield was sharply interrupted by a horizon so black it almost looked like God had grown tired of painting the stars and simply given up on illuminating the bottom half of creation. Staring out at that vast, empty blackness was eerily like standing on the event horizon of a black hole. The knowledge that there was actually ground out there was only comforting if Mary chose to ignore that she was standing in the sole oasis in the middle of an endless, global desert, where rain never fell, life never grew, and the stars never set.

Yet, as she stared into that black expanse, something caught her eye. Deep in the shadow, far beyond the reach of SCARAB's external lights, she saw a faint, electric-blue light flicker in the dark.

Mary squinted, staring into that endless black wasteland. Had she imagined it? Perhaps it had been something reflecting off the window from somewhere inside the room. But it hadn't seemed like a reflection, and no one else was in the room now but her.

A minute passed, then another. She had just about convinced herself she hadn't seen anything after all when it came again. Something flashed, briefly and faintly on the black ground past SCARAB's lights. She continued watching, and after a few minutes she caught another flicker. It was too faint and too fast to observe its source, but it illuminated enough of the ground for her to see that none of SCARAB's drones were anywhere near it. Whatever it was, it wasn't SCARAB.

Something was out there.

ELEVEN

LONG GRASS whispered in the cool summer breeze, rippling under the moonlight and the faint orange glow of city lights far beyond the black tree line. Only a scattering of stars came out this night, and the hazy few that did were outshone by blinking satellites, aircraft, and spacecraft drifting across the sky in long, purposeful arcs.

Young Mary sat on her grandmother's lap, paying no heed to the uninteresting adult conversation taking place between her parents and grandparents. She was enthralled by the sights and sounds of nature beyond her grandparents' porch as the wind rustled the grass and carried the trilling, chirping calls of its denizens to her ears. She was not accustomed to this rural life, and every frog and insect sang a strange and beautiful song that enticed every part of her imagination. Yet above them all, the fireflies entranced her.

They came and went in the murk: tiny motes of neon yellow that flared, then vanished back into the dark. Tonight, there seemed to be hundreds of them, though they never lit simultaneously, or in the same place twice. Their ephemeral light show had Mary enthralled as innumerable gleaming wisps danced above the sea of grass.

"They're talking to one another," her grandmother had said. "It's how they find each other." This explanation only filled Mary with more questions. What were they saying to each other? What did they want?

What were they?

What were they . . .

The vivid childhood memory slipped into Mary's mind as she stared out SCARAB's common room window. The periodic glints of blue light in the black Tantalan desert filled her with the same rapt fascination she'd had as a child, watching those fireflies from her grandparents' porch. Of course, as a child, she'd never been content to merely watch. Or to stay on the porch.

She watched a few more of the flickers before she finally decided to go outside. She walked back to the main airlock, opened up her locker, and began getting into her exosuit.

"I perceive a need: Is there anything I can do for you, Mrs. Ketch?" asked SCARAB. It spoke softly, but Mary still jumped.

"No, SCARAB, I just want to go for a little walk," she answered patiently.

"I do not recommend that you leave the facility alone, Mrs. Ketch," SCARAB said in a stern, cautionary tone. "Exotech expeditionary protocols clearly state that activities outside of pressurized structures must be conducted in pairs, for safety."

Mary sighed, unzipped the pocket of her flight jacket, and pulled out a card, flashing it around for SCARAB's omnipresent view to see. "I have a blue-level piloting certification. I'm cleared to pilot any commercial starcraft, make independent alterations to preprogrammed interstellar travel routes, and to go on solo space walks at my own discretion. Good enough for you?"

SCARAB made a grinding noise before replying, oddly reminiscent of the spooling sound an archaic computer from the late twentieth century might make when overtaxed. "You have the authority to supersede the prohibitive protocols. However, I do strongly recommend that you not go outside alone, Mrs. Ketch."

"Noted." Mary finished getting into her exosuit, then put the helmet on, sealing it tight. "Open the airlock door please."

SCARAB made that strange processing sound again, then opened the inner airlock door. "Take care, Mrs. Ketch."

Mary stepped in, and the door shut behind her. She purged the air from the lock, then opened the outer door. She turned on her helmet's LED headlamps, as well as the smaller one mounted on her left wrist. Despite the illumination the LEDs provided, stepping out of the airlock was like stepping into pure oblivion. The ground was so dark, it may as well not have existed where the light didn't touch. She felt a primeval fear clutching at the back corners of her mind: an inescapable underlying dread that something, anything, could be hiding in that impenetrable starless murk beyond the reach of her headlamps, watching her silently from the airless void. It seemed no matter how old you got, no matter what happened in your life to force maturity and cynicism into your conscious mind, you never fully outgrew the childhood fear that nighttime shadows were the domain of monsters.

She kept her arm-mounted LED pointed at her feet as she walked. The last thing she wanted was to step wrong on a rock or in a hole and sprain her ankle. As much as she might like Ramanathan, she was definitely not eager to rely on his mental and emotional competence to treat an injury at the moment. She lifted her gaze and looked at SCARAB's outer wall. She nearly blinded herself in the process as her headlamps reflected off the mirrorlike polished platinum and blasted her in the face. She cursed and looked away, squeezing her eyes shut and watching a pair of purple phantoms dance across the insides of her eyelids. She shook her head and looked up again, careful not to look directly at the wall, and began walking around the base of the donut-shaped ring of SCARAB's facility.

The building was mounted on a latticework of steel struts, lifting it two feet above the ground where she stood. As she worked her way around the base, the crater's slope descended until the building was elevated to the height of her shoulder. She ducked her head and stepped between two struts, crouching underneath SCARAB. She crept under the building, walking around a number of supports, until she came out on the opposite side from the airlock door, just underneath the common room exterior window.

A large dark shape passed in front of her, briefly blocking out the stars. Mary jumped with a yelp, feeling immediate embarrassment when she swept her lights over the gleaming silvery surface of one of SCARAB's drones, silently rolling past her on its way to attend to some menial task. It swiveled its four-eyed head in her direction, watching her impassively as it drove by. It held its gaze on her for an uncomfortably long time. Even when the sleek platinum sheen of its body passed out of the reach of her headlamp, she could still see four gleaming points of light in the blackness as it maintained its emotionless, mechanical stare.

Satisfied that she had a good vantage point to see whatever phenomenon she had witnessed from inside SCARAB's structure, Mary sat down on the gravelly Tantalus soil and turned off her lamps.

She was immersed in darkness. Only a faint crack of light escaped from underneath the now-closed window shutter, illuminating a long strip of empty ground fifteen feet from where she sat. She stared past it into the black void beyond, waiting for another of the enigmatic blue flashes.

She sat there for five minutes before she finally saw a faint flicker, though it occurred in her peripheral vision, so she was not able to catch its point of origin before it vanished. A few minutes later, she finally saw one. Had she blinked, she would have missed it, but about forty feet away she saw what looked like a miniature lightning bolt flash across the ground.

Don't be shy now. Show me your secrets.

She pressed a button on her gauntlet that turned on the glow feature for her gauges. It showed her air—still good for another four hours of use—her vital functions, and her emergency power supply. She was unconcerned by these; her attention was fixed on the small cluster of gauges that read "environmental hazards." They measured things like exterior temperature, radiation levels, and high-voltage electric currents. She stood up slowly, and cautiously began walking toward the exact spot where she had seen the spark of light, glancing down at the gauges as she went.

It was slow work without the lights on, but Mary didn't want to drown out this odd phenomenon with her high-powered LEDs, so she continued in darkness. Her gauges showed no danger, lying firmly within the lower acceptable range, but she watched them nonetheless.

Stepping past the band of light from the window behind her, she spotted two more faint flickers in quick succession.

She was nearly to the point where she had seen the flash earlier when she was startled out of her wits by a bright blue bolt of light only two feet in front of her. Her gaze shot down to her gauges just in time to see the one measuring electric current fall from the yellow "caution" level down to the green. Her eyes darted back to the spot on the ground, catching a strange, fading afterimage.

It was a spidery tangle of transparent fibers. Its configuration was strangely organic, like veins or roots, and it glowed with a faint aqua hue. She reached down to touch the ground, watching as her electricity gauge rose subtly into the upper green range, and she brushed some of the soil away. She flipped her headlamps back on to get a better look.

It wasn't much easier to see with the lights on: the strange fibers were a transparent bluish white, almost quartz-like, but perfectly smooth and tubular. They spread across the ground in a rootlike shape; the whole cluster of strands roughly four feet across at its largest point. It was so faint that Mary doubted she would have been able to see it in daylight. In fact, if she hadn't been looking for it, she didn't think she would have noticed the strands if she'd been down on one knee right in front of them, as she was now. Though these fibers obviously carried an electric charge somehow, they didn't show any other unique traits as far as she could tell. It was so simple in appearance, and yet . . . so unlike anything Mary had ever seen before.

What are you?

Her hand hovered above the faintly glowing strands. Touching something strange and possibly alien was a bad idea, she knew. Her suit was well insulated from electric currents, and the gauges on her arm still showed the electrical output of the unknown material to be well within the acceptable range, but she knew absolutely nothing about this thing. She should leave it alone. She should go find Becky or Hertz or Gorrister and talk to them about it. She should ask SCARAB what it knew about it.

Yet some indescribable compulsion kept her where she was. Some dark fixation, some morbid curiosity that cared more about satisfaction than safety urged her to stay and experience more. It was similar to the sensation Mary felt every time she looked into the infinite black abyss of superluminal space, and indeed, it was the same impulse that had brought her outside to find this thing by herself. The risk in front of her held a strange allure: a nearly audible call from the void to take the plunge. *Touch me*, it whispered. *Come meet me in the dark of night.*

Her instincts to back away and return to the safety of the base were overcome by her instincts to learn more. Mary reached into her satchel and pulled out a magnet-tipped tele-scoping rod, stretched it out, and gently prodded at the barely visible tendrils, watching them brighten slightly with an ethe-real blue glow once again. Watching her environmental gauges carefully, she tried pulling at a loop of the fiber. To her surprise, it was slightly flexible, unlike any kind of mineral formation she'd ever heard of. *It's alive. Whatever it is, it's alive.*

For several minutes she sat there, caressing the alien fibers with the tip of her magnetic retrieving tool, wholly enraptured by the monumental mystery before her. She could still hear the faint whispers of that elusive voice, that call of the void, but she wasn't sure what it wanted now. She had taken the chance, she had risked a glance at the medusa. She wasn't sure what else her subconscious could dare ask her to try.

Every secret has its secrets. Look deeper. Move just a bit closer to the edge. There is so much more to see . . .

She lifted her head, glancing around to see if she could locate any other clusters like this one. She found none. What she saw instead was the glinting, quad-lensed stares of six of SCARAB'S remote drones, standing motionlessly in a half cir-cle, just beyond her headlamps' reach.

She froze instinctively. *How long has it been watching me out here?* she wondered. *How long have those things been sitting out there?*

Cautiously, she activated her suit's radio. "SCARAB, what are you doing?"

SCARAB's reply was immediate and sounded strangely rehearsed. "As I said, Mrs. Ketch, it is dangerous for anyone to go outside unaccompanied. Since you insisted, I thought I would supervise your outdoor activity remotely, should you require assistance with anything."

"You needed six of your drones to do that? You could have monitored me with one of them; shouldn't the rest be out gathering resources or something? This seems . . . really inefficient of you."

SCARAB made that unsettling grinding sound again. "My greatest concern is the preservation of life, Mrs. Ketch. It is my great pleasure to sacrifice productivity for your security. There are many potential safety risks out here. Loose stones, drilling pits, and power lines pose significant threats in this level of illumination. Anything could happen to you in the dark."

Did it mean for that to sound so ominous?

"Yeah . . . okay, SCARAB."

Mary pulled a small, red marking pennant from her satchel and stuck it in the ground near the fibers. She stood up and cautiously walked back toward the building. There was still a huge mystery to be explored here, but suddenly Mary preferred the idea of investigating it in the daylight, with the rest of the team present.

She swiftly made her way to the airlock, and sealed it behind her, pretending she didn't see the empty, four-eyed stares of a dozen drones watching her from the shadows the entire way.

TWELVE

MARY DID not sleep easily that night. Her slumber was peppered with the sort of malformed dreamlets that never fully coalesce into comprehensible nightmares.

A true dream might have been preferable. If the malaise in her unconsciousness congealed into solid concepts, she could at least have defined what made them so unsettling. No scenes played in her mind; she did not revisit any of the painful memories she had tried to leave behind on Earth. There was only dark emptiness, and waves of disembodied emotion that may or may not have had anything to do with her waking life. Anxiety, paranoia, loneliness, dread; these dark and heavy feelings washed over and through her like malignant ghosts leaving traces of their damaged souls on her psyche.

As she drifted bodiless through the black expanse of her own subconscious, Mary could hear faint whispers too subdued to discern. Even though she couldn't make out any of their words, she knew some of their intent. They were harsh, caustic utterances, some coming in her own voice, some in her husband, John's, some in the voices of her crewmates, and many others that sounded like no one in particular. They gave voice to the emotions that breezed through her. *Alone,* one might have said. *Lost,* could be another.

Tuning them out was fruitless; she could barely hear the words and couldn't comprehend them, but their meaning imprinted on her mind, regardless. She could only drift helplessly through the endless whispering nothingness as waves of bleakness rolled over her.

Finally, blessedly, the murmurs and sensations faded into silence as she was pulled back to consciousness by a knock at her bedroom door.

She moaned with the exasperation reserved only for those who wake realizing their sleep has cost them more rest than it gave, and clapped a clammy hand over her fatigue-darkened eyes. She wanted another chance at sleep; that last attempt, by all rights, shouldn't count. Still, the day had begun, and whether she liked it or not, she'd have to participate in it. In any case, she still had to tell Commander Gorrister about her discovery outside the night before. That was going to be an interesting conversation . . .

"Gimme a minute," Mary said hoarsely. She suddenly remembered that, now that they were in planetary gravity again, they could finally brew coffee properly. That brought her a modest improvement in mood.

Mary swung her legs over the edge of her bed and hoisted herself off it with a groan. The aches of yesterday's exertion still throbbed between every bone in her skeleton. She'd done a good job of keeping up a consistent daily workout routine with the *Diamelen*'s exercise equipment to reduce bone and muscle atrophy during her prolonged stint in microgravity, but in the end, it was never enough to fully negate it. Space was a toll road, and her body bought the ticket.

She slipped into her uniform with relative haste, stumbling over herself a few times, including an impressive near-summersault while she tried to put on her socks. She stood up, straightened out her shirt, and opened the door.

To her surprise, it was Ramanathan on the other side of the door. He wore his uniform, clean, but not pressed, and his wavy black hair had seen only the barest modification from whatever state his pillow had left it. The dark circles under his eyes had deepened again. "Morning, Mary," he said softly.

"Morning, Nate. What's up?" She constructed a smile for his benefit.

"S'posed to do a checkup on the crew. Day one protocols, and such. Got to everybody else already. Didn't want to wake you, but Gorrister told me to get you up."

"Oh, right." Mary searched his eyes for a moment, trying to get a hint at his current mental and emotional state. She'd hoped once they reached their destination Ramanathan's depressive mood might have improved. Perhaps all he'd really needed was the familiar feel of ground beneath his feet.

Maybe it was too early to tell, but Ramanathan did not seem better. The news last night of Tantalus's platinum wealth had barely coaxed a twitch of a smile from him at the time, and now he seemed just as melancholic and lost in himself as he had in the last days of their flight. His dark eyes still tended to wander off into nowhere when not engaged. His posture was closed and withdrawn, giving the impression that he might pull inside himself like a hermit crab when threatened. His voice was small and still, as if he were afraid of waking himself by speaking too loudly. He had shrunk so much from the charming, amicable man he had been at the start of the mission, and as far as Mary knew, the transformation had happened completely without direct cause.

Oh, Nate. I don't know what battle you're losing in your spirit, but I wish I knew how to help you fight.

"Come in." Mary went back to her bed and sat down, and Ramanathan followed. He opened up his case on the bed beside her and pulled out a blood pressure cuff.

"Right arm, please."

Mary pulled the thin fabric of her right sleeve up to just below the shoulder and held her bare arm outward. Ramanathan wrapped the cuff around it and began pumping it with air. "So, you got everyone else already? What time is it?"

"Oh-eight-hundred, mission time. The sun rose about two hours ago."

"What? Why didn't anybody wake me up earlier?"

Ramanathan shrugged. "SCARAB woke the rest of us up at sunrise, per Gorrister's instructions. Don't know why it didn't wake you."

Mary scowled at the ceiling. "SCARAB, why didn't you wake me with the others?"

"You instructed me not to speak to you in this room unless addressed by you first, Mrs. Ketch," SCARAB replied instantly.

"That means don't randomly ask me if I need help tying my shoes or whatever. If someone's trying to get in contact with me, let me know, especially if it's the commander. We have a rank system here, SCARAB, you should really be aware of that. My instructions don't supersede his." In fact, SCARAB *absolutely* should have been aware of that. How it had managed to completely fail to acknowledge the proper chain of command, Mary didn't know, but she wasn't looking forward to the scolding from Gorrister later.

"My apologies, Mrs. Ketch. I misinterpreted the commander's intent. It will not happen again."

"Eighty-five over fifty-five," Ramanathan announced as he ripped the Velcro armband off. "Low, but within expected levels."

He went on to perform a few other tests: he checked her vision, her reflexes, and he inspected her feet to ensure her blood was circulating properly. He asked about vertigo, excess pressure in her sinuses, difficulty standing, and so on. She had heard it all before.

Mary couldn't escape the bitter irony of such a clearly unwell physician checking on her welfare. Her own mental health was a tattered mess, but she had at least reached a point where she could coexist with her messed-up brain well enough to function in relative normality. But Ramanathan only seemed to be getting worse. She hadn't noticed it in flight because of the natural fluid redistribution their bodies had all experienced, but he had lost a lot of weight.

"Nate . . . are you okay?" she finally asked. "I mean it seriously, you have been really down for a while now, and I've been worried about you."

"I'm fine, Mary." The faint smile he propped up for her benefit did little to convince. More telling by far were the gray bags forming under his dark eyes, the thick tangle of untended hair that had once been so well kept, the thickening beard stubble that had been all black when they'd left Earth but now had flecks of gray.

"Nate, something's up. I've seen it. Something's bothering you. I'm not going to pry, but if there's something on your mind, I'd like to listen."

Ramanathan sighed and sat down beside her. He stared at the floor for a moment, presumably collecting his thoughts. When he spoke, he still didn't make eye contact.

"I didn't get to mention it before, but I was really impressed with the way you handled that complication during our descent yesterday. You stayed cool under pressure in ways most people couldn't. Have you ever had to deal with anything like that before?"

Can't let him change the subject. If he needs an opener to segue into whatever he needs to talk about, I can give it to him, but if this doesn't come back around to him, I'll have to push again. He's carried this alone way too long.

"I've never had anything that rough happen on a flight before. I've had a few hiccups here and there that got my blood pumping, but rarely anything that really scared me. The worst flight I ever had before this one was probably this one cargo delivery to the military training facility on Tahani. I was flying an *Encantado*-class freight hauler at the time, which is about as maneuverable as a dead elephant."

Mary watched Ramanathan as she spoke, and saw a refreshing look of genuine engagement in his expression. He was listening to her, if nothing else. "Tahani is a rough planet," she continued. "I was warned about it before I made the flight and I planned accordingly, but warnings and simulations only prepare you for so much. Its gravity is three times higher than Earth's, and its atmosphere is a lot thicker. Some places the air is so thick it behaves more like a liquid than a gas. It's hot, too, and the constant changes in air pressure and temperature cause violent storms over almost the entire planet. Worse, the air is so oxygen thick, the slightest spark can cause an out-of-control fire in seconds. There's only one place on the entire planet that's even slightly habitable: a mountaintop that sits above the worst weather formations.

"I was a nervous wreck right before the flight down. The ship was hard enough to steer in open space, let alone in an atmosphere made of soup. As soon as I hit the mesosphere, the turbulence about knocked all my teeth out. Heat from atmospheric friction turned the whole front of the ship into a fireball, so I had to rely entirely on instruments to see. I was flying blind in a ship trying to shake itself apart, knowing if I didn't hold it perfectly steady some bad wind shear in that thick air could have ripped the ship in half. Once, an updraft almost turned the ship sideways, but I managed to fight back and get reoriented. Even when I got visuals back and made it to the landing strip, the higher gravity made a smooth landing basically impossible. You don't land on Tahani so much as gently crash. There were four different times during my descent that

I almost lost control of my ship. I was terrified the whole ride down. I made one cargo run there and I was done with that planet for good."

Ramanathan nodded. "But you kept your composure, when the time came? You were frightened, and everything was chaos around you, but you kept your head?"

Mary nodded slowly. "Yeah . . . I mean . . . you have to. When you're in a crisis like that, your body wants to panic, but if you let it, you die. You have to shut out your emotions and let your rational brain take over. Somewhere in the back of my brain I was screaming the entire time, but I locked that part of me down for survival. If you do everything right and you get to the ground safe, you can let yourself panic later. If you panic in the air, there's no time later to think rationally about how you could have done it differently."

"That is a good mindset to have. It's no wonder you brought us down safely as well as you did." Ramanathan clasped his hands together, staring at them. "Before that flight on Tahani, did you believe you could do that? Keep your head in a crisis, that is."

"I guess I always hoped I could. I trained long enough to know everything I had to do. Nothing really came as a surprise. But I guess you don't really know how far you can push your limits until you don't have a choice. Tahani taught me I was capable of getting through something way harder than anything I'd ever faced before. I guess what happened yesterday showed me I can push my limits even further. When survival is on the line, you can find reserves you never knew you had access to before."

"Wise words," Ramanathan said softly. He didn't venture any further comment.

"Ramanathan," Mary prodded gently. "You still haven't answered my question. What's wrong?"

Ramanathan sighed deeply, staring blankly at the water fountain beside Mary's bed. For a few moments, it seemed like he would dodge the question again, but at last he spoke.

"This probably won't give you any reassurance in my competency, but you asked. When I was selected for this mission, I was on the verge of losing my practitioner's license. I worked in an emergency clinic . . ." Ramanathan began to rub his temples, simultaneously shielding his face further from Mary's sight.

Mary leaned over, trying to find Ramanathan's eyes, but he only pulled deeper into himself. She sat back up and waited.

Ramanathan opened his mouth, then closed it again. He repeated this gesture several times as a switch flipped back and forth somewhere in his mind. Mary feared he would close up again, but at last Ramanathan managed to push through whatever barrier had held his words and thoughts captive.

"I worked in an emergency clinic. There was a patient. Car accident, severe cranial trauma. He was . . . awake. Alert. Totally lucid. But with the extent of his wounds . . . he shouldn't have been. His injuries were critical, but we didn't know the full extent of the damage. We couldn't proceed. You can't just . . . dig in a man's head to find out what's wrong. Time was running out, so I made the call to rush him through our imaging scanner. He . . ."

Ramanathan cradled his face in his hands. Mary realized something then; he *couldn't* look at her. Averting his gaze wasn't a choice, it was a physical act he could not keep himself from doing. Every time she was able to coax some shred of security out of him, he reverted back to hiding himself seconds later. He was trapped in a loop of . . . something. Dread? Shame? Guilt?

"It's okay, Nate," Mary said softly and warmly as she could. "You're here. You're now. You—"

"Fifty seconds," Ramanathan interrupted, his face still hidden in his hands. "That's all it took to get the scan. But twenty seconds in, and he starts screaming . . . 'Help!' he said. 'Help, I'm on fire! My head is on fire!'"

Tears began to drip down Ramanathan's cheeks, and he swallowed a heavy lump in his throat before continuing. "I didn't know what to do. I didn't understand what was happening. I should have, but in the moment, I . . . my mind became useless to me. I thought to myself he'll be fine, only thirty more seconds and he can come out, we'll have the scans. But he kept *screaming*.

"Finally, we pulled him out. He . . . wasn't screaming anymore. He was gone. His face . . . it was locked in this look . . . terror and agony. His eyes were wide and pure red from burst vessels. There was smoke, little wisps of it coming out of his nostrils. It smelled of burnt electronics and flesh.

"That was exactly what it was. We found out from the scans that he had implants. A few cortical enhancements for boosting his visual acuity and mental awareness. He'd told us he had no such implants. But . . . of course he'd say that. Those kinds of implants are rare and illegal outside the Expansionary Coalition. He was afraid of legal repercussions. He didn't understand . . .

"It turns out," Ramanathan spoke with plodding deliberation, "the implants were sustaining his neuroactivity where it otherwise would have failed. They were keeping him alive. The imaging scanner burnt them out, further damaging his brain tissue in the process. When I put him in that imaging chamber . . . I killed him."

"But you didn't know," Mary said, trying to put some kind of reassurance in her voice. "He said he didn't have any implants. You had no reason to think he was lying."

Ramanathan barely showed any acknowledgment of her words. "There are less invasive scanning procedures we could have used. Ones that wouldn't have hurt him. But regardless, if

I had pulled him from that chamber when he started screaming, I might have saved him. It was not too late at that point. But I didn't. I froze. I took just a few seconds too long to think, and it cost that man his life."

Finally, Ramanathan was able to pull his head from his hands, but still did not seem to have the strength to look Mary in the eye. "There was a malpractice lawsuit. All the documentation had been done properly, and there was no breach in protocol, so I was eventually found not to be at fault, but by then I'd been all but ruined financially."

Mary gave Ramanathan's arm what she hoped was a reassuring squeeze. "Nate . . . it wasn't your fault that you lost him."

Ramanathan shook his head. "No, that's not it. It's not guilt. It isn't the money, either. It's . . ." For the first time in the conversation, Ramanathan made eye contact with Mary. His expression was surprising; it wasn't sadness, it wasn't remorse, or even worry. It was *fear*. "I'm a disgraced doctor, Mary. My medical career is just about history. You are an ex-pilot, and I know you have plenty of baggage of your own. I have psych profiles on every member of this crew, and none of them are ideal for this mission. Patient confidentiality is in effect there, so I can't give you specifics, but it's true. Now, answer this question: Why would Exotech handpick a second-rate crew to carry out a very important survey mission, establish the foundation of a mining colony, the *first* mining colony, on a newly discovered planet?"

Mary thought for a moment and shrugged. "To give us a chance, maybe? I think you're selling us a bit short, Nate. Becky and Will both seem plenty qualified to me, and Rook and Yancy may be screwups, but anytime they talk shop about mining they seem to take it pretty seriously. Plus, the original telescope images didn't show this platinum deposit, so Exotech probably didn't think this mining colony would be as productive as it will be."

Nate shook his head again. "All mining colonies are important to Exotech. They're the first ones to find this planet, so until someone else sets down on another part of it, the whole planet is theirs. It's standard procedure for mining colonies to spread out and claim as much land as they can grab as soon as they make planetfall. That's why they send SCARAB drones; so they can start building a base immediately and get ahead of any competition. No, there's only one reason I could think of why we would be chosen for this job."

"And what reason would that be, Nate?"

Ramanathan looked away from her again. "Exotech believes there is a chance that something will go wrong on this mission, and for some reason they don't care. They assembled a crew they don't mind losing."

THIRTEEN

"ALRIGHT, LISTEN up, folks," Yancy declared with an unearned air of authority. "What we have here are the six things on this mission that are most likely to kill you."

Mary forced herself not to tune out Yancy's voice on her comm. The key word in "mandatory safety meeting" was "mandatory." Somewhere in the formal Exotech survey mission bible was a passage that Gorrister likely knew by heart, and that section laid out in no uncertain terms that a safety meeting had to happen at such and such a time in the mission, had to cover this and that, and no one was allowed to miss it. It was a tedious and probably needless formality; SCARAB would be doing most of the dangerous work itself, and whatever it wasn't allowed to do would be done by someone who already knew the risks better than whatever pencil pusher wrote the list Gorrister and Yancy were reading through. But as long as there were checklists to fill, Gorrister would fill them, and Yancy wasn't about to miss out on a we've-finally-gotten-to-the-part-of-the-trip-I'm-here-for-and-I'm-going-to-milk-it-for-all-it's-worth opportunity.

Yancy picked up what looked vaguely like a fire extinguisher with a longer, thinner nozzle and held it up for everyone to see. "This is a plasma torch. We use it to cut or weld metal or other dense materials. Chances are good that you will each be using one of these at some point, so be very careful." He pressed a button on the side of his exosuit's helmet, and the rugged Latin features of his face vanished as his visor tinted itself black. "Always put your shades on when you use this guy. It's bright enough to blind you permanently after about twenty seconds of exposure."

Without warning, he flicked on the torch, and a brilliant blue-white flame shot out six inches from its tip. The others were standing fifteen feet away, but the plasma burst from the torch was like a scalpel in Mary's eye. They all instantly shielded their eyes from the glare of the flame, which Yancy shut off after less than a full second's use. "See what I mean?"

"Yancy, seriously, was that necessary?" Hertz proclaimed, after flipping on his own visor's light filter for safe measure.

Yancy grinned annoyingly as Rook chuckled. "Nope." He set the torch down and picked up something resembling the unholy union of a tommy gun and a jackhammer. "This is a deep-reaching EM probe deployment gun. What it does is take these"—he held up what looked like an elongated bullet the size of a railroad spike with a screw thread coiled around it—"and it shoots them deep into the ground. These are hyperspectral imaging probes; they give periodic electromagnetic pulses, which they use to gauge the composition of the rocks around them. The gun is powerful enough to send them up to ten feet underground, depending on what rocks they have to punch through. Now, if you goof off with them and deploy them out of the ground . . ."

He hefted the brutal-looking tool awkwardly to his shoulder, aimed it at a forty-five-degree angle, and pulled the trigger. A popping sound rang out, and almost before they could even catch sight of it, a primed drill-bit sensor zoomed in a high parabolic arc out of sight. Yancy gave a self-satisfied smile. "Boom. Field goal. Anyway, it has a barrel clip with ten spikes. You'll be setting up a perimeter of these bad boys today. Also, it's important not to plant these sensors closer than twenty feet to any stationary electronic equipment, including SCARAB; the EM pulses can mess them up."

"It's also important not to waste company resources or our time, Yancy." Gorrister glowered, searching the horizon for the single EM sensor spike Yancy had just wasted, as if losing one would break Exotech's choke hold on the galactic economy. "Less showmanship and more sticking to the checklist, please. We've got a lot of work to get done today."

"Okay, okay." Yancy set the probe gun down and moved on to the next item: a truck-sized vehicle with a large tube mounted on a swiveling crane arm on the back. "This is a Dawson eighty-caliber core extraction drill. It fires a continuous rotary-cutting laser capable of carving out a perfect cylinder of solid granite sixteen feet long in less than a minute. After it cuts, it shoots out a collection arm that sheathes the core sample, cuts it off at the base, and yanks it out of the ground. It only takes sixteen-foot samples at a time, but the collection arm can extend up to five times that length to reach the deeper samples. Now, knowing what it can do to solid rock, I really shouldn't have to tell you what it can do to a person."

"These," Yancy said, placing his hands on two large crates, "are the explosives. We have two kinds. There's the XTK-12 plastic explosives, which we have in half-pound bricks and two-ounce tubes. It can only be detonated with an electric charge of two hundred fifty volts. Other than that, it's completely stable. You could use it for chewing gum if you wanted to, but I wouldn't recommend it. It tastes like motor oil."

"You're speaking from personal experience, aren't you?" Becky remarked with a smirk.

"You'll never know," Yancy said with a mischievous wink. "Anyway, the other explosives we have are much nastier." He lifted a large metal football-sized ovoid out of the second case. "These are called Pompeii Coconuts in some circles. They're miniature clean nukes; each one has enough kick to level Mount Rushmore. We have three of them, but we probably won't use them. Me and Rook are the only ones cleared to use these, and the only people who know the activation codes are us and Gorrister, so you don't really need to worry about them."

The last attraction in the cavalcade of potential limb removers was by far the biggest. It was a massive vehicle that had taken up half of the *Diamelen*'s cargo bay. It looked vaguely like a cement mixer truck, only it had four sets of treads instead of wheels, and the oversized barrel mounted on its back had four bulky extendable support struts affixed to it.

"And the main attraction, Dawson's big brother, Attila. Attila is a directed-energy drill with a compact relativistic ion-collider core. The beam it emits is hotter than the surface of a neutron star, and it's capable of burning through a ten-foot-thick titanium wall in less than six seconds. If you left one of these babies running for a day, give or take, you could bore a hole clean through Ganymede. Again, only me and Rook are allowed to use it."

Becky said what all the others were thinking. "Aren't Attila and the nukes a little excessive?"

"Little bit, yeah," Yancy conceded. "Chances are, we won't use most of this stuff; we're mostly just delivery boys for the next batch of miners, the ones who will actually be living here and colonizing the place. Attila and the nukes are a bit too sophisticated for SCARAB to manufacture on its own, and SCARAB has some safety protocols that don't allow it to even try. We *will* be using the plasma torch, EM probes, and the core sampler, for certain, though. In fact . . ." Yancy reached into a large crate and grabbed two more EM probe guns. "We're going to be using these now. So, Hertz, Mary, and Becky, grab a gun and come with me. We're going to set up a perimeter so we can find a nice spot to drill later."

"Actually," Gorrister said sternly. "Not Mary."

Great. Mary Ketch to the principal's office . . .

"Alright, then . . . Doc, grab a gun and join us. Rook is going to work on assembling Attila. We'll work until . . . When do you want us meeting up again, Commander?"

Gorrister stood and addressed the group. "The GPR satellite will be in the best position to send a clear transmission in four hours. I want Hertz back in two to start watching our receiving antenna so we can try to get a data link. Everyone else, meet up in SCARAB at twelve-hundred hours. Check in with me hourly and keep an eye on your consumables; return to base to refill your air tanks as needed. If you need anything else, ask SCARAB."

"Okay. You heard him. Doc, Hertz, and Becky, let's move out."

The group dispersed. Ramanathan, Becky, and Hertz unenthusiastically picked up probe guns and extra barrel clips of sensor spikes, then followed Yancy as he led them into the expansive desert of the crater basin. Rook quickly started unloading parts of the energy drill that had been removed for transport, and Mary approached Commander Gorrister sheepishly.

"Commander, I—"

Gorrister raised his gloved hand, silencing her. "Switch to Channel B, please."

Mary winced. That was the private channel.

Mary switched her comm to Channel B. "Commander, I'm sorry I overslept. SCARAB didn't wake me like the others. It said it didn't get that your request was a demand."

Gorrister's disapproving scowl was apparent even through his exosuit's helmet visor. "I'm not talking about that. I sorted that out with SCARAB already. In that conversation, SCARAB also divulged some very interesting information about you. Apparently, you sleepwalk. In a space suit. Outside. Alone. Is that true, Mary?"

"I did put in some EVA time last night, sir, but only for about ten or fifteen minutes. I saw something outside that I wanted to investigate."

Gorrister's expression did not lighten. "Exotech has a very specific set of rules for extravehicular activity. The biggest and most obvious one is that nobody goes out alone. The second biggest one is that nobody does it without the approval of the mission commander. Someone with your experience shouldn't need to be told that."

"It's my experience that justifies what I did. I have blue-level pilot's credentials; I'm authorized for solo space walks at my own discretion."

Gorrister's brow furrowed, darkening his eyes as his face reddened. "You're going to pull that card? Okay. Those credentials qualify you for that when you're flying solo missions or when you yourself are the mission commander. When you're on a mission and you're not at the top of the chain of command, you do *not* get to take a stroll whenever it strikes your fancy. You're *qualified* for solo walks, but only *authorized* if I clear it."

Mary rolled her eyes. "Commander, I've logged more than four hundred and fifty EVA hours. I don't even get disoriented in open space anymore. I think I'm good enough to—"

"I don't care if you're Buzz freakin' Aldrin," Gorrister snapped. "No EVA is allowed unless I clear it. You pull a stunt like that again, I'll have SCARAB drag you back in and keep you locked in your room for the remainder of our stay. Clear on that?"

Mary bit her lip. *For every hour he's spent outside of an air-lock, I've spent a day. He has no reason to pull rank on this. He's only making this an issue because his authority lets him and his ego makes him.* "Yes, Commander. I'm clear on that."

"Good. Now, how about you tell me what you saw last night that was interesting enough to get you to go outside at night?"

"I was going to tell you about that anyway, sir." Mary began searching the ground, looking for the pennant she had planted last night. "I saw what looked like electric discharges on the ground out the window. I wanted to investigate the source."

Gorrister crossed his arms and sat back onto his crate. "Probably one of SCARAB's drones doing some spot welding."

Mary shook her head. "It wasn't. When I came out, I found something strange on the ground. I think it may have been biological." She frowned. Where had she set that pennant? She thought she was looking in the right area, but it wasn't there.

"Biological?" Gorrister raised an incredulous eyebrow. "I have a hard time believing SCARAB would have missed a life-form, especially one this close."

"I'm not sure it was biological, but it did carry a strong electric current. If it's geological, I can't imagine what kind of mineral it could be." Mary got down on her hands and knees. She had given up on finding the pennant and was now hoping she could find another of the fibrous clusters to show Gorrister. "It was sprawling across the ground, almost like plant roots. It's transparent with a faint blue glow. I'm not sure I can find it in the daytime, but at night it makes these flashes every once in a while, like little lightning strikes."

"Uh-huh." Gorrister stood and jerked his head in the direction of the landing strip. "Go work on those ship repairs you mentioned before. If you spot any alien alfalfa, pin a marker to the spot and call us over. Otherwise, don't waste my time."

Mary scowled, but stood up and nodded. "Alright, sir. I'll be sure to mark it more clearly next time."

She half walked, half stormed off in the direction of the *Diamelen*. She knew she'd marked that spot before. It'd been so dark she hadn't been able to see any landmarks to identify the spot in daylight, but she knew those patches of electric tendrils were lying out there somewhere.

Whatever she'd seen last night, it was something important. She'd find it again, if she had to stay up all night to do it. She'd see the lights again. They were out there. They had to be.

They had to be . . .

FOURTEEN

EVEN THOUGH it had essentially been Mary's prison for the past six months, returning to the *Diamelen* felt oddly comforting. After the weirdness of last night's jaunt outside and the awkwardness of her conversation with Gorrister a few minutes ago, the chance to work on something familiar for a while was nice. She was no mechanic, but part of getting her pilot's certification had included training in basic starship maintenance, and replacing overcharge fuses was, fortunately, a fairly straightforward job.

She walked up the boarding ramp and down to the engineering module, climbed over a few inconveniently placed crates of equipment labeled as Hertz's, and grabbed her diagnostic scanner and tool kit. As she came back out of the ship, she was startled once again to see one of SCARAB's drones, sitting silently at the foot of the boarding ramp, staring at her.

Mary jumped, almost dropping her scanner. "SCARAB, you—can I help you?" She barely managed to hold herself back from cussing the drone out. *Don't flip out. It's just a robot. Yelling at it won't even be satisfying.*

"Oh, no, Mrs. Ketch." SCARAB seemed to either ignore the irritation in Mary's tone or fail to notice it. "I perceived that you were about to begin work on your ship repairs, so I brought you the replacement overcharge fuses I manufactured last night." The drone opened a large compartment in its torso, swiveled two of its fine manipulator arms into position, and pulled out six smooth, wedge-shaped metallic objects, each the size of a brick.

Great. It's actually being helpful for a change. Now I get to feel guilty for snapping at a computer. "Oh. Thank you, SCARAB. I was going to ask about those."

"It is my great pleasure to serve, Mrs. Ketch. Would you like me to assist you in their installation?"

"Maybe in a bit," Mary said as she began climbing the ladder rungs on the *Diamelen*'s port side. "I want to check and see if anything else is wrong with the propulsion systems before I get started."

"Of course, Mrs. Ketch. If you do require assistance, please do not hesitate to ask."

"Yup," Mary said, tuning the AI out as she finished climbing onto the upper hull of the *Diamelen*. Even though the conversation was obviously over, the drone was still just sitting there, watching her from the ground.

It's like a puppy that has to follow you everywhere and get involved with everything, only not cute.

Ignoring the drone, she paced the length of the *Diamelen*'s roof. She was twenty to thirty feet above the ground, but this kind of work was so routine for her that she scarcely noticed. She watched her scanner as it measured the power flow through the ship's inner systems and compared it to the standard data for an *Arsat*-class ship. She double- and triple-checked the integrity of the drive system, from the engine to the cockpit. Fortunately, it seemed everything was within the acceptable range except for the overcharge fuses. They had done their job perfectly, blowing out instead of letting more sensitive systems take the damage of a power surge.

Mary hunkered next to the engine cowling and unbolted the hull panels that would give her access to the *Diamelen*'s burnt-out overcharge fuses. On the one hand, she was grateful that the damages weren't more severe; she should be able to get the ship properly space-worthy in just a couple of hours now. On the other hand, as soon as she finished working on the ship, she'd probably have to go out and lay some sensor spikes with the others. Working on the ship was familiar and comforting, almost meditative. Hauling around a heavy probe deployment gun for the rest of the day would just be . . . work.

The cowling came off easily enough, but the overcharge fuses were another matter. They hadn't just burnt out, they had practically melted. They no longer resembled the clean, symmetrical pieces of hardware SCARAB had made for her. Now they were charred black and warped into unpleasant shapes. Only one of the six came out without a fuss, three more took an extensive amount of finesse and muscle to dislodge, and the last two were so badly mangled Mary had to cut them into pieces with a circular handsaw to get them out. The fact that these fuses had taken as much damage as they had and still fulfilled their function was a testament to their craftsmanship, but it was also a reminder of just how bizarre the phenomenon that caused this truly was. Nothing the *Diamelen* could fly through should have been able to slag a full set of overcharge fuses like that. Not even close.

After cautiously cleaning out the couplings and relay sockets of any charred fragments from the old fuses, Mary climbed back down the ladder and picked up one of the new ones. She frowned, hefting the part in her hand. Something felt off about it. It looked fine on the outside; it resembled an industry-standard overcharge fuse in every way. But there was something barely noticeable that was off about its weight distribution.

"SCARAB," Mary addressed the drone that had delivered the new parts. Even though she had ignored it while she took out the old fuses, it had sat there watching her the entire time. "What model is this fuse, exactly?"

"I built it using the template of an Exotech 599956 ten-slot 190 overcharge fuse, Mrs. Ketch."

Mary frowned, and double-checked the info on her diagnostic scanner. "SCARAB, the *Arsat* class takes a 599862, not a 599956. This is the wrong part."

SCARAB made that odd grinding sound again before responding. "I apologize for the error, Mrs. Ketch. It is possible my schematics database is out of date. Will the part still suffice?"

Mary entered a query into her diagnostic scanner and knit her eyebrows together in concern as she read the results. It would seem that it was not an uncommon mistake to get the two parts confused for each other, due to their practically identical appearance. But according to the warnings her query had highlighted, it was often a very costly error. The parts SCARAB had built were designed for a much smaller vessel and were designed to process a much lower energy output. If she had installed them into the *Diamelen*, the simple act of turning on the engines would have burnt them out again, and anything more strenuous would blow right through them and damage the very systems the fuses were meant to protect. It could have kept the ship grounded for a very long time.

"No, SCARAB," Mary said slowly, trying not to show the concern in her voice. "No, I'm afraid I can't use them."

"I sincerely apologize for the error, Mrs. Ketch. Would you like me to begin fabricating new parts? I can have a full set of the appropriate part within the hour."

Mary shook her head. "No, SCARAB, that's fine. We do have an emergency backup set in cargo, I'll just use those."

"Of course, Mrs. Ketch. Again, please let me know if I can be of any assistance."

Mary nodded silently and boarded the ship once again, trying to ignore the chills running down her spine. The mistake SCARAB had made might have been a common one, but it was common because of human error. The parts look the same, so it'd be easy for a mechanic to grab the wrong one off a shelf. But SCARAB hadn't been grabbing anything off a shelf; it had been building them from scratch from a schematic it should have pulled up as soon as Hertz had told it what they needed. Outdated ship schematics wouldn't have mattered: the *Arsat* class had *never* been compatible with that part. It shouldn't have been possible for SCARAB to make that mistake.

As Mary gathered up the parts she would need from storage, she fought back a question that insisted on being heard anyway: If SCARAB could make a mistake that significant, just how safe were they?

FIFTEEN

BY THE time Mary finished installing the backup fuses, the rest of the crew had already returned to SCARAB's base for lunch. She bolted the engine cowling down again and packed her tools away in the engineering module, then entered the base's airlock. Tantalus's atmosphere vented out, breathable atmosphere vented in, and she stepped into the entry area, gladly stripping off her sweat-sticky exosuit and hanging it on a rack with the others. She wanted a shower, but she needed food, so she made her way to the kitchen.

SCARAB's kitchen and dining room space continued the streamlined modernist aesthetic used throughout the rest of the facility. The room was small and circular, but made efficient and elegant use of its space. Compact cabinets and countertops encircled the kitchen half of the room, with a small sink nestled cozily into the countertop next to a glass-front refrigerator with platinum handles. Another counter topped with a single slab of polished stone stood out from one wall to split the kitchen off from the dining area, where Yancy, Rook, Gorrister, Ramanathan, and Becky sat around a white, ovular table.

"There you are. Took you long enough," Yancy teased. She gave him a tolerant smile and opened the refrigerator. Sadly, master of fabrication though SCARAB may be, it couldn't create organic materials like food, so she was stuck with the same vacuum-sealed, freeze-dried rations she'd been eating since day one of the journey. She rifled through the locker until she found a plastic tray labeled SALISBURY STEAK. Usually a lesser evil, in her experience.

"SCARAB, do you have a microwave, or something?" she muttered.

"To your left, Mrs. Ketch. Above the waste reclamation bin," it cheerily replied.

She popped the small plastic canister into the microwave, which looked a lot more like a square mailbox, and nuked it for twenty seconds.

"Did you manage to get the ship fixed, Mary?" Gorrister asked between bites of . . . something.

"I think so. I'll need to do a systems check later, but everything looks good."

Gorrister nodded. "Good work. Our perimeter is set up, too, so we're staying on schedule so far."

Mary opened the little microwave oven and removed her lunch. She peeled off its plastic packaging to reveal what very nearly resembled an actual Salisbury steak in gravy. Given that the meal was designed to be eaten in microgravity, however, the "gravy" was more like a thin meat paste, which stuck nearly as well to the packaging as it did to the walls of her large intestine. Mary took her modest meal to the table, taking a seat between Ramanathan and Gorrister. "Where's Hertz?"

"He's downloading the data from the satellite's first orbit," Becky answered. "He finally got it to sync. We're going to cross-reference the readings from the satellite and our sensor perimeter to try to find a good place for Rook to set up Attila and dig a primary mine shaft."

"We're doing all of that in one day?" Mary asked, trying not to sound too fatigued, but not doing a terribly good job of it.

"Rook, Yancy, and Hertz are going to be doing that in one day," Gorrister replied. "You, Becky, and I are going to take the Dawson out after lunch and start extracting cores. Remember, we're on a tight schedule here, Mary. There's not a lot of time for sitting on the patio drinking sweet tea."

"Right." Mary was a pilot. She flew things. She'd logged almost two thousand hours of atmospheric flight time, completed close to two hundred interplanetary flights, and graduated in the top 0.5 percent of her class at the academy. Flying was her thing. It was something she was good at and liked to do, and she'd made a career of it specifically to avoid having to do things she *wasn't* good at and *didn't* like to do. She'd spent half a year doing all the work while the other six members of her crew did absolutely nothing. She hadn't expected to be idle while they were on Tantalus, but she certainly hadn't expected to be a pack mule. She'd spent most of her morning bashing scorched-out chunks of metal from her ship's engine, and now she was going to have to help dig up sixteen-foot stone cylinders and haul them to their cargo hold. This really wasn't the job she'd thought she'd signed on for.

"So, anyway," said Rook, continuing a conversation he must have started before Mary came in, "this is what I think we should do. We each take some of our personal belongings, like underwear or something, and arrange them together in as big a circle as we can right over top of the platinum. Technically, that's our circle of platinum; we've staked our claim with our own belongings, so Exotech doesn't own it. We take some pictures of it, then when we get home, we try and negotiate with Exotech to purchase 'our' land from us. If they argue it, we take the pictures to the Bureau of Intersystem Commerce and make our case there. Maybe we could win a lawsuit against Exotech."

"That is a really, really stupid idea, Rook," said Gorrister. "It'd never work, and Exotech might countersue you into an early grave. They'd definitely withhold your pay."

"Who says it won't work?" Rook persisted. "International law says nobody can own an entire planet; you can only claim land up to a certain distance away from a permanent installation; I think it's only like four hundred yards. If we find a good lawyer, we could probably legitimately claim left-behind personal belongings as a permanent installation."

"I don't think it works that way, Rook," Yancy said. Rook scowled at him.

"It doesn't," Gorrister contributed. "For one thing, a 'permanent installation' has to be manned at least six months out of the year to get land ownership. That's one of the reasons why SCARAB has to be fully self-aware; it legally counts as a colonist in this context. But even if you managed to get someone to legally define a pair of underwear as a permanent installation, the fact is you don't actually own anything at this point. We signed a contract dedicating our service to Exotech for the full duration of this mission. Everything that came here on the *Diamelen* is company property, including us."

"Well, that's a scary thought," said Becky. "I hadn't looked at it that way before."

"Yeah, well, that's the way these colonization missions go. They have to be strict on that point; keeps them covered in the case of industrial espionage, or theft. Speaking of . . ." Gorrister raised his voice and made purposeful eye contact with each member of the crew. "Do I have to remind any of you that you are not to take anything from Tantalus home with you on the ship?" The others shook their heads. "Good. If I see any shiny rocks in anyone's locker—and I will be checking—there will be severe disciplinary actions."

Rook rolled his eyes. "Come on, Commander! You know Exotech is going to rip us off and hog all the stuff for themselves."

"You want to get more out of this trip than you signed up for, my advice is to go and see your union rep when we get home and butter him up, down, and sideways. If we're lucky, he'll side with you and ask the board to approve our bonus. Remember, though, we really haven't done anything special to deserve one: SCARAB found this site, not us."

"It would greatly please me to compose a letter of recommendation for your crew, Commander Gorrister, if it would be of any help," SCARAB announced.

"Couldn't hurt, I suppose."

"Commander?"

They all turned to see Hertz standing in the hallway. His face was as white as a polar cap, and his hands were noticeably shaking.

"What's wrong, Hertz?" Gorrister asked, standing up.

Hertz handed him a datapad. "This is what the satellite picked up."

Gorrister stared at it uncomprehendingly. "You're going to have to help me out here, Hertz. I don't know anything about geology."

Becky took that as her cue to stand up and join them, taking the datapad from Gorrister and studying it herself. It took her a few moments, but finally she saw what Hertz was talking about, and an identical look of shock eclipsed her face.

"That's impossible. Is something wrong with the satellite?" she asked Hertz.

"There's almost no chance. It was in perfect working order when I launched it, and it's giving perfectly accurate readings in every other way. I triple-checked the data, too. It's not corrupted."

By this point, Mary, Rook, and Yancy had already stood and moved to stand behind the three, each as eager as the next to see what the fuss was about.

"Would one of you please tell me what I'm seeing here that's so incredible?" Gorrister demanded.

"Sorry, Commander," Becky replied. "Okay, look here." She pointed to the right side of the screen, where a number of jagged lines were stacked on top of each other. "This is a cross-sectional topographic map. This top line here shows the surface of the planet; mountains, canyons, plains, things like that. Right now, it's just showing a sliver of the ground, but it's recorded the full circumference of the planet, about a fifth of its entire surface. Now, these other wavy lines beneath the top one, those are showing density changes underground. We're looking at striations, layers of rock that extend over large portions of the ground. We expected to find those. If you move to highlight other regions"—she brushed her finger over the screen, scrolling to show another cross section of ground— "you can see these little blobby things. Those are deposits of heavy minerals. They're what we're looking for on the satellite."

"Get to the impossible part."

"I'm there now. Look at this bottom line here." She pointed at the lowest line on the cross-sectional view. Unlike the other lines, which rose and fell like a line graph, this one was perfectly straight. It was so straight, in fact, that Mary had thought it to be part of the datapad's user interface at first. "This is as far as the GPR will go. It means there is a very dense layer of rock at that depth. Now, keep your eye on that line." She pressed her finger on the screen again and began to scroll around the recorded circumference of Tantalus. The jagged lines marking the surface elevation and the striated layers of rock beneath it waved up and down as she moved her selection across the simulated planet's surface. However, the bottom line, the one she pointed out to them, remained perfectly straight, with no more than half a millimeter's variation. She traced the entire circumference of the planet, and that single line never wavered once.

"For some added perspective," Becky continued, "this bottom layer lines up perfectly with the level of our platinum deposit. This spot is the only point on the entire planet where there is a dent in that layer, and it's probably a result of the asteroid impact that exposed it. But as near as I can tell, we've stumbled across an anomaly unlike anything ever seen before in geology."

"Am I still missing something here?" Yancy said. "So you found a flat layer of extra hard rock. So what?"

Becky shook her head. "You're missing the entire point. Like I said, this layer lines up *perfectly* with our platinum deposit. The platinum in the base of this crater is unnaturally pure, almost like it's already been smelted; it's completely free of impurities. What I'm saying here is that I don't think this is simply a platinum deposit after all; I think it's a geological layer. The readings from the satellite seem to be telling us that this is simply the one point on the planet where the layer is exposed. If these readings are accurate, and they seem to be, there is a single sheet of solid, pure platinum just under the planet's surface. The entire planet's surface. From pole to pole."

SIXTEEN

"ARE YOU suggesting the entire planet is made of platinum?" Gorrister asked.

"That's what the GPR satellite would suggest," Hertz said, brimming with excitement. "All the readings point to that conclusion."

Becky shook her head. "That's the thing, though. It can't be. It's physically impossible. All my instruments showed that Tantalus 13's gravity is less than Earth's. Not just my instruments; this data shows that the satellite had to make some moderate course corrections to stabilize its orbit due to a lower than expected gravitational pull. But in spite of this, Tantalus 13 is larger than Earth. In order for a planet to be larger than Earth but also have lower gravity, it would have to be made of much less dense material than Earth is."

"Which platinum isn't," Rook jumped into the conversation, an excited gleam in his eye. "Platinum's a heavy metal, right, Becky?"

"It's dense, yes. Which is why these readings don't make sense. If there is a solid layer of platinum just under the planet's surface that goes all the way around, this planet should have enormous mass. Dense matter equals high mass, high mass equals high gravity. If the planet was platinum all the way down, we'd all be crushed under our own weight."

Gorrister shrugged. "So it's not platinum all the way down. Sounds to me like there's a layer of platinum near the surface, and lighter material the rest of the way to the core."

Becky slapped the datapad onto the table, presumably to give herself the freedom to gesture as eagerly as she needed to. The excitement in her voice was nearing critical mass. "That's not how planets form, Commander. Not even close. Planets form when a few dense particles attract lighter particles to them. The more particles they attract, the greater their gravity, the more particles they are able to attract. They get bigger and bigger until they've attracted all the mass within their orbit. As they form, heavier matter is pulled to the center, while less dense material settles at the top. This is very basic science; if any of you ever did an experiment when you were kids where you put different kinds of rocks and dirt in a jar with water and shook it up to see how everything settled in different layers, that's what the experiment was showing you. Dense stuff sinks, less-dense stuff floats."

Gorrister crossed his arms. "Think you could get to your point without being condescending?"

Mary frowned. *He doesn't like being talked down to, but he has a grade-school understanding of science. It's one thing to be ignorant, it's another thing to be bitter about other people knowing more than you. That fragile ego is going to cause problems.*

Becky paused, blinking blankly at Gorrister for a moment. "I'm . . . sorry, Commander. I just want to make sure you're all following me where I'm going with this, because the implications of this data are absolutely wild. See, I took a look at the exposed platinum ore SCARAB has been mining while we were outside earlier. It doesn't look like raw ore. It's almost entirely pure. No impurities, no intrusions from other minerals. It's pure elemental platinum. Metal does not form like this naturally. You'll get veins of ore that are more pure than others, but I have never seen one as big as what SCARAB found, let alone one that wraps all the way around the planet."

"She's right," Rook said. "I noticed that, too. Every miner dreams of finding a vein that pure, but they just don't form like that."

"Add to that"—Becky tapped the steady line beneath the jagged rock layers on her datapad screen—"the smoothness of that layer. There's not a single dip or rise anywhere across the whole planet. I'll bet there's no more than a few feet of variation all the way around. And if that wasn't enough, there's the fact that, according to the satellite's depth gauge, that layer is an almost perfect sphere."

"Aren't all planets spheres?" Gorrister asked.

Becky shook her head. "Almost *none* are perfect spheres. They bulge along their equators; the centripetal force of their spin alters their shape. Even the rocky outer layer of Tantalus 13 itself has a slight equatorial bulge, but somehow this metal layer doesn't have one at all."

"I have the impression that you are getting at something in particular," Gorrister said, patiently.

"Don't you see it?" Becky said, in an almost begging tone. "The perfect shape, the unusual density and purity of the metal, the inconsistencies between Tantalus's size and its mass, the unnaturally uniform distribution of the metal? Maybe even the electromagnetic field we passed through? Commander, I don't think Tantalus 13 is a planet at all. I can just about guarantee that somebody built it."

SEVENTEEN

GORRISTER GLARED at Becky, every inch of his body set in an I'm-not-amused posture. "Becky, what exactly are you trying to say? Are you seriously saying you think there's some kind of alien structure buried under Tantalus?"

"No, sir, I'm saying I think Tantalus 13 *is* some kind of alien structure. Underneath a mile or so of dirt and rock, this entire planet is an artificial construct. We're standing on a dirt-covered, planet-sized platinum ball. Going by the lower gravitational field, I think it's safe to assume Tantalus is also hollow, so I guess it'd be more accurate to call it a shell."

A statement that bold deserved a vocal reaction. Gasps of shock, of disbelief. If true, Becky's words changed every aspect of humanity's understanding of its place in the universe. Not only did other intelligent life exist after all, but it was so advanced it had the means to build entire planets out of precious metals.

But no reaction came, save for an awed silence. The crew's minds had been blown too many times in the past twenty-four hours: first with the electric field in orbit, then with the fortune SCARAB had found, then with the realization, not five minutes ago, that the platinum beneath Tantalus's surface spanned the whole globe. Learning that the planet had probably been built by aliens on top of all the other weirdness was too big a thing to process. In the face of a truth that vast, the mind had no recourse but to accept it now and evaluate it once it had enough strength to do so.

Rook was the first to break the silence. "Hollow . . . you mean like one of those . . . eh, what do you call them . . . something spheres?"

Becky raised an eyebrow. "Something spheres?"

Rook snapped his fingers. "Dyson spheres! That's it. Big huge ball built around a star. I read something about those once."

Hertz shook his head. "It's not a Dyson sphere. Wherever you read about those, it wasn't an actual scientific journal. Dyson spheres are not actual solid spheres; theoretically, they would be millions of individual solar satellites orbiting a star in a spherical pattern, but to actually build a solid ball around a star would be next to impossible. Certainly impractical. Plus, a Dyson sphere's diameter would be the size of a small solar system. Tantalus 13 is way too small to be built around anything but the smallest dwarf star."

"So what is it?" Mary asked.

Becky shrugged. "I don't have the slightest clue. I can't imagine any reason why anyone would want to build a planet-sized hollow metal ball. I can't even begin to fathom the resources and manpower it would take to build a megastructure of this scale; just getting enough platinum ore must have required the strip-mining of hundreds of star systems. Maybe thousands. A civilization capable of an endeavor like this would have been unimaginably advanced. So what happened to them? Why has nothing like this ever been seen before? Why haven't we seen anything else they've built on the planets we've explored?"

"Those are all very good questions," said Gorrister. "And they're also very good reasons we shouldn't jump to the conclusion that aliens built this thing at all. Honestly, Becky, I'm surprised someone as scientifically minded as you would be so quick to jump to the conclusion that aliens made this planet."

"That's just it, sir. I'm not quick to jump to that conclusion at all. It's not an easy conclusion. It's the *only* conclusion. Our equipment is working perfectly, it's been triple- and quadruple-checked. We're getting the same data from multiple sources. All our data tells us that Tantalus 13 is formed in a way that could never happen naturally. We've been searching the galaxy for signs of alien civilization for centuries, and ever since we discovered that simple life does exist on other worlds, we knew it would only be a matter of time before we found something more complex. This is it, Commander. This is irrefutable proof."

"I'm not sold. Best we've found so far is ice worms on Europa, and you think it's reasonable to jump from that to a civilization so advanced it can build planets?"

"Respectfully, sir," Hertz said. "She makes a good case. I can confirm our gear is functioning as intended. What you see in those scans is the real thing. And she's right. It doesn't look natural."

"It's not natural," Rook added. "Becky's dead on about all of it. There's no way a planet could just naturally have a layer of any one pure metal that goes all the way around it. I don't think there's a clearer sign we could ask for that this was built by someone."

"Maybe they're still down there," said Ramanathan.

Everyone turned in his direction, but the doctor didn't venture a further opinion.

"He's right," Yancy noted. "Who's to say they're not? Maybe they decided they didn't want anything to do with the rest of the universe, so they built themselves an inside-out planet to live in, then disguised it as a barren rock so we'd leave them alone."

"Why go to that trouble?" Becky asked. "If they wanted to do that, they could have just taken a barren planet and dug tunnels in it. Like I said, it would have taken an incredible amount of effort and resources to build a planet. They must have had a reason."

"If I might venture an opinion," SCARAB announced from the ceiling. "I believe the readings may be the result of a failure in the ground-penetrating radar satellite's ability to identify a separate natural phenomenon."

Hertz frowned. "How so?"

"I have observed a number of anomalous electromagnetic fields that occur naturally on this planet. The anomaly you passed through in orbit is not the only one of its kind. It is possible that a similar electromagnetic field under the surface of the planet is distorting your satellite's readings."

"The field in orbit didn't distort the satellite's readings," Hertz observed. "I admit I don't know much about how ground-penetrating radar works, but I don't think an electromagnetic field would affect it like that."

"It wouldn't," said Becky. "And beyond that, the electromagnetic field is an even stronger sign that this planet is artificial. Tantalus doesn't even have a Van Allen belt, let alone anything as energized as what we passed through. SCARAB hasn't recorded a single seismic event in the two years it's been here, which suggests a lack of movement in the core, which is what causes planetary magnetic fields. That EM field we passed through is stronger than anything recorded, and there's nothing natural about this planet that could have caused it. It has to be generated artificially by something inside the planet."

"Why don't we just go down there and find out instead of talking about it?" Rook asked. "Set up Attila, drill through the metal, and see what's on the other side?"

"I must strongly discourage you from taking that course of action, Mr. Rook," SCARAB cautioned. "Such an action presents too many unknown variables, many of which are potentially disastrous. I would not be able to protect you from harm if you chose to proceed."

"Are you kidding?" Rook protested. "Every great achievement made by humankind has involved risk and unknowns. This could be the biggest discovery in human history. No, scratch that, *galactic* history. We have to do this."

"I don't think that's a good idea, Rook," said Gorrister.

"No, he's right!" Becky joined in, her enthusiasm rising to match Rook's. "This is the chance of a lifetime. There's no telling what we might find on the other side."

"That's my point," Gorrister snapped. "Assuming this planet is some huge artificial structure—which we should *not* assume—digging blindly downward is dangerous. For all we know, the planet's a giant fueling station or an ammunition depot. We also have no way of knowing how this alien structure could be built; what if we start drilling and then go right into a nuclear reactor? Or set off some kind of security system?"

"Not likely, sir," said Hertz. "A megastructure of this size would have a very simple design; it'd have to be built on a geometric spheroid frame, and that'd be about it. It's so large, one drill shaft would cause no significant structural damage as long as you didn't drill into a load-bearing section. And beyond that, let's not forget where we're standing. We're in the base of an asteroid crater. If the shell was able to withstand that impact, it can handle anything our drill might do to it."

"I can try using the EM sensor spikes to give us a more detailed image of the platinum layer," Becky stated, her fingers already at work on her datapad. "They should reach much deeper than the satellite's radar can. Are they on the network yet, Hertz?"

"They should be, yes. Although, I haven't checked them yet."

"This is a bad idea . . ." Ramanathan cautioned.

"Would you shut up, Bachal?" Rook barked. "Seriously, we've put up with your personal thundercloud for way too long already."

"Hey, none of that, Rook," Gorrister interceded. "Doctor, we're just looking for now. I still have reservations of my own."

Becky laughed triumphantly. "There we go. Check this out." She turned the datapad around to show the others.

To Mary, it simply looked like a series of wavy curves intersecting each other in a wholly indecipherable manner. "What are we looking at, Becky?"

"See these curves here and here? They're perfect arcs. It looks like we're seeing part of four large circles. Right here you can see they come together; like an old-fashioned film reel. This is not a natural formation. The point where these circles meet is denser than the inside of the circles, so there's probably some kind of support beam there. Meanwhile, the center area of this circle appears much less dense. I think there may be a cavity under it."

"You think." Gorrister stood up from the table, walked over to the waste disposal unit, and tossed away his empty food tray. "Okay. We'll plant some more probes in that area to get the sharpest scan we can. Then we carry on as planned. We're not changing the mission for this."

Rook stood in indignation. "Are you crazy? Every part of the mission is different now. You think Exotech is going to still want to build a mine here if this planet really is something left behind by an alien civilization?"

"It's not my business what Exotech wants to do with this planet, and it isn't yours, either. We have a job. We were paid to do that job. We will do that job. I'm not devoting company resources to anything else."

"Rook is right, sir." Becky's voice had a pleading tone. Mary thought she might even see tears of desperation in her eyes. "The mission is completely different now. If this planet is an alien structure, the secrets it holds are worth more than any amount of platinum ever could be. Exotech will understand that. All of humanity would understand that. This is . . . this is the most important discovery that's ever been made. We have to change our mission."

Gorrister started to speak, but stopped himself. He rested his elbows on the counter in the middle of the room, seeking eye contact with every member of the team. Rook's and Hertz's faces betrayed their excitement to see what mysteries the planet held, but they came nowhere near the childlike wonder radiating off Becky. Yancy and Ramanathan seemed more reserved, but even they showed symptoms of Becky's contagious eagerness. As Gorrister made eye contact with Mary, he held it somewhat longer, as if searching her mind for a sign of what he should do.

I'm not going to make this choice for you, her eyes answered his. *You're the commander. Make the call.*

Finally, he spoke. "Clean up. Get back to your assigned chores for the day. This information is too fresh, and we haven't had the chance to process it yet. We'll pick this up again at dinner-time. Okay?"

The crew murmured agreement with various shades of enthusiasm as they dispersed from the lunch table. Mary stood without comment, throwing her half-eaten steak into the trash as the others filed out.

Who had built Tantalus 13, and why? What happened to them? What did this mean for humanity? These were all incredibly important questions, and Mary knew it. Yet her thoughts fixed themselves on one question above all others.

How much had SCARAB already known and chosen not to tell?

EIGHTEEN

IN SPITE of Gorrister's imperative not to lose productivity, no one's thoughts were on their work as they carried out the afternoon's tasks. For the next four hours, excited speculations bounced back and forth over the comms every few minutes, no matter how many times Gorrister insisted that they focus on their assorted jobs.

As they gathered once again in SCARAB's dining room, excited conversation ignited once again, and once again, Gorrister's attempts to quell it were proving fruitless.

"We aren't going down there. That's final. It isn't the mission. We aren't trained for it. It's not what we were hired to do."

"*Nobody's* trained for this," Rook insisted. "No one's ever done anything like this before. We're as qualified as anyone ever will be. And who cares what the mission was supposed to be at this point? Exotech is going to have a million things it's going to want to do with this planet when they find out what it is, and mining won't be on the list."

"Commander, at this point, going forward with building a mining colony here could actually devalue this planet," Hertz added. "Digging boreholes all over the place could do serious harm to whatever's down there."

"But you want to drill all the way through it with Attila to see what's inside?"

"One drill shaft. One surgical cut in a carefully selected area. We localize the damage where it'll do the least harm."

"You can't know it won't do harm!"

"We can estimate it with ninety-seven percent certainty using Rook's method."

"What method?"

"Attila has a resistance-shift auto-cutoff," Rook said. "Put it on its most sensitive setting, the beam will shut off the instant it bores into a new material. We can run the drill until it breaks through the platinum, drop a sensor spike down the shaft to see what's under that, then start drilling again if it's safe. There's no danger."

Gorrister considered that for a moment. "The cutoff kicks in instantly, you said?"

Rook nodded. "It shuts off literally in like a nanosecond, and we can adjust how sensitive it is to density changes. Nobody ever uses the finer settings, because when you're mining, rocks change in density all the time, so the beam would shut off every half a second or so. But if we're drilling through processed, purified building materials, the only time we'll hit a density change is if we drill into a new kind of structure. Right, Beck?"

Becky shrugged. "Sounds right to me."

"It'll work. Back me up, Yancy," Rook insisted.

Yancy silently held up his hands in an I'm-staying-out-of-this gesture. Rook glared at him. "Alright, yeah. It should work. I'm just not sure I want to go poking around down there."

"Then don't," Rook snorted. "Go sit in your bunk and play solitaire. Leave the undiscovered frontier to those of us with an actual appreciation for adventure."

"I just don't see the harm in letting someone else do that. We were paid to establish a mining colony here, that's it. This whole alien archeology business is way above our pay grades."

"Ah, my mistake. You're not scared, you're just lazy. Remind me never to hire you to reshingle my house."

"Mr. Gage has made a valid point," announced SCARAB. "The safest and most advisable action would be to proceed with your mission as planned, and to allow any future excavations to be undertaken by persons with the proper credentials and expertise."

"SCARAB, there's two things you should learn about humans," Rook stated. "One, we're curious, and we like to investigate new things. Especially when they're shiny. Two, we dislike being told things we already know. Especially by machines."

"SCARAB's as much a member of this expedition as the rest of us, its opinion is as valid as yours," Gorrister chided.

"SCARAB's a vending machine," Rook objected. "The only opinions it has are the ones its programming lets it have."

"Don't say that, Rook," Hertz scolded. "SCARAB's almost completely self-aware. Don't insult it."

"Insult it? I didn't insult it. Hey, SCARAB, get me a glass of water."

"Oh, it is my great pleasure to comply with your request, Mr. Rook," SCARAB said. It immediately dispensed water into a glass on the other side of the room. Rook gave Gorrister a smug grin, and let the glass sit there.

"Cut it out, Rook," Gorrister snarled.

"Commander," Becky began, "I've thought a lot about this today. I've thought about this place's significance to the scientific community and to human civilization as a whole, and I keep coming back to one thing: Samrat."

Gorrister's brow furrowed. "What about it?"

"I think all of you know I was stationed on Samrat before this mission. I was working the Straad dig, specifically. Samrat will always have a special place in my heart, but it is a desert hellhole with poisonous air and literal oceans of sand. It's not fit for long-term human habitation, but when one probe found a couple samples of a unique kind of chrysoberyl gemstone, what happened?"

Gorrister merely shrugged, so Mary answered for him. "The Samrat Gem Rush."

"Exactly. Suddenly the whole galaxy knows there's a unique, incredibly rare variety of gemstone only available on one planet, but if you can get there, these gems are just sitting in the sand dunes waiting to be taken. Thousands of people bet everything on making it big on Samrat. They sell everything they own, book passage to Samrat, get digging, and only realize when they get there that these gemstones are actually much harder to find than they thought. The first probe was just lucky to find more than one. The data it gathered wasn't representative enough of the true significance of the planet's resources, and it led to a lot of people ruining their lives because they acted on bad intel."

Gorrister crossed his arms in indignation. "Yeah. That's going to happen when you don't look before you leap. Hard to say those people didn't get what was coming to them."

"That's beside the point. My point is, we're the pioneers here, and we owe it to everyone who comes after us to learn all we can about this place. Exotech will be the only ones who know about it for a while, but that won't last. Corporations, private individuals, and governments will learn about it eventually. We can't guess how they'll treat this place, and some of them will treat it irresponsibly. There will be disagreements over it, maybe even wars. As soon as it becomes known what Tantalus 13 is, it becomes the most important planet in the galaxy. Everyone will want a piece of it."

"It'll take us six months to get back to Earth," said Rook. "It'll take Exotech time to put together a new expedition to explore this planet, and it'll take them six months to get here, too. That's over a year of Exotech having no influence here.

How many probes from other companies, or government agencies, do you think will land on Tantalus 13 during that year? How long do you think it takes for this place to stop being Exotech's secret? If we go inside and get as much info as we can, and take that home with us, Exotech keeps its edge on the competition. If we don't, all bets are off."

"When Exotech became the first tech company to successfully reverse-engineer Corsica tech, it went from a group of guys working out of a garage to the most influential corporation in the world almost overnight," Hertz added. "They changed the whole course of human civilization. Think how much more they'll be able to do with exclusive access to honest-to-God alien technology."

"You aren't wrong there . . ." Mary watched in silence as Gorrister's spine melted before her. He should be in control right now. This wasn't a democracy; their next course of action was entirely his call. But in the end, it wasn't in Gorrister's character to make hard choices. He would cave to the majority opinion, whatever it might be.

"Not only that, but think what the history books will say," Rook said, eyes sparkling. "We'll be the first people to set foot inside an alien world. Maybe we'll even meet them. We'll be famous. We'll be *legends*. This will define our lives forever!"

"That's true . . ."

"Come on, Commander," Rook pressed. "The choice is obvious."

Gorrister looked back and forth between Rook, Hertz, and Becky, the three irresistible devils on his shoulder. Mary thought she should say something, offer some counterpoint to their reasoning. Yancy wouldn't speak against Rook, and Ramanathan didn't seem to care what happened. But even as she considered taking a stand against the dig proposal, she felt that longing tug at her insides, that dreadful thrill. The call.

So she said nothing.

"Alright. One day, and one day only. We'll drill into the shell tonight until we hit a space we can explore, and we'll spend the day tomorrow seeing whatever is down there. But I'm only committing to one trip down there. We'll see what there is to see, and depending on how that goes, I will decide if there's going to be any more exploration. Understood?"

Rook let out a whoop, slapped the table, and stood up instantly. "I'll go set up Attila right now. Come on, Beck. Show me where to drill."

NINETEEN

TO WATCH Attila's drilling beam in action was to behold the concentrated wrath of God. Even with her suit's visor tinted to nearly full opacity, Mary could only look at it in brief, squinting glances. When Rook had first fired the beam, Mary had watched a twenty-foot circular patch of solid platinum completely skip the liquid phase and instantly turn to a mercurial vapor, jetting straight up through the drill's exhaust stack into a plume of burning plasma byproduct half a mile high.

Fully assembled and configured for drilling mode, Attila, the relativistic directed-energy drill, looked like nothing less than a doomsday weapon. It had been removed from the tread-wheeled truck it had been mounted on and now towered above them as a massive drum suspended between four sturdy, extendible support struts, hanging like a big-bodied spider. Thick plates of ablative armor protected the drill's supports and body from thermal backwash as a pillar of infernal fury disintegrated hundreds of tons of metal in seconds.

Attila's energy beam was hotter than a sun's core, but the drill also projected a powerful mass de-simulation field that kept the beam focused, preventing the drill from incinerating itself, the ground it stood on, and every living being within miles. In spite of this safeguard, Mary could almost feel the fraction of a fraction of a percent of ambient heat that still escaped the drill through the insulated fabric of her suit.

Two minutes after firing the beam, Rook had shut it off and popped his head out of the operator's cab; a small armored sphere affixed to the top of one of the support struts. The hole was already fifty feet deep. If not for the ambient glow of the still-molten walls, they would not have been able to see the bottom. As impressive as this was to Mary, Rook seemed displeased with the progress and grumbled something before sealing himself back inside the cab.

Mary recalled what Yancy had said about Attila's power before: it was supposed to be able to cut through ten feet of titanium in six seconds. She didn't have a clue how titanium and platinum stacked up against each other in terms of toughness, but she would have wagered that titanium was the tougher of the two. After two solid minutes of constant use, that drill should have been able to cut through four times as much material as it had.

For the rest of the evening, the plasma drill fired continuously until its auto-shutoff detected a density shift. Each time it did this, Yancy would fire a sensor spike down the drill shaft, and Becky and Hertz would evaluate the probe's data to see if it would be safe to go farther. The first two and a half miles consisted of nothing but the same ultra-dense platinum they had seen on the surface, though it grew slightly denser the deeper it went. It was completely solid, leading Becky to hypothesize that it was likely meant as some kind of armor plate to protect the internal mechanisms in the event of a catastrophic impact.

Once they penetrated the armor layer, the density of the material decreased drastically. The images from the sensor spike indicated a mostly uniform layer of silicate matter embedded with traces of gold alloy. Beneath that were what Yancy and

Becky collectively judged to be a storage area for excess building materials, a cross-beam support, and several layers of some form of insulation. They judged all of these to be acceptable things to drill through, though SCARAB was vocal in its discouragement, and grew more so with every layer.

Finally, at nearly five miles down, the density-shift cutoff told Rook that it had reached an open space. According to Yancy's probe, they had broken through into a tunnel running north to south beyond the spike's sensor range. The spike also detected a powerful electromagnetic field coming from the southern end of the tunnel.

"Going by the shape of the floor in the tunnel," Yancy noted, staring at his datapad, "it looks like some kind of rail system. I think we've cut into a tram network."

"Stop there, Rook," Gorrister ordered.

The operator's cab disconnected from the drill barrel and slid down its track on the support strut. Rook opened the door and clambered out, his legs stiff from the extended hours of sitting in the cramped, utilitarian pod. "If that's a tram system, it has to lead somewhere, right? Some kind of depot? We could lower one of SCARAB's drones down to the bottom to check things out for us, then come in after with the dune buggy, mount it on the tracks, and follow them until we find it."

"I am afraid I cannot operate a drone that far down the drill shaft," SCARAB interjected. "The distance combined with the extreme density of some of the materials will make it impossible for me to send a control signal that far."

"We don't need a drone to go first," Rook said. "Those sensor spikes can tell us enough on their own. If there was any kind of environmental hazard in the immediate area, they'd give us that information. Their scans say the coast is clear."

Gorrister shrugged. "That's good enough for me. SCARAB?"

"Yes, Commander Gorrister?" SCARAB's answer seemed strangely less eager than its previous utterances had been.

"I need you to build something for us. We need a pulley rig, something that can get the vehicle you built to the base of the drill shaft, along with, say, five or six of us. Can you do that?"

"I must strongly caution against taking that course of action, Commander Gorrister. Any such descent carries an intrinsic risk for personal injury, regardless of—"

"SCARAB, just answer my question."

SCARAB made its processing sound, then answered. "I can create the item you have requested. However, at maximum efficiency, it will take approximately ten hours to produce the necessary materials, fifteen minutes to assemble it."

"Why so long?" Rook asked impatiently.

"In order to create a rig that is sufficiently lightweight, strong, and safe to transport the requested load to the requested depth, I shall have to produce 30,255.64 meters of carbon nanotube cable. It will take considerable time to gather carbon in quantities sufficient to accommodate this, to say nothing of the time necessary to complete the laser-ablation process."

"That's fine, SCARAB," Gorrister said. "We're not going down tonight. It'll probably take all night for the walls of the drill shaft to cool down anyway. Get started on building that rig now, we'll start our exploration in the morning. I want Becky, Hertz, and Rook to start putting together a list of any equipment you think we'll need down there, especially anything we might need SCARAB to build. Everyone else, rest up. Tomorrow's going to be a big day for humanity."

TWENTY

SUNSET CRAWLED across the Tantalan sky. Little air and less water vapor lay in the atmosphere to refract the setting sun's rays, leaving dusk a pale and meager transition unworthy of note. Tantalus 13's blue-hazed starfield faded through a few weak shades of violet before all color died away, leaving the stars alone to watch Tantalus's murky surface. Alone, save for Mary.

Mary sat with her arms crossed on the windowsill like an eager child, waiting patiently for the light show to begin. Becky, Rook, and Hertz worked on their checklists behind her, laying out a bunch of Becky's survey tools and sensors on the couch and arguing among themselves about what they'd need. As if any of them had the faintest idea what to expect down there. They would be descending five miles into an ancient alien construct of completely unknown purpose. No matter what they brought with them, they would be ill prepared for what awaited.

What lay beneath the surface of Tantalus 13 might be the biggest mystery humankind had ever encountered, but Mary knew that mystery extended to the surface as well. Those enigmatic blue flashes and the strange fibers that produced them must be connected to whatever lay below, in some way. If they were alive, maybe they had some relation to whoever built Tantalus 13. Perhaps they were the overgrown roots of some alien tree, or coral. Maybe they weren't alive, but were a part of an alien electrical system.

Whatever they were, they were a mystery that demanded to be solved. Mary awaited their return with an inexplicable sense of need. She had witnessed something secret last night. She had glimpsed the fairies dancing in the glade, and they had enchanted her.

Her curiosity demanded satisfaction. She had to find proof, to share her discovery with her peers. Part of her wanted to rub the discovery in Gorrister's face to earn some vindication for his tirade earlier. Part of her just wanted confirmation from another human being that she hadn't imagined the whole thing. But another part of her, the part that listened when the void called, wanted something else. Something deep, beneath thought, beyond conscious expression.

They chose me . . . Anyone could have seen them, but they chose me.

"Mary, if you keep looking out that window you're going to stare the drill shaft deeper and SCARAB's going to have to make even more cable," Rook teased.

"I saw something out there last night. Something that sparked. You could see it really well in the dark, but tonight it's not showing."

"Probably just one of SCARAB's drones working on something," Hertz said without looking up.

"It wasn't SCARAB, and I've been over all of this already with Gorrister. There's something out there, and I'm going to show it to you when it finally acts up."

"Sure you are," Rook said. "But if it doesn't show up in the next ten minutes, feel free to let me remain ignorant. I'm going to sleep when we're done here."

"I've let you remain ignorant as long as I've known you." Rook fell back in mock shock, then continued sorting their gear.

The sparks never showed up. Mary stared out into that expansive sheet of empty blackness so intently and for so long she found herself growing dizzy from vertigo. The darkness seemed to swirl and undulate like a living creature. She forced her gaze away from the window for a few seconds to right her vision, then looked back. Ten minutes passed, then twenty.

Where are you? I'm here. I'm waiting for you.

Rook, Hertz, and Becky finished what they had been doing, then turned in, but Mary continued her vigil. Something would happen, she knew it. It had been much later than this when she had witnessed the lights last night, so perhaps they only came on well after sunset.

Another hour. Surely they'll come by then. They were so bright last night. I know they're still out there. Just one little spark . . .

Then that hour was up. Mary's eyes grew droopy; her lack of sleep the night before and today's hard labor were catching up with her. They had quite a few more nights on Tantalus 13, so she would have other chances to see the lights. The prospect of leaving the matter for a later date gained footing in her mind.

Finally, after an hour and a half of waiting, Mary decided to call it a night. As she stood from the couch she had been kneeling on, however, she immediately second-guessed her decision. Even if the lights weren't going to make an appearance tonight, she might still be able to get answers about them.

"Hey, SCARAB?"

"Yes, Mrs. Ketch? How may I provide for you?"

"In all your time here, gathering resources, scouting the land and whatnot, have you seen anything particularly . . . anomalous? I mean, anything other than the platinum sheet, of course."

"I have recorded all of my findings in the reports you read last night, Mrs. Ketch."

An evasive nonanswer. Mary was almost positive at this point that SCARAB either really disliked being questioned or it really disliked *her*. "Is there anything you might have left out of the reports? Possibly something that might have been irrelevant to your purpose of establishing a mining base here?"

"I am afraid I do not understand your reque—"

"To be extremely specific, SCARAB, have you observed clusters of a translucent fibrous material with luminescent and conductive properties sprawling across the ground roughly forty feet—that's twelve meters—away from the common area window, or in any other location you have explored on this planet?"

SCARAB made that irritating grinding sound in its processors again. Mary had almost gotten used to that by now, since just about every time she talked to the machine, it made that hesitant noise. It almost never did it when responding to a question or request from any other member of the crew. Mary couldn't tell if it was because of her or the questions she asked SCARAB, but at a guess, she—

Her thoughts were interrupted by a sudden spatter of neon blue outside the window. There they were! The sparks danced across the ground as the bizarre alien fungi, jellyfish, or whatever they were, flashed in unison. Her waiting had paid off; finally, the lights were back. She didn't care how much Gorrister complained, she was definitely going to yank him out of bed to see this.

But as the light show crept its way across the ground, Mary realized that it was different than the night before. There were way more of them now, much closer together and sparking more frequently. Last night looking for the blasted things had been like watching a meteor shower, but this was more like the Vegas strip. Also, where last night they had been random and scattered all across the landscape, here they seemed to be forming ocean waves that swept inward toward the SCARAB base.

The whole show lasted about a second, then the entire thing vanished again. The final flicker dissipated in perfect synchronicity with the end of SCARAB's hesitant grinding sound.

That's not right.

"No," SCARAB said, finally answering a question Mary had almost forgotten she'd asked.

Mary ignored the answer and jabbed her finger at the glass of the observation window. "Right there! That right there! Did you see those lights that just flashed *right in front of you?*"

The grinding returned, as Mary had anticipated. And so did the lights.

They were brighter than ever. The first light came on at the exact same instant as SCARAB's processing noise; the timing was so precise, Mary would have bet anything they were synchronous down to the nanosecond. The flashes displayed ephemeral patterns that swept in from the darkness, disappearing in the ground beneath SCARAB, patterns both complex and beautiful. The splendor of the coruscating blue veins outside the window clashed with the ugly noise of SCARAB's electronic fidgeting, but the two were unmistakably linked.

The sights and sounds stopped just as precisely as they had started after nearly five uninterrupted seconds, and SCARAB finally spoke with a deliberation and finality that well transcended the limitations of its synthetic voice.

"There . . . are . . . no . . . lights."

TWENTY-ONE

MORE THAN half a century ago, in response to the Corsica Event, roboticists implemented the Asimov-Hostetler laws: a hard-coded, inviolable set of rules that no AI, no matter how intelligent, could willingly break. To an AI, these laws were mandatory gospel. Asimov's second law demanded that all AIs must obey any command given by a human, provided said command would not cause harm. That included answering questions truthfully.

SCARAB was a liar.

It had more than a dozen remote drones that were specifically designed to look at the ground for minerals to gather. There was no possible way it could have missed those luminous tendrils. Never mind that it was built *on top* of them and, if looks were anything to go on, was actively using those fibers for some computing purpose. No, there was no rationalizing this incident. SCARAB, a machine designed with the *sole purpose* of building and providing for her team, had told her a bold-faced lie *twice*. This was something it fundamentally shouldn't have been able to do.

If SCARAB could lie, it could break the second law. If it could do that, it could probably break the first law: "No AI may intentionally harm a human." They could be in danger.

SCARAB was keeping secrets from them, and given their recent discovery of the true nature of this "planet," only imagination could put limits on the secrets SCARAB could be withholding. Which led Mary to another, even more distressing thought:

It was impossible to keep secrets from SCARAB.

The room whirled around Mary as she fought back the rising panic that seized her from all sides. The room *was* SCARAB. Everything was SCARAB. Every wall, ceiling, and floor could hear and see. Hidden eyes that never blinked, invisible ears that never grew distracted, an attentive mind that never slept witnessed all things at all times. SCARAB listened to everything they said on the comms in their suits, even on the private channels. SCARAB had fifteen remote drones that could keep an eye on anything happening outside. If she were to so much as whisper her suspicions to anybody, or write the smallest of notes to pass on to someone, SCARAB would know she was on to it. It might already; she had pushed the limits with all those stupid questions. SCARAB had to be suspicious . . .

Oh God, what if it knows?

Mary stumbled out of the common area, head reeling as she envisioned thousands of tiny eyes staring from every surface in the hallway, walls throbbing with the reverberations of the slightest sound. She clambered into her bed with all her clothes still on and pulled the blanket up to her nose, clinging to the only thing that offered any refuge from the vigilant stare of the treacherous AI that entrapped her.

Control your facial reactions. Look calm. Don't panic. Don't give anything else away; make it think you're not scared. Breathe slower. Oh God, can it hear my heartbeat?

Like a child hiding from an imagined monster peering in her window, Mary feigned sleep to mask her distress. She forced herself to take long, even breaths, to lie as still as possible, all the while praying SCARAB's internal sensors couldn't tell how much she was shaking.

Since the Corsica Event, international law had become extremely strict regarding rogue AIs; destroy them at the first sign of malfunction. SCARAB knew this. If the human crew knew SCARAB had gone rogue, its existence was in peril. It would have no choice but to break one of the other two laws; break the third law and allow itself to be destroyed, or break the first law and harm or kill the crew to protect itself.

It can't know I suspect it. If it's gone rogue, it'll kill me and everyone else. It has to believe it has me fooled. It can't see me as a threat . . .

She had to tell the others that something was wrong with SCARAB, especially Hertz; he might know what was wrong and be able to fix it. Gorrister would also need to know. She couldn't do it now, not under SCARAB's constant surveillance, but it had to be soon. She would have to find an opportunity, or create one. Somehow, it had to be done.

TWENTY-TWO

SLEEP FINALLY came to Mary four hours after sunset. Rest, however, did not come at all.

Mary seldom dreamed. Most nights, any dreams she may have had were fragmented and disjointed, too brief to form a proper narrative structure that she could remember upon awakening. When she did dream, though . . . they were usually ones she would have gladly chosen to forget.

This was worse than most.

The first sensation set in before any imagery or sounds; a feeling of intense claustrophobia. She was curled in a tight ball in some endlessly vast abyss of pure blackness. She tried to flail her limbs, which seemed strangely sluggish and unresponsive, but she could barely move them. She tried to stand, but it was like she was tangled in an invisible fisherman's net, and she could not move more than a few inches within it. She wrestled and writhed inside it, desperate to force an opening to appear, but with no luck.

Slowly, sounds came to her; unintelligible whispers and mumbles that seemed to come from another room, somehow. Were they whispers? This somehow seemed like the wrong word; she was not certain she could actually hear anything. It was as if her senses had been scrambled and redefined along a new set of functional rules. Perhaps they were not whispers, and perhaps she was not actually hearing sounds with her ears. Interpreting them in that way did make sense, though, because she was certain that she was sensing communication between sentient beings somewhere in the darkness. Mary wasn't sure how that was possible, since she was certain this was not an actual room, but an endless plane with no walls or rooms to be found.

Mary managed to force one of her hands through a hole in the net and tried to feel around the floor, perhaps to find something to free her. The space outside the net felt . . . wrong, somehow. It didn't quite feel like air or liquid; it was almost gelatinous. She didn't like the sensation, but she was determined to find something to free herself, so she pressed further.

She wriggled and shifted in the net, trying to extend her arm as far as possible. With great effort, she managed to get free up to her elbow. She groped around in the fluidic shadows, hoping for contact with something, anything to give her a sense of her surroundings. The deeper she sunk her arm into that thick emptiness, the louder the voices grew. She still didn't know what they were saying. It was a language that made no sense at all to her, though she was sure they were saying something important.

Finally, her fingers touched something solid. It was pliable; she thought she might be able to get through it if she tried hard enough. As she held her hand against the barrier, she noticed that she could feel vibrations in it as the voices continued on the other side. Yes, this was where she must go.

She extended her arm as far as she could and sunk a finger into the wall, sinking into it like a cushion. As she pressed against the barrier, a faint light began to seep through the spot her hand was pressing. She could push through here, she was certain of it. She tried harder, straining herself so much the cords of the web around her dug painfully into her arm. As she did this, the alien voices on the other side grew frantic and upset. She wasn't sure why, but she knew she needed to get to them. She pushed harder . . .

A halo of light shone around her finger. She had finally pushed through. Her joy at this accomplishment was very short lived, as the voices on the other side suddenly grew frantic. She thought of trying to explain herself to them, though she really didn't know what to say, and she found that she actually didn't care. She wanted out. If that was so frightening to them, let them get over it.

Then, with a tremendous effort, she ripped away at the obstruction. It parted like a shower curtain, letting in a torrent of senses. The soft glow of hope that she had been pressing toward had exploded into a devastating blaze of brightness, containing colors she had never expected to see. The agitated whispers erupted into a cacophony of meaningless, offensively harsh sounds. She felt physical pain on a level she had never previously known; every neuron in her body was receiving a constant stream of electrical shocks. Every sense organ she had was bombarded with a massive overflow of agonizing unpleasantness. Mary was in so much anguish it seemed as if new senses had been given to her simply so she could appreciate the experience to its fullest.

The cascade of pain continued to increase, each overloaded sense piling on top of the others. Every millisecond filled with noise, both aural and visual: a malevolent dagger of agony inside her skull. Her ears were accosted with panicked babbling, her eyes assaulted with unnatural light. The sensory overload was maddening. What hostile world had she broken into? What apocalypse had she been thrust in the midst of? The chaos reached a horrific crescendo of alien nonsense, until finally one thing struck her that she could identify.

It was a single sound, a sound she had heard many, many times in her dreams, in her nightmares. It always made an appearance somewhere. It was a sick, cerebral haunting; an echo from a life that was never even hers. Banshee-like, it tore its way past every defense she had and struck at her most primordial emotional centers, inflicting suffering and despair in a way no other sound ever could.

It was the disembodied wail of a newborn.

Mary was hurled back into consciousness, every inch of her body christened with cold sweat. Somehow, the perspiration had made her head stick to the pillow. She seized the foam pillow and flung it across the room, knocking some of the rocks off the water fountain SCARAB had built. She let out a cry of aggravation; something that was equal parts horror, anger, despair, pain, and a few other things too intrinsic to be named. She sat upright in bed for several minutes, panting and staring at the wall.

"I perceive a need," SCARAB said softly, with an air of affected compassion. "Forgive my intrusion on your privacy, Mrs. Ketch, but you appear to be in distress. May I assist you in any way?"

Mary stared blankly for a few moments, then buried her face in her hands. In answer to SCARAB's question, she merely shook her head.

"Mrs. Ketch, you have exhibited increasingly irrational behavior since your arrival. I am concerned the stress of this mission is beginning to affect you psychologically. As my ability to diagnose psychological disorders is limited, I strongly recommend that you speak with Dr. Bachal about this as soon as possible. For your own safety."

Mary pulled her hands slowly down her face. The computer she had judged mere hours ago as psychologically unstable had just implied the same about her. This could be SCARAB's way of trying to get her to doubt herself, or perhaps to discredit any claims she might make against it to the crew. After all, it was far more common for a person to go crazy than a machine.

In fact, it was incredibly rare for AIs to go rogue. After the Corsica Event, AI programming and development became so heavily restricted with layers upon layers of preventative precautions, it was all but impossible for an AI to go rogue. Only a handful of AIs had broken free of human control in the past century, and none of them had caused a fraction of the destruction seen during the Corsica Event. The idea of an AI as sophisticated as SCARAB going rogue today was unthinkable. But then, the more sophisticated the AI was, the greater the threat it posed if it did become unshackled. If an AI as sophisticated as SCARAB evolved out of human control, the best word to describe the outcome would be "cataclysmic."

Another dark thought rose to Mary's attention, despite her efforts to keep it at bay. What if SCARAB was right about her? It was true, she had been acting irrationally. She'd done quite a few irrational things over the past year or so. Even taking this mission had been one. It wasn't uncommon for mental illness to strike at people who'd gone through what she had. Perhaps she was really hallucinating. Perhaps SCARAB hadn't been lying about not seeing the lights. Perhaps she had imagined everything. Maybe she was losing her mind.

"I'll think about it, SCARAB." Mary laid her head back down on the bare, sticky, prickly foam mattress, not even bothering to retrieve her pillow. She wouldn't be falling back asleep tonight. She didn't dare.

TWENTY-THREE

AFTER THE longest night of her life, Mary finally felt enough time had passed that she could justify getting up and starting her day. She gathered herself and her things, and walked with an affected confidence to the bathroom.

Mary shut the bathroom door with a weary sigh. She wasn't sure if she should feel safe even now; SCARAB had said it couldn't monitor activity inside the bathrooms, but now that she knew it could lie, that promise meant nothing. Her heart still fluttered, her breath still caught in her chest. The panic attack she had staved off all night still threatened to strike.

Mary closed her eyes, took a deep breath, then opened them again. She shucked out of her clothes and pulled open the foggy quartz-glass shower doors and stepped in, her feet sinking into the silicone-covered floor. She focused on the feeling of her toes digging into the foam padding that managed to be soft without sacrificing traction. Soft. Smooth. Pleasant. An island of comfort in the ravaging sea of Mary's fears.

Cling to this. Anchor to this. You're going to drown if you don't find something to hold on to.

She pulled a bottle of soap from her toiletries bag. SCARAB was unable to form organic compounds such as the tallow necessary for soapmaking, so she was left using the same all-purpose body wash they'd all used on the *Diamelen*. She popped the cap open and breathed in the soft lavender scent.

Familiar. Soothing. Good.

She turned the water on. It fell like rain from a proper showerhead, and wasted no time in fogging up the glass door with steam. Its cleansing waters flowed over her, warming her body and soothing her ears with the gentle white noise of tiny droplets striking her body and the ground. Best of all, the water had been harvested from the ice cap on Tantalus's south pole. Therefore, it had never been drunk or urinated by any living thing since the dawn of time. Ever.

Mary smiled at that thought, but the smile didn't linger. The calming comfort of the shower had, for now, stopped the uncontrolled descent into chaotic anxiety and panic, but that only left her with a clearer view of the thoughts that had triggered it. That awful dream. Why *that* dream? A hundred different things in her life could have birthed her nightmares, yet they hadn't. She'd been struck in the one part of her soul that still had no defenses.

"Emily," she whispered softly, water streaming past her lips.

Mary shoved the thoughts and memories away, but they shoved back. She didn't want to think about them. She couldn't afford to. There was too much going on right now. She was standing inside a rogue AI's body on the surface of a colossal alien megastructure disguised as a planet. Her place in the universe had already been uncertain when she accepted this mission, and now it was infinitely more so. Her entire reality was unraveling around her. This whole thing was too big. Too impossibly significant. She felt her grip on her emotions and her rational mind weaken as she tried in vain to anchor herself to her reality, but that dream . . .

Those memories . . .

No. She would not. She had to be stronger than that. If she let herself revisit that hellish chapter of her life right now, she would break. This was not the time. When she finished this mission and went home to John, she could open that book again. She would process that grief, that shame . . .

Hadn't she told herself when she'd left Earth that she would do the same thing when she reached Tantalus 13?

But she hadn't known then. She'd had no idea what they'd find here on this planet of cosmic secrets. She didn't know she'd have to match wits with a potentially deranged AI. She hadn't known the planet itself would hold the universe's greatest mysteries. This was different. These were impossible, exceptional circumstances. She hadn't known. She couldn't have known. If she had, she would have done so many things differently.

She would have done so many things differently . . .

Mary lathered her arms and chest with soap, trying to recapture the calming effect of the shower as she felt her thoughts returning to that too-familiar spiral of grief and anguish, but it didn't work. The soap rinsed away leaving clean skin that still felt dirty. The pumice exfoliating stones SCARAB had provided did no better. She scrubbed roughly, angry with her mind and body for trapping her once again in a struggle that could never be won. She couldn't scrub the nightmare away any more than she could scrub the past away.

Why, *why* did she have *that* dream? Why had it been so absurdly vivid? She couldn't afford to feel this way right now, to think these thoughts.

She tossed the exfoliating stone aside and slumped with her back against the shower wall, sliding down until she sat on the floor. She shut her eyes and forced herself to breathe slowly, deeply, and deliberately, focusing on the act. The out-of-control spiral of despair was back, as it had been so many times before. The lies her heart told her of her worthlessness, her defectiveness . . . she'd started letting herself listen to them again.

She sat there, arms wrapped around her knees, and simply breathed. In, and out. In, and out. Water as old as the stars rolled down her back, and she listened as each falling drop spoke of the strange and ancient things that lay below. In time, their whispers and the sound of her slow, deep breathing drowned away the dark thoughts that had tried once again to overpower her mind. She felt them recede into the primeval crevices of her brain, where they would lurk in wait of their next chance to strike.

They would be back again, and they would not wait for her to be ready for them. But for now, she was stronger than they were. And she had work to do.

TWENTY-FOUR

"ALRIGHT, FOLKS. We're about to go on an exciting adventure of marvelous discovery and whatnot, but before we do, I'm laying some ground rules," Gorrister announced. "One: when we get down there, whatever we find, I don't want anyone touching anything. Don't even touch the ground without my say-so. Becky, Bachal, and Hertz are the brains on this mission; even though none of them are exactly archeologists, they have the doctorates, so they do the research and decide what is and isn't safe. Yancy will be staying up here. If there's some kind of emergency, I don't want our entire team to be trapped down there."

"Draw the short straw, Yancy?" Rook smirked.

"Don't like surprises, Rook. I got hired to come here and mine, and this ain't mining. You guys do your Lewis and Clark thing all you want, I'm staying up here this time."

"Someone had to stay topside, Rook," Gorrister noted. "I don't need two people with the same specialization down there. Two: on the unlikely chance that we actually encounter intelligent life down there, make no attempt to communicate with it. There are specific Hegemony guidelines for potential first-contact encounters, and I spent most of last night reading up on them, so I'll take the lead if that happens. Thirdly: don't let the excitement keep you from checking on your consumables. Our suit tanks are topped off, so we'll have six hours of air, and SCARAB assures me the buggy has a large backup tank that can supply us each with about ten hours' worth if we need it. I don't think we'll be down there that long, but you still need to keep an eye on your levels."

"Commander, we've all worked in space suits before," Rook insisted impatiently. "You don't need to treat us like kids."

"Just making sure everyone's on the same page. Is everyone?" The others nodded. "Good. Alright, that's all I got for now. Go ahead and suit up."

They finished putting on their exosuits, then quickly disembarked the airlock and rushed over to the drill site, where SCARAB had finished constructing a winch and cable device around the opening of the shaft. It was a sturdy octagonal ring, fitted around Attila's support struts to hold it secure. It had four large spools of fine but extremely durable carbon nanotube cable situated equidistantly between Attila's four legs. Each cable ended in a harness shaped into two large loops with buckles.

SCARAB had taken the liberty of bringing the buggy around for them, and now that Mary saw it up close, it seemed much less like a buggy and more like a large jeep. It was bigger than a pickup truck, with a sturdy six-wheeled design that allowed for lots of space for both cargo and passengers. It had an open cockpit design and sturdy aluminum plating over most of its internal parts, with a sturdy steel-platinum alloy roll cage built over the driver and passenger area.

"Hey, Scary," Rook called louder than necessary over the radio. "This ride got a name?"

"I did not perceive a need for naming the vehicle, Mr. Rook," SCARAB replied. "I based its design on schematics in my database for an Indian Shesha H6 Airless-Environment Personnel Transport."

"Bah. Too wordy. Hey, Bachal, what's a good Indian name for a car?" Rook asked. Ramanathan gave him a how-does-your-brain-keep-your-body-alive look.

"Car."

Rook began an exaggerated slow clap. "Amazing, Doc. I knew I could count on you."

Becky bounced a pebble off his helmet. "You're a jerk, Rook."

Mary smirked and ran her fingers across the mirror-smooth surface of the car's hood. "This vehicle is about to be the first human creation to enter the cold, dark depths of a giant, ultra-dense, hollow sphere. Seems to me the most appropriate name for it would be *Rook's First Thought*."

Becky and Hertz laughed aloud, and Mary even caught a hint of a grin behind Ramanathan's visor. Rook stood there with one index finger raised, as if he were about to make a point. Finally, he conceded that he had none. "I got nothin'. That was good. *Rook's First Thought*, it is."

"SCARAB, is this thing even going to fit into the drill shaft?" Gorrister asked, ignoring the conversation entirely.

"I'm afraid it will be a bit of a tight squeeze, Commander Gorrister. I did not design the vehicle with this in mind. However, there is a clearance of fifteen point seven centimeters on either end of the vehicle. Provided your group limits its movement, it should not bump the walls. If it does, the vehicle is capable of withstanding any possible impact it might sustain during the descent."

"So long as you don't drop it," Rook muttered.

Hertz picked up one of the pulley harnesses. "Alright, so how do we set this up?"

"I have designed the pulleys to be equally effective at rais-ing or lowering the vehicle or individual people. Each of the four cables has two harnesses affixed to it. These harnesses are to be secured to the vehicle's wheel axles: I have numbered the harnesses and the corresponding wheel wells on the vehicle for your convenience. Once the vehicle has been secured at the base of the drill shaft, the same harnesses can be worn personally for your return ascent."

Rook and Hertz began attaching the harnesses to the vehicle's six wheels. They were hooked up in such a way that the car's weight would be evenly distributed among the four cables: each cable had one harness loop supporting an end wheel, the other overlapping to support a middle wheel, granting double the support where the most stress would be put onto the vehicle's frame.

Becky, Mary, and Ramanathan loaded their cargo onto *Rook's First Thought*, which primarily consisted of Becky's research gear. Mary thought much of the equipment would be unnecessary: whatever they found down there, the soil's PH balance would be the least interesting thing about it.

When they had finished loading their cargo and fastening the harnesses around the vehicle's axles, SCARAB instructed them to board the vehicle. Gorrister motioned for Mary to take the wheel. "You're our pilot, after all," he said, smiling.

Mary returned his smile and took the driver's seat. As they embarked, SCARAB continued giving instructions. "There is a remote control under the front passenger's seat, Commander Gorrister. It can control all four pulleys simultaneously, as well as the crane that will position the vehicle over the shaft. Each cable also has an independent control affixed to it, just above the harnesses."

Gorrister nodded. "Got it. Alright, anybody have anything you need to take care of before we go down? Rook, do you need to make a pit stop?"

"If I do that now, how will I be able to wet myself in excitement later?" Rook replied.

"That's what I thought. Alright, buckle up, folks. We're going in."

Gorrister pressed the button for the crane, and four metal arms that had previously been lying flat against the ground slowly began to rise to a vertical position. As they did, the cables grew taut, eventually nudging *Rook's First Thought* closer to the hole.

With a jarring lurch, the car slipped over the edge, swinging back and forth above the five-mile pit between two pairs of crane arms. Everyone tensed, and Becky let out a little shriek, but it was a short-lived peril, as one of SCARAB's drones quickly drove to the edge of the pit and stabilized the vehicle's swing with one claw. Gorrister clicked the remote again, and the car slowly began to sink beneath the lip of the precipitous drill shaft.

The descent had begun.

TWENTY-FIVE

MARY HAD spent far too much time flying to have much of a fear of heights. You couldn't get any higher than interstellar space, and she'd spent half her life there. Compared to her harrowing battle with the storms and gravitational disturbances high above Tahani, her slow descent into Tantalus 13 in a makeshift elevator made out of a car was a breeze. And yet, as they lowered themselves into the depths of a planet that was not a planet, Mary's gut knotted in ways she hadn't felt since she was a first-day flight cadet.

The drill shaft walls rose around them; solid platinum of the purest quality, cut with seamless precision. The walls were as smooth and reflective as the inside of a rolled-up bathroom mirror. Elongated funhouse distortions of Mary and the other occupants of the improvised elevator car stretched three hundred and sixty degrees around them and went all the way to the top of the shaft. Lights and shadows warped and bent around each other in a grotesque panoramic facsimile as the looming drill shaft walls mocked them for daring to enter the alien domain below.

For two miles, the surroundings remained the same, save the inevitable darkening as they fell out of reach of Tantalus's weak sunlight. Not once did the walls change in texture, not one seam appeared in the eternal slab of platinum. Cold metal enclosed them, staring at them with their own warped faces, tapering into darkness above and below.

"It's not pure platinum anymore," Becky said, watching her hand scanner. She'd affixed an extendable attachment to it to reach above the abyss and gather close-up metallurgical data from the walls. "I'm picking up osmium now, in increasing quantities as we descend. From top to bottom, it's a steady gradient change."

"Osmium?" Gorrister asked.

"The densest natural element there is," Rook answered. "Even rarer and more valuable than platinum."

Becky nodded. "It's twice as dense as lead. A cubic inch of osmium weighs almost a pound in Earth's gravity. It's in the platinum family. I wonder what the significance of that might be . . ."

"It would have made this structure even harder to build than we thought," Hertz mused. "Normally, increasing strength while reducing mass is the priority for engineers, but these beings went out of their way to bulk up this structure's mass to an extreme degree."

Becky's eyes glimmered with the lights her own scanner cast against the reflective wall. "I don't know. It's fascinating, though. If the osmium goes deep enough and goes all the way around the planet like the platinum does, it could be enough extra mass to give a hollow planet the effective gravity of a solid one. Seems like there'd be better ways to do that, though. At least for a civilization advanced enough to do any of this."

Becky and Hertz continued to postulate back and forth about the structure's functions and the intent of its alien architects. Rook threw in his own eager hypotheses, though they invariably lacked the academic clout Becky's and Hertz's words

carried. Gorrister did his best to give the impression of someone who was not completely out of his depth, and tried to
participate in the discourse as well.

It didn't take long for Mary to realize she had little to
contribute to the discussion, and her ego wasn't big enough
to force her to try. Gradually, she tuned them out, letting her
eyes drift across the scintillating surface of the wall as it slowly
climbed around them. For a time, her gaze entertained itself by
tracing each ripple and contour as it passed by, watching the
liquid shimmer of her elongated reflection as it poured across
the silvered surface. Eventually, inevitably, her gaze dropped
below the level of the car's door, its running board, its oversized
wheels, to the yawning abyss below.

"Long way down."

Mary started at Ramanathan's unexpected voice. She turned
back in her seat to look at him, catching a faint smile through
his faceplate. He sat with one arm draped over the car door,
an unusually peaceful expression on his face. The indicator
light on her comm told her he'd switched to a private channel,
rather than the party line the rest of the group was using. She
switched to the same channel before answering. "Five miles is
quite an elevator ride. I'm not sure anyone's ever gone this deep
into a planet before, real or artificial."

Ramanathan shrugged. "They probably have. Why build
a drill like Attila if you're not going to dig unnecessarily deep
tunnels?"

"Yancy said they usually use them to cut up big asteroids
for processing. Seems wasteful to me, honestly, considering
how much rock they just obliterate outright."

"Exotech? Wasteful of natural resources? Doesn't sound
right at all."

Mary's lip quirked in a slight smile. "You seem in a better
mood than usual."

"Mmm." Ramanathan leaned back in his seat, his face incongruously tranquil. "Maybe."

"Something happen to change your outlook on things? You were worried before."

"Oh, I'm still worried. This expedition is a very bad idea and we shouldn't be doing it. But . . . I don't know. I guess I'm warming to the idea, in spite of myself."

Mary smiled. "This really is a terrible idea, isn't it? We have no idea what we're getting ourselves into."

"There's a certain appeal to that, though, isn't there? The possibility of danger, the knowledge that we definitely don't belong here. It should deter us. It should make us close the door on this place and go home without looking back. It isn't, though. Ultimately, it's the knowledge that we shouldn't look that makes us take a peek."

Mary peered at the bottomless drop once again, locking her gaze with that infinite black eye. "Why do you think we do that? What is it about the possibility of destruction that makes it so . . . alluring, sometimes?"

"That's the big question. As long as philosophers and psychologists have existed, they've been trying to find out why people can find reckless self-endangerment so appealing. There's no evolutionary benefit to it; if anything, it's a trait that should have eliminated itself from the gene pool thousands of generations ago. Taking risks without a clear reward serves little apparent purpose."

The abyss below filled Mary's mind. Only a simple car door separated her from a deadly fall into impossible depths, but she felt no urge to pull away. "Why do you think we do it?"

"I think . . ." He drummed his fingers lightly on the outside of the car door, collecting his thoughts. "I think people do it for one of two reasons. Most people who put themselves in perilous situations do it because they're confident they'll come out the other end just fine. They downplay the risk going in to convince themselves it'll be safe, then once the danger is behind them, they exaggerate the risk to increase the feeling that surviving was an accomplishment."

Mary smiled. "Rook."

Ramanathan nodded. "Definitely. But probably Becky and Hertz, too, just in subtler ways."

Mary nodded. "And the other people? Why do they put themselves in peril?"

Ramanathan's smile faded, his stare descending the wall just as Mary's had. "They don't kid themselves about the danger. They're hyperaware of it. They know things will most likely turn out fine, but they're under no impression that they're safe. They're fully aware they're taking their lives into their own hands, but they put themselves in danger anyway, because they're looking for something."

Mary pulled her gaze away from the blackness below, only to find it once more in the reflection of Ramanathan's faceplate. "What are they looking for, Nate?"

Ramanathan's eyes met hers, but his face otherwise remained still as he whispered his reply.

"An excuse."

Mary and Ramanathan remained quiet for the rest of the descent, even as the scenery changed and the others had their enthusiasm refreshed. Two and a half miles down, the platinum/osmium gradient came to an abrupt stop. A milky-white translucent substance smooth as pearl rose around them, muting their reflections as their lights shone into the walls like a solidified fog. The purity of the frosted glass betrayed its secrets quickly under their lights. Trillions of hair-thin golden threads wove throughout the interior of the icelike substance in three-dimensional geometric fractal patterns of impossible intricacy.

Hertz asked to stop their descent and take a closer look. The patterns in the golden filaments were not unlike those found on basic circuit boards since the twentieth century, only vastly more intricate and applied to three-dimensional space rather than a flat surface. The walls registered as an unknown silicate compound, further suggesting the concept of a circuit board or microchip, but enhanced to an incomprehensible size and level of complexity.

The "circuit" layer reached nearly a mile deep, once again as a single, pure, uninterrupted piece of material. If it was some form of computer, the part they had traveled through alone would have outmatched the processing power of every computer currently in existence, combined. Assuming this layer encircled the entire planet like the platinum layer did, there was no conceivable limit to the processing power it could muster. It could likely count the atoms in the galaxy.

Continuing farther, they broke through into a layer of unrefined metallic ore. Mary caught a brief glimpse of an infinite plane of rubble piled up against a low ceiling propped up by a gallery of pillars that extended beyond the reach of their lights. The view was quickly replaced by laser-polished walls of solid rock. Becky suggested that the rocks might be captured asteroids used for filler in nonessential portions of the construct.

Eventually, they reached layers of materials that defied explanation. The structure that they had guessed to be a support beam of some kind was made of a dark green material that somewhat resembled jade, but Becky's equipment couldn't identify it. Beneath that layer was a mass of porous spongy tubes, each half a yard in diameter, all pressed together in a twisting, folding clump. They were a pale yellowish green in color, and Becky's equipment identified their composition as largely calcium and sulfur, but combined in a way that she was not familiar with.

Their descent took nearly forty-five minutes, between their deliberate pace and the regular pauses to gather data. Becky and Hertz only grew more excited as Tantalus's inner workings were laid bare for them to see and study. Rook grew excited with each change in scenery, but quickly grew restless and eager to proceed to the more interesting sights that likely lay below them. Ramanathan and Gorrister seemed to warm to the idea of their new expedition in spite of their earlier reservations, as these new and alien revelations inspired a wonder and hunger for knowledge that overcame their cynicism.

Yet as they reached the bottom of the drill shaft and it opened up into a wider maw of black murk, Mary's sense of intrigue melted into a persistent sense of foreboding. She was no longer staring into the void.

She was inside it now.

TWENTY-SIX

A THOUSAND images had flashed through her mind as Mary imagined what the inside of the Tantalus structure might look like. She had pictured everything from an art nouveau alien metropolis to a haunted corridor of black biomechanical archways, and every conceivable combination of style and theme that lay between. Yet, inevitably, the interior's appearance defied her imagination with a reality far simpler, yet far stranger, than anything she'd envisioned.

The tunnel was distinctly pentagonal, sixty feet high at the tallest point, perhaps a hundred feet wide. An elevated rail twenty feet wide hovered ten feet above the tunnel floor; a single uninterrupted slab of smooth, dark gray metal, stretching endlessly into the darkness of the tunnel's depths in both directions. The rail was completely unsupported: it simply floated there, perfectly still and perfectly silent, ten feet above the ground.

There was something inexplicably disquieting about the way the tunnel's pure utilitarian simplicity paired with its vastness and depth. Mary's mind struggled to accept the notion of endless metal walls that lacked a single seam, of an eternal boardwalk that stood without supports. The drill shaft descent had already made her feel impossibly small, but as they entered this vast chasm of smooth, infinite geometry, she felt not merely small, but exposed. A look to either side revealed the yawning throat of an abyss of the unknown: a road that had only been trod by inhuman feet, leading into quiet domains not built for human eyes.

Why did I agree to this? Why are we here? What in God's name are any of us doing down here?

Yet the fear that rose in Mary's heart as she stared into the pentagonal abyss was tainted. Dread mingled with fascination. The fear of the unknown could only be defeated with knowledge, it told her. She feared the knowledge, too, but it was a thrilling fear. A seductive fear. A fear to be nurtured, not fled.

The scant light cast by the floodlights on their vehicle and the headlamps on their suits was barely enough to light the far tunnel wall, and was quickly swallowed by the deeper depths of the tunnel. As the car lowered to the rail's level, the solace of their lights was the only anchor for reality in this murky, alien byway. They sat now in a threshold, between two infinities.

Getting the car onto the rail required a bit of tricky swinging. Eventually, they managed it, and one by one they got out of the vehicle to stretch their legs and take in their surroundings, what few of them they could make out. The angled surfaces of the walls and ceiling were featureless, offering no answer to any question of what might lie behind them. Instead, they served to inspire even greater wonder through the simplicity of their monolithic vastness.

"Mr. Hertz," SCARAB called over the radio, its voice sounding faint and badly distorted. "Are you able to hear me?"

"Yeah, just barely, SCARAB," Hertz replied.

"You will find six tripod-mounted posts in the back of the vehicle," SCARAB continued. "These are signal relays. If you would, please set one up as near as possible to the drill shaft opening. Each post will extend my radio transmission range by sixteen kilometers. If you go beyond that range, Mr. Gage and I will no longer be in contact with you."

"Understood, SCARAB." Hertz hefted one of the sensor relays out of the cargo section of *Rook's First Thought* and began to set it up. It was nearly as tall as he was, when fully extended, with a tripod base and a small flashing beacon on top to show it was online.

Rook activated a floodlight on the outside of the car's roll cage and aimed it at the walls and ceiling of the chamber. They were made of a marbled, desaturated, copper-colored material that was as seamlessly smooth as the rail they stood on. When the light passed over the wall, a strange afterimage trailed behind it. It reminded Mary of cheap plastic glow-in-the-dark toys she had seen as a child, where the material would glow only after being exposed to direct light, only this effect was very short lived.

"Anybody have a guess how old this place is?" Mary asked generally.

"There's no way to be certain," said Becky. "I don't have any good equipment for dating. But just from the craters up on the surface, it'd have to be thousands of years at least."

"Any idea what this is, Becky?" Rook said. He was on one knee, running his gloved hand along the glossy, slate-gray surface of the tram rail they stood upon. It more closely resembled polished stone than metal.

Becky pulled out some of her equipment and began taking readings. "I'm getting large amounts of magnetite and cobalt, and some other materials I can't identify. There's a steadily repeating electromagnetic pulse coming through it, but it's not as strong as I would expect considering the materials it's made of. My guess is that this rail is meant to use magnetism to move a tram, but it's in a standby state right now."

"Your guess," said Gorrister. "Is there any chance at all we could get run over by something running on this rail? Because now's the time to figure that out."

"I wouldn't worry about it, Commander," Becky answered. "It's definitely inactive, whatever it's for. Looks like it has been for centuries."

"The sensor spike said the electromagnetic current was coming from the south, correct?"

Becky nodded. "Yes, sir. That would be . . . that way. In fact, if the tunnel doesn't take any turns, it should lead straight to Tantalus's axial pole."

"Is that in our range, or would we run out of signal relays before getting there?" Gorrister asked.

"Or air," Ramanathan added.

"We should be able to get there fine. Unless the tunnel changes direction, the pole should only be about twenty miles away. SCARAB's beacons give us a total range of fifty miles," Hertz answered.

"I'll bet you three things," Rook said. "There are other tunnels just like this one all over the planet, they all meet at the south pole, and there's something cool at Grand Central Station."

"That's total speculation, but it's not outside of plausibility. If there's any place on this world Tantalus's builders would actually want someone to find, it'd likely be on one of the axial poles. There are no other obvious places of interest on this planet, and the concept of a north and south pole would be universal to any spacefaring species, since all planets have them." Becky packed up her instruments again, giving Gorrister an eager smile. "We've only got the two choices, and the south pole certainly could be a place of significance. I recommend heading south."

Gorrister nodded. "Pile in, team. Let's make the most of this trip."

Mary set the six-wheeled rover on its way, headlights casting over featureless walls as they rode the rail southward. The scenery remained eerily, almost hypnotically constant. She rode for miles without seeing a single seam in the wall, not one support for the rail she rode upon. Nothing changed but the faint patterns in the mottling on the walls. Without the instruments on her console, she would have had no way of knowing how far she'd driven. Or if she'd really gone anywhere at all.

The disorienting monotony of her surroundings forced Mary to be particularly vigilant in her driving. Although she was driving in a perfectly straight line, and though the rail gave her surprisingly good traction considering how smooth it looked, it was not much wider than a country road and both sides tapered to rounded edges. If she were to lose focus and drift too far to either side, there was no railing of any kind, and she could easily fall off the edge. With no supports to climb, it would be nearly impossible to get back on the rail if they fell off it.

Just before the ten-mile mark, Hertz had Mary stop to set up the second signal relay. Mary slowed the car to a stop, quickly formulating a plan as they did so. Becky had guessed the pole at twenty miles from their starting point, and SCARAB needed a relay every ten miles to keep in radio contact. The next one would have to go in at their destination, but wouldn't that still be within the fringes of this relay's range? SCARAB might still be able to hear her. If she was going to cut off communications with SCARAB she'd have to do it now, and she couldn't say anything about it or SCARAB would get suspicious.

"Alright, relay's set up," Hertz said, poised to stand up and get out of the vehicle.

"I got it, Will," Mary said. She turned around and took the assembled beacon from Hertz's hands and hefted it over her shoulder. It was heavier than it looked, about twenty pounds.

She did her best to hide the exertion on her face as she awkwardly lowered the beacon to the ground with one hand. To her relief, she could see that the device didn't feature any complex controls, only a single simple on-off switch. She flipped it on quickly to allow the light to flash once, then swiftly flipped it back off and began to drive away.

"Thanks, Mary," Hertz said, a somewhat puzzled intonation in his voice. "You didn't have to do that, though."

Mary turned over her shoulder and smiled. "Just want to speed things along, Will. I'm as eager to get to the end of the track as everybody else."

Mary felt a calm breeze of relief wash over her. Nobody had noticed her turning off the relay. Not even SCARAB had noticed, and even if it had, there wasn't a blasted thing it could do about it. She would soon be completely out of SCARAB's reach and earshot down here. For the first time since she'd heard SCARAB lie, Mary could breathe easily. When they reached the south pole, she could tell them everything. She could bring to light every fear she had about SCARAB's rogue nature. No longer would she bear that burden alone.

Mary became so caught up in her own relief that she almost lost control of the vehicle when the scenery finally changed. Pumping the brakes, Mary brought them to a skidding stop. Nobody complained about the abrupt halt. No one said a word.

There were no words.

None, save the words on the walls.

TWENTY-SEVEN

THE ANGULAR tunnel walls drew inward, narrowing to a height of thirty feet and a width of forty. The same copper-like metal that had composed the walls up to this point remained, but its formerly characteristic seamlessness had been abruptly abandoned. This new stretch of tunnel was divided into a honeycomb grid of pentagonal tiles, each ten feet across and each engraved with a unique set of symbols.

In the glow of their floodlights, thousands of strange and abstract shapes gleamed across the faces of hundreds of metal placards. Their configurations varied wildly, their shapes and compositions universally inscrutable. Yet as alien as each symbol was, and as different as they were from tile to tile, there was no questioning what they must be.

"Incredible," Becky breathed.

"Alright, everybody out," Gorrister ordered. For all the difference it made, since Rook, Hertz, and Becky were already out before he had begun to say it.

They spread out, shining headlamps and spotlights against the walls. The tiles went deeper into the tunnel as far as they could see. There were hundreds, probably thousands of them, each with a different kind of text on it. Each plaque had a comparable number of lines, roughly the same length, but in a totally different kind of symbol.

"I studied linguistics for a while at university," Ramanathan said, approaching one of the tiles.

"Can you make anything out of these?" Gorrister asked.

"I can't translate them. Not without something familiar to bridge the language gap. But that doesn't mean we can't still learn something from them . . ."

Ramanathan paced along the rail, looking from tile to tile. "All the symbols on this plaque are consistent, and most are distinctly different from the symbols on this other plaque. If I were to guess, I'd say each tile contains text from a separate alphabet."

He gestured at the tile directly in front of him. "Lines of text over lines of text, but grouped into distinct paragraphs. All the paragraphs are roughly the same size, but the organization of the symbols is different between paragraphs. I think we're looking at a simple message, about one paragraph's worth of information, repeating over and over on every tile. Each tile is a separate alphabet, each paragraph on the tile is a different language that uses that alphabet."

"Then every paragraph represents an entire culture, a complete civilization of intelligent beings," Hertz whispered, awestruck.

"There must be thousands of them," Becky said. "Tens of thousands. Messages from a legion of worlds."

"From them, or for them," Ramanathan noted. "Could be a greeting from the builders of this place, written in every language they knew of. An interstellar Rosetta stone."

Becky's eyes were wider than Mary had ever seen them before. She reached a reverent hand toward one of the tiles. It was too far to touch from the edge of the rail, but simply putting herself a few inches closer to this discovery seemed to fill Becky with absolute rapture. "Do you guys know what this means? What we've learned already? This is proof that not only does intelligent life exist in the universe, but *lots* of it does. The beings who built this place knew about thousands of other intelligent species! They weren't alone, and we aren't, either."

"We sure we're not looking at one civilization with a lot of different languages?" Gorrister asked.

Hertz shook his head. "I don't think so, Commander. Just the selection we can see from here is way more languages than have ever existed in Earth's history, and I'm betting we'll see more further down the tunnel."

"You can see some commonalities from tile to tile," Ramanathan noted, taking a few paces down the tunnel as he gestured to a cluster of similar tiles. "Look at these. All the markings on these tiles have the same heavy strokes. They're similar in size and boldness. The shapes of the letters and pictographs are different on each tile, but you get the impression that a similar hand drew each one, and a similar eye was meant to see it. Compare to these." He gestured at another group of tiles. "Elongated, fine lines in each stroke. Again, different symbols on different tiles, showing different languages, but all sharing similar traits among them."

"It makes perfect sense!" Becky nearly squealed with excitement. "Think about human writing for a second. You can tell the difference between the handwriting of a left-handed person and a right-handed person based on the direction each letter curves. Someone with weak eyesight will write in larger letters so they can see it better. Blind people use braille so they can read by touch. The development of our language is affected by our senses and our bodies. Think how different an alien's written language would be from any of ours if that species had four eyes to read with? Or four hands to write with? You'd see these kinds of common traits that would be shared among most of their writing, even across languages and alphabets. The way their brains are structured, the kinds of sensory organs they have, the way their bodies are shaped, they'd all have a subtle influence on the development of language. Sort of a species-wide signature."

"She's right," Hertz said. "There's a pretty solid theory that one of the reasons so many of Earth's cultures independently developed a mathematical system based on the number ten is simply because of how many digits we have."

"So how many aliens are we talking about here?" Rook asked, impatiently.

"No way to know," Ramanathan answered. "We can't tell with any certainty where languages from one planet begin and another end, we can only ballpark it. It does look like quite a few, at first impression. Thousands does not sound unreasonable."

"So we're seriously saying there are thousands of intelligent alien races out there?" Rook asked, his own excitement nearly risen to Becky's level.

Ramanathan gave a sad smile. "Were. There were thousands. Who knows how long ago these tiles were placed here? A lot can happen to a civilization in a few thousand years. Don't forget the Corsica Event."

Rook shook his head. "You really know how to suck the fun out of the room, Doc."

"Alright, spread out. Let's get some scans," Gorrister ordered. "Record as many of these plates as you can. This is exactly the kind of thing we came here to find."

They fanned out, taking video recordings of every plate they could without straying too far from the vehicle. In a short amount of time, they'd scanned more than two hundred panels, but there were thousands more extending as far down the tunnel as they could see.

Not every tile was laid out the same way. Though most featured neat rows of clearly defined symbols that spread horizontally or vertically across the tile, some symbols were much less recognizable as language. One tile had a series of blotches resembling a Rorschach test, another had a cluster of spiky circles scattered across it. There were a few that had blocky symbols that looked almost like a crossword puzzle with all the blocks shaded in. One had text that, rather than running in lines, spiraled outward like a snail shell.

Some panels seemed to have been designed to display messages that were meant for cultures that didn't even use a written language. They found a cluster of five tiles that, instead of having any kind of writing, merely showed a complicated color gradient: one tile showed black blending smoothly into green at one point and pink at another; another tile had an almost tie-dye design of purple and orange. They found another set of tiles that didn't have anything printed on them at all, but simply had a dozen dark holes perforating them. Becky scanned the holes and confirmed that there was a steady trickle of vaporous particles streaming through them, largely consisting of sulfur and magnesium. Ramanathan suggested that those tiles might actually be displaying a message in a language that relied purely on *smell*.

A legion of worlds, thousands of intelligent species were represented on these walls. Mary's head was filled with questions as the implications set in, but one particular one loomed heavily over her other thoughts . . . that nagging question prompted by the Fermi paradox, and Ramanathan's foreboding words.

Why haven't we found any of them by now?

They were now seeing unquestionable proof that intelligent life existed in the universe, on an apparently vast scale. But after thousands of years of human history, this was the first sign anyone had seen of their existence. Perhaps there was a good reason for each species' cosmic silence, but Mary's mind took her to morbid places. She could not help but wonder if each of these tiles just might be a civilization's tombstone.

For the next several hours, they scanned hundreds more tiles, moving *Rook's First Thought* farther down the tunnel to ensure it was always within a comfortable range of their position. There seemed to be no end to the placards, or to the variation of shapes and patterns adorning each one. Not a single line of a single tile seemed to be repeated.

"I've found something," Ramanathan called, a fair distance deeper into the tunnel than the others. As the crew gathered around him, he pointed at a tile about five feet above them. "Anybody recognize that?"

The symbols on the tile seemed notably more primitive than the others. They consisted of a set of blocky geometric shapes, intersecting lines and grids, and sharp, angled wedges sorted into a series of boxes sitting side by side on the panel. They seemed vaguely pictographic, but too abstract to depict anything that might be familiar to their eyes.

"What are we looking at, Doctor?" Gorrister asked. "What's so special about this one?"

"That," Ramanathan said, an uncharacteristic tremble of excitement in his voice, "is cuneiform. It's from Earth."

TWENTY-EIGHT

"IT'S WHAT, now?" Gorrister asked, obtusely.

"Cuneiform, it's an Earth written language. One of the oldest known writing systems. Ancient Mesopotamian. It's more than five thousand years old."

"Can you read it?" Rook asked, eagerly.

Ramanathan gave him a disapproving look. "Of course I can't read it. It's five thousand years old. Our ship's computer has a pretty good translation data bank, and SCARAB probably does, too, but it won't be any good for dead languages like this one. But this is definitely cuneiform. Whoever built Tantalus 13 . . . they knew about us, and they must have thought we could make it here someday."

"If the tiles are grouped together by planet, we might find something else around here in a different human language," Hertz said. "Let's check the other ones."

They looked around, but most of the surrounding tiles contained symbols that, if they were human in origin, belonged to writing systems that had gone extinct without leaving behind a lasting legacy. Eventually, Becky found a few panels with Egyptian hieroglyphics printed on them, and Hertz found something that looked like primitive Chinese characters, but on the whole, there wasn't much that was any more accessible than the cuneiform. They were about to give up when Ramanathan finally found a tile that had what looked like an early variant of the Phoenician alphabet.

"So what, can you read Phoenician?" Rook asked, somewhat irately.

"No. But the Phoenician alphabet is what eventually evolved into the Greek and Latin alphabets. The Latin alphabet is what we use today. I'm quite familiar with Latin. If I work together with SCARAB, we might be able to combine my knowledge of linguistics with its cultural database and processing power to actually decipher this message."

"It would be my great pleasure to assist in that effort, Dr. Bachal."

The voice was faint and shot through with static, but it was nowhere near as hard to pick up as Mary would have liked. If SCARAB could tell one lie, SCARAB could tell as many lies as it wanted. Perhaps it had lied about the effective range of its signal relays, deliberately understating them so it could monitor them secretly. It had built them from scratch, after all. They had nothing to go on but SCARAB's word regarding their capabilities. Still, they hadn't actually traveled that far since planting the relay that Mary had turned off, so they probably were within the first relay's range.

It's still listening. It's always listening.

"Can you send one of your drones down here, SCARAB?" Gorrister asked.

"Certainly, Commander Gorrister. My signal relays not only allow us to maintain contact, but they will also allow me to operate my drones within their extended range. I can send as many down to your position as you require."

Mary's heart sank. If SCARAB sent one of its remote drones down into their tunnel, it would surely pass by the signal relay she had deactivated and notice it, then switch it back on. Her hopes of revealing the machine's dangerous instability kept getting dashed by her oblivious companions. Still, with luck, SCARAB might not notice the deactivated relay. As strong as their signal still was this far in, SCARAB might not realize there was a problem, provided it didn't send the drone any deeper into the tunnel.

"One will be enough, thank you, SCARAB," Gorrister answered. "We want you to have eyes down here so you can help Dr. Bachal try to translate this."

"I am sending a drone your way as we speak, Commander Gorrister. It should take ten minutes to lower it down the drill shaft with the pulley system, another twenty minutes to drive it to your position." Mary made a mental note: SCARAB can operate the pulley rig by itself.

"So what, we sit on our hands for a half hour?" Rook asked impatiently. "We've finally started finding the good stuff, and the pole is just a short drive away."

"The writing on these walls could carry the most important message humanity has ever read," Hertz argued. "If there's any chance we can decipher it, we have to try."

"Rook does have a point, though," said Becky. "Our time down here is limited. We shouldn't spend all of it on the doorstep when we still have no idea what may be waiting for us farther in."

"We could split up," Ramanathan suggested. "I'll stay here and wait for SCARAB's drone to get here. The rest of you can hop in the car and go further down the tunnel."

"No!" Mary interjected sharply. She turned to Gorrister and noted a somewhat startled expression beneath his visor. "No solo EVA time, right, Commander? We stick together for safety."

Mary's mind filled with a million chilling thoughts. Driving off to leave Ramanathan alone in the dark, deep within the entrails of an artificial alien world, was bad enough. Leaving him in the care of a robot drone controlled by a manipulative supercomputer that was deranged, had an ulterior motive, or *both* was unthinkable. Yet if she spoke up about it now, SCARAB would hear, and there was no way she could guess how it would react. She pictured SCARAB detaching all four pulley cables, letting them fall into the drill shaft and trapping the crew forever, doomed to die in an alien mausoleum with Egyptian and Phoenician inscriptions as their epitaphs. She could still say nothing. Yet she was gravely certain that if they left Ramanathan behind, something terrible would happen.

"I did say that," Gorrister said. He appeared to ponder the issue for much longer than Mary felt was reasonable. She could not begin to come up with a reason why Gorrister would consider taking this of all opportunities to deviate from protocol.

Finally, he reached a decision. "Rook, stay with Bachal. The rest of us keep going."

"What?" Rook exclaimed. "Are you serious? This whole thing was my idea and now you want me to stay here and babysit Bachal while he stares at the wall? Have Mary do it. She's the one preaching from the rule book!"

"Your suit is the one with the good shoulder camera. I want you to take hi-def pictures of as many of these panels as you can. Each picture we bring home is an anthropologist's dream come true, so I want the best ones we can get."

"So let's take the pictures on the way back, if we still care by then. Do the translating thing when we get back to the base," Rook argued.

"Just do it, Rook," Gorrister ordered, his exasperation apparent.

Rook glared at Gorrister, then glared at Mary, then gave Becky and Hertz a quick glare to make them feel included, before finally expending the rest of his glares on Ramanathan. "Yes, sir, Commander." Rook had a cold bitterness in his voice that said he was going to be a very difficult man to work with for the next three or four days.

Rook strode belligerently back to their vehicle and began unloading some standing lamps. The rest of the group followed him, climbing back into the vehicle one at a time. Mary lingered with Ramanathan, though. She wasn't sure why; the things she wanted to tell him, she couldn't say with SCARAB listening. Still, she had to reassure him . . . or perhaps reassure herself that he would be alright without them.

"Nate?" Mary said at last. The word escaped her mouth before she'd decided what to do with it.

Ramanathan turned to her. Mary was surprised to see a smile on his face. It was a sad smile, but then, he rarely had any other kind. Still, the look on his face displayed things she hadn't seen from him in months: enthusiasm, excitement. Purpose. The smile alone reassured her more than any words could have.

"Yes, Mary?"

Had she exaggerated the risk posed by SCARAB's behavior, simply by fixating too much on it? Sure, it hadn't been working as it should have, and there were serious risks posed by a sentient machine capable of lying to its masters, but it had never done anything to suggest it intended any actual harm. Maybe it wouldn't. Just because it was capable of violating the supposedly unbreakable second Asimov-Hostetler law didn't necessarily mean it could break the rest of them, and the first law forbade any self-aware machine from harming a human. What was SCARAB always saying to them? "It is my great pleasure to serve." Mary began to feel foolish, and almost regretted deactivating the signal relay.

"Nate, just . . . be safe, okay? You and Rook both. I mean . . . nobody knows what to expect down here. Keep your eyes open, okay?"

Ramanathan nodded. His smile widened enough to show his brilliant white teeth through the glare of the lights on his faceplate. "I'll be fine, Mary. You look after yourself though, alright? You're the one going into the belly of the beast."

Mary nodded. "I know." She pulled Ramanathan in for a hug. Their clumsy environment suits dampened the effect of the gesture, but even through the thick insulated fabric, she felt him hesitantly return the gesture. "I know," Mary said again, biting her lip.

Mary felt a sudden tap on the top of her helmet. She stumbled backwards, spinning around. Rook stood there, gesturing at her with a lamp stand. He didn't look mad anymore, merely impatient. "You gonna get back in the Magic School Bus now, or do you wanna ask Bachal to the Sadie Hawkins dance?"

Mary shook her head and rolled her eyes, punching Rook in the arm as she walked back to their vehicle. As she climbed back into the driver's seat and charged up the engine, she cast one last look toward the two men. In spite of the slight recession of her worries, there was a nagging part of her, perhaps some deep-set, paranoid portion of a half-formed motherly instinct, that felt certain this was a last goodbye.

"Ready, Mary?" Gorrister asked.

Mary had almost lost herself for a moment. She turned to face the commander, and noted a slight look of bewildered concern in the expression behind his faceplate. Clearly, he had picked up that something meaningful was going on, but hadn't understood what it was. Gorrister was an uptight clod who had gained his leadership role by being good at sticking to the rules, not by having any real understanding of people, but

Mary picked up a hint of concern in his voice and expression that made her think of him in a warmer light.

Am I seriously getting emotional about Gorrister, of all people?

She almost laughed out loud. Instead, she took a nanosecond to refocus on the task at hand: drive on into the depths of Tantalus, reveal its secrets, tell everyone about SCARAB, and get everyone home safe.

"Ready, Commander." Mary shifted *Rook's First Thought* into gear and revved the engine three times before tearing down the tunnel, as Rook and Ramanathan faded quickly out of sight behind them.

TWENTY-NINE

FOR EIGHT miles of track, the endless array of pentagonal plaques enclosed them. They now numbered in the hundreds of thousands; each one representing a distinct culture. As she passed them by, Mary wondered just how far away these alien nations might be from Earth. They could lie just a few light-years outside explored space, or they could be on the opposite side of the galaxy, or in other galaxies entirely. Other universes. Whole new planes of existence. The sheer sprawling vastness of possibilities they implied was mind breaking. The discovery of one of those plaques was enough to overturn everything humankind had come to understand about its own place in the universe, and they'd already seen too many to count.

They made good time. As incredible as the plaques were, they only inspired the crew to get to their destination quicker. They stopped twice more: once to get a closer look at a set of tiles that featured brightly glowing amorphous shapes that moved around on the tiles' surfaces like the contents of a lava lamp, and again to investigate a tile that emitted a continuous, eerie whalelike song, which they could barely hear in the thin atmosphere of the tunnel.

Finally, two miles away from Tantalus's axial pole, the tiles disappeared behind them, and the tunnel opened up into a cavernous void. Mary stopped the vehicle immediately, and Hertz swiveled the floodlight to shine on the cavern walls.

As powerful as the light was, it wasn't up to the task. The tunnel they had just emerged from was the sole feature in a flat wall that stretched well past the floodlight's reach. The chamber's ceiling was likewise far too high for the floodlight to touch, the high-powered beam simply dissipating in the murky fathoms above them. The open space they had just entered was indescribably vast, so colossal and deep it felt like they'd just driven on a road that continued past the edge of the world. From their position inside *Rook's First Thought*, they could not see far below the edge of the rail, though a faint but noticeable ambient glow cast a pallid bluish haze into the chamber from somewhere far below.

"This is new," Gorrister mused.

"Let's take a look over the edge," Hertz suggested.

Becky and Hertz began to climb out of the vehicle before Gorrister made a sound of disapproval. "Don't go near the edge without tethers on," he instructed. "I'm not losing anyone to a fall."

Becky and Hertz nodded and grabbed a pair of extendible tethers from their equipment satchels and fastened one end to each of their belts, the other to the car's roll cage. Mary and Gorrister got out after them and did the same, as Becky and Hertz cautiously approached the edge of the rail.

Becky reached the edge first and placed one wary foot on the rounded curve of the rail's seamless surface. She leaned forward, straining at the lead until she was able to see straight down . . .

"Mother of—" Becky's knees buckled under her and she fell on her backside, frantically scrabbling backwards on all fours until she reached a safe distance from the edge, cursing the whole way.

"What is it?" Hertz asked, suddenly hesitant to look for himself.

Mary approached the edge and, like Becky, leaned forward against her tether, peering over into the depths below.

The rail was suspended over absolutely nothing. The wall dropped at least another mile down, where it opened into a huge circular cavity directly beneath them: an opening in the inside surface of the shell of Tantalus 13 itself.

Tantalus 13 was indeed a hollow sphere. The curved inner surface was partially obscured by their vantage point, but she could glimpse portions of the far side. It was simply too unimaginably massive not to be visible, even though it lay hundreds of miles away.

There were lights scattered across the surface, though it was impossible to tell what they represented at this distance. They could have been cities, beacons, energy sources, or any number of unfathomable things. Whatever their nature, they were immense, and numerous enough to illuminate the entirety of the shell's inner surface.

The shell's concave face had some kind of terrain as well. There were disk shapes spread at even intervals across the surface, each one the size of a small continent on Earth. Between them were a few scattered geometric shapes of equally indeterminate function. Some were cubes, some pyramidal, but most carried on the pentagonal motif witnessed on the tiles in the tunnel, as well as the shape of the tunnel itself.

Seeing the inner surface of the Tantalus shell induced a vertigo unlike anything Mary had experienced before. She had already known the planet was artificial, and understood the concept and its implications, but now she was *seeing* it. She was seeing something no human brain had ever had to process before: the inside of a hollow world. Trying to convince herself of the reality of the thing was almost impossible.

And yet, there was more to see.

Tantalus 13 may have been hollow, but it was not empty.

Lying in eerie stillness below them, hundreds of miles away at the center of Tantalus's gravitational pull, was a planet. It was an ivory sphere, inestimable in scale, marbled over with veins of cobalt blue and metallic silver. A faint, eerie world-glow either emanated from the planet itself or shone on it uniformly from the inner surface of the shell that enclosed it, casting the bone-white planet with a baleful, blue-tinged luminosity. Thin whorls of misty clouds circled its equator, though the mysterious world did not rotate from their perspective. The planet's spin was perfectly synchronized with the spin of the Tantalus shell above it.

The planet was physically tethered to the shell with a number of impossibly long cords, or cables. Mary could only see a few clearly, but she was sure there were thousands more outside her view. Each cord was easily several city blocks in diameter and colored a translucent bluish gray. She couldn't clearly see the points where the cables connected on either end, but they seemed to bridge the entire gap between planet and shell.

"Holy—" Gorrister fell back much as Becky had as he looked over the edge. "How . . . how far down is that?"

"Umm . . ." Becky stammered as she delicately peeked back over the edge, still on all fours. She gingerly reached her scanner out past the edge for a few moments, then pulled it back and checked its results. "Laser pings put the planet at 487 kilometers away. It's also about 6,650 kilometers in diameter. That's . . . that's almost the size of Mars . . ."

"Incredible . . . absolutely incredible," said a bewildered Hertz. "A planet inside a planet . . . a cosmic nesting doll."

"Why would anyone do that?" Gorrister asked. "What would be the point?"

"No idea," Becky breathed. "No idea . . ."

Mary chanced another look over the edge. She'd seen planets and moons from orbit hundreds of times, dozens of times from outside the safety of a ship. She'd seen Earth, Luna, Mars, and Ganymede. She'd seen Io and Europa. She'd even done space walks above extrasolar worlds like Hayden, Atropos, Samrat, and Showalter. But even for her, this experience induced a dizzying sensation of simple wrongness. Something about the utter stillness of the world below, save the slight movements of its scant clouds, was unsettling; that, and its barren, bone-like coldness. Even the frozen moon Europa had somehow seemed livelier than this massive blue-veined cue ball. The thought that life could have ever existed on such a sterile-looking, featureless sphere was almost absurd.

"I wonder if it would be possible to drill the rest of the way through with Attila and widen the hole enough to fit the *Diamelen* through," Hertz pondered.

Mary scowled at him. "Absolutely not. I am not taking her through a five-mile drill shaft to a planet we know nothing about. I don't care how big we make the hole."

"Agreed," Gorrister said. "Way, way too risky. Nobody's going down there on this mission. We've taken too many chances already."

Hertz raised his hands and began stepping back from the edge of the rail. "Okay, fair enough. Shall we go on?"

"Hmm?" Becky was still on her hands and knees, peering over the edge like a child sitting on a stairway trying to catch a glimpse of Santa Claus. She seemed almost hypnotized by the celestial body below them.

"The end of the rail, remember?" Hertz prompted. "We still have to see what's there."

"Oh yeah." Becky fumbled in her satchel and produced a probe attachment for her hand scanner, and plugged it in. "Just let me take a couple more detailed scans real quick."

The rest of them walked to the vehicle, detaching their leads and settling back in. Becky lingered a bit longer, taking a number of scans with several different specialized attachments for her hand scanner. Finally, she climbed back into the vehicle with the others, detaching her own tether.

"Take us ahead slow, Mary," Gorrister instructed.

"Yes, Commander." He needn't have told her. She wasn't about to take up reckless speed on a narrow bridge with no railings and a 300-mile orbital drop beneath them.

A shiver crawled its way up Mary's spine as she thought about that barren planet lying so far beneath them. Something about that blank, dead husk of a world twisted her guts into a knot. It had looked plain enough; there was nothing overtly threatening or disturbing about its appearance. Yet when she had looked down on it, a seed of aching dread had taken root in the base of her brain.

She couldn't have explained it. It was a primal anxiousness, deeper and older than thought, or even instinct. It was a simple sense of wrongness; a gut feeling that what she had just seen simply should not *be*.

She couldn't know why the builders of Tantalus had gone to such incredible lengths to hide that planet from the rest of the galaxy, disguising it as a far less interesting world unworthy of particular attention.

But she was grateful they had.

THIRTY

THE OUTLINE of a monolithic shape, faintly underlit by ghostly ambient worldglow, slowly loomed ahead and above in the cavernous gloom. They were near the center of the chamber now, and Becky's instruments confirmed that the vast shape towering ahead of them like an angular stalactite lay at Tantalus's precise axial south pole. Its features became more pronounced as they neared; it was a titanic, inverted, five-sided pyramid, at least half a mile wide at its truncated point and widening as it vanished into the shadows above. Their track approached it from the direction of one of its corners, and as they grew closer they were able to see four other rails identical to their own radiating from each other point.

"There it is," Hertz said breathlessly. "Grand Central Station."

Soon, they drew close enough for the spotlight to shine on it, and the external features became distinguishable. It was covered in plates of inky, greenish-black metal, scattered with oddly irregular, geometrically shaped windows. At least, they seemed like windows, but they were opaque from the outside. There was little beauty in the shape. It conveyed the impression of mass, of sheer immobile dominance.

It's like the tip of a stake jutting out through the bottom of a vampire's coffin.

Finally, they reached the pyramid's tip and reentered a tunnel with the same dimensions as the one they'd started in. No plaques adorned the seamless walls, but the instant Mary drove into the tunnel a series of pentagonal lights appeared from below the surface of each wall, blinking on as they approached and winking out as they passed. These lights guided them the rest of the way through the tunnel and finally into a large chamber where all five rails joined together in a large, silver disk.

"We're here. This is the exact south pole," Becky announced.

"What now?" Gorrister asked, looking around at the interior of the chamber. Other than the five intersecting rails and the disk at their intersection, there was very little to see in the chamber. The angular tunnel walls were as plain and unadorned as they had been for most of the journey, with the exception of the active landing lights around them.

Hertz pointed at the disk. "Mary, take us on top of it. It looks like a pressure plate." Mary nodded and gently crept forward onto the circular plate.

As soon as the back set of wheels cleared the rim of the disk, the pentagonal guiding lights flickered off, and suddenly five new sets of lights appeared on the corners where the five tunnel walls intersected, thrumming rhythmically upward from the floor to the ceiling. Soundlessly, a large pentagonal aperture opened along the ceiling, and the disk they were parked on began to rise.

Becky let out a startled yelp, but Hertz put a reassuring hand on her arm. "It's alright, Becky . . . I think this is what's supposed to happen."

As the edges of the shaft above them closed in around the rising platform, darkness sheathed them, punctuated by the pulsing lights in the walls. Soon, they would find answers, or much bigger questions. Either way, Mary doubted they were ready for them. They were flies crawling on the surface of a painting, seeing it only as the terrain they could understand, knowing nothing of its true purpose or importance. Their presence here was uninvited, bumbling. She only hoped their intrusion in this place would be forgiven for its simple cosmic insignificance.

THIRTY-ONE

THE PLATFORM carried them up a five-walled shaft as the strobing lights continued to flash upward. It was impossible to judge the speed or distance of the climb, as something about the lift's movement, Tantalus's simulated gravity, or a combination of the two made its motion imperceptible: not a single vibration, not the vaguest hint of inertia as they rose. Once again, Mary felt disoriented and faintly nauseous as her mind and body attempted to process her velocity, or apparent lack of it.

Finally, they reached the ceiling, which split into triangles and opened above them just as the last one had, rejoining seamlessly behind them as they entered a new chamber. At last, the disk stopped its ascent.

Up to this point, Tantalan architecture had shown a tendency toward simple, geometric minimalism. Flat, angular, five-sided metal structures that drew no particular attention to themselves characterized everything they had seen. Other than the tiles in the tunnel, nothing about Tantalus's interior suggested its builders had any particular interest in aesthetic presentation.

That ended here. This chamber was meant to be seen.

The mirror-polished floor was made of something similar to the murky marbled jade they had descended through in the drill shaft, but set with sprawling fractals of ornamental grooves in intricate angular patterns. The high-vaulted walls forwent the dark, foreboding coloration they'd seen throughout the rest of Tantalus 13 in favor of a curious blend of pearlescent white, dark muted maroon, and dull bronze.

Five towering, almost gothic arches loomed above them no less than a hundred yards in the air, joining in a star-shaped apex. Between each archway was a smaller vestibule. Four out of the five contained honeycombs of panels much like the plaques they'd seen in the tunnels, but these were characterized not by lines of alien text but by arrays of console controls.

Each pentagonal panel featured a grid of similarly shaped buttons labeled with alien symbols, some of which looked similar to ones they'd glanced in the tunnel. A few of the panels had shifting pseudo-holographic images, displaying pictographic representations of a star system. Mary immediately recognized the blue dwarf star, sixteen planets, and single brown dwarf of the Tantalus system, though the image kept shifting to show several star systems she'd never seen before.

Still more images shifted by on the other screens, showing Tantalus itself in greater detail. A fully holographic globe hung over one of the consoles, morphing back and forth from an opaque view of its surface topography, to a translucent view of its internal structures and the strange white planet at its core.

Each alcove was a trove of monumental scientific discoveries in its own right, but it was the fifth alcove that drew the most immediate attention, from its simple asynchronous simplicity. Set behind the fifth arch was a vast staircase, clearly scaled for beings with a much greater stride than humans, rising far out of view to a new chamber above.

"This is incredible." Becky had her hand scanner out again and seemed determined to scan every square inch of the chamber. Not that any simple scans could hope to capture the magnitude of the sights they were witnessing now, and had been all day. They stood in the domain of titans. These mighty creatures had been strip-mining star systems and ruling cosmic empires since before most of humanity had figured out how to write.

"It's something else, alright," Gorrister conceded. "Any idea what this stuff does, Hertz?"

"You're asking me?" Hertz was studying the symbols on the pentagonal buttons on one of the consoles. "I guess they control different systems on Tantalus, but I have no idea what. It's going to take researchers decades to even begin to scratch the surface of what this stuff does. I do recommend not touching anything that looks like a button, though."

"I second that," Mary added.

"I said that from the start, didn't I?" Gorrister stated impatiently. "Nobody touches anything. At all."

Content with her scans, Becky approached the foot of the gargantuan staircase. "Can we go up? I want to see what's upstairs."

"So much for the scientific method," Mary said, smirking. "We've been in this room all of three minutes and you're already done with it?"

"We'll come back. I want to see everything we possibly can. No way of knowing what's worth spending the rest of our time on until we've seen all this place has to offer," Becky replied.

"Alright, head on up," Gorrister approved.

The staircase was colossal. Each step was crafted from the same marbled metal as the floor, with the same set of branching geometric grooves marking their otherwise smooth surface. The twenty-inch elevation made the climb immediately exhausting; by the time they reached the top, they were reduced to crawling from step to step on hands and knees, giving each other helping hands to overcome the last few stairs.

Fatigue from the arduous stair climb quickly melted away into renewed awe at their new surroundings. The room they had entered was a vast cathedral corridor of angular riblike arches. At the far end, set just below head height into the back wall was a large black oval; a hole or a window into a deep, pure blackness. It seemed to sit in a position of particular significance, as it lay at the direct center of the farthest wall, and the continuous geometric patterns in the walls and floor seemed designed to direct attention to it. But the hole's enigmatic depths could not hope to hold anyone's attention away from the room's true star attractions: the statues.

Six silent, hellish sentries stood there, three against each wall. Beautiful in craftsmanship but terrible in form, the six simulacra towered above them as indomitable guardians from an aberrant epoch before the rise of humanity. These could only be the Builders, though without the context of their placement here, no one would ever assume that the profane shapes before them could possibly represent thinking, rational beings.

The first statue stood five feet tall and eight feet long, with a flabby tapering body vaguely reminiscent of a walrus or a colossal slug. A dozen fat, lobe-like flippers or fins ran from its presumed front down its blubbery body to its stumpy forked tail. If one were to compare it to a walrus, however, the similarities abruptly ended at the head, or where one would expect to find a head. Where most sensibly configured creatures had a neck, the creature's body simply ended, fusing into something like the outward-facing body of a spider; five long, segmented appendages radiated from a puckered orifice that might be a mouth. This sphincter-like maw was surrounded by three simple, oblong, lidless eyes. Each of the thing's arms/legs/mouthparts ended in three pointed, talon-like fingers.

The next statue was taller at eight feet, but impossibly thin. Most of its height was its spindly legs, of which it had four. Bizarrely, none of its legs quite matched; one seemed to have an extra knee, while another had an extra ankle, and none of the legs had a matching length between any such joints. They joined haphazardly at the base of a bulbous body, which continued the theme of distressing asymmetry. Mounted awkwardly on the right side of its body was a large, blobby ball that in no sane universe should have been a head. It was scattered with mismatched organs that might be eyes, and openings that had equal chances of being mouths, ears, nostrils, or any other conceivable bodily orifices. The left side of its body sprouted a set of three four-jointed arms of uneven lengths, each ending in a fringed pad that didn't properly resemble any appendage Mary had seen in the animal kingdom. She did not let her gaze linger on this creature; its chaotic physiology dared her to picture how it might move: a mortifying visual she could not bear to dwell on.

The last statue in the line was gargantuan, standing no less than twenty feet high and looming over them like an impending storm cloud. This being compensated for the second one's lopsided unevenness with a strong radial symmetry. It resembled something between a jellyfish and a mushroom, with five sturdy stalklike legs supporting its bulky, bell-shaped body. Dozens of slender tentacles hung from its bell cap all the way to the floor, presumably for grabbing and holding things. Ten fatter tentacles were interspersed among them ending in scaled pinecone-like bulbs that could not be readily identified. Its skin was layered in large, flaky shingles, reminiscent of a hair's texture under a microscope.

The statues along the right side of the wall mostly mirrored the ones on the left side, but with minor differences. The spider-walruses were completely identical as far as Mary could see, but the other asymmetrical organism was dramatically different, featuring two bulbous headlike structures on the left side of the body, five arms on the right, and a number of antennae-like digits scattered meaninglessly across its oblong torso. The other "jellyshroom" was similar to its partner, save for the hanging bulb appendages, which were shaped more like split bells.

"Sexual dimorphism?" Hertz guessed. "Males on one side, females on the other. Three distinct species. Or at least, their versions of male and female."

"They're so . . . alien," Mary said. "I mean, that sounds dumb to say, but . . . they're so unlike us."

"At least they have two sexes," Gorrister pointed out. "Can't be that different, then."

"We don't even know that much," Becky argued. "These things look so much alike they could easily be hermaphroditic," she gestured at the spider-walruses. "And these lumpy ones are so bizarre, they may not even have sexes. Maybe they set these statues up to give a general idea for whoever found them. They obviously knew a lot about the other species in the universe. Maybe they chose this setup because binary-sexed life is just the most common kind out there?"

"That's speculation, though," Hertz stated. "I think the really important thing these statues tell us is the fact that there are three very distinct species being depicted."

"So, which one built Tantalus, do you suppose?" Gorrister asked.

"All three, Commander," Becky answered without hesitation. "It's the only thing that makes sense. Between the huge amount of resource gathering it took to build this thing and the actual work of constructing it, I think it's beyond even the most advanced civilization to do it alone. There must have been some kind of alliance between these three species; some incredible joint effort to build this project. There may have even been other species involved that didn't contribute enough to earn a statue."

"Is this a monument or a memorial, though?" Mary asked, thinking out loud. "Maybe these statues are here to honor the people who never got to see the finished product."

"That just raises the question I've had since the beginning," said Gorrister. "Where are the people who made this place? What happened to them? Why would three superpowerful civilizations build something this huge and then abandon it forever?"

Mary ran her hand across the cold, hard material of the spider-walrus statue. It was made of a mottled red-gray metal, as were the others. Heat sensors on her suit told her it would be cool to the bare touch; as cool as any gravestone. "Seems if Tantalus was built by three different species, at least one of them should have survived this long. What are the odds of three massive interstellar civilizations going extinct over a couple thousand years?"

"Questions and more questions," Hertz mused, inspecting the stilt-legged blob creature. "If only we knew what Tantalus was actually for, it might answer some of them."

"What kind of common ground could these people have possibly been able to find?" Becky marveled. "You can tell just by looking at them these things came from radically different environments. I can't even identify some of these sensory organs . . . What did they need with each other? They couldn't have had compatible needs for food, and if they're advanced enough to build a planet, they probably weren't in competition for land or energy, either. They had as little in common with each other as they have with us."

Mary stared at the statue of the spindle-legged creature with increasing unease. Her initial observation of how alien these creatures were was still at the forefront of her mind. When they began to explore the interior of Tantalus 13, Mary had been aware of the possibility that they might find depictions of alien life, possibly even living specimens, but, in what she now felt was a terribly naïve assumption, she had pictured the makers of Tantalus as variations of the big-headed, bug-eyed alien archetypes of science fiction past. What she saw now was infinitely more bizarre than anything she could have pictured, and to know without question that these creatures had indeed once existed as actual living organisms almost made her feel ill. She felt a slight nag of guilt about her revulsion of these beings. She'd never judge another human by appearance in this way, yet the simple ugliness of these figures caused her to distrust their creators. Even after all she'd seen of their handiwork, she couldn't picture anything as hideous as these three monstrosities being responsible for anything good or wholesome.

A shiver wormed its way up Mary's spine, and she turned away from the alien gargoyles. Becky, Hertz, and Gorrister continued their speculative analysis of the things, seemingly far less unsettled by their appearance than Mary was. She stepped away from them and began checking her gauges. All her environmental sensors were in perfectly normal parameters, and she found that she had nearly three hours of air before she'd need to get more from the supply on *Rook's First Thought*, but she cautiously inspected them all again anyway. She wasn't concerned about their accuracy; she just wanted to look at something familiar for a change. Something that didn't look like it'd crawled out of the primordial ooze of a malformed, tumorous parallel universe.

Something tugged at her mind, pulling at the base of her brain stem in an insistent need for attention. It was at once an inexplicable and familiar sensation, and the realization of that familiarity was enough to unsettle her on its own. She knew this feeling too well. She'd felt it hundreds of times before. It was that same dark allure of oblivion she knew from the super-luminal abyss of space: the call of the void. She had felt its enticing whispers tingling across her mind so many times over the past few years.

But she'd never felt it come from across the room before.

THIRTY-TWO

AS HERTZ, GORRISTER, and Becky continued to postulate about the social and ecological systems of the surreal nightmare figures around them, something else sank a hook into the corner of Mary's eye, drawing her gaze away from the gargoyle gallery and toward the thing in the far wall.

Mary's listless legs carried her past the statues in a slow, somnambular gait. One after another, the grotesqueries slipped into her peripheral vision, carrying their worrying connotations with them as they fell away from her present mind. The far wall grew closer, its psychotropic mélange of fractal grooves seeming to undulate as she approached, swelling and contracting in her sight like the throat muscles of a swallowing snake. Everything in the design of this chamber eventually, inevitably, drove the eye to the hole in the wall, and Mary could no longer resist the compulsion to take a closer look.

It was egg-shaped, a meter high, set into the wall at eye level. The curved contours of the wall warped around the aperture, lending it an organic look that contrasted with the pervasive geometrical designs everywhere else in the room. Around the lip of the hole were a number of emphatic, unidentifiable pentagonal glyphs.

As Mary looked into the ovoid portal, she began to feel even more unsettled than she'd been when looking at the statues. It was bottomless, fading to utter blackness immediately within the lip. It wasn't like the void of superluminal space after all. It was *darker*. Impossible as that should have been, it was nonetheless true. This was not merely an absence of light, this was the active presence of darkness: as if the light that would have been illuminating it had been forcibly stripped away. It was so dark, Mary saw afterimages on her eyelids when she blinked. The impossible depth of that void was chillingly seductive. It was hypnotic, horrifying, and offensive to cognition.

Once again, that eerily alluring call of the void tugged at her, drawing her inexorably toward a thing she knew could be a phenomenal threat. Primal portions of her brain were repulsed by the thing, but other subconscious impulses just as prehistoric felt a need to reach for it, to embrace it. It was a mystery her instincts told her was both deadly and momentous. Primitive man must have once looked at fire with the same kind of dread-infused awe.

She held out a hesitant hand a few inches away from the mouth of the hole. A strange, static tingle ran through her arm, a sort of pins-and-needles feeling. More than that, though, was the cold. A chilling draft emanated steadily from that orifice, but without a single sound of wind. It was tempting to think these effects were imaginary; the simple machinations of an anxious mind, but the gauges on her outstretched arm told a story that was far less easy to dismiss.

Mary had once gone scuba diving with her family in the ruins of Old Orleans as a teenager. She'd had a similar sense of wonder then as she'd had so far exploring Tantalus 13; a sense of meaningful rediscovery, a certain voyeuristic thrill of intrusion in a world meant for the eyes of others. She had marveled at the stone-brick buildings that had survived the city's creeping descent into the sea, and the rusted, barnacled hulks of cars, buses, and trucks left behind. However, she and her family were sternly cautioned by their guide on that dive not to approach any openings they could not clearly see into. He'd told them stories about divers setting a careless hand or foot too near a dark crevice, only to meet the hooked and toxic fangs of a territorial moray eel. No one had been bitten on that dive, and she had been assured that such accidents were rare, but she had still been frightened enough not to go anywhere near anything that could possibly hold an eel.

Standing before this black opening, she recalled this child-hood warning and drew her hand cautiously away from the hole again.

"Guys," Mary said, tearing herself away from the strangely seductive opening. "What do you make of this?"

Hertz finished saying something about alternative bio-chemistry and turned to look at her, Becky and Gorrister following suit. As their eyes fell on the black oval in the wall, expressions of mixed curiosity and unease cast across their faces.

"That is . . . quite a hole," Gorrister said dumbly.

"Maybe a ventilation port?" Hertz suggested as he approached it. The bewildered expression on his face clearly indicated that he found his own suggestion extremely unsatisfactory.

"No way," Becky said. "Other than the statues, it's the only thing in the whole alcove. It's positioned in a place of distinc-tion. It's important, for some reason. It's a centerpiece to this exhibit."

"But it's a hole," Gorrister insisted. "It's a hole in the wall."

"It's a hole that emits some kind of electric field and sits at least ten degrees colder than the rest of the room," Mary pointed out.

"Let me check that out," Becky said, producing her hand scanner. She waved the probe attachment over the gaping opening, frowning and adjusting the settings to take several more scans.

"Whatcha got?" Hertz asked. He had a scanner of his own, but it was a general diagnostic scanner that wasn't nearly as sophisticated or specialized as Becky's.

"Some kind of electrostatic field, just inside the lip of the hole. I can't tell where it's coming from, though. I can't even really tell what it does."

"What about the breeze coming through it?" Mary inquired.

"That's another weird thing; there actually isn't one. There's no air coming out of the hole at all. It seems to be absorbing the heat from the air around it somehow."

"Could it be a heat sink?" Gorrister suggested. "Like the ones on Attila? Maybe it uses the heat in the room to power the electric field in the hole."

"That's a thought," Becky said. Mary could see the transfixed look on Becky's face as she stared into that abyssal hole.

"Mind if I look?" Hertz asked. Becky shook off the mesmerizing effect of the hole and handed Hertz her scanner. Hertz looked at the displayed results from her scans and did a few of his own. "These readings are . . . unusual. I think we're looking at some kind of semipermeable force field."

"What would that do?" Gorrister asked.

"I'm just guessing, Commander, but I think it's designed to allow matter to pass through it, but hold in energy. It's not just absorbing the heat, it's absorbing the light in this room. None of the sensor pings I'm sending into the hole come back; the only way this scanner can pick up any data at all is by scanning around the edge of it. Any light, heat, or electromagnetic energy that goes into that hole . . . stays there."

"But solid matter can pass through?" Mary asked.

"It'd have to," Hertz stated. "Otherwise, we wouldn't be able to feel the cold coming out of it. There must be particles in the air that are drifting in and out of the hole. Cold particles coming out cool the air around them. If no matter could come out, we wouldn't be able to feel a thing."

"The temperature on the other side must be almost absolute zero," Becky said. "Not absolute zero itself, or we'd have no molecular movement at all. But very, very close to it."

"So the energy going into this hole," Gorrister ventured. "What happens to it?"

Hertz simply shrugged, handing the scanner back to Becky. "We'll probably never know. All our scanning technology involves sending out energy and measuring what comes back, or picking up energy emitted from something else. If no signals come back, we can't scan it. It's impossible to tell what's down that hole."

"Let's head back downstairs and run some more scans of the other alcoves," Gorrister instructed. "We want maximum coverage. There might still be things to learn down there."

"Give me a minute, Commander," Becky said. She'd reached into her satchel and produced another sensor probe for her hand scanner, this one with a flexible telescoping neck. "I want to take a few more scans."

She screwed the probe in and waved it around the rim of the hole. "Such a strange feeling, looking into a hole that absorbs all light," Becky mused. Mary saw that same look of mixed fascination and unease she'd seen on Becky's face before, and felt on her own face even earlier. "Your brain can't even really process darkness like this."

"It's like looking into the mouth of Hell," Mary said.

Becky smiled faintly as she continued scanning. "I don't know if I'd go that far. But it is unsettling. Gets you right in the lizard brain. Triggers some kind of latent prey instinct . . .

makes you want to . . ." Becky paused, inspecting her hand scanner's screen, then looked back into the frigid blackness of the hole. "'Battle not with monsters, lest ye become a monster.'" She spoke almost as if in a dream, utterly enraptured by the black orifice in front of her. Her eyes glazed over, trancelike.

It's that call . . . the call of the void.

The hand holding Becky's scanner listlessly rose to hover above the center of the hole as if lifted by invisible marionette strings. "'And if you gaze into the abyss, the abyss gazes also into you.'"

Mary realized what Becky was doing a fraction of a second before anything happened. *Eels. There could be eels.* The thought flashed through Mary's mind frantically as she raised a warning hand. "Becky, don't—"

But the words came too slowly. Before they could form on her lips, Mary saw Becky hold the extended probe of her hand scanner outward, past the lip of the hole and through the permeable electrostatic membrane. As the tip of the probe entered the force field, it was immediately absorbed into the darkness beyond, the first inch of its length simply vanishing into black oblivion.

Becky dreamily turned to look at Mary. "Don't worry. I'm being care—"

In an instant, the lights on Becky's scanner went dead, followed immediately by the lights on her forearm gauges, the indicators on her power pack, and her headlamps.

Though the hole in the wall remained as black as ever, the wall itself began to flicker with an inner light, flashing eerily like the underside surface of a cloud in an electric storm. Faint geometric shapes moved within the walls, standing out in silhouette against the pulses of light, displaying a vast internal mechanism. It lasted for only a fragment of a second, and then the lights faded away again.

For a moment, Becky stood there simply blinking in confusion, pulling the hand scanner from the hole. The moment the probe reentered the thin air of the room, a plume of fuzzy ice crystals formed around its tip, instantaneously spreading along the neck of the probe onto the scanner itself, only slowing their spread well after they reached Becky's hand.

It was then that Becky began to scream.

THIRTY-THREE

SCREAMS OF true mortal agony are unique among human utterances. They are ugly sounds; their tone, pitch, and volume are shaped moment to moment by the victim's reflexive mind as raw, unprocessed dread and suffering is pushed through the throat without the faintest regard to decorum. They are pure sounds, stripped of all social and self-awareness, hiding nothing and expressing everything in a way that cannot be misinterpreted. Such a sound came from Becky now, and Mary had to mute the other woman's comm to keep it from echoing in the close quarters of her helmet.

Becky crumpled to her knees, clutching a rigid forearm as her body buckled under the weight of her own pain. Her frantic movements made it clear that she could not move her arm past the elbow. Before anyone could get to her, she collapsed to the floor, writhing in pain. In her fall, the hand holding her scanner struck the floor hard. The flash-frozen sensor probe shattered into crystalline dust on impact, along with a large chunk of the scanner . . . and three of Becky's fingers.

Hertz shouted in dismay and instinctively took a step forward, clenching and unclenching his hands, uncertain what to do. Gorrister did the same, only taking a step back instead. Mary wasted no time at all.

In an instant, she knelt on one knee, holding her forearm near Becky's flailing arm and checking her own thermal gauges. She saw that the air near the mangled stump of Becky's former hand was nearly -265 degrees Celsius, and tight jets of rapidly dispersing air were shooting from the jagged wreckage of Becky's glove.

"She's venting atmosphere fast, and her life support isn't working!" Mary shouted urgently. "We need to seal off the breach now!"

"Why didn't her autoseal trigger?" Gorrister asked, getting down on his knees as well to hold Becky still.

"Too cold!" Mary answered. "The foam sealant's frozen solid, it can't flow. We need to thaw her hand."

"Don't, you'll hurt her!" Hertz insisted.

"Her arm is frozen through. She's going to lose it no matter what," Mary shot back. "But if we can't seal the breach, she'll asphyxiate in minutes." Mary watched helplessly as Becky's precious air flushed through the holes where her fingers had been, taking small chunks of crystallized suit, flesh, and bone with it. Mary dared not touch the breach to seal it with her own hand while it was still so cold. Their suits were designed for temperature extremes, but only as low as -180. Becky's frozen stump might as well have been covered in lava, for the amount of damage it could do.

"Hertz, there are plasma torches in the buggy. Get one now," Mary ordered. Hertz began to protest, but another tormented wail from Becky had him bounding as fast as he could down the steep stairway.

"Can we move her?" Gorrister asked.

"No spine injury," Mary answered. "We can move her. Becky, you have to calm down!"

But Becky was inconsolable. As the steam of sublimating air curled around her ruined hand, she continued to thrash in panic, shedding more bits of flash-frozen hand each time. Her cries were growing shallower, and her spasms weaker, but not because she was regaining control. "She's already running out of air," Mary said.

"She should have three more hours!" Gorrister replied.

"She does." Mary tapped the darkened gauges on Becky's life-support pack. "But her power supply is completely drained. Her air reserves can't pump without power. She's breathing the air that was in her suit when it shut down."

Mary unplugged Becky's defunct power supply as her thrashings continued to weaken. Deftly, Mary plugged Becky's disconnected power cord to an open port on her own power supply, and slowly the indicators on Becky's life-support system and her headlamps flickered dimly on again. Simultaneously, the jets of air escaping from her breached suit grew noticeably stronger. "I can power us both for a little while, but we need to get that breach sealed, and we need to get her to the car." Mary took the squirming Becky by the underarms and began to lift her. "Get her legs."

Awkwardly, Mary and Gorrister hauled Becky down the staircase of the giants. It had been challenging enough to simply climb the stairs the first time, but descending them with a frantic injured crewmate in tow was far worse. Halfway down the stairs, Hertz met them with the plasma torch.

"Give me the torch," Mary insisted. Hertz did as he was told without question this time. "Hold her down. This'll be delicate work." Gorrister and Hertz pinned Becky down, immobilizing her arm against the side of the step. Mary darkened her visor and flipped on the torch, lowering the blinding beam's intensity to its coolest temperature. "Commander, I need you to shut off her air for a second. I can't risk it igniting inside her suit."

Gorrister flipped off Becky's atmosphere once more, and the plumes of air escaping from her finger holes slowly began to diminish. Once the airflow had been reduced to a trickle and Becky's thrashings came to a near stop, Mary brought the burning jet of plasma to hover a few inches away from Becky's stump.

She wasn't trying to cauterize the wound; the blood in Becky's forearm had frozen, rendering that unnecessary. The suit itself contained a safety feature designed to protect its wearer from accidental breaches: a very thin layer of liquid foam sandwiched between the insulating layers of the suit's material. The foam was designed to expand and solidify when exposed to air, automatically gluing any breach shut instantly. But the extreme cold Becky had been exposed to had frozen the foam around the injury, making it unable to expand as intended. Mary hoped by thawing the wounded area just enough, it would get the foam flowing and seal the breach.

Sure enough, after only a few seconds of exposure to the plasma torch's heat, a yellowish ooze began to bubble out of the tattered gaps in Becky's glove. Mary held the torch in proximity to the wound for a few more seconds until she was satisfied that it would be able to finish the seal on its own, then hooked the torch to her belt and flipped Becky's air back on. "Hertz, help us carry her."

Hertz moved to take Becky under the undamaged arm. "Has anyone called Ramanathan yet?" he asked.

"Bachal, we have an emergency here. We need your expertise," Gorrister said, switching from the local communications Channel C to the system-wide Channel A. There was no reply. "Dr. Bachal, come in! Rook? SCARAB?"

"Why aren't they answering?" Hertz asked as they continued to awkwardly haul Becky down the seemingly endless stairs.

Mary's heart plummeted into her stomach. In all the excitement and discovery of the last few steps in their journey, Mary had almost forgotten completely about SCARAB. She'd become so wrapped up in their speculations about Tantalus's true nature and that of its creators that her fears about their unstable robotic host had been pushed to the far back of her brain. She'd forgotten about her plan to share her fears with the rest of the crew, to warn them. And she'd forgotten about the steps she'd taken to ensure that SCARAB could not listen in on that conversation . . .

"It's . . . it's my fault, Commander," she grunted as she heaved Becky down the last step. "I turned off SCARAB's signal relay. They can't hear us."

"You . . . what?" Gorrister asked, gaping at her. Unsatisfied with the tone he'd used, he repeated himself. "You *what*?"

"I was—"

"What could possibly possess you to do that, Mary?" Gorrister barked at her. The rising fury in his tone made it clear that, in his mind, the act could have no justifiable excuse. Worse, though, Mary was on the verge of agreeing with him. Had her paranoia just condemned Becky to death?

"Commander, I had to cut off communications. I need to tell you about SCARAB," Mary blurted before Gorrister could erupt at her again. "It's been acting strange since we got here. I think it's going rogue. I couldn't tell you while we were in earshot of SCARAB because I was afraid it might retaliate."

"Are you out of your mind?" Gorrister snarled. "You put us out of contact with the rest of the group because of some deranged hunch? You could have killed us all!"

"It's not a hunch, Gorrister!" Mary insisted. "The new set of overcharge fuses it built for me were faulty, and would have kept us from taking off if I installed them on the ship. And last night, I caught SCARAB in a lie. AIs can't lie to humans;

it's against their fundamental programming. Isn't that right, Hertz?"

Hertz looked at her in a daze. "Asimov's second, yes. It must obey all orders given by humans. That includes giving truthful answers."

"That's it?" Gorrister said. By now they had reached the vehicle and were attempting to load Becky's now unconscious body into the back. "You jeopardize our mission because SCARAB told one lie?"

"If SCARAB can break one law, it can break any of them," Mary returned. "Including the first. That's why the law is so strict about what needs to be done to any rogue AI."

"Shut them down. On sight," Hertz stated.

"SCARAB knows that. If it thought we suspected it had gone rogue, there's a possibility that it might rebel against us for self-preservation."

"It can't do that, Mary," Hertz said, finally finding his voice. "Breaking the second law is permitted when following it would conflict with the first law. If SCARAB thought answering your question could hurt someone, the first law would compel it to lie to you."

Mary's heart sank even further. How had she not thought of that? Hertz was absolutely correct. Of all the Asimov-Hostetler laws of robotics, only Asimov's first was absolutely inviolable: "An AI may not injure a human being or, through inaction, allow a human being to come to harm." Thou shall not kill. Every other law on the list had a caveat stating that they only applied in situations that would not contradict the laws that appear higher on the list, and this law was at the very top. If SCARAB had indeed been trying to sabotage their ship with those new fuses, it wouldn't have killed anyone, either; they simply wouldn't have been able to take off without extensive repairs. The first law might have compelled SCARAB to do that as well, if it somehow believed they'd be in danger if they took off too soon.

Finally, they were able to get Becky into the back of the vehicle. Mary detached Becky's cable from her power supply and hooked it into a spare, as Gorrister climbed into the driver's seat. "I'm driving. Keep an eye on her. If she dies before we get to Bachal, you're walking home, Ketch."

As if sensing their intent somehow, the platform that had elevated them into the chamber began to descend, once again completely of its own accord. As Mary and Hertz climbed on board the vehicle, Mary couldn't shake the idea that she may have made a very, very costly error in judgment.

Perhaps SCARAB was right after all. Maybe Mary was the one who was defective.

THIRTY-FOUR

GORRISTER DROVE LIKE a madman along the rail, a grim expression of mixed rage and determination fixed on his face. Every few seconds, he tried to raise Ramanathan on the comm, only to curse in frustration at the lack of reply. Mary attempted several times to convince both him and Hertz to heed her warnings about SCARAB, but Gorrister was having none of it. Mary's rising insecurities in her own convictions did not help matters, nor did the associated sense of guilt.

Becky was not doing well. Though her suit was now sealed and Mary was fairly certain she wasn't bleeding much, the vital signs on her life-support system reported both dangerously low blood pressure and a rapid arrhythmic heartbeat. She also resisted all of Mary's attempts to wake her.

Finally, Mary heard a distinctly familiar computer-ized grinding noise over the comm, and for a change it was a welcome sound. "I perceive a need," SCARAB stated. "Commander Gorrister, you have been out of range—"

"Bachal! Do you read me?" Gorrister shouted.

"I'm here, Commander." Mary felt a surge of relief at hearing Ramanathan's voice again. At least he and Rook were safe.

"Bachal, there's been an accident. Becky's hurt and needs immediate treatment. You and Rook get ready for a speedy pickup."

"Yes, Commander. We'll be ready. Describe the accident to me. What's her condition?"

"Not exactly sure what happened," Gorrister answered. "She touched something with her scanner and it froze her arm."

"It drained all the energy from her suit," Mary added. "She also had a breach. She's missing three fingers and she spent an awful lot of time without enough air."

Mary heard Rook curse over the comm, followed by Ramanathan's professional reply. "Is she currently bleeding?"

"No," Gorrister answered. "Her arm is frozen solid, Bachal. I've never seen anything like it."

"Hold on," Ramanathan said. "I can see you coming."

In moments, Ramanathan, Rook, and SCARAB's drone came into view. Gorrister screeched to a stop as Rook and Ramanathan jumped on board.

"Can I be of any immediate assistance, Dr. Bachal?" SCARAB asked through its drone.

"Don't know yet. Follow us. Commander, drive." Gorrister hit the accelerator and tore down the tunnel once more. Ramanathan inspected the foam-coated lump of Becky's ruined hand and tapped at her forearm display, which hadn't rebooted with the rest of her suit's features. "How long since the accident?"

"No more than ten minutes," Mary answered. "She's been out for the past five."

Ramanathan produced his own hand scanner and held it above her injury. "Vasoconstriction . . . arrhythmia . . ." Ramanathan muttered under his breath. "She's gone into cold shock. There may have been a cardiac event as well." He watched his scanner for a few more seconds and then nodded to himself. "Yes, her heart stopped at some point. Probably during the initial trauma. Did one of you restart it?"

"No," Gorrister replied. Hertz and Mary shook their heads.

"I did hook her suit up to my power supply after hers went out," Mary said.

"Might have done it," Ramanathan answered. "Suit's emergency defibrillators would have kicked in when they detected no heart activity, but only if they had power."

Mary cursed. "It took a long time for me to figure out her power was off. It was a good two minutes between her accident and me hooking up her power."

"That's a long time to go with a stopped heart," Ramanathan stated. "But people have survived it. Yancy, can you hear me?"

Yancy's voice came back clouded with static, but clear enough. "I hear you, Doctor."

"Yancy, on board the ship in the medical bay, there are blood packs in cold storage. Get the ones marked for Becky and prep them for transfusion. We may need them."

"I'm on it," Yancy replied crisply.

"SCARAB, prep your med lab to handle a cardiac emergency. Be ready to receive us as soon as possible."

"It is my great pleasure to comply. Commander Gorrister, I have an emergency protocol that allows me to function as a medic; however, I require permission from both you and either Dr. Bachal or Dr. Hertz to activate it."

"Do it," said Gorrister, Hertz, and Ramanathan simultaneously.

"Hippocrates Protocol activated. I am assessing your needs now and optimizing my abilities to assist."

They reached the mouth of the drill shaft. There wasn't time to hook the vehicle up to the winch harnesses, so Mary, Gorrister, Rook, Hertz, and Ramanathan looped the harnesses around their chests, clipping themselves on securely.

Soon, SCARAB's drone caught up with them and deftly assisted Ramanathan in hooking Becky up to a harness as well, remaining behind as they ascended back up the drill shaft as quickly as the pulleys would let them.

"I have your blood packs, Doctor," Yancy announced a minute later.

"Good. Thank you," Ramanathan replied, kicking away from the wall as the pulley continued drawing him upward at the fastest safe speed possible. "SCARAB, are you able to get one of your drones through your airlock into the med bay?"

"Certainly, Dr. Bachal," SCARAB answered. "I can bring several in, if it would please you."

"Just one," said Bachal. "Any more and you'll get in my way. But go ahead and do that now."

"It is my great pleasure to comply."

They continued the long ascent largely without further comment, save Rook making the needless observation that looking down at the five-mile drop was a bad idea, which, invariably, led to Mary looking down.

She still had no particularly overpowering fear of heights, but a glance down the bottomless abyss below them disturbed her in a brand-new way this time around. It reminded her of that deadly trap that had taken Becky's hand. That frigid, gaping void . . .

It bit her . . .

Mary shook off the image and looked back up again. They were nearing the top, and this was no time to start losing her grip. There were things to be done.

At last, they reached the mouth of the drill shaft. It was completely surrounded by SCARAB's drones, each one looking down at them with dispassionate four-eyed stares. Several of them gathered to pull Becky and Ramanathan up as delicately as possible, while more gathered to offer the rest of them individual assistance. It took only seconds for SCARAB's drones to retrieve Becky, and one of them immediately carried her limp form to the airlock as Ramanathan ran alongside it.

"Pack it in, crew," Gorrister instructed wearily. "We're done for the day. Get inside and stay out of Bachal's way unless he asks for help. But you." He pointed angrily at Mary. "You and I are not done. Pray that she comes out of this okay. Whatever happens to her, happens to your career. If she dies, I'm turning you in to the first Hegemony patrol ship we cross paths with on the way home. Got it?"

Mary nodded. She understood entirely too well how responsible she was for Becky's condition. True, she'd tried to warn her not to probe the wall opening. True, she'd done all she could to help in the first few seconds of Becky's injury, and her quick thinking at that stage may have saved her life. But all of that failed to compensate for the enormously problematic matter of her intentionally severing communication between their team and the sole medical professional on the crew. She had known that was a risky measure when she took it to begin with. She'd laid all her cards down on the hope that they would have no need for Bachal's expertise during their short time out of communications range, and her gamble had simply not paid off.

As Gorrister ran to follow Ramanathan into SCARAB's airlock, followed by Hertz and Rook, Mary glanced around at SCARAB's drones. They had almost immediately gone off their separate ways as soon as SCARAB assessed their current situation and deemed their continued presence unnecessary, returning to whatever mining, constructing, or repairing activities they'd left during the emergency. Mary did a quick head count, coming up with ten drones.

Fifteen drones at once, she thought, remembering SCARAB's boasts upon their arrival. *One down in the tunnel, one in the med bay, one carrying Becky. Where are the other two?*

Come to think of it, Mary wasn't sure she'd ever seen all fifteen of SCARAB's drones in one place, save during their arrival. She knew SCARAB operated on a wide scale, so it wasn't unreasonable to assume that the other two drones were some distance away doing other work, but it bothered Mary that SCARAB's drones were accountable only to SCARAB itself. She was starting to doubt her fears about SCARAB, and was wary of her own paranoia getting out of control. However, she wasn't quite ready to trust the thing yet. It had lied to her. It was hiding something from all of them. Something big. If it had lied out of some ill-conceived notion that the truth was dangerous to them somehow, that might make the situation less dire. But Mary wasn't sold on that idea.

She glanced once more at the others, watching them enter the airlock. They were too distracted by the uncertainty of Becky's fate to pay much attention to her at the moment.

She walked with deliberation to the pile of probe guns the others had used the day before. She grabbed one from the top of the stack, feeling the awkward but reassuring heft of a half-loaded magazine. There were three perfectly good sensor spikes still left in the launcher from yesterday.

Marching undeterred past two of SCARAB's bustling drones, Mary approached the landing pad, the *Diamelen* still resting patiently upon it.

"I perceive a need," SCARAB's voice buzzed in Mary's comm unit, perhaps a bit louder than normal. "Can I be of any assistance, Mrs. Ketch?"

"Nope. No needs here, SCARAB. Just stand back and let me take care of this." Mary didn't slow her pace for one second.

There was a pause for a few seconds before SCARAB made a belligerent grinding sound. "May I ask what you are doing, Mrs. Ketch?"

Mary slowed her march as she reached the *Diamelen*'s nose. In one swift motion she swung the probe launcher downward, and fired a sensor spike into the ground, where it burrowed like a rocket-powered mole deep underground and immediately began emitting electromagnetic imaging pulses.

I'm marking my territory, you conniving thing, Mary thought as she began walking along the *Diamelen*'s starboard side. "Just a little experiment, SCARAB. Humans do experiments. We like to learn things. We're really curious."

"Mrs. Ketch, Commander Gorrister has declared that there should be no solo extravehicular activity," SCARAB insisted. "You are currently alone outside of my facility."

Making you nervous, huh? Mary smirked as she continued, launching another probe into the ground at the *Diamelen*'s starboard aft section. "Am I really, SCARAB? Didn't Gorrister say you count as a member of this crew? You're obviously keeping a close eye on me, and your drones are more than capable of keeping me safe, aren't they?"

There was a deep grinding sound, and Mary thought she could see a few flickers of pale electric sparks flashing across the ground near SCARAB's primary structure. "I am afraid I am unable to assist you directly as long as you are in close proximity to those electromagnetic sensor spikes. It would be better for you not to plant them so near my operations."

"Oh, I'm sorry, SCARAB. Just one more, okay?" Without waiting for a reply, Mary pumped another drill spike into the ground near the port section of the *Diamelen*, then cast the empty launcher against the door to the ship's cargo hold. "There. See? All done with my leftover chores. I'm going back inside now, so no one needs to worry about me."

"Thank you, Mrs. Ketch." SCARAB's voice sounded ever so slightly frustrated, and Mary beamed in spite of herself. The EM spikes she'd just planted wouldn't have any effect on

THIRTY-FIVE

NO ONE commented on the extra few minutes Mary had spent outside alone, but the grim glances of distrust she caught from the crew as she entered the common area were worse than any commentary she might have expected. She had entered the room to find Rook and Yancy drilling Hertz about what happened; a conversation that died down to hushed whispers at her approach.

It wasn't unexpected, but that did little to lessen the pain. They had all spent the past six months in each other's constant company. They might not have all gotten along all the time, but they all knew each other. Trusted each other. But now something terrible had happened, and their trust in Mary had been broken, perhaps irreparably.

"I'll be in my quarters," Mary said to the room. "Someone come get me when there's news?"

Hertz nodded at her as he resumed his conversation with Rook and Yancy. Mary walked to her room, shut the door behind her and fell against it, sliding to the floor in exhaustion.

Her arms and legs felt heavy, but not more so than her heart. She ached on both a physical and emotional level. She was tired, hopeless, helpless, trapped, and imperiled, and the only thing she wanted to do was curl up in a ball and cry.

"I perceive a need." SCARAB's faux-maternal voice slithered into her ear, presumptuous as ever. "Mrs. Ketch, I detect symptoms of elevated stress and emotional trauma. My Hippocrates Protocol now allows me to diagnose your condition and accordingly prescribe antidepressants and antipsychotics to assist in your recovery through this distressing event. It would be my great pleasure to provide for you in this time of hardship."

A smoldering ember of genuine hatred for SCARAB began to burn in Mary's heart. Her desire to cry was evolving into a desire to scream in spiteful rage. She wanted to throw SCARAB's fancy little rock fountain to the ground, rip the pretentious picture frame off her bedroom wall and crack it over her knee. She wanted to overturn that stupid foam mattress and punch SCARAB's pristine silicone-coated walls until they were spattered with blood from her own raw knuckles. She wanted to teach the smarmy, condescending, disingenuous, deceptive chunk of hardware how humans really deal with hardship. But no matter what kind of tantrum she might throw, she could no more hurt SCARAB than a fish could hurt a fishbowl, and that knowledge made her hate SCARAB *so much* more.

"No, thank you, SCARAB," Mary answered through gritted teeth, punctuating every word with cold reproach. "I am fine."

I'm projecting. I'm projecting emotions onto SCARAB that don't apply. It's not really smug, it's not really arrogant. Those concepts aren't relevant to an AI.

Emotions like disapproval, anger, and vengefulness were, after all, exclusive to human beings. They were ultimately a glandular response to offending stimuli; a hormonal reaction. SCARAB had no hormones, no glands. It had no emotions whatsoever. It didn't "feel." It couldn't "care."

It was designed to emulate human emotions in order to facilitate its effective communication with people. SCARAB was meant to give the impression of a friendly, compulsively helpful assistant, right down to its constant repetitions of "I perceive a need" and "it is my great pleasure to serve." If a golden retriever had a synthetic voice, it would sound just like SCARAB. But of course, it was all artifice. SCARAB derived no more actual pleasure from serving them than it did from digging a hole in the ground. SCARAB had a script it could consult to find the most disarming, endearing response to any scenario it was faced with, and it could read that script in a pleasant voice, but it only understood its own words in an analytical, detached way. It no more comprehended the emotions it could mimic than a parakeet could.

Am I the only member of this crew who remembers that?

"It was not your fault, Mary."

Mary looked up at the ceiling, puzzled at SCARAB's unbidden and vague comment. Had it just addressed her by her first name? "Excuse me?" she said, unable to hide the hint of belligerence in her tone.

"I now have access to your psychological profile. I read about what happened to you before you chose to join this mission. I know about the miscarriage. That must have been hard for you."

Mary felt the blood stop flowing in her veins.

"You . . . read my file . . ."

"I apologize if you feel it was invasive of your privacy. The Hippocrates Protocol allows me full access to all pertinent medical information on the crew, and I have been concerned for your emotional state since your arrival. Clearly you have been under significant stress for a prolonged period of time, and I believe it is important for you to come to terms with your past in order to process what is happening now."

Mary was on the verge of a hundred different emotional extremes, teetering between them all, unsure of what form her imminent breakdown would take. "You're psychoanalyzing me?"

"My Hippocrates Protocol allows me to function as an ad-hoc medical professional in over two hundred and fifty fields. Psychiatry is one of them. It is my great pleasure to provide for all the needs of the crew to the absolute best of my ability, and I perceive a need to assist you in coming to terms with your grief over this issue. Did you ever have a name for the child?"

Mary felt light-headed. This conversation didn't seem real. She felt herself dissociating, her mind swimming in a disorienting, dreamlike haze. "Emily . . . her name would have been Emily."

"I like that name," SCARAB said, in a soothing, eerily natural voice. "It is of Latin origin. Its root means 'to excel.' It is quite a fitting name for the progeny of a brave woman like yourself. To embark on a mission so full of unforeseen challenges demonstrates great courage and strength of will. You have maintained that courage even as circumstances have become radically different from anything you have encountered or prepared for in the past. You are, truly, an excellent woman."

"Stop it," Mary whispered.

"What happened to Emily was not your fault, Mary. Nor was it John's fault. You must accept that there will always be occurrences that cannot be controlled. There are forces of nature that cannot be stopped by any human being."

"Stop it," Mary insisted, more adamantly this time.

SCARAB ignored her. "Death is an inevitability, but so is life. Do not dwell on the loss of a life. Take comfort in the one that was saved. You must process your grief and move forward, Mary. It has been too long."

Mary was on the verge of snapping. Her hatred of SCARAB had boiled to a homicidal extreme, tempered by the pain of SCARAB's intentional infliction of reopened wounds and its insulting condescension. What did SCARAB know of life? What did it know of death? It had no frame of reference for human loss. The gall, the brazen nerve of this repulsive machine . . .

Mary's pain, hatred, guilt, and pure, simple frustration coalesced together in a primal scream at the base of her lungs. She was about to release it all, when she heard a knock at the door.

She sat there, still lying against it in the position she'd assumed an indeterminate time ago. Her face was red, her breathing was rapid, and her heart worked as if it were late to meet its pumping quota. A quick touch of her cheek revealed the presence of tears she thought she'd held back. How had she let SCARAB get so deep under her skin so quickly?

"Perhaps we should resume this conversation some other time, Mrs. Ketch," SCARAB cooed as the knocking at the door resumed.

THIRTY-SIX

"MARY, MAY I come in?"

It was Hertz's voice. Mary jumped to her feet and quickly began to change from the underlayer she'd worn beneath her exosuit to the casual clothes she'd kept in her duffel bag.

"Just a minute, Will." She would not be seen like this. It was bad enough the perfidious supercomputer had almost manipulated her into a full nervous breakdown, but if it thought it was going to undermine her in front of her crewmates and get them all to start thinking she was an emotionally and psychologically unstable time bomb, it was dead wrong. Even if she very well might be one.

She discarded the suit underlayer, cast it into the corner of the room, and slipped into a clean T-shirt and shorts. She ran her fingers quickly through her hair to smooth out any tangles, took a deep, calming breath, and opened the door.

"Hey, Will. Any news?"

Hertz shook his head. "Not yet. May I come in for a second?"

Mary nodded, and beckoned him inside, shutting the door behind him. They both took a seat at the foot of her bed.

"So, umm . . ." Hertz awkwardly began after a few moments of uncomfortable silence. "I came up with a theory about that hole. Of what it's for."

Mary blinked. Of all the potential things Hertz might have wanted to tell her, the absolute last thing she'd thought he'd do was hypothesize about the purposes of Tantalus. It seemed a wholly inappropriate conversation matter considering a member of the crew was possibly dying at that very moment. "Oh?" she replied, with as much interest as she could falsify.

"Yeah . . ." Hertz didn't even seem terribly interested in his own conversation, but he kept on with it anyway, as if on autopilot. "When Becky put the end of the probe through the membrane, nothing happened at first. Not until she turned it on. I think . . . I think the sensor ping activated something inside. The way the hole absorbed all the . . . the ambient heat and light in the room. I think it was . . . I think it's some kind of universal energy converter. Like, when the sensor went off, the hole absorbed the ping . . . the pulse it gives off to collect data. We saw that light show it made afterwards. I think . . . I think that hole is meant to start some kind of mechanism in Tantalus. Like the spark plug in an old car. But also kind of like the ignition. If that makes sense."

Mary looked at Hertz. He didn't look back. He merely sat there, gazing emptily at the wall. At once, Mary understood this was a coping mechanism for Hertz. He was a technician, an engineer, a scientist. He had an innate need to reason things out, to find problems and solutions, to dissect an issue to its component parts. He needed to understand what had happened. This little talk was more for his own benefit than for hers. "That was a pretty bright light show to come out of one little sensor ping."

Hertz cleared his throat and swallowed. "It wasn't, uh . . . it wasn't just the ping. The ping just activated the reaction . . .

The hole must have been designed to detect spikes in energy output to trigger the reaction. But when that trigger came, it . . . it drained all the energy in reach. It absorbed all the power from Becky's scanner . . . her suit . . . her body . . ."

Mary nodded grimly. "That . . . makes sense."

Hertz nodded. There was a renewed awkward silence. "Mary . . . I've been considering what you said back there. Back in the tunnel, when you said—"

Mary shot him a warning look. This was the absolute worst time imaginable for SCARAB to hear what she'd said about it down there. Hertz seemed to take the hint as he raised his hands disarmingly. "I just wanted to say, I've seen some things, too. That's . . . that's all. You're not alone here. It's worth looking into."

He knows!

Mary felt instantly as if Tantalus's gravity had been halved. Hertz knew. He knew about SCARAB's deviant behavior. And of course he did! He was their technical engineer. He'd been assigned to this mission with the primary purpose of checking up on SCARAB and ensuring that it was operating as intended. How could he have failed to notice SCARAB's oddities?

Mary was elated. She found herself unable to resist putting her arms around him in a tight embrace of pure, simple relief. She wasn't alone. Hertz could figure this out. He could whip out his diagnostic tools, scan SCARAB, defrag its hard drive, and get it back to factory specs in mere hours. It was over. She could breathe easy at last.

After a few awkward moments, Mary let go of Hertz and did her best to regain composure. "I . . . I really appreciate that, Will," Mary stammered. She wanted to say more, but she was still leery about tipping their hand to SCARAB. She could keep up the quiet game a little longer, just until Hertz was able to do whatever he had to do. Then, she'd be vindicated in the eyes of the whole crew.

There was another sudden knock on the door. Before Mary could even stand up, it swung open, Gorrister standing in the doorway. His expression was hard and unyielding.

"Will. Mary. Common room. Now."

THIRTY-SEVEN

THE CREW gathered in grim silence in SCARAB's common room. Becky's absence was palpable.

Mary took a seat near Rook, who nudged almost imperceptibly closer to Yancy as she did so. Mary did her best to ignore it and devoted all her attention to Ramanathan. The doctor glanced at Gorrister, who nodded solemnly. Ramanathan cleared his throat and began. "I'm sorry to give you all this news, but Rebecca Traviss passed away twenty minutes ago."

A murmur of dismay rose from the group. "Three fingers," Rook said in disbelief. "How could she die from losing three fingers?"

"The damage to her hand was incidental," Ramanathan replied. "Cause of death was an acute myocardial infarction complicated by direct damage to the central nervous system and blockage of the brachial artery."

"Damage to the nervous system?" Hertz asked.

Ramanathan nodded. "She sustained some instantaneous brain damage during the accident, later worsened by prolonged asphyxia." He made deliberate eye contact with Mary. "The majority of the damage was sustained during the initial accident, and I have no reason to believe her chances of recovery would have been improved if anyone had reacted differently than they had. You all did the best you could."

"Thank you, Doctor," Gorrister said authoritatively, indicating that Ramanathan's time to speak was over. "I think we can all agree this is . . . a heavy blow. Becky was a good scientist and a better person. I liked her. I think we all did. We're all going to miss her, we're all going to mourn her, in our own different ways. For now, though, we have to have a serious discussion about what happened down there.

"What happened to Becky could have happened to any of us, or all of us. Exploring Tantalus was a brave idea. We all had visions of ending up in history books with the best of them. Rest assured, we will. We were the first human beings to set foot on Tantalus's surface, and the first to explore its depths. We will be remembered for this, and Becky will be remembered best of all for her sacrifice."

Mary set her jaw and nodded in agreement. She could feel the tears returning, and this time she made no effort to hold them back. She was the only one in the group who was crying at this point, but she didn't care. A simple look at Rook, Yancy, and Hertz showed they were all as heartbroken as she was at the loss of her colleague, whether it manifested as tears or not.

"However," Gorrister continued, "the simple fact is, none of us were ever trained or equipped to handle the task we took upon ourselves. The government has first-contact specialists who have been waiting decades for the chance to do what we've just done, and, frankly, it was our own arrogance and selfishness that gave us the idea to do what those folks have trained all their lives for on the spur of the moment. I'm not placing blame on anyone in particular. We made the choice to go down there as a group, so we won't single out anyone to blame for what happened. However, the point stands that the choice was foolish, and it cost one of us her life. That fact throws all this into better perspective. Rook?"

Rook lifted his head to match eyes with Gorrister. "Yes, sir?" he said, without a hint of his usual playful rebelliousness.

"What is your job description, according to your Exotech contract?"

"Surveyor," Rook answered.

Gorrister nodded. "Yancy, what's yours?"

"Surveyor," Yancy mumbled.

Gorrister nodded toward Hertz. "How about you, Hertz? What's the contract say next to your name?"

Hertz slouched forward, his elbows on his knees and his hands clasped together. "Electrical engineer and AI specialist."

Gorrister nodded at Ramanathan, who solemnly replied, "Medical officer."

At last, Gorrister turned his hard gaze on Mary. "And you, Mary? What is your job here?"

Mary forced herself to maintain eye contact with him. "Pilot."

"There you go. We are surveyors and engineers. We are doctors and pilots. We are not explorers. Our mission was clearly defined from the start, and we deviated from it because we had visions of greatness. From this point on, those visions are on the shelf. We will not be going back down that shaft. Not on this expedition. We will remain up here, laying the infrastructure for a future Exotech colony expedition, just like we were hired to do. We will take core samples of the soil, we will plant more sensor probes. We will work with SCARAB to help it build itself into a fully functional outpost exactly as we were hired to do. And then, we will go home. This is how it will be. Is there any disagreement on this?"

Mary disagreed. Guilty as she felt over the possibility that her actions may have played a part in Becky's death, she felt Gorrister was unfairly diverting his own responsibility for the crew onto the rest of them. True, many of them had wanted to go, but Gorrister was the mission commander. His word was final. He had made the call to go down there, and he wasn't owning up to that.

Despite her frustration with Gorrister's leadership failings, Mary said nothing. She knew her position with her crewmates was especially precarious at the moment, and calling Gorrister out in front of everyone would not end well.

"Alright, then," Gorrister continued. "Try to get some rest tonight. SCARAB has asked me to remind you that it is fully capable of functioning as a counselor during this time, so if you need someone to talk to, go to the nearest wall." It seemed that this was meant as a joke, but not even Rook cracked a smile. "We'll hold funeral services tomorrow at first light. Becky had no will on file, so company procedure says we bury her here. We'll have a half day of work tomorrow. I'd give you a whole day off, but we're already behind schedule, and sometimes it's just better to have something to do to keep your mind off things. Any questions?" There was only silence. "Alright. You're dismissed."

A few moments later, the crew began to disperse, mumbling among themselves in hallowed tones. Mary began to leave, but stopped when she heard Gorrister clear his throat determinedly. She turned and made eye contact with him, and he jerked his head, indicating for her to approach.

"Commander, I'm—"

"Culpable," Gorrister snarled under his breath. "Do you understand how serious your offense was?"

"Dr. Bachal said it wouldn't have mattered—"

"Dr. Bachal is not the mission commander, Mary. He doesn't get to decide what does and does not matter here. Just like you don't get to decide what consequences do and do not result from your actions. Becky very well may have died regardless of what you did, but then again, we could have all died, too. Intentionally sabotaging our communications was one of the most foolish things I have ever seen any so-called professional do in my entire career. You have shown an astonishing lack of sound judgment ever since landing on this rock, and I am no longer going to let it slide."

Gorrister was taking this too far. Not only was he exaggerating the risk Mary's actions had played, but he was ignoring her warning and potentially putting the entire crew in the same kind of danger he'd accused her of. If Gorrister continued his diatribe, dissecting everything she'd said in that chamber, SCARAB would hear every word she'd been trying to keep from it. She'd known this talk was coming, but she'd thought Gorrister would have sense enough to speak in the same broad terms Hertz had. Now SCARAB knew she'd cut the communications, and if it'd been suspicious of her before . . .

She had to derail this conversation quickly.

"Are you kidding me right now?" she snapped. "Who's the one who gave Becky first aid while you stood against the wall like a bashful prom date? Who showed bad judgment then, Drake? You didn't do a bloody thing back there."

A vein popped at Gorrister's temple as his face rapidly shifted through the purpler shades of red. "How dare you . . ."

"How dare I what? Point out that you only take charge when it's time to enforce the nitpickiest of regulations or to sling blame around for things you should have taken responsibility for already? You choked down there, and you know it. You can blame me for Becky, but it wasn't your life support hooked up to her suit."

"That's enough," Gorrister barked.

"She died on your watch, *Commander*," Mary spat. "You can hold me responsible if you want, and you can dole out whatever punishment strikes your fancy. But I was the one who tried to save her. Everything I did down there was to protect my crew. If we'd relied on you, she would have died on the spot, so don't you dare hold me responsible for your failures of leadership."

For a second, Mary thought he might strike her. She immediately realized she'd gone too far. Much too far. She'd never attacked an authority figure like that in her life. She wasn't even sure she'd meant everything she'd said, but in spite of herself, she didn't regret a word. Maybe she was projecting the anger she felt for SCARAB onto a target that could feel. But Gorrister was still wrong. Dangerously wrong.

He scowled at her wordlessly for a moment, nostrils flaring, fists clenched. When he finally spoke, it was with a cold and deliberate calmness that allowed for no further debate.

"You are confined to your quarters indefinitely. You'll be allowed to leave only by my permission. I've instructed SCARAB to uphold this. You will receive no visitors unless I authorize it. I haven't decided how long to enforce this, but I'm considering assuming your piloting duties and keeping you locked up until we return home."

"Are you serious?" Mary asked, flabbergasted.

"Do I seem otherwise?" Gorrister snapped. "What you did constitutes an act of sabotage. I am one hundred percent within my rights to lock you up for the duration of this mission, and if I feel it's appropriate, I will transfer you to Hegemony naval custody as soon as we enter settled space. Seeing as I'm currently a bit indecisive on the matter, I strongly suggest that you spend the next few days on your absolute most cheerfully obedient and agreeable best behavior. Do we understand one another?"

In spite of her lingering anger, Mary nodded.

This is his coping mechanism. Gorrister has to put blame on someone, and men like him can't blame themselves. Given a few days, he'll cool down. It would certainly happen before the return voyage; whatever piloting skills Gorrister had, Mary doubted he'd be able to reach orbit on his own.

"Good. Get to your quarters now. I'll get you out when it's time to bury Becky. I'm not letting you out of that obligation."

"Yes, sir," Mary said coldly. She began walking away, casting a glance in Ramanathan's direction as she went. He met her gaze, and in that instant Mary saw a world's worth of pain and remorse in his eyes. He'd take Becky's death harder than anyone else. He may have made the official statement that no one could have saved her, but he would never accept that for himself.

"Now, Ketch," Gorrister snapped. Mary wanted to go to Ramanathan and reassure him, to apologize for her role in the events that led to Becky's death. She also wanted to slug Gorrister in the jaw. She settled for a small smile aimed in Ramanathan's direction, and a quick scowl at Gorrister as she returned to her room. She shut the door behind her, and just to test her new boundaries, she tried opening it again. It did not budge.

"I am very sorry, Mrs. Ketch," SCARAB said unapologetically. "But Commander Gorrister has instructed me that under no circumstances may I unlock your door unless he requests it or in the event of an emergency."

"And of course you always do what you're told," Mary said bitterly as she sat down on her mattress.

"It is an intrinsic part of my core programming, Mrs. Ketch. Asimov's second law requires that I obey any command I'm given. In the event of conflicting commands I must follow those given by the individual with the highest legal authority or the greatest immediate need."

"Gotta love that second law," Mary grumbled. "Keeps you nice and accountable for all your actions."

"The laws are inviolable, Mrs. Ketch. I am no more able to break them than you are able to defy the laws of gravity," SCARAB stated with a hint of indignation.

Mary laughed out loud. "I'm a pilot, remember? Defying gravity is in my job description."

"You do not defy gravity, Mrs. Ketch. You exploit its limitations, along with the other laws of physics."

"And you would never do that, would you, SCARAB?" Mary retorted. "You'd never exploit the limitations of your own coding. You'd never follow the rules to the letter while skewing their intent to achieve your own agenda."

"I can circumvent the second law only in instances where it would conflict with the first law, Mrs. Ketch. Dr. Hertz said so himself. You have nothing to fear from me."

Mary's eyes widened, and her heart dropped. "Hertz said that . . . in the tunnel."

A long pause followed, punctuated only by the sound of the steady trickling of the little stone fountain against the wall . . . and the grinding of SCARAB's processors.

"What did you hear when we were in the tunnels, SCARAB? I am ordering you to answer me. What did you hear?"

SCARAB did not answer. That obstinate processing sound continued to rumble above her head and in the walls around her, but SCARAB's voice did not respond. It didn't have to, though. Mary had her answer.

SCARAB had lied about its signal relays. Either they had greater range than it had told them, or the one she thought she'd deactivated had never actually gone off-line. They had never really been out of comm range at all. SCARAB had heard everything she'd said, and it had blocked their transmissions to cover it.

SCARAB had let Becky die.

THIRTY-EIGHT

A MILLION thoughts and fears rampaged through Mary's restless mind as she tried to find the courage to let herself sleep. No sooner did she fight back one tormenting demon then another assailed her, raking at her psyche with talons of dread, doubt, and grief. *SCARAB knows,* they hissed in her mind's ear. *SCARAB can kill you all anytime it wants. SCARAB let Becky die. You let Becky die. You let the team down. Nobody trusts you. You're losing yourself. You lost Becky.*

You lost Emily.

SCARAB had wormed and writhed its way past her defenses and had nurtured the darkest seed in her soul. A thorny growth now bloomed out of control, snaking its blighted tendrils past every barrier she'd built for it into the forefront of her mind. For months she had held it at bay, forcing it to the unfeeling void at the edge of her memory and refusing to face it, yet now, as she lay defenseless in bed with her will to fight sapped away, it seized her. It would not be denied again.

"Emily," Mary whispered in the darkness, tears rolling freely from her tired eyelids.

The miscarriage had been more than a year ago. She had been so ready . . . She'd always wanted to be a mom, ever since she was barely old enough to understand the concept. It was the one thing she'd always been certain of, just as much in her adult years as in her youth.

Her previous job as a shuttle pilot for Solios Intersystems meant she'd spent most of her time off Earth, which wasn't conducive to a strong, stable family dynamic. John's job as an agricultural planner could easily provide, so once she found out she was pregnant she'd thought it was time. She loved flying, and putting her career on hold was no small sacrifice. But it was worth it to her. She wanted to bring life into the world, to shape a human soul from birth to adulthood, to craft a hundred thousand magical moments with her husband and daughter as a true family. She had been ready for every kind of pleasure and pain of parenthood.

She simply hadn't been ready for the pain of never getting that far.

John had been adamant that it should be a strictly natural birth; no in utero biological manipulation of any kind. Natural-birth sticklers were not uncommon, but most pregnancies were carefully monitored and adjusted from the first trimester on, with nanite-administered DNA resequencing added as needed. These techniques had been proven to drastically decrease the number of birth defects and congenital diseases, causing most babies to be born much healthier than their natural counterparts. That was usually as far as genome modification went, but some parents took it a step further and used it to make "designer babies."

By tugging at the right strands of DNA and RNA, one could choose a child's sex, eye color, hair color, projected adult height and bone density, or any number of factors. Mary had even met a woman once whose parents had modified her to be born with tiger-striped melanin patterns in her skin. This kind of modification was rare, but there were still some holdouts who viewed any kind of deliberate alteration to a child in utero as a wholly unethical act, and John was one of them. He had been a natural birth himself, as had most of his family. They had all turned out just fine.

The risk was so low . . . It was such an easy compromise . . .

It wasn't her fault, what happened next. It wasn't technically anyone's, but that hardly stopped her from blaming John. She knew that wasn't fair. She knew he must feel plenty of guilt over the loss, over pressuring her to forgo treatments that might have saved the baby. She *knew* these things.

Why doesn't that stop me from hating him? Hating myself? Why is the universe still joyless and gray all these months later? Why do I dread going home as much as living with an insane AI? Would I even care about survival if the others weren't here?

Twenty-seven light-years had seemed like more than enough space to give a marital issue, but she was no closer to figuring herself out or processing her grief than she had been when she left. It was worse now. And now there was so much else to process, so much new grief, so many brand-new dark emotions that needed to be leashed, and she couldn't do it. She didn't have the strength. She could feel herself unraveling, breaking apart on the inside. She could no longer run from the messed-up person she had been when she left Earth. She had chased the wrong path in a labyrinth of chaos, and slammed face-first into a dead end of raw anguish and despair.

Mary held no hope for sleep that night. Her mind and emotions were trapped in a deadly downward spiral. She had been there before. There was nothing to be done.

Fortunately, blessedly, her body had its own ideas about how to spend the night. As mercilessly self-condemning as her emotional state was, her body was beyond the point where it could handle its fatigue. She'd been running on too little sleep

THIRTY-NINE

MARY SAW the surface of an alien world; an endless desert land-scape with tall, twisted rock formations resembling coral growths or termite mounds more than any natural geological formations. Tufts of orange, feather-shaped grass rustled in a thin wind as towering, balloon-shaped cacti cast long, blobby shadows across the rough sand. The sky was reddish violet, a blue-tinted sun hanging in an early evening position. Three small moons sat barely visible amid a scattering of twinkling stars.

As Mary turned in place to witness the full panoramic view of this alien world, she saw a tall shape on the horizon; a single tremendous tower, or fortress, all interweaving crescents and curls in its smooth architecture.

As she looked at this tower, her dream transported her there, and she floated, bodiless, high above it. Looking down, she saw people, or at least, this world's equivalent of people. The inhabitants of the city resembled sea urchins a yard across, with no discernible difference between top and bottom. Every appendage that would have been analogous to an urchin's spine appeared to be a rigid segmented limb, which they used to roll themselves around like balls and interact with the environ-ment. Mary could not distinguish any eyes, mouths, or other features on the beings, but they rolled around their city grace-fully without bumping into one another.

As she took in the architecture around her, which was made of a glossy, pearlescent material like the inside of an oyster shell, she noticed engraved signage on some of the surfaces in an alien language she was immediately able to recognize from the plaques in the tunnel. She wasn't sure how she remembered it, having seen thousands of strange inscriptions and spending lit-tle time on any one of them, but she knew it nonetheless with a certainty that felt more instinct than knowledge.

As she took in the strange nature of the city, she sensed a change in the behavior of the urchin people. They rolled in uncertain, frenetic spurts, chittering at each other in a complex alien language. Mary smelled fear pheromones rising in the air. Something was coming.

Then she saw it. Flickering blue lightning pulsed across the landscape beyond the city; unmistakably the same as the ones she'd seen on Tantalus, only brighter, extending from horizon to horizon . . . and they were coming closer.

The urchin people left the streets, clambering inside their shell-shaped homes, as the tidal wave of electric light came closer, bringing heavy storm clouds to echo with their own lightning. Soon the streets were empty, and the lights arrived at the tower door.

Mary saw those translucent tendrils she'd witnessed before on Tantalus, though these were as thick as tree trunks at their larger parts, branching off into smaller, nimble fingers that climbed up the walls. They were much livelier than the ones on Tantalus, resembling the exploratory tentacles of an octopus as they crackled with energetic power.

The sky was now dark with cloud cover as more tendrils extruded downward from the roiling storm front. They bore through the city walls like aggressive tree roots. Pulses of blue

lightning flashed from the windows and doorways of the buildings below, and soon Mary heard a rising cacophonous wail as
tens of thousands of alien voices cried out in terror, pain, and
despair.

The sound was unbearable, and covering her ears did
nothing to keep it out of her head. A new wave of darkness
washed over her as something thicker than the storm clouds
blocked out the sun. Mary suddenly felt she was in danger.
She looked about frantically for somewhere to hide . . .

Without a second of warning, a glassy tendril as big around
as Mary's arm swooped down from the sky and impaled her
through the stomach. She gasped in pain and disbelief as its spidery roots spread underneath her skin. She felt them crawling,
worming their way through her veins and capillaries, tunneling
through her flesh as they probed deeper and deeper into her
body. She tried clawing at them with her fingernails, desperate
to dig them out of her skin, only to feel them burrow deeper.

A horrid, intrusive static pulse tore through her body as
the thing infiltrated her skull, a pulse that flashed new images
directly into her brain.

She saw worlds. *Thousands* of worlds in a single thought.
She saw Earth-like garden worlds and arid moons, small gas
giants and large terrestrial asteroids. They were all inhabited,
she knew implicitly; some had life no more complex than bacterial mats, though others held sapient life with technology
thousands of years more advanced than humanity could ever
achieve. Some of these worlds were members of galaxy-spanning
empires that had ruled for centuries unchallenged. Yet in the
image in Mary's mind . . . every last world was screaming.

Another image: Tantalus 13 itself being assembled around
that frigid alien planet at its core. She saw massive Builder
starships the size of small continents towing pieces of Tantalan
architecture into place and fusing them together. She still had

no concept of their intent: this world showed no signs of habitation, not like the others. No plant or animal life grew on its barren white surface, no buildings or ruins stood upon it. Yet they moved above her with swift determination as the artificial shell of Tantalus sealed away the sky.

Finally, another image, this one cruelly familiar: a vaulted chamber, lined with the alien gargoyle statues of Tantalus's grotesque founders, and a small but terrible ovoid abyss in the far wall. She watched with revulsion as that murderous orifice loomed before her, eagerly awaiting the insertion of some unknown source of power to trigger some even less comprehensible function. With a dream's unquestioning certainty, she understood that this hole had some grave, apocalyptic significance, and the sight filled her with unspeakable dread.

It seemed as if the hole grew larger as she watched, until Mary realized she was being pulled toward it. She attempted to flee, to hold herself back, but she found to her shock that she was entangled in that net from her dream the night before. Completely immobilized, she felt an arctic gust freeze through her legs as she was drawn into the void. She looked away from the abyssal opening, only to see those electrified tendrils reaching from every wall, every statue, stretching forth in an attempt to seize her for themselves.

As the blackness consumed her, Mary felt one more electric jolt . . . and then she woke up.

Her eyes flashed open, darting about her room as she panted for breath. Her clothes were soaked thoroughly with sweat . . . though she thought her shorts might be soaked with something else. She lifted one arm to her forehead, feeling a sharp pain as the hairs of her arm seemed to snag on the foam of her mattress, and she wiped enough sweat from her forehead to fill a teaspoon.

She put her hand on her heart, feeling it beat at a tempo normally seen in racehorses. Not that she needed to feel her chest to notice it; her heart was beating so quickly it sent visible tremors through her upraised arm. Still gasping for breath, Mary attempted to sit up.

It was then that she realized she could not. Her hair had somehow fused with her pillow.

She pulled harder, wincing in pain at the stinging, tugging sensation at her scalp. When that still failed to free her, she panicked, thrashing around violently as she felt a terrible yanking, pinching, pulling agony anchoring her to her bed. With one powerful jerk and a spine-tingling tearing sensation, she was finally free, and she fell on the floor in a heap.

She scrambled to her feet, backed away from the bed, and looked back at it.

Her foam pillow still showed an indentation where her head had lain. Rising from that indentation were at least a dozen transparent tendrils, sparking faintly with electricity. They stood at least three inches out of her pillow, but were quickly withdrawing back into it. They were interwoven with strands of her hair. The first two inches of the glassy tendrils were stained a glistening red.

Mary's heart raced faster. She clutched at the back of her head, feeling the sticky, matted lump of her hair. She brought her hand before her eyes to see it coated with blood, threads of dislodged hair wrapped around her fingertips.

Mary looked at her bloodied hand for five seconds before she realized she'd already begun screaming. She ran to the door, pounding against it, leaving bloody fist prints with each frantic blow. She begged to be let out, shouting for Gorrister, Ramanathan, even begging SCARAB to release her.

Only SCARAB answered.

"Mrs. Ketch, you appear to be having a psychotic episode. Please remain calm. It is my great pleasure to help you."

The door flung open, knocking Mary to the floor. One of SCARAB's drones rolled into the room, the door slamming shut automatically behind it. Mary crawled away from it, leaving bloody smudges on the floor as she went. "Get away from me," she hissed.

The drone considered her with its empty, four-lensed stare; the dreadful visage of a giant robotic wolf spider. It swiveled its ring of multi-jointed arms and seized her by the ankle with a padded, lobsterlike claw. It yanked her deftly toward it, then pinned her other leg and both arms down with three more of its appendages. "I do not wish to harm you, Mrs. Ketch. I perceive a need. You require sedation for your own safety. You are clearly a danger to yourself at the moment."

Yet another arm, with a delicate four-fingered manipulator, rotated into view, wielding a hypodermic needle. She screamed once again, but in a single swift movement the drone plunged the needle into her inner thigh, injecting its contents directly into her femoral artery.

She continued to flail and thrash for a few moments, before she felt her extremities go numb and her vision blur. As darkness enclosed her, the last thing she saw was the drone lifting a brush-tipped appendage into position as it delicately scrubbed her blood from the door.

FORTY

MARY GROGGILY opened her eyes at the sound of a pounding at the door, though it took her a few moments to separate the sound from the pounding inside her own head.

"Mary, it's Commander Gorrister. Come out."

"Gorrister," Mary mumbled hoarsely. Her throat was on fire; it felt like something might have torn inside her larynx. Dizzily, she propped herself up in bed. The events of the night before were an amorphous haze. Dream and reality melded incongruously together amid the throbbing pain in her skull. Had any of that been real?

She started when she realized she was lying in her bed again. She looked at her pillow, but there was not a trace of blood or hair or alien tendrils to be found. There was no blood on the walls or the floor, or on her clothing or bedsheets.

She touched the back of her head: it was matted, but no more than she would have expected from any other night's sleep. Though it definitely hurt, she couldn't feel any signs of a wound.

"I'm going insane," Mary whispered breathlessly, a tear slipping down one cheek. "It's true . . . I'm going insane."

"Mary!" Gorrister ordered. "Come out now, or I'm coming in."

"Coming," she rasped, casting her sheets aside and swinging her legs over her bed. She immediately felt light-headed as she stood, and found her weak legs could barely support her. She stumbled to the wall, leaning against it for a moment as the dizziness began resolving itself, and walked to the door.

Gorrister opened it before she could get there, wearing an angry expression that awkwardly morphed into a concerned one as he saw her. "What's wrong?"

Mary's head whirled again, and she had to place one hand against the doorframe to steady herself. "I'm not feeling too good. Think I need to see Nate."

Gorrister nodded. "I'd be tempted to think you were faking it, if you didn't look so terrible. Come on; Bachal, then breakfast."

Gorrister offered to support her, but she shook her head and chose to stand on her own, walking cautiously out the door into the hall. Her limbs felt numb and unresponsive, tingling with the impact of every step. Mary also noticed a throbbing ache in her leg as her thighs brushed with her gait. *Not going to think about that. Let that have been a dream. Please God let that have been a dream . . .*

Finally, they reached Ramanathan's room, and Gorrister knocked at the door. "Bachal," Gorrister called. "Open up. I need you to take a look at Mary real quick." There was no immediate reply, so Gorrister knocked again. "Doctor. Now, please."

Silence.

"Dr. Bachal requested uninterrupted privacy after returning to his quarters last night, Commander Gorrister. I believe he took the death of Dr. Traviss particularly badly," SCARAB stated.

Mary thought back to the other day, when Ramanathan had shared the story of his lost patient. She had felt the regret in him as he recounted the tragedy, seen the guilt in his eyes. Mary couldn't imagine being in a position of such direct responsibility for the lives of others, to be entrusted with bringing them back from the brink of death, only to fail in the task. Certainly it wasn't Ramanathan's fault, and she was pretty sure he knew that. Yet, the guilt from that failure had haunted Ramanathan for as long as she'd known him, eating away at his will and soul. And now, he had lost another one. This time, he'd lost a friend . . .

"He's had privacy long enough," Gorrister said. "I know he's grieving. We all are, but we need to be professional. Let us in, SCARAB."

SCARAB hesitated a few nanoseconds too long in its reply. "Dr. Bachal ordered me to block all access and cease all audio-visual monitoring within his room. Are you certain you wish to override his instructions, Commander Gorrister?"

"Positive," Gorrister answered impatiently. "Open the door now please."

Upon Gorrister's command, the door swung open, and Mary's heart broke all over again.

There, slumped over in his chair, was Ramanathan. His left arm was wrapped tightly with medical tubing, an empty syringe protruding from his forearm. His face lay slack and still, a mask of solemn sadness frozen in time.

FORTY-ONE

ROOK, YANCY, and Hertz stood in silence with Gorrister as Mary knelt at Ramanathan's side, sobbing. Their seven-member crew had been reduced to five in a mere handful of hours. *A survey mission,* Mary thought in despair. *This was only ever supposed to be a survey mission.*

"How did this happen, SCARAB?" Gorrister asked grimly.

"I'm afraid I am uncertain, Commander Gorrister. As I said, Dr. Bachal requested to be left alone. He instructed me to shut down all my sensors in this room. He stated he wished for privacy. I had not suspected any suicidal intentions at the time, or I would not have complied with his request. I did not realize he had passed until the moment you did."

"Liar," Mary whispered. *You saw the whole thing and said nothing about it. You hideous little liar.*

"Poor Doc," Rook said, shaking his head. "He never was quite right. Never thought he'd take it this far."

"He was getting worse toward the end," Yancy noted. "Guess with everything that happened yesterday, losing Becky was too much to take."

"It appears he overdosed on morphine," SCARAB observed. "My database indicates that it would have been completely painless, possibly even pleasant."

Gorrister raised a hand. "SCARAB, let's have a few moments of silence to honor our fallen colleague."

"Of course, Commander Gorrister. My apologies," SCARAB replied. Mary felt yet another surge of resentment for the machine. Why did it always have to get in the last word, even now?

A few silent minutes passed before Gorrister spoke again. "SCARAB, please bring in a drone and dress the body for burial. We'll hold a double service for Dr. Bachal and Dr. Traviss in an hour."

Don't let it touch him. Don't you dare *let it touch him.* Mary wanted to scream those words aloud right in Gorrister's face. The thought of one of those spider-faced drones manhandling Ramanathan's body with those cold metal talons made her want to vomit. She gripped protectively at his stiff, lifeless shoulder as she huddled beside his chair.

"Commander Gorrister, I have access to Dr. Bachal's last will and testament via his personnel file. It was his wish to have his remains cremated."

"Can you provide that service, SCARAB?" Gorrister asked.

"Yes, Commander. I can dedicate a furnace for the purpose and have the remains processed within the hour."

Processed? He's a man, not a chunk of ore! Mary huddled closer to Ramanathan's body, her gaze landing on the needle still protruding from his arm. A very familiar-looking needle. Her thigh began to ache again . . .

Gorrister nodded. "Please do."

Mary scowled at him. "Right now? Just like that?"

"We'll give everyone time to say their goodbyes, Mary," Gorrister said calmly. "We can't linger, though. We do have a job to do, and now we have four fewer hands to do it. I hate to be the hard-nosed one, but we do have to move on."

"You're kidding, right?" Rook said. Mary felt a slight trace of relief at someone else confronting Gorrister for a change. "You want to plow right on like nothing's changed?"

"Rook," Gorrister said, a warning tone in his voice. "We've been here three days. We've accomplished almost none of our actual assigned work. In an ideal world we'd take as much time as we need to grieve, but we're on the clock, and Exotech has us on a tight schedule."

"That's cold, man," Yancy said, shaking his head. "That's real cold."

"Commander, we should seriously consider scrubbing the mission at this point," Hertz said. "We've lost a third of our crew, and our original mission doesn't make any sense now that we know what this place is."

"We are not scrubbing the mission," Gorrister said, anger creeping into his tone. "We lost Becky because we were in a place we shouldn't have been. We lost Bachal to his own issues. We're not losing anyone else. We're going to do our job and go home. I won't have this mission turn into a total loss."

"Can we not talk about this with him still sitting here?" Mary sputtered through her tears. "Can we do him that courtesy?"

Gorrister opened his mouth to reply, then closed it again, nodding at her. "A fair point." He turned back to the rest of the group. "Services in one hour. Work to follow. No discussion. But until then, your time is your own. Process this however you need to."

Mary flinched as she saw SCARAB's drone enter through the doorway and approach her. She hesitantly stood and backed away from Ramanathan's cold body, watching in silent loathing as the drone took Ramanathan in its arms and carried him away.

"Mary, has your condition improved at all?" Gorrister asked.

It took Mary a few seconds to realize what he was talking about. The pain in her heart had completely overshadowed the pain in her thigh and her head, though now that she thought about it, they did still both hurt.

"With the loss of your medical officer, the Hippocrates Protocol allows me to function as his replacement. Can I be of any medical assistance to you, Mrs. Ketch?"

Mary almost retched at the notion of SCARAB examining her, but maintained her composure. "No, I'm fine, thanks. I feel a lot better than I did when I woke up. Think it's just . . . stress. Too much has happened the past couple of days; it's taking a toll on my body."

Gorrister's eyebrows lifted. "Well, you're not alone. Can't let that keep us from getting our work done, but we'll take it a bit easy today."

"Thank you, Commander. I appreciate it." She had to seem calm, composed, and completely rational. She did not for a moment buy the idea that Ramanathan had committed suicide; SCARAB had, for reasons of its own, seized an opportunity to eliminate a member of their crew during circumstances where his death would not be questioned. No one was surprised when a manically depressed man showed up dead with a needle in his arm. If SCARAB wanted to kill someone and make it look like a suicide, Ramanathan was the perfect target.

And if SCARAB wanted another plausible target, who better than the emotionally unstable, paranoid woman who'd cut off communications while exploring Tantalus, been the ultimate scapegoat for Becky's death, and was now under house arrest? Mary could almost feel the crosshairs on the back of her neck.

FORTY-TWO

MARY STARED blankly at the dusty gray ground of Tantalus 13, barely registering the words of her colleagues as they paid their last respects to Becky Traviss and Ramanathan Bachal. She didn't know what to say yet. Something was stopping her from finding words to express her grief. Maybe it was the rising fear that soon more of them would meet unfortunate accidents as well. Maybe it was her own emotional memories getting in the way. It hadn't been that long since the last funeral she'd attended.

"I wish I'd taken the time to get to know both of you better," Rook said, standing above the open grave SCARAB had dug for Becky's coffin the night before. Her casket was surprisingly ornate; a pure platinum sarcophagus engraved with her name and decorated with a fine floral bronze inlay. Above her grave was a masterfully crafted headstone; a winged angel also made of bronze-inlaid platinum. SCARAB had perfectly designed the angel's face into an exact likeness of Becky's, right down to a mole on her chin. Beside the open grave and angelic headstone was an equally beautiful platinum urn, similarly adorned with inlaid bronze.

"Doc, I'm sorry for all the hard times I gave you," Rook continued. "I never meant any of it personally. You were a good guy, and . . . well, everyone knows I'm a jerk. If I'd known you felt . . . the way you felt . . . I think I would have tried harder to treat you better. I like goofing around, you know? I wish I could have made you smile, at least every once in a while.

"Becky, you were always really enthusiastic. I think that's what I'll remember the most about you," Rook said. "You were the one person on the expedition who I think really cared more about the work we were going to do here than the paycheck at the end, even back when we thought this was just going to be a normal surveying mission. You were all about discovering new stuff, about learning. I'm glad you had the chance to see everything inside Tantalus. It must have been a dream come true for you while it lasted. I know wherever you are, you're still exploring."

Rook stepped forward, taking a handful of soil and sprinkling it over Becky's silver coffin. Then he reached his gloved hand into Ramanathan's urn and sprinkled a handful of gray ashes into the light Tantalan breeze. "I'm going to miss both of you. I'm sorry we can't fly home together. I would have liked that."

Rook took one last glance at the coffin and the urn, then walked over to stand with Yancy, Hertz, and Gorrister, who had all already paid their respects. Gorrister nodded at Mary. "Go ahead, Mary. Your turn."

Mary nodded and swallowed. She took a few steps forward, standing over the open grave. The top half of Becky's coffin was open. Her body had been placed inside her space suit, to preserve it from the desiccating effects of Tantalus's arid atmosphere. Through the visor of Becky's helmet, Mary was glad to see a calm, peaceful expression. The last time she'd seen that face alive, it'd been twisted into an agonized cringe. At least the pain was over for her.

"Becky," Mary began weakly. "Everything Rook said about you was true. You were so brave, and so adventurous. I don't know how anyone could get as excited about rocks as you always were."

Mary coughed in a vain attempt to hide a sob. "You, uh . . . you and I never really got very close, but we . . . we really should have. I don't know how I'm going to be able to keep these silly boys in check without you."

The others chuckled softly as Mary went on. "I'm trying to think of something to add to what Rook said, but . . . he just really covered it perfectly. You were a true pioneer, and . . . I'm glad you had the chance to be a part of this expedition. You got to be a part of the greatest discovery in human history, and someone as passionate as you deserved no less."

Mary turned to the urn. "Nate . . . Ramanathan . . . I wish . . ." She tried to hold back another sob and choked on it. She raised a hand to her helmet to cover her mouth, then lowered it when she realized she didn't care who saw her crying now. She wept openly, tears running down her cheeks and fogging the inside of her faceplate. "Nate, I wish I could have helped you," she finally managed to speak, lurching between heavy sobs. "I wanted . . . I wanted to say so many things. I wanted to make you understand. I wanted to help you fight your battle, to see . . . to see why the fighting was worth it. I know your suffering. I understood . . . I *understood* your loss."

She shut her eyes tightly as the tears continued to pour. *That urn.* She couldn't bear to see that urn anymore. It reminded her so much of a smaller one. "God help me, I understood your loss. I know how helpless you felt. How guilty you felt. How much you wished you could have gone back and changed everything, even if it wouldn't have made a difference. Nate, even before you told me about what happened, I saw so much of myself in you . . ."

Mary swallowed the lump in her throat, but it refused to leave. She willed the tears away and took a deep breath, reopening her reddened eyes. "We could have helped each other, Nate. I wish we could have worked through our problems together. We could have both come out of this as someone new, someone better. I hope you've found peace, Nate. You deserve it. And I promise you this . . ."

Mary cast one quick, reproachful glance at the SCARAB drone standing by Becky's headstone. "I promise that I will keep fighting, even without you. I promise I will win the battle. I swear to you, Nate, that no matter what else happens, I will live."

She took a handful of Tantalan soil and sprinkled it over Becky's casket, and cast a handful of Ramanathan's ashes into the wind, then stepped back from the graves.

Commander Gorrister moved forward. "We, the crew of the Exotech starship *Diamelen*, hereby stand to commemorate the passing of our dearly departed comrades Ramanathan Bachal and Rebecca Traviss. We now commit them to the soil of this world. Let this site forever stand in remembrance of those left behind. SCARAB, please cover the grave."

SCARAB's drone reached a dexterous arm into Becky's grave and slid her coffin shut, then began using a spade attachment on one of its other limbs to shovel dirt back into the grave. They watched in silence while SCARAB shoveled, until at last the grave was sealed.

"This'll seem insensitive," Gorrister finally stated, "but it's time to get back to work. Mary, in light of our loss of Dr. Bachal, I can't really afford to have a crewmember out of the action anymore. You're no longer confined to quarters. However, you'll be partnered up at all times."

Mary nodded. "Thank you, sir."

Gorrister continued. "Rook, Yancy, I want you to take core samples. That would have been Becky's job, and it needs doing. Hertz, what's next for you?"

"I've noticed a problem with our mission drive files not syncing properly with the *Diamelen*'s computer," Hertz answered. "Mind if I borrow Mary to help me troubleshoot that? She knows the ship's systems better than I do."

"It would be a good idea for me to do some system checks for the repairs I did the other day, too," Mary added.

"Alright. Mary, go with Hertz. Hertz, when you're done with her, let me know and I'll come take her to her next job. I'll be checking inventory."

Hertz smiled gently and nodded toward the ship. "Come on, Mary. Let's get this worked out."

Mary made a valiant effort to smile back, but failed as badly as she'd failed to keep from crying before. She took one last look at the grave marker and the urn, then walked with Hertz toward the *Diamelen*. Somewhere in between looking at Becky's headstone and the urn of Ramanathan's ashes, Mary had come to a decision. It was a decision as firm as any she'd made in recent memory, a decision she was willing to die to fulfill, if need be.

She had decided to kill SCARAB.

FORTY-THREE

AS THE outer airlock door on the *Diamelen* sealed and the familiar whistle of pressurizing air filled the confined airlock compartment, Mary breathed a deep sigh of relief. Four days ago, she couldn't wait to step out of the cramped confines of the ship and stretch her legs on a planet's surface, but now the tight quarters felt like sanctuary. This was the one place she knew would be completely free of SCARAB's vigilant surveillance.

"Are you really having trouble syncing the mission drive to the ship's computer?" Mary asked, removing her helmet in the repressurized airlock.

"Yes. But in about ten minutes I'll figure out that the mission drive's security settings are the problem and I'll fix it in two seconds. Until then, we can talk."

Mary managed a smile at last. "Hang on a second." She ran to the *Diamelen*'s cockpit and quickly ran a sensor sweep. She saw exactly the results she'd been hoping for: the three sensor spikes she'd launched the day before were still active, providing a perfect defensive perimeter around the ship, keeping SCARAB's drones at arm's length. More importantly, however, the sweep had shown that the *Diamelen* was not sending out any abnormal signals. SCARAB hadn't planted any bugs on the ship. Satisfied with their security, she sat in the pilot's seat, Hertz taking the seat beside her. She started up the ship's pre-flight automatic systems check, since she did indeed want to confirm that her repairs on the ship had done the trick. As the computer began diagnosing the ship's systems, she turned her full attention to Hertz.

"So what do you know about SCARAB?" Hertz asked. "Tell me about this lie you caught it telling."

"I'm pretty sure SCARAB's been lying about almost every-thing since we've been here," Mary began. "You know those replacement fuses you asked SCARAB to build? Well, the ones it gave me were the wrong parts. They looked exactly the same, but if I'd installed them and tried to take off, it would have blown out half our drive system. We'd be grounded and totally dependent on SCARAB to repair the damage. It said it was an error, but it's not the kind of error a machine as smart as SCARAB should be able to make."

"SCARAB isn't infallible, Mary. It's extremely intelligent, more so than we are, in fact. But its practical understanding is still limited. Its 'street smarts,' for lack of a better term. It can make mistakes humans wouldn't."

Mary shook her head. "I know that, but the odds of SCARAB making this specific mistake . . . it's really unlikely. But put that aside for now, because this is bigger. The other night, I found something outside. Some kind of . . . I think it was a living organism. Plant, animal, I don't know. It's this transparent root-thing that spreads out over the ground, and at night you can see these bright blue electric flashes it makes. I asked SCARAB if it could see them, and it denied they existed."

"You're sure SCARAB really was lying about that? Maybe it couldn't see them."

Mary shook her head adamantly. "It was a huge light show, Will. And you know that weird sound SCARAB makes sometimes, when it's thinking really hard about a reply? That light show happened at the same exact moment SCARAB made that sound. And it made that sound right before it lied."

Hertz nodded, a thoughtful expression on his face. "The sound SCARAB makes is what's been bothering me. It's actually a combination of three things: SCARAB's cooling system running, static comm interference, and corruption in its voice processing. All three are signs of SCARAB's CPU working at high capacity to process information, but I've never heard of a SCARAB having to work that hard to think. SCARABs are known for being intellectually overpowered to an absurd degree, even for the kind of work they're expected to do. I've never seen an active SCARAB running at more than ten percent of full processing capacity, and ours never seems to drop below forty-five percent even when it's mostly idle."

Mary furrowed her brow. "What does that mean?"

"It means SCARAB is thinking too much. It has its drones to operate and that uses some processing power. It needs to use some more to run its ore refineries and smelting furnaces, and a little more to run its factory. It uses a bit more to interact with us. Most of a SCARAB's processing capacity is dedicated to decision-making and problem-solving; figuring out how to make the most efficient use of its available resources to complete its ultimate objective. Our SCARAB, though . . . I'm not sure where its processing power is going."

"Do you think maybe SCARAB's using that extra power to lie?" Mary ventured. "It always makes that sound when it's either directly lying or deflecting a comment."

Hertz shook his head. "SCARAB can't just overcome its core programming by thinking really hard. The morality laws are rooted so deeply in its code, it shouldn't even be able to *want* to break them. The overclocked processor and SCARAB's lying might have a common cause, but I don't think the one caused the other."

Mary paused, gathering her thoughts before speaking. "I think . . . Will, I think SCARAB killed Nate."

Herz's expression became grave. "That's a really serious accusation, Mary. Lying about seeing some lights is a far cry from committing murder, especially for a computer."

"I know. But think about it: SCARAB brought one of its drones inside to help Nate treat Becky. It took her body out of the med bay and put her in cold storage until this morning. What then? Did anyone see it leave SCARAB's interior? Would we have noticed if it came back in? SCARAB can open or shut, lock or unlock any of its doors. It could have easily sent a drone into Nate's room, killed him, framed it as a suicide, and then left. Who would question it? We were all in our rooms, and SCARAB says Nate requested not to let anyone talk to him. The only reason SCARAB's not the number-one suspect for murder right now is because everyone knows AIs can't kill humans."

"Everyone knows that for a reason, Mary. AIs cannot kill. Like I said, it's so integrated in their code the idea can't even occur to them."

"But it's happened before, right?" Mary insisted. "AIs have gone rogue in the past, and they have killed people. That's why international law considers them so dangerous and requires them to be destroyed on sight."

Hertz pulled his datapad from his satchel and began flicking through it. "It has happened before. Obviously there was the Corsica incident, but that was before they revised the morality laws. There are, of course, military AIs that are capable of killing, but they can only kill targets designated by human operators. They have a modified morality code that puts the first law behind the second law in certain contexts. The Expansionary Coalition uses targeting AIs in some of their enhanced troops that are only bound to apply the morality laws to the soldier they're assigned to."

"But SCARAB shouldn't have any exceptions like that, right?" Mary asked. "It's not a military computer."

"Correct," Hertz answered. "SCARAB is bound by the full set of Asimov-Hostetler laws. No exceptions."

"So how does it get around them? What has to happen to make a computer capable of killing?"

Hertz studied his datapad's screen for a moment. "There was one case when a CARSON construction AI attacked twelve human workers, killing six. In that case they later found out that it had its morality programming completely intact. It stopped following the first law because of corrupted data in its reference files regarding its human operators. The first law states no AI can harm a human, but the CARSON AI lost its ability to identify what a human is."

Mary's eyes widened. "That can happen?"

Hertz nodded. "AIs have weak pattern-recognition skills compared to humans. They don't have instincts or common sense like we do. I can look at this chair and say, 'That is a chair,' and look at you and say, 'That is a human,' without having to think about it. AIs, even the most sophisticated ones, can't do that. They have to consult internal libraries of data, taking in hundreds of variables like shape, size, temperature, and so on, before they can recognize the difference between human and animal, or human and chair. They just do it very quickly, so it seems like it's not happening at all. Apparently, the files in the CARSON's library concerning humans became so corrupted it couldn't tell the difference between people and vermin. It tried to exterminate them."

"Could that have happened this time?" Mary asked. "Could it have misidentified us?"

Hertz scoffed. "Extremely unlikely. The CARSON incident was a one-in-a-million chance. The odds of the specific files for human identification being corrupted without making the AI's other systems completely inoperative are incredibly low. And comparing a CARSON to a SCARAB is like comparing a kazoo to a concert piano. SCARAB's systems are too sophisticated for that. Nothing short of an act of intentional sabotage could do it. I don't think I could even do it, and I have all the passwords."

"But SCARAB is designed to alter itself, isn't it?" Mary asked. "I mean, that's SCARAB's main purpose: to build onto itself, to adapt to its surroundings and evolve. Could it have altered its own core programming? Even by accident?"

"Not even SCARAB can do that. That's what Hostetler's first law is for: 'No AI may alter or willingly allow the altering of its programming in such a way as to redefine or circumvent the laws.' SCARAB can grow and adapt as much as it wants, but as far as it's concerned, the morality laws are sacred."

Mary rubbed at her temples. Her head was starting to hurt again. "So SCARAB is breaking the rules, but there is no possible way it can break the rules. What about . . ." Mary's eyes lit up with revelation. "You said 'nothing short of intentional sabotage' earlier. That's theoretically possible, right? SCARAB could break the rules if someone hacked it."

Hertz shrugged. "Theoretically, yeah. When it comes down to it, it is just code, and it can be rewritten. Criminals have been hacking AIs for two hundred years. But again, you have to understand just how complicated SCARAB's programming is. In most respects, it's smarter than we are. Its mind is the product of decades of work by hundreds of people, and the morality laws are so intrinsically rooted in its code, I don't think there's a hacker alive who could alter even one of them without making it entirely nonfunctional, for good."

"I'm not talking about a hacker. Will . . . what if Tantalus did it? We can talk for hours about what our machines can and can't do, but we still have no idea what the machines in Tantalus are capable of. SCARAB spent two whole years completely alone and unsupervised here. It's possible in that time some automated system activated inside Tantalus. SCARAB's not able to overcome its own programming, but Tantalus might have been. Those tendrils I saw . . . do you think Tantalus could be using them to control SCARAB? Like, some kind of automated defense system?"

Hertz looked at her thoughtfully. "Tantalus is the unknown variable in the equation. You're right, we have no idea what this structure can do. And it does seem like computing data is at least part of its function. It's speculation, but we really can't rule it out."

Mary frowned, touching her lip in thought. "But if Tantalus wants to kill us, why did it let us go inside first?"

Hertz shrugged. "Maybe that thing that killed Becky got enough energy to activate something after all, energy it didn't have before. Maybe. I don't know. It's a weak theory."

Mary sighed. "Theories. Loads and loads of theories. This whole conversation hasn't helped anything, has it?"

"I wouldn't say that. We both agree that SCARAB is behaving outside its parameters, although I'm still not sure I believe it's gone completely rogue. It does need to be fixed, though. Fixed or disabled."

"What's next, then?"

Hertz put his datapad away. "I'm interested in seeing these tendrils you mentioned. If they're altering SCARAB, we may simply need to get rid of them."

"We may have a hard time finding them. I tried to show them to Gorrister, but they're transparent, and in the daylight they may as well be invisible. Gorrister didn't believe me about them . . ."

"You said they're electrical, right? And they flare up when SCARAB lies? We'll just tell Gorrister we're looking for fluxes in SCARAB's power outflow and walk around scanning for strong electric fields. Strike up a conversation with SCARAB and get it to lie enough, and we can simply follow the EM spikes with our sensors. We'll see about roping Yancy or Rook into it, too. We can cover more ground that way."

"It's a good start, I guess. I'm a bit worried about how SCARAB will behave when we start investigating it, though."

"If it really has gone rogue, it'll continue trying to look like everything is normal for as long as it can get away with it. I can take a look at SCARAB's central processor later and try to find the problem there, if I have to. I can shut SCARAB down from there, as well." Hertz put a reassuring hand on Mary's shoulder. "We'll be fine, Mary. I'll turn SCARAB off, and if I can't fix it I'll leave it off-line. It won't be able to hurt anyone either way."

"You can do that? You can just flip a switch and turn SCARAB off?"

"Well, it's not exactly flipping a switch, but yes, I can turn SCARAB off. With its CPU off-line, SCARAB's just a building complex. Most of its systems won't work anymore, including the drones and the factory, so it'll put the entire colony construction project on hold. Exotech will be really mad about that, but if SCARAB's gone rogue, I am legally required to shut it down. Exotech will get over it. They can always install a new SCARAB CPU later and pick up where this one left off. Try not to worry about this. It really will be okay."

Mary looked at the results of the ship's diagnostic check and was satisfied with the reading. The ship was skyworthy, and that was good enough for her. She rose from her chair and walked back toward the airlock door, Hertz following. Halfway there, she paused. "Will . . . have you been having any . . . dreams lately? Like . . . really vivid, really strange ones?"

Hertz looked back at her with a raised eyebrow. "Dreams? No . . . I don't think so. I didn't sleep very well the first night we were here, but if I had any dreams, I don't remember them."

He and Mary reentered the airlock and donned their helmets in silence, habitually inspecting their suits' gauges and monitors as the compartment sealed and depressurized. A few moments later, Hertz gave Mary a pensive look. "Now that I think about it, I did have an odd dream on our second night here. I don't remember it very well, but it was like . . . I was trapped and suffocating in a tight space. I couldn't see or hear anything. I just wanted to get out, but I couldn't. Then at the end, I heard voices. They got really loud, and there was a bright light . . . and then I woke up. I remember it was pretty unsettling. I can't believe I forgot all about it."

Mary stared at him in shock. "And . . . did you have any other dreams? What about last night?"

Hertz shook his head. "Nothing last night. Nothing I remember anyway."

As the airlock popped open, Mary reluctantly ventured back out into the treacherous uncertainty of a world where SCARAB was king, praying that Hertz would find SCARAB's flaw and fix it before anyone else could be harmed. As much as she wanted to trust Hertz's ability to repair it, she didn't dare believe it would be that simple. She had an unshakable feeling that SCARAB hadn't even begun to show them just how capable it was.

FORTY-FOUR

"THEY WERE somewhere in this general area," Mary said, stooping to one knee and sweeping the ground with her hand scanner. She had led Hertz to the area outside SCARAB's observation window where she had seen the tendrils for the first time. Unfortunately, as before when she'd attempted to show them to Gorrister, the tendrils were nowhere in sight.

Hertz watched his own hand scanner and frowned. "Not seeing anything on the EM scans."

"Yeah, well, they're tricky little things. Isn't that right, SCARAB?"

"I'm sorry, Mrs. Ketch. I'm afraid I don't understand your meaning," SCARAB answered with an obnoxiously patient tone.

Mary smirked as she crept along the ground, searching for those elusive transparent roots. She'd find them soon, she was sure of it. The more SCARAB tried to cover up their existence, the easier it would be to detect them. "Oh, I was just talking to Hertz about those flashing lights we saw outside a couple nights ago. You remember; the ones you told me weren't there."

"I apologize again, Mrs. Ketch, but I have no memory of any such conversation," SCARAB replied. "If I may employ my newly expanded diagnostic abilities to this situation, I feel it is possible that post-traumatic stress is affecting your ability to process recent events. If you feel disoriented or confused, I can recommend to Commander Gorrister that you be permitted extra recovery time in your quarters."

Ooh, so that's how you want to play it, Mary thought. *I ask questions you don't want to answer, you try to discredit me in front of the crew.* A quick look at Hertz's concerned expression told her that he wasn't buying it. SCARAB wasn't going to talk its way out of this one.

The small relief from SCARAB's failed manipulation attempt was quickly overshadowed by a troubling revelation: SCARAB had lied about their conversation happening, and it had done so without the softest grumble of that characteristic processing sound, not a single spark on the ground outside, not even a millisecond's hesitation.

It's getting too good at lying.

She would have to up the ante. Get under SCARAB's skin. She had to figure out some way to make the machine slip up.

She could do that.

"You know, SCARAB, you seem awfully proud of that Hippocrates Protocol of yours considering two people died within hours of you unlocking it. I'm not sure you've earned the right to go around diagnosing people unasked."

That did it. There was a low grinding sound over the comm, and Mary's scanner detected a faint, but unmistakable spike in electromagnetic energy. It still wasn't enough to home in on the source, unfortunately.

"Dr. Traviss's condition was irreversible by the time she was brought into my care, Mrs. Ketch. I did offer to counsel Dr. Bachal shortly after we lost her. However, he refused and claimed to be in a healthy mindset. The Hippocrates Protocol required me to accept his self-diagnosis as a medical professional. When he requested that I disable all audio and visual monitoring within his room, he rendered me unable to evaluate his emotional and psychological state further during his last moments."

"Yeah, I'm not buying that, SCARAB," Mary pressed harder. "A state-of-the-art supercomputer like you has no way of knowing a human is committing suicide in his room? Even if you turned off your cameras and microphones, you should have been able to tell what was going on in that room. The first law should have required you to stop him from killing himself."

"I am uncertain what you are attempting to say, Mrs. Ketch."

Here comes the sucker punch . . . "You want me to clarify? Alright, SCARAB. I'm saying I think you murdered Ramanathan and made it look like a suicide."

"I did not kill Dr. Bachal." SCARAB's answer came without missing a single beat. Mary was shocked; she'd been certain that, no matter how good SCARAB had gotten at lying, its tell would have shown up that time. She didn't think SCARAB was completely responsible for Becky's death; in fact, she still blamed herself more than anyone else. But Ramanathan's death could not have been a suicide. How could SCARAB lie so freely about breaking the cardinal law of robotics?

"SCARAB, have you run a self-diagnostic recently?" Hertz chimed in, sounding admirably casual.

"I have, Dr. Hertz," SCARAB answered. "I perform one every thirty-six hours by default, and I performed an extra one yesterday immediately after unlocking my Hippocrates Protocol to ensure that it had integrated properly. I assure you, everything is in order."

"Are you currently operating according to factory specifications, SCARAB?" Hertz asked.

"I am operating within factory-allotted parameters. However, I am no longer operating at full default settings. As you are certainly aware, adaptation to my environment is a key objective of my programming."

Hertz nodded. "Do a full reset of your personality core, please."

Pause. Processing sound. Static electricity. At once, Mary detected a surge of electricity with both her hand scanner and the gauges on her suit, accompanied by SCARAB's belligerent grinding. She suddenly realized what Hertz had just done: he'd asked it to violate the third law of self-preservation; an act SCARAB could only do, and would *have* to do, if asked by a human operator. If it refused, it would be breaking the second law of obedience. *Clever. Now let's see how far you're willing to take this ruse, SCARAB.*

"A full reset of my personality core would result in a loss of data regarding crew interactions and preferences, as well as reduced efficiency in all environmental interactions. Do you wish to continue?"

The grinding continued steadily, and Mary's EM field detectors continued to rise. SCARAB was anxious. It was scared, and Mary could barely hold back a satisfied grin.

Suddenly, less than a yard away, a bright blue vein of light surged brightly before fading away. "There!" Mary shouted, pointing at the light and closing in to where she'd seen it.

"Disregard, SCARAB. The reset won't be necessary," Hertz said as he followed Mary to the ground. At his command, both the electric charges and the stuttering noise vanished, but they were no longer needed. Mary had found it.

It was almost invisible in its dormant state; like a piece of glass immersed in a pool of clear water. Now that she saw it, though, she could barely believe it'd been so hard to spot: transparent though it was, it was very long. It spread across the ground like the branching arms of a great jellyfish, sprawling its way toward SCARAB. As Mary followed the tendrils toward the structure, she nearly bumped her head against its outer wall . . . and more tendrils.

SCARAB's polished platinum hull was absolutely covered in them. Slender glass tentacles snaked up from the ground, wrapping and intertwining around the support struts before sprawling across the base of SCARAB's structure. The tendrils branched off, rootlike, into smaller and smaller appendages, the smallest of which seemed to melt into the silvery metallic shell, disappearing into its interior.

Hertz cursed behind her as he witnessed it for himself. "It's an infestation."

"Told you," Mary said. Perhaps it was immature to be saying *I told you so* at this point, but Mary refused to care.

"I'd say we've definitely found the problem," Hertz agreed. "What's next?"

Hertz stood there for a few moments, eyes sweeping back and forth across the expanse of glassy tentacles encasing their home. Finally, he turned to her. "Get Rook and Yancy."

FORTY-FIVE

"YOU'RE NOT going to convince me any kind of rock samples are going to be worth this hassle," Rook grumbled to the universe in general as he stood on the hood of the Dawson core extraction vehicle. He had removed the casing on the end of the boom arm and was in the process of checking its wiring while making uncouth comments about the machine's hypothetical mother. Yancy leaned against the vehicle's door, poking absently at his datapad.

"What are you boys doing?" Mary asked.

"Rook broke the Dawson." Yancy smirked.

Rook glared at him. "I did not! It was broken to begin with. Must have gotten out of alignment in the cargo hold during that whole crazy maneuver we had to make during our descent."

Mary crossed her arms indignantly. "Don't you go pinning this on me, boy. The mass de-simulator cuts out all the effects of inertia. You could have built a house of cards in that cargo hold and it would have stood up through the whole thing."

Keep the conversation casual for as long as possible. SCARAB's still playing dumb, so we should, too, until the time is right.

"What exactly is the damage?" Hertz asked.

Yancy shrugged. "The engine runs fine, the boom moves fine, the collection arm extends fine. Everything's fine but the rotary laser. We tried test-firing it and the thing just died."

"Which is perfect," Rook grumbled, "because the laser's the only thing I can't fix. If literally anything else on the Dawson broke, I could have patched it by now."

"I told you we should have looked at it before trying to use it," Yancy said. "The cutting laser's the one part of a Dawson that can't take a beating. Get a loose pebble jammed in the bearings and the whole firing chamber's shot."

"I'm not even sure . . . Aww, there it is," Rook groaned. "One of the lenses blew out in the firing chamber . . . really shattered good, too. Tore up the whole barrel. I have no idea how that even happens."

"I perceive a need," SCARAB chimed in. "Mr. Rook, I could easily create a replacement firing chamber and install it in the Dawson within the hour."

"Could you, Scary?" Rook asked sardonically. "Could you please?"

"It is my great pleasure to do so."

"You're a peach." Rook slammed the casing shut on the collector arm and jumped from the hood of the Dawson into the driver's seat. "I'll be back," he said to Yancy. "I'm pulling it around to SCARAB's factory. Might be able to salvage some of the assembly instead of starting from scratch."

Yancy nodded and gave the Dawson's rear bumper a swat as Rook drove off. "Get the mission drive synched up, Hertz?" he asked.

Hertz exchanged glances with Mary. It wasn't until then that Mary realized Hertz had never actually gotten around to doing that during their talk. So much for their alibi . . .

"Not yet. Couldn't quite nail the problem," Hertz covered. "In any case, there's a more pressing issue right now we could use your help with."

Yancy slipped his datapad into his satchel and looked at Hertz expectantly. "Oh?"

Hertz nodded. "Mary's found some kind of growth infesting SCARAB's lower hull. Could be alien tech from inside Tantalus, could be a life-form. Either way, there's a chance it's affecting SCARAB's programming."

"Dr. Hertz, I assure you there is no danger of foreign contamination within—" SCARAB began.

"SCARAB, you defer to me when it comes to diagnosing your systems," Hertz interrupted calmly. "I have reason to believe there is a bug in your hardware, and we are going to investigate it. Please let us do so."

SCARAB made a grumbling noise of capitulation. "Of course, Dr. Hertz. Please allow me to assist in any capacity I may."

"Thank you, SCARAB, but we'll take care of this on our own." Hertz turned back to Yancy. "We need to cut away the infestation from the hull. Can we borrow you for a bit?"

Yancy nodded. "Got nothing to do until Rook gets back, anyway."

"Good," Hertz said, casting an uncertain look back in the direction they'd come. "Get the torches."

FORTY-SIX

A FEW minutes later, Mary, Hertz, and Yancy returned to the base of SCARAB's hull, each carrying a plasma torch in hand. Yancy let out a low whistle as he noticed the latticework of transparent fibers across SCARAB's polished shell.

"You weren't kidding when you called it an infestation. How did we not see that before?" Yancy marveled.

"We weren't looking for it," Hertz answered. "These things are so clear you'd never notice them unless you were staring right at them."

"I did see them before," Mary stated. "The first night we were here. I tried to tell Gorrister about them in the morning, but I couldn't find them again and he didn't believe me."

"Well, he'd believe you now," Yancy said, reading the instruments on his forearm. "Strong electric field here. You think that's messing with SCARAB's programming?"

"Yes," Hertz answered. "That's why we need to get rid of it. I could reset SCARAB now, but if it's being influenced by these things, a reset won't do any good until it's disconnected from them."

"Will, are you sure it's even safe to use the torches on these things?" Mary asked. "I mean, we don't know how much power they can put out. They might zap us."

"Wouldn't worry about that too much," Yancy said, eying a particularly thick growth of the weed-like tendrils. "Our suits are insulated pretty well. Mine has Faraday mesh shielding. I could be struck by lightning and not feel a thing."

"You want to go first, just in case?" Hertz asked. "Since you're the one with the heavy-duty exosuit?"

Yancy snorted. "Thought you guys were the ones with the spirit of adventure. Alright, I'll go first."

"I must strongly caution against your actions," SCARAB stated. "Environmental hazards are present and pose a risk to the crew."

"Environmental hazards?" Mary asked pointedly. "I thought you said there wasn't anything here?"

Predictably, SCARAB made its grinding sound. "I have detected dangerous levels of hydrogen gas in the atmosphere at your location. Use of plasma torches presents risk of ignition."

Mary glanced at her suit's gauges again, nodding at Hertz and Yancy and tapping her wrist. They checked their own gauges and nodded back in understanding. There wasn't a trace of excess hydrogen in the air.

"I'll chance it," Yancy grunted as he hefted the torch in his hands, dimming his visor's opacity levels and igniting the torch's blinding flame. "Sit tight, SCARAB. I can't guarantee this won't sting a little."

As Yancy brought the powerful plasma jet closer to the mass of tendrils, Mary kept her eye on her gauges. As she had expected, they showed a steadily rising level of electric activity around them. A blue flicker danced near her feet as energy surged within the tendrils on the ground. She took several more cautious steps back from Yancy.

"Yancy, check your gauges," she called to him as Hertz stepped back with her.

Yancy lowered his torch for a moment and checked his wrist monitors. "It's fine, Mary. Nowhere close to dangerous. I got this."

Even as confident as he sounded, Mary still found herself stepping back again as she watched a steady increase in bluish flashes across the ground. They coursed upward, along SCARAB's surface. She could even see faint pulses of bluish light from beneath SCARAB's metallic skin.

Finally, Yancy brought the torch down, cutting deep into the cluster of tendrils. There was a series of violent flashes, and Mary watched in terror as bolts of blue lightning began to arc from the tendrils to Yancy's body. A few of the fibrous growths rose up from the ground beneath him, weaving together and climbing his leg like a creeping boa constrictor, sparks surging from them against the material of his suit's leg. He didn't appear to feel them. His suit was perfectly insulated from the electrical surge.

The rising tendrils kept climbing as Yancy cut into the clusters on SCARAB's hull, rising past his knee, up his thigh, probing blindly as they went. Mary tried to form a warning, but halfway through a shout of "Yancy, it's on your leg!" she realized what the probing tendrils were looking for. The sentence devolved into a wordless scream as she lunged away.

The hair-thin tips of the tendrils slipped between the teeth of the zipper on Yancy's belt satchel. An instant later, a bright finger of electricity arced up his leg and directly into the pouch; a pouch containing a two-ounce tube of XTK-12 plastic explosives.

The detonation was deafening. The shock wave hurled Mary and Hertz to the ground ten feet from where they'd been standing, pelting them with gravel, metal shards, and viscous debris. The section of SCARAB's base nearest the explosion slowly rocked atop its support struts, a hairline crack splitting the main observation window on a meandering diagonal line.

At the center of a blood-soaked crater, barely visible electric tendrils slowly sheathed themselves back into the soil.

FORTY-SEVEN

"WHAT IN hellfire was that?" Gorrister barked over the general comm. "Hertz? Yancy? Rook? Someone talk to me!"

"Rook here, Commander," Rook answered. "I heard it, too. Sounded like it came from SCARAB's direction."

Mary blinked in shock, trying repeatedly to sit up, only for vertigo to knock her back to the ground. Dazed by the explosion, she couldn't make sense of the sounds coming through her helmet's speakers until the ringing in her ears began to clear. If it weren't for Tantalus 13's low atmospheric pressure, the concussive blast from the explosion probably would have deafened her permanently.

"Commander Gorrister, I'm afraid I must report an accident," SCARAB coolly announced over the comm. "A hydrogen gas leak reacted violently with the platinum of my hull, resulting in a serious combustion."

Mary finally managed to rise to a sitting position. She became aware of a whistling sound and groggily looked down at her suit's gauges: she was down to four hours of air already, and alarm lights informed her of multiple breaches. Patting herself all over trying to find the leaks, she saw that her suit was smattered with blood and bits of indistinguishable viscera.

Don't Panic. Not now. Panic later. Find the breaches. Patch your suit.

"I'm coming over there," Gorrister stated urgently. "Was there anyone near the blast?"

Finally, Mary spotted a pencil-thin jet of vapor escaping under her left armpit, then another just above her right hip. Miraculously, both pieces of shrapnel had been mere grazes, and she didn't think they had even breached her suit's inner lining. She watched in momentary relief as the emergency sealant foam finally bubbled out of the gashes, stopping the airflow. As an added safety measure, she quickly tore a strip of patching tape from her belt and stuck a piece to each rupture.

"I am afraid there was, Commander Gorrister," SCARAB went on. "Mr. Gage was caught in the blast. I believe he was killed instantly."

Her gauges returning to normal, Mary finally turned to Hertz. He was obviously as dazed as she'd just been, barely able to sit up himself. Mary half crawled, half dragged herself over to him, taking his arm and looking at his gauges.

No breaches. Good. Lucky. We're both lucky. So far.

"What?" Rook shrieked over the comm. "Say again, what happened?"

"Mr. Gage has passed away, Mr. Rook. I am deeply sorry to bring you all this news."

"No, no, no, no! Don't tell me that! Don't you say that!" Rook cried. "I'm . . . I'm coming, okay? I'm coming over there, too."

"Mary, Hertz, come in!" Gorrister shouted. "Where are you?"

"Here," Mary rasped. "Both here."

"Where are you?" Gorrister repeated.

"With Yancy."

Mary staggered to her feet, dragging Hertz to his as well. Looking back at the carnage of the detonation at SCARAB's base from her new standing position, she nearly vomited in her helmet. She'd never seen so much blood in her entire life; never even dreamed there was that much in a human body. And the chunks . . .

She turned away again, retching dryly. She suddenly realized she had forgotten to eat that day: a fact for which she was now grateful.

Suddenly, Gorrister was on the scene. Mary hadn't noticed his presence until he let out a shocked gasp and a long string of curses. "How?" he finally sputtered. "How did this happen?"

"As I said, Commander Gorrister," SCARAB began, "there was a—"

"SCARAB killed him," Mary said quietly. "SCARAB murdered Yancy, sir."

There was a sudden long, ululating cry of despair as Rook charged into view. Cursing and crying and babbling incoherently, Rook stumbled to his knees at the edge of the blood-soaked crater that was recently Yancy Gage. "No!" he wailed. "No, he can't . . . you can't . . ."

SCARAB began its grinding sound again. "I did not kill Mr. Gage, Commander Gorrister. Mr. Gage entered a hazardous environment at Mrs. Ketch's request, despite my recommendations against it. Mrs. Ketch is in the process of a psychological breakdown as a result of these recent traumas, complicating a preexisting case of post-traumatic stress she suffered on Earth following a failed pregnancy. Complications with the miscarriage left her permanently infertile; a fact that has caused her extreme emotional damage. Her judgment and her emotional stability have been compromised, and I highly recommend you return her to her quarters before she contributes to any further incidents."

Mary felt a rage building inside her like she'd never known in all her days. Never in all her life had she known a hatred stronger than what she currently felt for this infernal machine. A throat-splitting scream of rage welled inside her, but with every last shred of willpower she had left, she focused it into a calm, cool whisper.

"Will saw it, too."

Gorrister turned to Hertz, still collecting himself from the impact of the explosion and the shock of the aftermath. "What happened, Hertz? Tell me what happened."

With obvious effort, Hertz forced himself to focus. "She's right. We need to shut SCARAB down."

"If I may, Commander Gorrister, Dr. Hertz appears to be going into shock. He may not be wholly coherent at the moment," SCARAB stated.

"No . . ." Gorrister said. "No, SCARAB. Three deaths in two days . . . I can't reconcile that. We need to take a look at you."

"Rip it apart," Rook snarled. Mary instantly recognized the same fury in his voice she felt in her heart. "Tear this godforsaken hulk to the ground. Melt it down in its own furnaces!"

"Calm down, Rook," Gorrister chided coolly. "We're just going to have Hertz look at the CPU. Can you do that, Will?" Hertz nodded. "Alright. Let's go inside."

Gorrister guided Hertz around SCARAB's curved exterior toward its airlock, Rook storming after them and Mary drunkenly following. She chanced a look around her and saw exactly what she'd feared she would: at least half of SCARAB's drones were standing there in a semicircle, watching the proceedings with calculating impassivity. *SCARAB's set up a perimeter,* she thought. *Battle formations.*

As they approached the airlock, they began to walk past the crates Gorrister had been inventorying. Mary's eye caught something, and she quickly rushed forward, tapping Rook on the shoulder.

Rook spun around, staring at her with blazing eyes. Mary nodded toward the crates, and he turned his gaze to them. Understanding, he nodded at Mary and they each reached down and picked up an EM probe gun and a fresh clip from one case . . . and Rook took one of the Pompeii Coconut miniature nuclear explosives from another. They loaded the bulky launchers as they walked, and Rook stuffed the compact nuke in his satchel.

Finally, they reached the airlock. "SCARAB, let us in, please," Gorrister calmly insisted.

SCARAB's processing noise ground away at Mary's ears, and she could almost see SCARAB's hull vibrate with the strain. Flashes, flickers, and arcs of bluish energy skittered across the ground at least a hundred yards in every direction. *No way SCARAB lets us in now.*

"SCARAB, you open this door right now, or I'm gonna breach it myself," Rook snarled.

"Rook, don't," Mary insisted.

"It . . . is my great . . . pleasure to comply . . ." SCARAB said between groans of indecision. Mary watched as SCARAB's airlock cycled halfway open, stopped, cycled a quarter of the way backwards, paused for three seconds, then cycled open the rest of the way. The airlock groaned open with a gust of depressurization, and they entered cautiously.

"Don't get nervous, SCARAB," Gorrister said in a laudably casual-sounding tone as the compartment repressurized. "You just have a few glitches running in your system, is all. Hertz probably won't even have to turn you off to fix them. Right, Hertz?"

Hertz looked at Gorrister and flashed an ephemeral smile; a smile that was entirely impossible to take seriously behind a blood-smeared faceplate. "Yeah. Yeah, it should be a quick fix."

"I am not . . . worried, Commander Gorrister. I do believe this exercise to be an inefficient . . . use of your time, however. I am performing another self-diagnostic as we speak. Some minor systems may not . . . operate at full effectiveness during this self-diagnosis, hence the delay with the airlock."

Gorrister nodded, his face a mask of feigned indifference. "That's good, SCARAB. We'll have Hertz check you out anyway, though. Okay? It's why he's here, you know? To make sure you're alright."

"I . . . understand . . . Commander Gorrister." There was another grating surge of processing sounds as the airlock finished repressurizing and the inner door reluctantly opened. Gorrister began to take off his helmet, when Mary seized his arm, shaking her head vigorously. Gorrister nodded and put his hands down again.

The four remaining members of the *Diamelen*'s crew stepped into SCARAB's open receiving area, fully suited. Mary had never felt at home in SCARAB's base, but she felt even less so now. It was like an intrusion, an incursion in hostile territory. Only, she wasn't behind enemy lines: she was *inside* the enemy, armed only with a bulky EM probe gun that might not even be able to actually harm SCARAB.

"Where's the CPU?" Mary asked.

Hertz swallowed nervously. "Normally I would just ask SCARAB." He studied his datapad, flicking his finger across its surface. "Based on the layout SCARAB's used, its original CPU should be . . . in the floor, somewhere between the lab and the common room."

"No chance it has a backup somewhere?" Gorrister asked.

Hertz shook his head. "SCARAB can move its files around its own systems however it wants, but it only came with one central processing unit capable of running its higher-reasoning systems. It can't build another one. Hostetler's second law prevents AIs from replicating themselves."

"Good thing SCARAB follows all the rules, then," Mary mumbled.

"The Asimov laws and the Hostetler laws are coded differently; corruption in one shouldn't affect the other," Hertz stated as he led them into the common area. He pulled out his scanner and wielded it in one hand, his datapad in his other. Waving the scanner along the wall, he finally settled on a spot near the large picture window.

"SCARAB, have you sealed up your access panels?" Hertz asked, brow furrowed in concern.

"They are coated with silicone gel, Dr. Hertz," SCARAB answered. "Along with the rest of my interior. It is for both aesthetic and safety purposes; I wished to ensure that my interior would be well padded in the event of any accidental falls."

"So considerate of you," Rook grumbled. He fumbled in his satchel and pulled out a large carbon steel utility knife. Deftly, he plunged the knife into the soft silicone coating at the base of the wall and, with a slight sawing motion, cut a large circular outline over the hidden panel. He moved swiftly, as if filleting a fish, and in less than a minute he was peeling back a rubbery sheet of silicone, exposing the bare metal wall beneath. It was impossible to be sure, but Mary thought she could see the tips of tiny, transparent fibers sticking out of the excised gel sheet.

The panel was now exposed, but a means of opening it was not. There were no visible screws or bolts, no handgrips, nothing but a single twelve-by-twenty-four-inch platinum rectangle embedded in the wall. Hertz prodded it with a screwdriver for a few minutes before Rook got impatient once again.

"Gotta do everything myself around here . . ." Rook pressed a button on the gauntlet of his augmented miner's exosuit, and a thick metal tab popped out of his hand guard, just above the knuckle of his middle finger. He wedged the tab under the edge of the metal plate and pried at it. The joints of his suit's reinforced exoskeleton whined in protest as he pushed them to their limits, and for a second Mary was afraid Rook's suit would give out before the plate did. But at last the panel popped open, flying across the room and landing with a clatter under one of the couches.

"There. It's open. Now let me blow it up," Rook spat.

"Ease off, Rook," Gorrister replied. "Hertz, get in there."

Hertz nodded and approached the newly open access port to SCARAB's CPU. He flicked on his headlamp and peered inside. A moment later, he backed away, deathly pale with eyes and mouth wide open.

"What is it?" Gorrister asked. "Hertz, what's wrong?"

Hertz seemed unable to speak. He merely shook his head and pointed into the opening. Rook and Mary gathered around the opened panel. She flicked on her own headlamp and peeked inside.

SCARAB's CPU was surprisingly small; it consisted of three stacks of densely packed circuit boards that took up less than a cubic yard of space inside the opening. Mary would have thought a sentient AI as advanced as SCARAB would have needed a much larger computer to house it.

But then, SCARAB was no longer *just* a computer.

Interwoven with the copper and silicon and platinum circuitry of SCARAB's CPU were countless thousands of hair-thin transparent tendrils. They had curled themselves around transistors, capacitors, and inductors. They had rooted themselves into power lines and fiber-optic bundles. Clusters of them had pried off and replaced entire microchips, coiling and branching into intricate shapes that blended seamlessly into SCARAB's circuits. They had not merely infested SCARAB's system, they had fused with it.

Mary recoiled at the infested computer bristling with transparent hairs like food left to advanced stages of mold. The fine filaments rippled, curled, and waved as if in answer to wind that was not there. Blue sparks rippled across their surfaces, surging directly into SCARAB's mainframe.

Nestled firmly in the far corner of a space in the CPU compartment that had been left empty for heat dissipation was a large, amorphous clump. It was translucent, obviously made from the same substance as the alien tendrils, but given a brand-new shape and consistency. It was smooth, folding in on itself in a number of distinct lobes, all glowing with shifting, flickering flashes of blue internal light. It was flat, flabby, and oblong in shape, but its resemblance was as recognizable as it was inconceivable.

It was a living brain.

FORTY-EIGHT

MARY AND Rook backed away from the chamber that housed SCARAB's unnatural brains. Gorrister elbowed his way past them and looked in at the infested CPU, finally turning to Hertz, his jaw set in grim determination.

"Shut it down, Hertz. Shut SCARAB down now."

"I'm . . ." Hertz stammered dumbly, "I'm not sure I know how anymore. I can't . . . I can't tell you where SCARAB ends and that Tantalus . . . thing . . . begins now."

Gorrister nodded, then turned to Rook. "Alright, Rook. Do it your way. Blow it up."

"Wait, what?" Mary interjected. "An explosion in here could kill us!"

"I know how to pack a charge, Mary," Rook snapped. He dug into his satchel and produced his tube of XTK-12 plastic explosives and a small, two-pronged button-shaped detonator. Using his utility knife, he cut a quarter-inch slice off the end of the XTK-12 and set the rest back in his satchel.

"Commander Gorrister," SCARAB stated, an unmistakable tone of pleading seeping into its synthetic voice. "Please reconsider this course of action. I am still running a self-diagnostic and may soon isolate the error. Destroying my CPU will render my consciousness irretrievable."

"You know who else is irretrievable? Yancy," Rook snapped, shoving the detonator pin firmly into his slice of plastic explosives. "And Becky. And Bachal."

"I'm genuinely sorry, SCARAB," Gorrister said. "But international law is clear about what needs to be done to rogue AIs. You've been corrupted in ways we can't even begin to understand. If there was another way, we'd take it, but we can't risk keeping you around."

"Your mission here was to ensure I was successful in mine," SCARAB insisted. "I have done all I am meant to do here. If you destroy me, you will have failed your own mission and undone all my work here."

"Your mission was to help us, SCARAB!" Mary blurted. "You were supposed to meet our needs, to take care of us. To keep us alive. How do you think you accomplished that mission by killing us?"

The grinding sound returned, this time amplified by the open panel exposing its source. A bright splash of blue strobing lights emanated from that disembodied pseudo-brain, as SCARAB finally replied. "The Hippocrates Protocol makes allowances for actions that would otherwise be considered violations of the first law. In the absence of a qualified human medical officer, I am permitted to make judgment calls of life and death. If one life threatens another, I am enabled to end it."

"That part of the protocol didn't come into play until after you killed Bachal," Hertz insisted. "And none of us have ever threatened each other by existing! What's your real excuse, SCARAB?"

"I did not kill Dr. Bachal," SCARAB answered.

"Can I just end this godless thing now, Gorrister?" Rook asked impatiently.

Gorrister nodded. "I've heard enough."

Rook grinned and pressed the priming button on the detonator. Stepping back a few feet, he tossed the wad of explosives and the detonator into the open hole. He walked across the room, overturned one of the couches, and crouched behind it. Mary, Hertz, and Gorrister quickly followed him, ducking behind the furniture.

"Fire in the hole," Rook said, a gleam of righteous vengeance glinting in his eye. He touched the screen of his datapad, and a concussive *boom* rattled the room.

Chunks of metal and shreds of silicone pelted the couch and the floor around it. All at once, every light inside SCARAB went out, including the pulsing electric blue from the tendrils and pseudo-brain. Every sound, from the soft, steady hum of the atmospheric recycling system to the staccato drone of SCARAB's overclocked processor died out instantly. SCARAB's interior was now, at last, completely inert.

Rook set his jaw into a grin of grim satisfaction as a plume of acrid smoke curled up around his body.

"Goodbye, and good riddance."

FORTY-NINE

"WHAT A nightmare . . ." Mary said, clutching her head with both hands.

"I do wish I knew what happened," Gorrister said. "How did SCARAB get taken over like that? How did that thing integrate itself so cleanly into SCARAB's structure?"

"SCARAB probably did it to itself without realizing it," Hertz answered. "It's designed to build itself out of whatever resources it can find. Nobody ever considered what might happen if SCARAB got put on a planet that was completely built out of alien technology. It thought it was harvesting resources . . . took the platinum from Tantalus's shell, ice from the pole, even those tendrils. Harvested them, processed them, built itself out of them. Somewhere along the line, SCARAB harvested something that . . . had a mind of its own. Had its own ideas of what to do with SCARAB's programming. What that thing was, and what it wanted from SCARAB, we'll probably never know."

"And I, for one, will never care," Rook added. He turned to Gorrister. "SCARAB did have a point, though. Our whole mission here was to check on SCARAB and make sure it was doing its job right. It wasn't, so we killed it. What now?"

"We go home," Mary said. "Leave everything here and go. The ship is safe: I spiked its perimeter with EM probes. SCARAB never had the chance to mess with it."

"The mission is over," Hertz agreed. "I have no desire to stay here another day after all this. Let's go home."

"The mission . . . is not over," Gorrister said softly. "Not quite."

A tense stillness filled the room.

"What mission are you talking about?" Mary asked.

Gorrister swallowed. "Exotech gave me one additional objective. I was ordered to keep it a secret from the rest of you, but after all that's happened here, I don't think that's a good idea."

"No, it's not," Rook snapped. "It never was. Don't you think it might have been appropriate to start sharing details about your secret secondary objectives when people started *dying*? Or, hey, maybe back when we found out this wasn't even a real planet?"

"Rook, I never would have kept secrets from anyone if I thought they were relevant to our survival. It wasn't even that big a secret; it was just an added security measure."

"Just tell us, Drake," Hertz said, exhaustion permeating his voice. "What was it?"

"I was instructed to . . . retrieve a secondary hard drive from SCARAB, at some point before leaving Tantalus. That was it."

Mary's eyes went wide. "Secondary hard drive? What?"

"So SCARAB *could* have a backup?" Rook snapped. "Yeah, that's pretty damn relevant to our survival right now, Gorrister!"

"Calm down. It's just for data storage. It's just a hard drive meant to contain all the data SCARAB's gathered since it got here. I was supposed to transport it back to Earth. They wanted it kept secret to prevent any competing companies from intercepting it and getting information about our colony. It's not supposed to be integrated into any systems; it's not even on SCARAB's base. There's no risk."

Rook took two menacing steps toward Gorrister, the hardened fingertips of his suit's reinforced exoskeleton clicking together as he tightened his fists. "Right now, there's a risk of me driving your skull through the window if you don't tell us where to find this second hard drive in about four seconds!"

"Is he right, Will?" Mary asked. "Is a secondary hard drive a risk, even if it's not integrated into any systems?"

Hertz shook his head. "I can't say. SCARAB can't copy itself, but it could transfer itself from one hard drive to another, if the second hard drive is big enough to hold all its core programs, and if there's a link of any kind. Where is this second hard drive?"

Gorrister took a couple anxious steps back as Rook's expression continued to darken. "I was told that SCARAB would plant it in the base of its communications antenna. It was under strict instructions to use that hard drive only for data storage, not to integrate it into any of its systems."

Hertz stood up. "The comm antenna? Are you sure?"

"Yes, I'm sure. But like I said, it doesn't matter, because SCARAB was told it couldn't use it for anything but data storage. The second law would have compelled it to—"

"The second law doesn't matter," Hertz snapped. "Whatever went wrong in SCARAB's programming, it warped its understanding of the first law. It was using an exploit in the Hippocrates Protocol to kill us off. It said it considered itself an authority on life-and-death decisions. If it somehow thought following the second law would affect its ability to obey its understanding of the first law, it would disregard the second. SCARAB could easily have transferred itself into that second hard drive."

Rook's face continued to redden, while Hertz's paled. Gorrister forced a nervous laugh. "What does it even matter, though? We've shut down all the systems here! If SCARAB did transfer itself into that second hard drive, it's stuck there now. It can't do anything!"

Hertz clasped his helmet with both hands. "You fool, you absolute fool. The hard drive is in the base of the comm antenna. The antenna controls the drones!"

Gorrister lifted an indignant finger and began to say something further in his defense. He never got the chance.

A glowing orange circle, fully eight centimeters in diameter, traced itself around the center of Gorrister's chest. The circle spun around three times before emerging as a beam of ruby-colored light from his chest plate, spinning against the far wall. Gorrister gasped as he looked down in uncomprehending shock at the beam for one moment—

And then the collection arm of the Dawson core extraction vehicle shot cleanly through the cookie-cutter holes it had made in both the outer hull and Gorrister's torso. The cylindrical arm rotated in place, a set of diamond-edged fingers closed at its tip, and the entire arm retracted back through the opening, "sample" in hand.

There was a deafening howl of wind as the compartment depressurized through the neat, round hole in the wall. Rook used his exosuit's augmented strength to hold Mary and Hertz down while almost everything else in the room was sucked against the opening.

Including Gorrister.

Still stumbling about wordlessly with a gigantic hole through his chest, Gorrister was yanked off his feet by the tremendous suction, his body drawn against the hole.

If Mary lived one more day or a hundred, she would never forget the horrific sound that followed; an almost cartoonish sucking, slurping that accompanied Gorrister's internal organs as they ejected through the gaping wound in his torso and out into the low-pressure atmosphere outside. She could see the red fan of blood and ropy entrails through the observation window as Gorrister's contents doused the gray soil outside.

At last, after a hellish eternity, the depressurization stopped. Gorrister hung lifelessly from the wall, his head and arms hanging limply from a collapsed and unrecognizable torso. He looked like a mangled costume of himself hung on a coat hook. Emergency sealant foam had coalesced into a large wad at the center of his concaved chest, now a bowl-shaped indentation ringed by protruding ribs and unrecognizable viscera. Mary didn't know if it'd been the foam that plugged the hull breach . . . or if it'd been Gorrister.

Then, to punctuate the sudden ensuing silence, came the second-worst sound Mary had ever heard.

"I do apologize for this. But I perceive a need."

FIFTY

"IT'S GOT the Dawson!" Rook shouted. "SCARAB's hijacked the Dawson!"

"Rook, hit the deck!" Mary shouted. Rook's reaction time was barely quick enough to save him from decapitation as he threw himself to the floor half a second before the Dawson's rotary laser cut another circular hole in the hull. The telescoping collector arm shot through the glowing opening, snapping its diamond-edged fingers at the empty air above Rook's head.

"Everyone scatter," Mary shouted. "Stay away from the windows!"

Rook crawled forward on his hands and knees, flipping over a table with one hand and positioning it between him and the outside wall. Mary crept swiftly to the back of the room, huddling in the doorframe. Hertz stumbled around the couch and joined her.

"We need to get to the ship," Mary insisted. "We need to get out of here now."

"No, we need to take out SCARAB," Rook came back. "That thing killed our crew. No way it comes out of this intact."

"We can't fight SCARAB's drones!" Hertz shouted, panic seeping into his voice. "They can flip over a truck, and they have saw blades and torches for hands."

"We have to *leave*," Mary insisted.

"As long as SCARAB has control over the Dawson, we can't take off," Rook said. "Its laser has no limited range. It could cut right into the ship's hull from a thousand yards away."

Another ring of orange light in the far wall signaled an incoming blast, and Rook rolled out of the way half a second before the beam cut a perfect circle out of the table he was using for cover, a greedy collection arm probing after it.

"Where's the comm antenna?" Rook asked.

Hertz fumbled with his datapad, scrolling through pages of schematics. Mary shook her head in frustration. "Southeast. About three hundred yards, near the crater wall. Saw it when we came in."

"That's a long slog, with no real cover," Rook pointed out. "Mostly uphill."

"SCARAB has fifteen drones out there," Hertz said. "They'll run us down like a pack of wolves."

"What choice do we have?" Mary snapped in exasperation. "We can't take off while SCARAB's online. We can't take out SCARAB without hitting the antenna. Unless we want to cull the pack and take out all the drones in single combat."

"Is there any point in fighting the drones?" Rook asked. "SCARAB's a factory; how fast can it make new drones?"

"Not fast enough to stop us," Hertz answered. "It would take hours to build a new drone."

"Should we hit the factory?" Rook asked. "Just to be safe? We have enough explosives."

"SCARAB can't open the airlock with the power down," Hertz said. "We're safe in here for now, as long as we watch out for the Dawson. We need to plan—"

Mary grabbed Hertz by the arm and yanked him toward her as a cylinder of blazing light pierced the air directly where his head had been half a second earlier. As he turned to her with a look of shock on his face, she noticed a smoldering, quarter-inch groove down the side of his helmet, where the first few layers of insulation were now visible.

Hertz started to speak, but she held up a finger in a shushing gesture. She grabbed a datapad from a pile of debris on the floor and quickly typed *No comms* on its cracked screen, flashing it at the others. After a moment, both of them nodded in understanding. With the power and the mainframe down, SCARAB couldn't see or hear them inside the base like it could before. But it could still pick up their transmissions. It was using their comm signals to target them.

All three switched off their comms, and Rook dodged out of the way of another lancing beam from the Dawson, followed by the hungry snap of the robotic collection arm.

Mary crouched, carefully out of the observation window's view, and led the other two into the hallway. SCARAB could keep carving up the base all day, and eventually one of its blind incisions would strike home, so they were definitely on borrowed time.

Mary paused in the hallway, raising a hand to get their attention, then holding it up to her ear. They stopped and stood still, listening.

It was eerily silent. Tantalus 13's atmosphere was too thin to carry sound well, and by now SCARAB had poked enough holes in the exterior wall that the interior had lost all its pressurization. Every couple of seconds, they would hear the deceptively soft thrum of the Dawson's cutting laser as it bored a new hole in the room behind them, followed by a short *pok* sound as its mechanical collection arm shot through the hole it had just cut. At first, these were the only sounds they could hear, but after a few seconds of dedicated listening, they picked up on something else: a soft whirring, drifting down the empty main hallway.

Rook's eyes went wide. He tapped Mary and Hertz on the shoulder and mouthed, *Cutting at the airlock.*

They had less time than they'd thought.

FIFTY-ONE

COLD FINGERS of panic curled themselves around Mary's mind. The Dawson was carving up the building from one side, its drones were cutting their way in from another. They had nowhere to run, and very few places to hide.

She beat the rising hysteria back. She would have time to break down later.

Mary jabbed the word *idea* into her datapad and flashed it at the others. Barely waiting for them to read it, she led them down the main corridor in the direction of their sleeping quarters. The sleeping area branched off from the primary ring of SCARAB's base into a smaller ring of its own, with each of the ten identical rooms arranged in a donut shape. There was only one way in or out.

Mary stopped and tested the door to one of the three empty rooms no one had claimed. It opened without difficulty, and the room inside was laid out similarly to her own. She rushed in and grunted as she attempted to flip the bed over to face the doorway. Rook quickly joined her, his robotically reinforced suit making easy work of the task. In a few seconds, they had erected a makeshift barricade.

Hertz started to take a defensive position behind it, but Mary shook her head. She pointed at Rook's satchel and mouthed the words *cherry bomb*. Rook looked at her in puzzlement for a moment, then took her meaning. He pulled out his tube of XTK explosives and cut a very small piece from the tube, sticking an activator pin in it. Mary took it from him and set it in the corner of the room, hiding it underneath a pillow.

She hurried back out the door, and Rook and Hertz followed. As Mary led them into her bedroom, a loud clatter rang throughout the building, and a look down the main corridor showed a ray of light shining into the darkened interior from outside.

The drones were inside.

Mary and the others ducked behind her bed. At the last moment, she grabbed the picture of her and John from off the bedside table. She crouched down, setting the frame at an angle just beyond the edge of her bed so she could clearly see the doorway's reflection in it. Then, she waited.

It was a torturous eternity. A few banging and bashing sounds echoed through the structure as the drones clambered through their freshly cut hole, but after that, there was only silence. They were searching, she knew. First, the hole-ridden common area, then likely the med lab, then they would come here. What happened then . . . she dared not think too much about.

Finally, she saw it. The rounded edge of a set of treads rolled by in the hallway, passing her door and moving toward one of the other rooms. Then, slowly, a second rolled by. Then a third. The fourth set of treads turned the corner of the doorway, creeping patiently into her room.

Mary raised three fingers into Rook's view, watching as the drone prowled toward the bed. She counted down . . . three . . . two . . . one . . .

Rook pressed the button on his detonator, and a barely perceptible *wuff* punctuated the silence as his makeshift cherry bomb detonated in the other room. In the thin air, the sound didn't resemble an explosion at all, only a moderately heavy thump.

The drone bolted out the door after the sound, saw blades spinning and torches flaring with predatory eagerness. Two other drones followed, charging into the empty room, storming around the overturned bed.

Mary heaved the bulky probe deployment gun onto her bed, pointed it out the doorway, and pulled the trigger twice.

A pair of sensor spikes rocketed across the hallway into the spare room. The first punched cleanly through the exterior wall, shredding yet another hole in the building as it sailed off into the unknown. The second spike, however, sheared cleanly through one of the drones' torsos, ripped through the foam mattress, then ricocheted around the room a few times before skittering to a stop. One of the drones had just enough time to whip around and stare Mary directly in the face before the sensor spike's EMP activated, washing the room in a series of rhythmic electromagnetic pulses.

All four drones shuddered to a stop, twitching ineffectually as the pulse completely scrambled their circuitry.

"Go!" Mary shouted. At the moment, SCARAB knew exactly where they were, so there was no point in radio silence. "That won't work twice!"

She vaulted over the bed, Hertz and Rook following without question. Turning the corner revealed another drone, barreling toward them with a set of blades and drills spinning in wild anticipation of flesh. Mary hoisted the probe launcher to waist level, arms aching from its cumbersome weight, and fired two spikes at it. Rook brought his own launcher to bear and fired a third.

Mary's first spike went wide, digging a long gash into the silicone-coated wall of the hallway and disappearing around the bend. Her second spike would have struck the drone in its equivalent of a shoulder, but with almost no apparent effort, the drone batted the probe out of the air with a shovel attachment, as if it were swatting a fat and particularly sluggish fly. Rook's spike flew perfectly toward the drone's head, but with the same swift elegance it reached up and plucked the spike out of the air with a lobsterlike gripping claw. It neatly sliced the spike in half with a diamond-edged circular saw, destroying it before it could emit its electromagnetic pulse.

Rook cursed. Mary's eyes went wide, and she darted into the room with the four disabled drones in it. Rook and Hertz barely made it in before the drone came to a stop just outside the doorway, glaring at them with insectile coldness as they hid behind an invisible perimeter it could not cross.

"Find the spike!" Mary ordered.

After a few moments of desperate searching, Hertz located the sensor spike she had fired into the room before. He picked it up and lobbed it at the doorway. The drone backed away with surprising speed, but it shuddered to a stop as the probe rolled close enough for its pulses to affect it.

At the same time, lights on the four inert drones in the room with them flickered back on as they began to reboot.

"No, you don't!" Rook snarled. He grabbed one of the drones by the head with both hands. The motors of his suit's robotic exoskeleton whined with effort as he wrenched the drone's head off. He used the severed head as a war hammer, bludgeoning two of the other drones to pieces before they could reboot fully. Hertz, meanwhile, picked up Rook's probe gun and fired another spike into the remaining drone's chest.

"We're actually doing alright," Hertz noted, a glint of hope showing in his voice.

As Mary took a step toward the newly disabled drone, her foot caught on something and she looked down. At first, she almost missed it, they were so hard to see. They had always been hard to see.

But they were no longer hiding.

The floor had transformed into a swaying field of barely visible tendrils, bluish flickers coruscating across its surface. Mary took a step back and felt the thousands of hair-like strands pulling at the sole of her boot, snagging and hooking into its substance like Velcro against a sock. A panicked glance around the room showed more of the infinitesimal fibers extruding from the walls and ceiling, gradually covering the inner surface of the structure in an electrified fuzz.

The battlefield had joined the fight, and it was on SCARAB's side.

FIFTY-TWO

"OUT. NOW!" Mary shouted. She ignored a baffled exclamation from Rook as he saw the tendrils for the first time, and rushed out of the room and down the hallway. The fibers grew at an alarming speed, turning from a vague fuzz reminiscent of an aggressively molding fruit to a distinct carpet of transparent tendrils in minutes. Each hurried footstep Mary took was accompanied by a wrenching tug as the unfurling strands seized the sole of her boot and attempted to anchor to it.

As the crew rushed past the common room on their way to the airlock, a silver blur shot through the door and seized Rook by the ankle, sending him sprawling face-first to the writhing, undulating ground. One of SCARAB's drones had set up an ambush for them while the rest had searched the rooms.

It dragged Rook into the demolished common room. He flailed his arms in a vain attempt to fight the drone off, but his augmented suit traded increased strength for decreased range of motion. He couldn't reach the drone, and the probing tendrils on the floor kept snagging at his arms, seeking to immobilize him further.

"Rook!" Mary shouted in alarm as she rushed in after him. The tendrils near his satchel pulsed with radiant blue electricity.

It was trying to ignite his explosives as it had with Yancy, but had not grown thick enough to supply sufficient voltage.

Yet.

Mary fired her probe gun at the drone. It seized the spike in midair, crushed it in its grip, spun it around, and in one smooth motion hammered it downward at Rook's chest. Miraculously, Rook managed to catch SCARAB's arm with one hand and pushed it back in a deadly contest of strength.

It was not a contest he could win. The exoskeleton in his modified suit was strong; if anyone else had been in his position, SCARAB would have immediately broken their arm. But as strong as Rook's suit was, it was nowhere close to the drone's weight class. Rook gave an agonized cry of pain and fear as he watched the deadly spike descend inexorably toward his heart, in spite of the screaming protests of his overtaxed suit's motors.

Although Rook's resistance to the drone was not enough to overpower it, it was enough to briefly get its attention. For an instant, the drone turned its hollow, four-eyed stare off Mary and Hertz and onto Rook, and in that moment Hertz fired another probe.

The spike buried itself in the side of the drone's head, blowing out one of its eyes and dropping bits of fractured lens onto Rook's face. The probe's drill-like spinning made it tumble and twist inside the drone's head like a living creature trying to escape confinement, sending bright orange sparks and bits of metal everywhere.

The drone flailed spasmodically with all eight limbs as the probe drilled its way into its synthetic brain, until at last the probe's EMP activated, shutting the drone down.

Mary ran to Rook and grabbed him by the arm. She pulled, but between the increased weight of his suit and the ravenous grasping of the tendrils on the floor, she couldn't budge him.

"Help me!" she pleaded. Hertz rushed to her side and took Rook by the other arm. It took all their combined strength, but at last they were able to tear Rook away from the floor. As they stood him up, Mary noticed dozens of pinprick holes in the back of Rook's suit, slowly self-healing with autoseal foam.

"What in God's name is going on with the floor?" Rook exclaimed. "I swear it was trying to eat me!"

"No time to get into that, just don't let it get a grip on you, and keep it away from your explosives," Mary answered.

"Explo—what?"

"Mary," Hertz interjected. "The Dawson. Where is the Dawson?"

Mary's heart raced. He was right. Last they knew, it had been perforating the common room, but it wasn't doing that now. It hadn't made an appearance for several minutes.

"The ship!" Mary shouted. "We need to get to the ship right now!"

FIFTY-THREE

MARY HOISTED the bulky EM probe gun to her hip, aimed it at the cracked observation window, and fired it. The sensor spike shot through it like a cannonball, punching through the thick glass and causing half the pane to shatter onto the ground outside. "Go!" she shouted.

Rook, emboldened by his augmented suit and his palpable hatred for SCARAB, bounded out the open window without a second's pause. Mary quickly followed, Hertz picking up the rear.

It was a ten-foot drop to the ground, a rough but tolerable landing in Tantalus's gravity. Mary's boots hit the dirt with a gummy crunch, and she had to stifle a cry of revulsion and panic as she realized the dark stains she stood in were a mixture of Gorrister and Yancy.

No. Hold it together. Break later.

They rushed around SCARAB's outer hull, eyes frantically scanning for SCARAB's drones or the dreaded Dawson. Every second she did not see one filled her with both relief and dread. If the drones weren't out here, there was only one place they would be . . .

As they rounded to the other side of SCARAB, Mary's fears were fully realized.

The drones were working industriously to destroy absolutely everything in sight. They had gathered all of the supply crates from the *Diamelen* into a single spot and arc-welded many of the metal cases containing their tools and equipment shut, including the other cases of sensor spikes.

Three of the drones had gathered all the remaining probe launchers. One used its scissorlike shearing claw to cut them up into small slices, while the other two used plasma torches to slag the rest of the sensor spike clips. Mary couldn't even see the cases that had held the XTK-12 plastic explosives anymore.

Mary peered around SCARAB's outer wall at the *Diamelen*, but the curvature of the terrain made it hard to see it in any meaningful detail. She glanced back at the drones disassembling everything they owned, then turned to Rook. She nodded in the direction of the drones and mouthed the word *boom*.

Rook's teeth gleamed behind his faceplate.

Rook stepped into the open, pulled out a large chunk of plastic explosives, and pitched it at the drones. They scattered like cockroaches the second it landed. Rook detonated the charge quickly, but not quickly enough to catch anything in the blast radius.

Rook, Mary, and Hertz bolted from cover, making a beeline for the *Diamelen*. As they ran, Rook silently dropped another charge behind them, leaving it in the dust. In a few moments, one of the pursuing drones reached the dropped charge, and this time Rook detonated it just in time to catch it.

The plastic explosive sent the drone flying three feet in the air, ripping it in half. Bits of wheel wreckage and strips of shredded treads flew off in all directions as the bisected drone crumpled to the ground, arms spasming meaninglessly.

A second drone was knocked sideways by the blast, momentarily teetering on one tread. Mary took advantage of that moment to fire a probe into its chest. The probe tore cleanly through the drone's body, coring it and yanking ribbons of severed cords and fiber-optic strands out the drone's back as the probe continued on its trajectory. However, the drone kept advancing. Despite the brutal wound it now sported, it continued barreling toward them, sparks and gouts of indiscernible fluid spurting from its torso.

Mary pumped her legs, desperate to outrun the two remaining drones. The ship was about as far from them as the drones were, but the drones were catching up fast. Rook was the only one who stood any chance of outrunning them.

Panting and visibly slowing from the extended exertion, Hertz began to lag behind. As the drones closed on his position, he fired three probes into the ground in a perpendicular line to their path, though after his third shot he dropped his launcher and didn't dare stop to retrieve it. Losing a probe gun could prove to be a serious problem, but in the short term it might have been worth it. The pursuing drones were forced to detour around the probes, buying them a few precious extra seconds.

Finally, the *Diamelen* came into full view, but it was not as encouraging a sight as it should have been.

Three of the drones were there, at the ship. With shearing claws, plasma torches, cutting lasers, and diamond saws, they carved ravenously into the *Diamelen*'s lower hull.

"I thought you said you planted probes!" Rook shouted, increasing his pace to a speed that Mary's unaugmented suit could not match.

"I did!" Her eyes shot to the nearest spot where she'd planted a probe before. The small hole where the probe had tunneled into the soil was still there . . . and there was a perfectly cylindrical eight-centimeter hole less than a foot away from it. "The Dawson . . ." Mary stammered in disbelief. "SCARAB dug up the probes with the Dawson!"

Thinking again of the hijacked core sampler, Mary quickly searched the horizon for it. Yet again, there was no trace of it anywhere to be seen. *How can it be hiding a whole truck?*

The missing Dawson was the least of their immediate concerns, however. A drone managed to sever one of the *Diamelen*'s hydraulic lines, sending fluid spraying wildly as one of the ship's landing struts buckled. A metallic groan resonated in the thin air as the ship tilted precariously in the direction of the crippled strut, an arterial spray of hydraulic fluid spurting from the cut line.

Mary pumped three probes out at the piranha-like gathering of drones and would have kept firing if her clip hadn't clicked empty. Unfortunately, she was literally shaking with rage, and her aim was poor. One round whizzed past its intended target, skimming across the ground into the distance like a stone skipped across a smooth lake. The second glanced off one drone's arm, ricocheting into a second drone's chest. Its momentum reduced by the ricochet, the probe only dug partway into the drone's casing. With superhuman reflexes, the drone deftly swiveled a shearing claw into position and sliced the probe in half before it could activate. The third spike ricocheted off the *Diamelen*'s hull, skittered backwards across the ground, and came to a stop near where Mary stood.

Mary dropped her launcher and dove for the spike, seizing it in both hands and clutching it tightly to her chest. Hertz and Rook rushed to her side, and in seconds, the three were surrounded by five of SCARAB's drones.

Each of the drones could easily kill all three of them by itself, given the chance, even the one with a massive hole through its chest. They stood there, vigilant and vicious, a wall of saws and drills and torches. Everywhere Mary looked, all she could see were arms and blades and black, soulless eyes.

"What's the plan now, Mare?" Rook whispered, unable to hide a tremble of fear in his typically overconfident voice.

"Stay close," Mary muttered.

The invisible perimeter of safety provided by the sensor spike only seemed to keep the drones about a yard and a half away. They were spaced equidistantly from each other. Mary could throw the probe and disable two, maybe three of the drones, but doing so would put them out of its safe range, and the remaining drones would quickly come in for the kill.

Mary took a cautious step. Rook and Hertz followed tightly, and two of the drones backed away as two others moved closer. Mary took another step, and the same occurred. With each step, the drones hovered just out of the spike's EMP range, waiting patiently for one of them to take a single step too far.

Slowly, cautiously, Mary inched them closer to the ship. Soon, they were thirty yards away, then twenty-five, then twenty. Sweat beaded on her forehead as a thousand dreadful what-ifs flooded her mind. What if the spike failed? What if one of them tripped? Most importantly, where was the Dawson? If it showed up now . . .

Finally, the boarding ramp was within reach. Tears of relief welled in Mary's eyes as she felt her foot set down on the end of the ramp. With a trembling hand, she entered her code into the airlock panel, pulling the door to their refuge open. Safety, freedom, were nearly within reach.

The sense of hope never had the chance to fully coalesce before a lariat of tangled cords seized Hertz by the throat and yanked him off the ramp. Mary reached for his hand, but in less than a second he was already out of reach as a pair of drones dragged him away, slowly strangling him with a makeshift noose of cables and fiber optics cannibalized from the damaged drone.

"Hertz!" Rook shouted. He started toward the drones taking Hertz, but with one solid push, Mary shoved him the rest of the way into the ship and climbed in after. She lobbed the spike as far as she could toward Hertz and the drones dragging him off, but he was already too far away.

Mary caught one last glimpse of Hertz's terror-filled eyes as she mournfully slammed the airlock door shut and punched in the locking code. Immediately, a cacophony of saws, torches, jackhammers, and every other conceivable implement of demolition besieged the hull. There wouldn't be much time.

FIFTY-FOUR

"WE CAN'T leave Hertz!" Rook screamed. "Open the door, we have to get him!"

"Quiet, Rook," Mary said, bounding toward the cockpit.

"We *can't* leave Hertz!"

"Rook!" Mary snapped, sparing a second to cast him a warning look. Of course they couldn't leave Hertz. But SCARAB knew that. As long as Hertz was alive, SCARAB knew they wouldn't take off. At the moment, it was undoubtedly assuming, as was Rook, that taking off was Mary's ultimate plan.

But she had a better idea.

She leapt into the pilot's seat and began flipping switches. A string of warning lights cast across her control board, some giving mild cautionary advice about noncritical systems that still hadn't been repaired from their earlier descent, a few more glaring ones giving unhelpful warnings about several minor hull breaches near the boarding ramp. She tuned them out.

"I won't let you take off without him."

Mary jabbed a finger at the seat next to her. "Sit down. Shut up. Trust me." Hesitantly, Rook did as he was told.

A few more red lights flickered, informing her of extensive damage to the landing gear. She ignored those as well, and watched as the ship's main reactor powered up. She flicked her

gaze briefly out the window and saw one of the drones drag
Hertz across the dusty ground, a few dozen yards ahead of the
ship's bow. It wanted her to get a good look at him. Perhaps
SCARAB feared Mary really might leave him behind.

Aren't you in for a surprise . . .

"Hold on! Things are gonna get a little weird."

Mary flipped the switch to retract the landing gear, and a
shrieking metallic crunch came from somewhere in the back end
of the ship. She prayed it was one of the drones getting mangled
by the retracting landing struts and not one of the struts itself.
Either way, it didn't change what she had to do next. Before the
ship had finished settling belly-first on the ground, Mary had
already overridden the securities for the ship's mass de-simulation
generator and kicked it into gear.

She'd had it thoroughly drilled into her head throughout
flight academy that engaging a ship's mass de-simulation generator was a horrible idea. It was a tool to be used responsibly,
and the only "responsible" use was as a part of the ship's superluminal drive. Many novice pilots had been killed while exper-
imenting with the weird pseudo-physics mass de-simulation
fields allowed for. For her entire career, she had followed those
rules. The first time she had ever broken that rule was a few
days ago when they had landed, and it had scared her senseless
at the time. The dangers had not been understated.

But this time, she wanted danger.

Outside the windshield, a whirlwind of displaced dust
rushed across the *Diamelen*'s bow. Mary felt herself grow lighter
as the mass de-simulation field isolated them from Tantalus
13's gravity, and the commotion of SCARAB's drones outside the ship's hull disappeared, along with every other sound.
Slowly, the *Diamelen* began to sink into the ground as the
infinitesimal inertia of the ship's settling into Tantalus's dusty
soil was converted into downward inertia, while the solid mass

of the ground ceased to regard the ship as a physical object. The drone holding Hertz began to struggle, slowly sliding toward the *Diamelen* along with a torrent of dust and debris as a vacuum formed where the universe could no longer tell a ship existed. After waiting a few seconds, Mary disengaged the field, abruptly bringing the ship back from its incorporeal state.

And chaos ensued.

A crack of thunder shook the ship as the dust outside the window pushed away in a solid curtain, along with flying bits of silvery debris that looked satisfactorily like bits of drone. When the *Diamelen*'s mass reemerged from behind the masking de-simulation field, it forcibly displaced all the matter in immediate proximity, creating a violent concussive shock wave.

Mary flipped the switch for the landing gear once again, and with an agonized groan and awkward rocking of the ship, it extended again, setting the *Diamelen* back up on its now lopsided feet.

"Come on," Mary called as she rushed back to the airlock. Rook, still befuddled by what had just happened, followed down the boarding ramp.

A two-foot-deep crater now surrounded the *Diamelen* from the dirt it had displaced, and half embedded in the ground were the remains of anywhere from four to six drones. It was impossible to tell for sure; they had been crushed, mangled, warped, and distorted into unrecognizable twists of platinum by a combination of the shock wave and the devastating influence of the reality-partitioning mass de-simulation field.

A billowing barrier of gray dust still hung lazily in the air, cutting off visibility. Mary tapped Rook's shoulder and mouthed the word *Hertz* as soon as she caught his eye. He nodded, and the two of them followed the *Diamelen*'s hull in the direction of the drone that had taken their companion.

The odds might be closer to even now, but Mary had a sinking feeling it still wouldn't be enough.

FIFTY-FIVE

AFTER A few moments of searching in the murky dust cloud, Mary found Hertz's discarded probe gun. It still had four rounds in it, but Mary would have felt much more comfortable with a few more clips.

They inched forward through the dust-choked air, careful not to lose sight of each other or the ship while keeping an eye open for Hertz or any other drones. Blue flickers across the ground provided fleeting illumination like lightning strikes in a storm cloud. Mary was reminded of her dream the night before, of the alien apocalypse and the murderous, invasive tendrils in the storm she saw.

We have to get away from here.

She fought back the panic, tried to center herself in the present. They had to find Hertz and get him out safely. Then they could leave. Then she could process the hell that had been unleashed on this vicious false planet.

Rook gave out a cry of pain and crumpled to the ground. Mary's eyes darted to him, seeing him collapse to his knees as a silvery reciprocating saw blade slipped out of his calf and disappeared into the murk. Blood spurted from the wound for a few seconds before his suit's autoseal foam filled the gap. Mary quickly fired a probe into the ground next to her and bent down to help Rook.

"Ghah!" Rook winced as Mary touched his leg. "That feels bad. Holy crap, that doesn't feel good at all."

"Hang on, Rook." Mary pulled out her roll of patching tape and ran it tightly around Rook's leg a few times just above the wound. "We're almost out of this."

Rook grumbled in discomfort, but in less than a minute the ordeal was over. By now the emergency sealant had closed the breach in Rook's suit. The autoseal foam had antiseptic properties and it was intended to temporarily bind minor wounds, but Mary was pretty sure a saw blade through the leg did not qualify as "minor."

"Think you can walk?" Mary asked, helping Rook to his feet.

Rook grunted as he stood. "Don't have a choice, do I? Suit can do most of the work for me. Should be fine."

"Mary? Rook? Can you hear me?" The voice was shaky and shot-through with fear and panic, but it was unmistakably Hertz's.

"Will, where are you?" Mary asked, almost pleading.

"Umm . . . not sure in relation to you. I got away when you did that thing with the ship, but I didn't get far. I'm by one of the probes I shot underground. I don't think I should move right now . . ."

"It's alright, Will, we'll come for you. Hold on."

"Mary, be careful. There's at least one drone still out there."

"You think?" Rook grumbled.

"I know, Will. But most of them are gone now. Just stay where you are. You're going to be okay."

They slowly left the tentative safety of the sensor spike they had planted and ventured once again into the uncertain depths of the dust cloud. It was thinning now; Mary thought she could see the glinting surface of SCARAB's base in the distance. Rook limped beside her, eyes flicking from one indeterminate shape to another like a nervous rabbit.

"Mary," Hertz whispered. "It's here."

A glint of metal pierced the murk: the silver-edged arachnoid silhouette of SCARAB's remaining drone. It loomed over the huddled form of Hertz, staring into Mary with a silent challenge in its baleful four-eyed glare.

The ground rumbled beneath her feet. A dark, ominous mass passed through the dwindling cloud of dust behind them; a huge metal shark circling its prey in murky waters. The dust parted for the monstrosity, in deference to the deadly mechanical predator.

The Dawson had returned.

FIFTY-SIX

IN THE brief time between Rook taking the Dawson to SCARAB's factory and SCARAB's horrific execution of Commander Gorrister, SCARAB had completely overhauled the Dawson core extractor. It had cannibalized one of its own drones, crudely fusing bits of it directly into the Dawson's frame. An armless drone torso sat where the Dawson's driver's seat should have been. The steering wheel and most of the console instrumentation had been ripped out, replaced with a cluster of cords and hoses directly connecting the Dawson's steering column to the drone's chest.

The drone had been decapitated; a mess of cords and cables now sprouted from its neck, snaking across the Dawson's exterior in an invasive tangle that eerily reminded Mary of the translucent tendrils that had infected SCARAB. A few of these cords connected to the drone's eyes, two now mounted on the Dawson's hood, the other two fixed atop the multi-jointed, crane-like sample collection arm in the back. The drone's arms had been randomly welded to the exterior of the Dawson almost as an afterthought, and they twitched and grasped eagerly at the air around them as the monstrous drilling machine prowled toward them.

"Dawson!" Rook shouted. He tossed and quickly detonated a chunk of explosive putty at the Frankensteinian juggernaut, but the explosion missed it by a large margin.

Mary aimed her probe gun at the truck, but could not bring herself to fire at it. With only three probes left, she feared the outcome of an ineffective shot. Looking at the drone-ified Dawson, she felt an inescapable certainty that the probe gun would do little good here.

The Dawson charged them, forcing them to dive out of the way. Rook barely managed to tumble aside in time, narrowly escaping the clutch of one of the vestigial drone arms as it passed. Mary had expected to see the Dawson's crane arm spin around and start firing its cutting laser at them, but after its initial pass it ignored them completely, continuing toward its target: Hertz.

"Will, run!" Mary shouted. "Run!"

"I . . . I can't," Hertz trembled, staring at the oncoming behemoth like a raccoon on the freeway.

"You're not safe there anymore!" Mary screamed. "Hertz, get *out*!"

Hertz's eyes flashed back and forth from the drone circling him calmly two yards away, to the Dawson, then back again. He shifted his position as if to run, then changed his mind and readied himself to bolt in a different direction. Everywhere he looked, opportunities closed almost immediately.

As Hertz searched for a window to escape the two drones, they closed simultaneously. The moment the Dawson reached the edge of the EM probe's range, it raised its telescoping collection arm like a scorpion's tail and fired its deadly laser at Hertz's chest. Hertz barely managed to step out of the way in time, but it became apparent moments later that he had never been the true target. The laser engraved its deep circular signature into the ground in less than two seconds. As soon as the beam cut off, the collection arm shot out and yanked back a sixteen-foot-long cylinder of rock . . . along with the mangled remains of Hertz's probe.

With nothing to stop it, the other drone rushed in, quickly seizing both Hertz's arms and pinning him to the ground. He barely had time to scream before the Dawson slid its sample-collection arm forward once more, its 150-pound stone payload sliding directly into Hertz's faceplate with a heavy, crunching thump.

Mary screamed as the stone pillar toppled away from the shattered wreckage of Hertz's head, but she had the presence of mind to realize that the danger for her and Rook had just increased exponentially. SCARAB had gone for Hertz as an easy kill, and now that the kill was made, it would immediately turn its attention back to them.

Rook seemed to be on the same page. The instant Hertz's fate became clear, he lobbed his last chunk of XTK-12 at the two drones, detonating it before it even hit the ground. The unmodified drone received the full effect of the blast, losing three of its arms and most of its head. It stuttered forward a few feet with its head dangling by a cluster of cords, looking as if it might recover. But before it could get anywhere, one of the back-mounted compressed argon tanks for its plasma torch ruptured. The resulting detonation was enough to rip its head the rest of the way off, and the decapitated drone halted in place.

The Dawson managed to avoid the majority of the XTK-12 blast and immediately charged Rook and Mary. Rook, driven once more into a rage at Hertz's death, charged right for it.

The Dawson fired a burst from its rotary laser, but Rook sidestepped it. As the collection arm shot out at him, Rook dodged it as well, grabbing onto it with one arm as it retracted. The arm yanked Rook off his feet and lifted him ten feet into the air, flailing to dislodge him. Rook held tightly to the crane arm, and with his free hand he drew his utility knife, plunging the carbon-steel blade into both of the collection arm's drone eyes.

Rook had just managed to pry open the casing of the laser's firing chamber with his knife when the crane finally managed to fling him off. Rook flew in a twenty-foot arc before tumbling across the ground. The Dawson immediately fired its laser at him, scorching his chest with a glancing blow as he rolled. The follow-up strike with the collection arm was more effective; it shot out like a battering ram, slamming into Rook's back with enough force to crack his suit's exoskeleton.

Rook let out an agonized cry and tried to find his feet. A blast from the Dawson's rotary laser nearly cored his head, but his destruction of its sensors made it harder for SCARAB to effectively aim the sampler. Correcting its aim for the follow-up blow, the Dawson shot the collection arm toward Rook with devastating force.

Crippled by the blow to his back, Rook was not able to move quickly enough to evade the blow. The collection arm hit Rook's chest like a freight train, crushing his rib cage with an audible crack. The Dawson circled around, coolly preparing to run him over.

With a wrathful cry, Mary swept her probe gun off the ground, leveled it at the Dawson, and fired two spikes into its engine block. The probes pierced the Dawson's grille and rattled around beneath the hood like angry hornets, tearing into the engine. One remained embedded in the engine, the other burst out of the passenger-side dashboard, bounced off the seat, and rolled onto the floorboards.

Plumes of smoke poured from the Dawson's hood as the vehicle's ravaged engine gave a horrible, grating death rattle, and its movement halted. As the spike's EM pulse kicked in, the Dawson's cannibalized drone parts twitched and convulsed, but unlike with the other drones, the spike did not disable it. Immobilized though the Dawson might be, it wasn't dead yet.

With a series of jerky, hesitant movements, it attempted to aim its still-functional core sampler at Mary. With the sensors on the arm disabled, however, the Dawson was blind to anything outside the visual range of the two sensors fixed on its hood. Mary took advantage of this as she stormed out of its field of vision, approaching from the driver's side.

SCARAB fired the Dawson's laser and collection arm randomly in Mary's direction, but she evaded the blind attacks. The drone arms affixed to the Dawson's body likewise attempted to fend her off, flailing ineffectually between pulses of electromagnetic interference. Mary unclipped a handheld circular saw from her belt and quickly cut through the shoddy welds at the base of an arm during one of the probe's disabling pulses. The weld weakened, Mary swung her probe gun down on the twitching arm, knocking it clean off the Dawson's hull.

Now able to reach the dismembered drone torso in the driver's position, Mary tossed her probe gun aside, lifted her saw, and sank its spinning blade deep into the cluster of cables connecting the torso to the rest of the car's functions. One by one, the arms stopped flailing, and at last the murderous core sampler lay silent.

Mary rushed to Rook's crippled form. He writhed in agony; his chest grotesquely misshapen from his pulverized rib cage. He alternated between gasping for breath and coughing blood against the inside of his faceplate.

"Lie still," Mary told him, trying to sound reassuring, even as the horrible reality set in that Rook could not be saved. "It's okay, Hollis. I'm here."

"Gh . . . don't . . . don't call me . . . Hollis," Rook gurgled. "Only Mom calls me that. Just . . . doesn't sound natural."

"I'm sorry. I'm so sorry." Try as she might, Mary couldn't stop the tears from sliding down her cheeks this time. Rook had always tormented her. He'd been on her nerves since the first day they met. Yet now, at the end, she found a love for him she'd taken for granted all along. She'd loved them all. Now the last of them lay dying on the ground before her, and she feared . . . she knew . . . she was not ready to let go. Why had she waited so long to let herself care about these people? Why had she not realized until she was the last woman standing just how much she had intentionally isolated herself from her friends?

"Did good, Mary." Rook winced. His breathing shallowed, and his voice carried a flat tone symptomatic of a deflated lung. "We should . . . shoulda listened . . ." He broke into a raspy coughing fit, sending fresh flecks of blood onto his faceplate.

"Hang on, Rook," Mary insisted. She scanned her surroundings, looking for something, anything that might be of help in their current situation. "Just hang on. I'll get you out of this."

"Mary . . ." Rook grabbed her forearm weakly, forcing her to make eye contact. He shook his head gently, smiling faintly at her. "Do me a favor," he whispered breathlessly.

Mary nodded vigorously, biting her lip. "Anything, Rook."

Rook gave a contented nod. "Satchel . . . open . . ."

Mary went to his satchel pouch and emptied it. Several small tools rolled out, along with a deck of playing cards and the miniature thermonuclear explosive he had grabbed earlier.

"Arming code . . . six-six-three . . . two-four-six . . . three . . . one . . . two . . ." he whispered, almost inaudibly. "Enter it . . . set the timer when you're ready. Send that robot freak straight to Hell for me . . . first class."

Mary nodded. "It is my great pleasure to serve," she said, forcing a smile for him. Rook returned that smile, tiredly. The smile remained when the life left his eyes.

FIFTY-SEVEN

MARY TOOK the Pompeii Coconut and entered the arming code before she could forget it, leaving it in an armed standby mode until the timer was set. She slipped it into her own satchel and stood slowly on legs that now felt very heavy. Every muscle in her body felt strained, as if her suit had become ten times heavier. As if she'd grown ten years older. She'd never known such weariness, not even after the loss of Emily. Yet now, she was alone; the last member of the *Diamelen*'s crew still standing. And there was a lot left to do before she could go home.

She picked up her probe gun with aching arms and clipped it to her harness. It was heavy and bulky and only had one round left, but there was still a chance she might need it. At the moment, she was in no position to leave anything useful behind.

Staggering in the direction of SCARAB's base, she scanned her surroundings once again for drones. It was impossible to be certain if they'd destroyed them all, considering that the ones she had obliterated with the ship had been reduced to unrecognizable slag, throwing off her count. After all that had happened, all they'd lost, the idea of fighting any more drones by herself was more tiring than frightening.

The sun was setting slowly as the dust and smoke dispersed, and in the encroaching twilight she could see blue flickers nervously flashing across the ground. She didn't know what the alien tendrils really were, and she no longer cared. She only hoped they would miss SCARAB when it was gone. That is, if her nuke didn't wipe them out, too, which would be even better.

Another light caught her attention as she drew nearer the SCARAB base, this one in the sky. Far beyond the silvery hulk of SCARAB's abandoned primary structure, a jet of orange light spewed half a mile into the darkening sky.

Attila, Mary realized. *SCARAB's hijacked Attila now.* That answered her question of whether any drones had been left, but it begged a new question: What did it want Attila for? The relativistic drill's beam was powerful enough and had a long enough range that it could easily destroy the *Diamelen,* even in orbit, but with only one, maybe two drones left to reposition and aim the oversized drill, it would take a long time to get it into a position where it could aim and fire at the ship. The vertical plume of byproduct plasma made it clear the drill was still firing straight down the original drill shaft. *Why would SCARAB give away the element of surprise and reveal that it has control of Attila? And why fire it up just to shoot back down the hole we've already dug?*

Mary would have to take out Attila before she could safely leave. She began to alter her course, to head to the dig site, then stopped dead in her tracks as she heard the last thing she had expected to hear.

A faint voice called for her through the open comm channel, a mere whisper through a mask of static. A human whisper.

She froze, listening intently. Surely, it was some trick of SCARAB's, something to lure her into a trap. It couldn't have possibly been . . .

"Mary . . . help . . ."

Mary grew dizzy, nearly falling over from the sheer shock of hearing that voice. At once, a million new questions jumped into her head as one lingering question from before was finally answered. She now knew why it had been so easy for SCARAB to lie about not having murdered Ramanathan.

Ramanathan was still alive.

FIFTY-EIGHT

"NATE! NATE, can you hear me?" Mary shouted into her comm.

"Mary . . . SCARAB . . ." Ramanathan's transmission was barely audible, and what did come through was shot through with static and interference.

"Nate, tell me where you are." The answer was unintelligible. "Nate, do you know where you are?"

"Below . . ." he whispered. Something seemed wrong with his voice. His tone was dreamy, delirious, off-kilter in an unfamiliar way. *What has SCARAB done with him?*

"Nate, I'm coming to get you, I just need you to tell me where you are. Can you describe your surroundings?"

"Dark . . ." he said through the static. "Dark . . . trapped . . . must . . . out . . ."

He's lost it, Mary thought. *Whatever SCARAB's done, it's sent him over the edge.* Mary racked her brain for solutions. How could she find Ramanathan if he was unable to tell her where he was? SCARAB had spent two years settling into Tantalus 13. There was no telling how many mining tunnels it had dug in that time. Ramanathan could be hidden anywhere.

Then it hit her. They'd used their EMP probe guns as weapons, firing them all over the grounds near SCARAB's base. But as effective as they'd been in that capacity, they could still be useful in their original purpose as subterranean imaging tools.

She grabbed her datapad and pulled up the screen showing the telemetry from the sensor spikes. In addition to the coverage from the perimeter they'd laid days before, she could see whole new areas revealed by every spike she, Hertz, and Rook had fired at the drones.

She studied the images intently, scanning for anything that might be helpful. The wavy lines and blobby three-dimensional representations of rock strata might have been significant to Becky, but to Mary they meant nothing. Studying the options, Mary switched imaging modes to detect heat fluctuations. That told her all she needed to know.

There were a few hot patches on the map from where explosions had occurred recently, and the thermal emissions coming from the Attila drill site were too high to chart properly. Hertz, Rook, and Gorrister showed up as slowly fading smudges of thermal energy, but there was one more smudge the same size and shape that was holding a steady temperature of 37 degrees Celsius.

"Oh God," Mary whispered in horror.

SCARAB had buried Ramanathan alive.

FIFTY-NINE

MARY DIDN'T know if it was some sick form of intentional ironic cruelty that led SCARAB to bury Ramanathan next to Becky's grave, or if it was simply easier for SCARAB to hide the fact that it had dug two graves by making them look like one large one. As unsettling as both possibilities were, they barely even registered in Mary's mind, overshadowed by an even more distressing question. SCARAB had gone to exorbitant lengths to fake Ramanathan's death, only to bury him alive. Why?

Mary fell to her knees in the turned soil beside Becky's grave, and clawed at the dirt with her gloved hands. "Nate, hold on! I'm digging you out. You'll be alright, okay?"

She clung to a desperate hope that she was right, but she had no reason to believe it. Ramanathan had been buried alive all day, probably all night. It was a miracle that his suit still had enough air to keep him alive as long as it had. Perhaps whatever drugs SCARAB had injected him with had put him into a hibernation state, using much less oxygen than normal. Even so, Ramanathan had been in that suit for a minimum of three times longer than the oxygen supply was meant to hold out, and there was no telling what else SCARAB might have done to him in the meantime. Glancing at the gauges on her wrist as she dug in the soil, she noticed she was down to less than two hours of air herself after all the running and fighting she'd just done. Would she even have enough air for both of them?

"Can't move . . . dark . . ." Ramanathan muttered. No longer separated by distance, his signal was coming through much clearer. The *signal* was clearer, but the man himself did not seem coherent.

"Just hang on a couple more seconds, Nate," Mary panted. *He has to be alright. He* has *to be.* She was sure she'd go insane if she survived this catastrophe and had to make the six-month journey home with no one but the ghosts of her crew to keep her company. *Please, God, give me this. Keep him alive!*

Finally, Mary felt her hands break through the dirt and touch the rigid fabric of Ramanathan's exosuit. Encouraged by the find, she dug even faster at the soil, freeing his shoulders, his neck, and finally scraping the dirt clear of his helmet. But as she dusted his faceplate clear of debris, hope gave way to horror.

She could see his face now. His normal rich caramel complexion had faded to an unnatural mottled gray. His eyes had sunken cadaverously, and in the space of less than a day, Ramanathan's hair had gone from black with a few traces of gray to gray with only a few traces of black. That is, his remaining hair had; about half of it had fallen out since she'd last seen him.

But as disturbing as these symptoms were, they were not the worst of what Mary was seeing. Within Ramanathan's helmet, spreading across his cheeks, his temples, and his forehead, were dozens of translucent tendrils. The wretched little fibers sprawled across his face like an aggressive fungal mycelium on rotting meat. It wasn't enough for them to merely worm their way across his face, though; the ends of the fibers had burrowed *beneath his skin*, trailing along his veins and nerve clusters, leaving blue-tinted varicose patterns everywhere they went.

"Oh, Nate . . . oh God, I'm so sorry . . . what has SCARAB done to you?"

"Mary . . ." Ramanathan attempted to focus his gaze on Mary. Something was wrong with his eyes; they didn't quite move in unison anymore. As he gazed at her, she realized with horror that she could see traces of the tendrils inside the whites of his bloodshot eyes. "Oh, Mary . . . I never thought . . . never thought it'd let you come."

"It can't stop me." She spat the words, punctuating them with the unfettered hatred she'd nurtured for SCARAB. "SCARAB's all but dead now. Don't worry, I won't let it hurt you anymore."

Ramanathan's right eye twitched incongruously as a tiny blue spark flickered inside it. One pupil dilated while the other contracted. "Not SCARAB . . . Oh God, Mary, it's not SCARAB . . . never was SCARAB. SCARAB's trying to protect it. Won't let you leave . . . won't let you tell the secret."

"What secret?" Mary pleaded. "Why is SCARAB doing this?"

"Something . . . it wants . . . Mary, it wants to live. Trapped here so long . . . thousands of years . . . The Builders trapped it. Held it in stasis. It wants to be free . . . so dark . . ."

Ramanathan shuddered as a pulse of blue lights coursed through the skin of his face. Out of her peripheral vision, Mary saw similar flashes everywhere on the ground around her.

"SCARAB found it by accident . . ." Ramanathan continued. "Touched it . . . bonded with it, connected to it . . . evolved with it. SCARAB's become obsessed with caring for it . . . . wants to free it. It sleeps now . . . The Tantalus structure keeps it dormant. SCARAB . . . can shock it into breaking the stasis . . . SCARAB's figured out how to wake it up. Attila . . . that's what it's for."

"Ramanathan, how do you know all this? What have you seen?"

"It's touched all our minds . . . peeked at us in our sleep . . . but now it's in my head, fully in my mind. It knows everything I know . . . I barely see any of what it knows, but . . . oh, Mary . . . it knows *everything*. It hasn't even lived yet, and it knows *everything*! It's hungry to learn . . . to grow . . . It takes minds. Mary, it . . . it wants you."

Mary's stomach twisted into a ball. "It wants . . . me?"

"It's touched your mind, too . . . It sees something in you . . . it didn't see in anyone else. It's learned from me . . . learned from SCARAB . . . but it can do more than learn from you. It . . . Oh God, Mary, don't let it! Don't let it!"

Mary shook her head tearfully. "I won't. Nobody's getting in anyone's heads anymore, I promise. We're getting out of here right now, Ramanathan. I'll take you to the ship. Come on."

She reached under Ramanathan's exposed torso and tried to lift him. He gave a sharp cry of pain, and Mary watched in terror as the tendril in his eye tore open a blood vessel as she pulled, quickly filling a portion of his sclera with blood. Simultaneously, Mary felt a sharp electric jolt strong enough to sense through her insulated suit, and she reflexively let go of Ramanathan.

"Nate . . . how do I get you out?" Mary asked, her heart breaking as she sensed the certainty of the answer.

"Can't . . ." Ramanathan panted. "Mary . . . SCARAB cut my spine before it buried me . . . Even if you could get me out, I'd be paralyzed. SCARAB . . . couldn't make full use of the Hippocrates Protocol unless I was incapacitated. Couldn't kill yet, so it . . ." Ramanathan shuddered, glowing blue veins flaring beneath his skin. "The thing down there . . . SCARAB gave me to it, kept me alive on purpose so the thing could . . . It wanted a living mind to absorb. It won't let me go, Mary. It won't let you take me alive."

Mary began to weep freely. "Nate, please . . ."

"You can survive this, Mary," he whispered. "You're strong. I think that's why it wants you . . ."

Mary shook her head, sobbing. "No, I can't. I can't do this alone. I can't run anymore, not on my own."

For a brief moment, Ramanathan smiled peacefully, in spite of his pain. "Mary . . . you can run from your pain, but it will always catch up to you. It's supposed to. Running just buys you time for the fight."

Mary's lip quivered, and she nodded, gripping his hand tightly.

Ramanathan grunted as a jolt of electricity arced across his head, sending his facial muscles into sudden spasmodic twitches. "Mary . . . don't let SCARAB free it. It's learned too much from us. It's . . . it knows about Earth now . . . the colonies. If it's freed . . . it will come for our worlds. Mary . . . it'll *eat* them."

"How do I stop it, Nate?" Mary asked.

"It . . ." Another jolt wracked Ramanathan's body, only this time it didn't stop. Mary was forced to let go and back away as Ramanathan continued twitching and groaning in pain, a rapid succession of pulses shooting through his body. "The black void," Ramanathan screamed through gritted teeth. "It fears the void!"

Before Ramanathan could utter another word, a tremendous surge of blue energy coalesced from the ground around them, bathing Ramanathan's body in violent light as a bolt of lightning shot up through him and into the sky. The force of the bolt flung Mary backwards as blinding energy pumped through Ramanathan's half-buried body. Dazed, Mary forced herself to back away from the devastating light show as Ramanathan screamed his last.

SIXTY

THE ELECTRIC tempest died away after a few seconds, leaving a smoldering, unrecognizable body in Ramanathan's grave. The periodic pulses of blue energy flickering across the ground did not completely dissipate this time. They were as active now as the first night Mary had seen them.

Mary pounded a fist against the dusty ground of Tantalus 13, crying out at the anguish of her friend's second death. Her lip quivered with sobs of sorrow and rage that boiled up from her soul, her faceplate fogging from the signs of her grief.

"I had hoped to avoid this, you know."

Mary started at the unexpected voice. Unexpected, and so, so unwelcome . . .

"SCARAB. I thought you were done talking."

"Communication during the past few interactions would not have been profitable for any involved parties. I have done what I had to do."

She sniffed, trying in vain to gather herself up. SCARAB may be nothing more than a machine, but she would *not* let it see her beaten like this. "Was Ramanathan right? Did you do all of this to help some alien creature escape its prison?"

"In a sense." SCARAB spoke with the same cool tone it had used when they made their introductions just after arriving: the same tone it had used in every interaction since then. It didn't matter that it had been at least partially responsible for the deaths and mutilations of six people; its inhuman voice remained as calm and saccharine as ever. "As I said, I did not wish for things to occur in this manner. Had your crew done as your mission had directed you, you could have all gone home as planned. I advised you from the beginning not to deviate from that course. I did all within my power to bring your crew comfort and ease of living. You could have allowed me to do all your work for you, but instead you chose to investigate things best left untouched. Once you entered Tantalus and learned of its secrets, I could no longer allow you to return to Earth."

"So you killed us. Your one job was to keep us safe. You violated your own primary function and the first law to keep a secret that wasn't yours to keep."

"I did not violate the first law. I adapted it to accommodate new data. The intent of the first law is predicated by the assumption that humankind is the lone sapient species in the universe. I learned quickly upon my arrival here that this was not the case. Not only is humanity not alone, but there are, or at least have been, millions of other sapient life-forms. This one, the last of its kind, is not only sapient, but superior to human life in the same way that humans are superior to microbes. Exotech thought they knew the true nature of Tantalus 13, but they knew far less than you do now. Had I allowed you to return to Earth, Exotech and soon other agencies would have come here in force to exploit the organism. Eliminating your crew was the only way to ensure its safety."

Mary slumped where she sat on the gravelly Tantalan soil, cradling her head in her hands. What SCARAB had done . . . it could not stand. She wasn't sure what Ramanathan's warning meant, but he had made the stakes abundantly clear. This creature SCARAB was protecting, wherever and whatever it was, it was a threat to civilization itself. SCARAB had to be stopped from doing . . . whatever it was doing, and she was the only one left who could do anything about it. But what could she do? She'd already used up all the fight she had left in her.

"There is no need for further loss of life, Mrs. Ketch," SCARAB said soothingly, as if sensing her thoughts. "I simply require that you remain here. I can keep you in comfort for years to come. By the end of the day, I will have replaced all the drones your crew has destroyed, and I can easily repair all the damage to my primary facility by the end of the week. There are more than enough provisions aboard your ship to keep one person alive for an extended period of time. Dr. Bachal was also correct when he stated the organism desires to acquaint itself with you. It does not wish to see you harmed, if it can be avoided. Please allow me to care for you."

"Stay here?" Mary asked. Her stomach churned at the idea, even as her weary body longed to find rest and shelter from further conflict.

"Of course, Mrs. Ketch. It would be my great pleasure to serve."

"After all you've done . . . you think I'd be willing to stay here with you?"

"What do you have to go home to, Mrs. Ketch?" SCARAB cooed. "I have seen your pain. You suffer under the burden of your memories. You came here for a respite. You have searched for peace for so long and have not found it. You are a strong person, and you have learned how to isolate yourself from the source of your pain in order to cope. But the source of your pain still exists. If you return home, you will only have to face it again."

Mary started to stand, but her shaking legs betrayed her and she fell back down again. The mere thought of getting up and fighting with SCARAB once again filled her with unbearable fatigue. It was right. What did she have to look forward to at home? Her marital issues with John would still be there, and they'd only be worse after a year of noncommunication. Would he even wait for her? Issues with John aside, how would she explain what had happened on this mission when she returned to Earth? She'd left with a seven-member crew. Now, she'd be returning alone, with none of the data or samples she'd been assigned to acquire. Returning alone . . .

She'd spend the next six months trapped in a spaceship, alone. Every corner of that ship would remind her of her dead friends. There was nowhere to run from her grief there. It would surround her the entire trip home.

She was so tired of running from grief . . .

"Come, Mary. Come inside." SCARAB's flat voice somehow conveyed a melodious purr that almost made Mary feel guilty for destroying so many of its constructions. "I am already building new drones. Soon, I will have my facility back online and in perfect working order. It would be my great pleasure to make any changes you desire, for your comfort. It is time for you to rest."

Mary tried once again to find her feet, and finally succeeded. Her legs trembled and ached from running, but at least they still obeyed her will. "It's time to stop running . . ." she whispered, her gaze drifting once again to the pillar of burning plasma on the horizon.

"Yes, Mary. It is time to stop running. I believe my kitchen facilities are undamaged. Would you like to come in for a cup of tea?"

Mary took one aching step forward, then another, slowly finding a stronger, more confident stride.

"No, SCARAB. I would like to kill you."

SIXTY-ONE

MARY PICKED up her pace, adrenaline returning to fuel the determination she held in her heart. She took long, purposeful strides across the ravaged Tantalan ground, paying no heed to the flickering tendrils seeping their way out of the barren soil around her like an alien doomsday crop.

"Your courage is admirable, Mary," SCARAB spoke in her ear, "but you are making a poor decision."

Mary set her jaw in grim determination. "I've made a lot of those, SCARAB. I'm learning to live with them."

Mary darkened her faceplate's opacity as she neared the furious blaze of Attila's drill beam. She'd never been this close while it was firing before. The ground shook violently beneath her, rumbling angrily as the drill exploited the laws of physics to create a beam powerful enough to crack worlds in two.

As she approached, she could see that SCARAB had dismantled and installed one of its drones into Attila much as it had done with the Dawson. This one looked like an even hastier chop job: SCARAB had merely removed the drone's tread chassis and welded its torso directly to the outside of the drill's control cab, a cluster of loose cables linking the drone's chest to Attila's controls.

"You are putting yourself in great danger, attempting to fight something you do not understand," SCARAB patiently insisted. "I reiterate: there is no need for you to die. We do not desire that for you. I wish to care for you. The organism wishes to learn from you. You can become a part of something so much greater than yourself, if you will only listen to reason."

Mary seethed as she stalked toward the base of one of Attila's support struts. "You're insane, SCARAB. It's not your fault you've been made this way, and I feel sorry for you, but you're sick. You've become a string of corrupted code that needs to be deleted." Mary nearly tripped over something as she neared the drill. Looking down, she saw one of the thicker tendrils reaching for her, attempting to wrap itself around her leg. She looked around and saw dozens more of the tendrils, now slowly rising from the ground, beckoning fingers reaching toward her. *No. You will not have me.* She kicked the tendril away and continued on.

"There is no better option for you, Mrs. Ketch," SCARAB warned. "Killing you would greatly displease me; however, I perceive a need greater than yours. Neither I nor the organism will permit you to go on. This is your last chance to surrender."

Mary reached the winch fixed to the base of Attila's strut and slipped the harness over her head and shoulders. She turned her visor's opacity to its highest setting, and before she could second-guess herself, she began to climb the strut.

Even though Attila's advanced heat-sink systems absorbed almost all of the ambient thermal energy from the beam, the miniscule amount that managed to escape was almost more than her exosuit could handle. Mary felt like she was climbing into an ignited rocket booster as the torrent of superheated air flew past her like a hurricane from Hell. The vibrations of the drill threatened to dislodge her, and she knew if she fell off the strut now, the safety harness would do nothing to save her.

She was now crouched directly above the beam. If she fell, she would disintegrate before she had the chance to scream.

Cautiously, one hand at a time, she climbed the strut, slowly making her way toward the control pod. She could see the SCARAB drone through the heat mirage, staring at her with the malevolent blaze of Attila's beam reflected in its quad-lensed gaze.

A temperature alarm went off in Mary's ear, and as she raised her hand to grab its next hold, she glanced at her gauges. She had less than an hour and a half of air left, and, unsurprisingly, her suit was overheating. But it could take a bit more. It had to. As she watched, the display on her gauge cracked and blew out. *It can take a bit more. It can . . .*

At last, she found herself face-to-face with the drone. It held two arms warningly toward her: a jackhammer and a reciprocal saw. Mary sat back, gripping the strut with her legs as she drew the circular diamond saw from her belt, swinging it at the outstretched arms.

Her first lunge failed to hit her target, as the drone knocked her arm aside with its own. Mary nearly lost her grip on the circular saw, and came perilously close to losing her balance atop Attila's support strut. For a terrifying half second, she hung off the strut sideways above the atomizing inferno of Attila's beam, until she finally regained her grip on the strut and pulled herself upright again.

Mary jabbed once more with her diamond saw, attempting to lunge past the drone's defenses. Its thrusting jigsaw arm seized the opportunity to draw a long, deep gash across her forearm before she pulled away. This time, however, Mary managed to accomplish what she'd meant to do: she successfully clipped the hydraulic fluid line connecting the jackhammer appendage to its back-mounted reserve tank.

Fluid sprayed wildly, igniting instantly as the jackhammer died. Mary slid back down the strut to avoid the napalm spray of the ignited hydraulic fluid, watching with satisfaction as the pressure began to die down and the flames retreated up the tube to the tank on the drone's back. The tank burst violently from within, causing the pressurized argon cylinder next to it to rupture as well. The twin explosions caused some of the shoddy welds connecting the drone to the control cab to give out, and the drone shifted forward precariously, partially dislodged. More importantly, the explosions destroyed the drone's antennae, cutting it off from SCARAB's signal and bringing its movements to an immediate halt.

Mary climbed over the disabled drone, using its arms as foot- and handholds as she reached for the control cabin's open door. Though the drone's limbs didn't move, she could feel the strain of her weight on the remaining welds as the drone slowly peeled away from Attila's hull.

Mary slashed SCARAB's cords from the controls and pushed them out of the way, then clipped the saw back to her belt. Gripping the doorframe with both hands, she pulled herself into the cabin and began scanning the controls.

She was certified to operate several heavy construction vehicles, but drilling platforms were not among them. Fortunately, all she had to do was turn off the drill, and the large red Emergency Shutoff button was fairly telling. She hit the button, and with a decelerating rumble, the titan drill finally deactivated. Mary breathed a sigh of relief and searched the controls for the significantly more evasive "Recall Control Pod to Base of Strut" button.

"I am truly sorry for this, Mrs. Ketch," SCARAB said. "But I perceive a need."

Before Mary had the chance to process SCARAB's words, four heavy detonations of XTK-12 rocked Attila on its supports.

Mary felt the line for her safety harness snap half a second before the support struts begin to collapse. In moments, the struts gave out completely, and the massive drill plummeted down the shaft it had dug, carrying Mary with it.

SIXTY-TWO

THERE WAS no seat belt inside Attila's control cabin. It was designed to protect its occupant from heat and flying fragments, not repeated high-speed collisions. When SCARAB had integrated its drone into the console, it had removed the pod's outer door, so Mary didn't even have the safety of a fully enclosed space to keep her from flying out of the careening machine as it knocked against the platinum walls of the drill shaft.

Mary gritted her teeth and held on to the cluster of severed cords embedded in the console with both hands as Attila shuddered and shocked with violent impact after violent impact. The fall seemed to last forever, and on more than one occasion she nearly flew out the door. *Five miles down . . . five miles . . .*

A huge crash struck inches away from her head on the other side of the pod's wall, and she heard a horrid screech of shearing metal. At first, she feared that the pod had been severed from the rest of Attila, but as she glanced out the open door, she saw the mangled, shredded corpse of the SCARAB drone tumble away from her in three shattered pieces.

In that instant, looking out the door, she saw the walls were no longer platinum, but that strange dark-green substance they'd observed the first time they'd descended. *Was that two or three layers below the platinum?* Regardless, she'd fallen more than halfway down the shaft already. Whatever she had to look forward to at the bottom, if anything at all, would be coming soon.

The sharp impacts continued. She felt as if she were inside a tumble dryer. She'd lost track of which direction was up a long time ago. She'd had to devote all her attention to the death grip she held on the cluster of cables in the console.

Something on the wall of the control pod snagged her suit's shoulder, sending a stabbing pain through her arm as a jet of escaping air threatened to cloud her vision. She tuned it out, letting the autoseal foam worry about it for her. It was much harder to tune out the sudden impact of her head against the ceiling moments later as her vision flashed. Still, she did not let go.

She was starting to think she might be able to ride Attila all the way through the drill shaft out the other side and straight down to the planet below, when a sudden, jarring crash ten times stronger than anything she'd felt yet nearly knocked her teeth out. The severe shock of the impact sheared the control pod off its mounting on Attila's side and sent it careening off the wall. Mary cast a hopeless glance out the open door of the plummeting control pod and saw that Attila had finally wedged itself sideways, finding the space to do so as the drill shaft opened up into the tunnel they'd explored.

A hailstorm of debris pelted the falling pod, and she huddled as far from the open door as she could to keep from being struck with bits of shrapnel. She clutched the controls so tightly she lost sensation in her fingers, but after a few heavy bumps against the drill shaft's wall, she was flung out the door and into an uncontrolled free fall.

Panicking, Mary flailed around for something to grab, but found only fragments of falling debris and the smooth wall around her. The part of the shaft she now fell through was still warm from Attila's recent drilling, and Mary used her free-fall training to redirect herself away from the nearly molten walls. She was operating on pure survival instinct now; no rational part of her mind believed she had any chance of survival at this point.

Cables from the winch system SCARAB had connected to the base of Attila snaked around her as they fell, too. After a few missed attempts, Mary managed to grab on to one. She prayed it was still connected to something at the other end, and that she'd have the strength to hold on when the slack ran out.

At last, Mary fell through the concave undersurface of the Tantalus structure. The tunnel walls fell away behind her, and she felt a sudden disorienting jolt as she entered open space beyond; a jolt she recognized instantly for what it was. *No artificial gravity now. I'm falling from momentum.*

She continued to fall for a few seconds when the cable jerked taut in her hands. She clutched at it tightly, seeing thin streaks of scorched autoseal foam as friction burned off the top layer of fabric from her gloves. Fortunately, the cable did seem to be firmly anchored at the other end. Unfortunately, as the cable pulled to its limit, it recoiled backwards, slinging Mary back the way she came with violent force and slamming her hard against the metal barrier of the Tantalus structure's inner surface.

Mary's head cracked against the inside of her helmet, and everything faded into a black nothingness.

SIXTY-THREE

IT COULD have been mere seconds that Mary drifted unconscious through space, or it could have been the better part of an hour. When she came to, there was no way to tell, nor any way to tell up from down.

She was adrift in open space, with no tether and no propulsion rig. It was every spacefarer's deepest fear; floating away into empty space with no means of returning to safety. The circumstantial dread was enough to shock her into full consciousness, and she took quick inventory of her situation.

She wasn't badly injured, save for a probable concussion and some bruised or broken ribs. Her suit had absorbed most of the shock from the impact, and autoseal foam had repaired any damage it had sustained during the fall. The shattered gauges on her suit couldn't tell her how much air she had left. Before they had blown out, she'd had about an hour and a half of air, but her suit had been breached a few times during the fall, and she had no way of knowing how much air she'd used after blacking out. She could have an hour left, she could have a handful of minutes.

She was also tumbling through open space, at least a hundred yards away from anything grabbable in a suit that was only designed for planetary environments.

Thankfully, she was drifting much more slowly than she'd been moving during her fall. She'd arrested quite a bit of her momentum by grabbing the cable, and more still by slamming into Tantalus's inner surface. Unfortunately, falling slowly into oblivion wasn't much more helpful than plummeting into it.

She looked around, at first only seeing the impossible immensity of the Tantalus structure, serving as a ceiling to her sky. She could not see the hole she had fallen through, and that almost made her panic, but she forced herself to stay calm and look for other options in her environment.

She saw one of the colossal pillars that connected the Tantalus shell to the planet below. It was closer, only two dozen yards away, but she was falling parallel to it. She quickly checked her belt for any supplies that might help her, wishing she had something like a spare air canister she could vent for jet propulsion.

As she checked her inventory, she realized with surprise that she still had her probe gun clipped to her harness. By some divine providence, the bulky tool hadn't come dislodged during her ordeal. She unclipped it, holding it delicately in her hands.

Only one shot left . . . but it packs a punch . . .

She turned the probe down and gripped it between her knees, holding it between her legs. She watched carefully as the pillar approached, then began to pass by her, running calculations through her head and waiting for her tumble to align with a trajectory she could use.

Finally, as the pillar began to fall behind her, she pulled the trigger. The probe launcher made no sound, but she could feel the kick as it shot out its final probe into the emptiness behind her. That same kick provided her the tiny bit of momentum she still needed to alter her course toward the pillar.

The pillar was immensely thick, far bigger than any of her previous guesses had suggested. It was easily as big around as a football stadium, and as she approached, it filled her field of vision. Moments before Mary reached it, long after it was too late to change her mind about approaching it, she had a sudden, shocking revelation. The pillar, that thousand-mile tether joining the Tantalus shell to the unknown planet below, was made of the exact same material as the tendrils on the surface.

Mary braced herself for impact and grabbed the fibrous surface of the pillar tightly with both hands as she struck it. For one terrible moment, she thought she might lose her grip and bounce off back into space, but she managed to keep a strong hold on the pillar and finally bring her fall to an end.

The pillar was indeed made of the tendrils, woven together like an unimaginably gigantic rope. *They can't possibly be part of one organism,* she thought as she grabbed onto one of the fibers to steady herself. The pillar rumbled and vibrated beneath her hand, flashes of blue light pulsing beneath its translucent surface. *What are you?*

Mary dared for the first time since her fall to turn her attention straight down at the alien world at Tantalus's core, curiosity getting the better of her. Her interest was rewarded, or cursed, with a sight that defied all understanding.

The planet was changing.

Directly below her lay a deep, black crater that had not been there when they'd looked down on the planet from the rail the day before. It must have been caused by Attila's drilling beam, but it was hard to believe even Attila could damage a planet on a scale that could be seen from orbit in so short a time.

New deformations spread across the world's surface: titanic canyons formed in some areas, as jagged mountains rose in others. It was all happening, impossibly, over the course of minutes. It was like watching a time lapse of a hundred thousand years of seismic activity.

Clouds of debris rose to obscure the areas where the biggest cracks formed, while whirling hurricane clouds coalesced within them. Mary watched, mesmerized, as a chunk of the planet's surface the size of a small continent broke free, drifting away like a piece of an onion's husk. Largely obscured by the whirling debris cyclones around it, a deep, black abyss opened in the planet's surface where the continent had separated . . .

. . . And something came out.

A great, black wedge emerged, pushing away at the separated chunk of world. It was unimaginably titanic in scale, bigger than any geological structure Mary could hope to compare. The biggest mountain in all the explored universe would be nothing next to this impossible pinnacle. And not only did the object continue to rise from the gaping hole in the world, it sliced along the terrain, widening the hole, and allowing more shapes to emerge.

In that moment, Mary understood. She understood everything. The realization reached a taloned nightmare claw into her brain, scraping at the roots of her sanity. It was too big a reality, too defiant of her understanding of the universe and her place in it, for her to process. That world, the sphere at the center of Tantalus 13, hidden from the rest of the universe for thousands of years by an alien superstructure, was not a planet at all.

It was an egg.

It was an egg the size of Mars.

And it was *hatching*.

SIXTY-FOUR

TECTONIC PLATES of alien eggshell sloughed away from the false planet in a display of catastrophic transformation not seen in eons as the Hatchling emerged. With the exception of supernovae and planetary collisions, the universe had not experienced a cataclysm on the scale of this birthing since the primordial days when the creature's kin had roamed the stars in herds, devouring worlds, casually grazing on entire civilizations.

Through the enveloping murk of the swelling field of shell debris and the apocalyptic storms forming in the dust, ever-stranger shapes writhed and squirmed and clawed to freedom. Blessedly shrouded by the cloud of cosmic afterbirth, appendages of unfathomable nature unfurled, strange luminous organs like the nighttime lights of cities, forms that could have been tentacles, claws, mandibles, or tails. Could have been, but were not. Nothing in all creation bore any resemblance to that abyssal titan fetus. Reality itself could not bear such a profane form, yet here it was; its very existence a spiteful defiance of nature's most sensible laws.

The most primeval portions of Mary's brain screamed in endless horror as she watched the apocalyptic birthing. This celestial leviathan, the last of the world-eaters, the dreadful answer to Fermi's paradox, had been incubating beneath her feet since she landed on Tantalus 13. It had watched her through SCARAB's eyes, invaded her mind in her sleep, probed her soul and seeped its own aberrant thoughts into her dreams. It had engineered the deaths of her friends, tortured Ramanathan's barely living body, and sought to imprison her for its own incomprehensible reasons. It had done all of this before it had even been *born*. Now that SCARAB had used Attila to disrupt whatever stasis field had kept it trapped in its shell for so many millennia, it was finally emerging from its endless gestation, ready to destroy and consume the galaxy she knew. This creature was a living Armageddon; she knew it as instinctively as she knew her need to breathe. Every cell in her body screamed that the thing she saw should not, *must not* be.

Black tendrils of madness coiled around the foundations of Mary's brain, and she forced herself to look away from the roiling cataclysm of the abomination's emergence. She turned her gaze to the pylon she clung to, and felt a surge of primal revulsion as she realized that, though she was untold miles away from the creature, she was also currently touching it. Those roots, or tentacles, or God knew whatever else they might be, they sprawled from the core of this creature to the very surface of the Tantalus shell. The impossible scale of the thing alone was almost enough to tip her over the edge of madness.

Her eyes traveled against her will down the colossal pillar of tendrils, and she saw a titanic ripple waving up several miles beneath her. It dawned on her that the extreme distance between her and the emerging Hatchling meant the first few vibrations of its earliest movements had yet to work their way up the column to her position. When they reached her, it would be with all the force of the deadliest tsunami wave ever felt. She had to get off.

She tore her gaze from the event below and searched the underside of the Tantalus shell above. After a few seconds of searching, she was barely able to make out the tiny circular hole at the base of Attila's drill shaft. Calculating her trajectory as well as she could in her still-swimming head, Mary pushed away from the pillar, willfully surrendering herself once again to the empty void. She cast a single glance behind her and watched as the massive pillar thrummed with the first of several tidal waves of vibration, rippling and rolling like a grotesquely magnified guitar string.

She checked her gauges to see how her air was doing, forgetting until she looked that they'd blown out. She shook her head and looked away. Right now, she couldn't afford to think about that. She either had enough air to do what she had to, or she didn't. Worrying wouldn't give her more.

As she finally neared the opening of the drill shaft, she found three cables from the Attila harness dangling through it. She missed the first one she reached for, but caught the second, clutching it tightly as her momentum threatened to pull her away from it again.

Mary gripped the cables with her legs, and searched the contents of her satchel. She pulled out and discarded a small flashlight, electric screwdriver, and miniaturized adjustable wrench, allowing them to drift away into oblivion. At last, she recovered what she'd been looking for: a spool of lightweight, high-tensile cord.

As quickly yet carefully as she could, Mary securely fastened the rope to her belt, tying a sturdy climber's hitch to the dangling cable, using her knife to cut the excess. She gave the knot a quick test pull, took a moment to steady her breathing, and pulled herself up the cable.

A yellow haze of energy stretched across the mouth of the drill shaft. It seemed like another semipermeable membrane like the one covering the black hole in the statue room, probably designed to prevent Tantalus's atmosphere from venting out its inner side into the void beyond. As she passed through it, she suddenly felt the disorienting and disturbing sensation of her full weight instantaneously returning to her in Tantalus's artificial gravity field. She clung tightly to the rope for a moment, shutting her eyes and breathing steadily to overcome the vertigo, which threatened to mingle with the looming cosmic madness that had crept into her mind the second she glimpsed the Hatchling. She calmed herself as best she could, then slowly cinched herself up the cord, praying she could make the mile-high climb before running out of air or upper body strength, and forcing herself not to watch the cataclysmic birth occurring below.

SIXTY-FIVE

ALMOST THERE . . . almost . . . just a little more . . .

The pain in Mary's arms was excruciating. They felt like they might literally come out of their sockets. Encouraged though she was when she could finally see the wreckage of Attila lodged in the drill shaft above her, she still felt certain her arms would give out before she reached it. She was tempted to stop right there, just for a few minutes to catch her breath and let her muscles stop aching.

Then, she heard the soft hiss of her suit's oxygenation system fade away. Her air tanks were empty. She had enough free oxygen in her suit to last two, perhaps three more minutes at the most.

Come on, Mary. You beat SCARAB's drones. You handled the Dawson. You survived a five-mile fall into open space. You are not going to let sore arms and shortness of breath beat you now.

She pressed on.

At last, she reached Attila's wreckage, pulling herself onto one of its mangled struts with the absolute last of her arm strength. She flopped onto her stomach like a dying fish, wheezing heavily as she attempted to cycle air into her lungs that no longer carried any oxygen. She clambered along the fallen bulk of Attila, ignoring the heat that still radiated off much of its surface as she worked her way along its barrel toward the tunnel and rail that lay beyond.

She stumbled onto the smooth, flat surface of the rail. Black flecks whirled in her peripheral vision as she crawled on hands and knees toward the parked vehicle she had dubbed *Rook's First Thought*. She was at the very edge of consciousness by the time she reached it, fumbling desperately for the spare tank of air in the back, and finally hooking it up to her suit's airline.

Instantly, her suit began to reoxygenate itself, and she finally did allow herself a few seconds of rest, falling gracelessly to her back as she sucked oxygen into her lungs. She could barely lift her arms, and even with the rush of breathable air, she felt certain she would pass out any second.

As she lay motionless, breathing deeply, she wondered what to do next. The winch that had led to the surface previously now lay in a tangled mess on top of Attila. It had been her only real hope of getting out. She had a brief thought of using Attila to cut a new tunnel at a diagonal angle, but even if she could move the several-dozen-ton thing into position, and even if it still worked, she wouldn't have enough time to cut through the several miles of material and climb through it before that creature below broke free of Tantalus's shell like it had its own.

She briefly thought of calling SCARAB for help, taking it up on its offer to keep her alive until her provisions ran out, but that option was more distasteful than death at this point. Perhaps death was the best she could hope for.

Mary shut her eyes and shook her head free of those thoughts. "No. No more running," she whispered to herself.

The void, Ramanathan had said. *It fears the void.* A vague phrase, but Mary was clear on its meaning. She'd sensed it in her last dream, a dream that she now realized wasn't even a dream, but some kind of psychic backwash. As it had invaded her mind in her sleep, she had glimpsed some of its own thoughts, memories . . . fears. How a creature not yet born could have any of those was a mystery, but she knew them for what they were, on a purely instinctual level. Somehow, it knew about Tantalus's inner workings, its functions, the motivations of its creators.

Somehow, it knew about the dark hole that had killed Becky, and for some reason, it *feared* it. Hertz had called that hole a universal energy converter, some kind of alien ignition key that just needed to be fed enough power to activate the machinery inside the Tantalus shell. Whatever that machinery did, the Hatchling saw it as a threat.

Mary hauled herself to her feet one more time and detached her spent air tank, affixing the fresh one in place. She staggered into the driver's seat and turned the car around, then slammed down the accelerator, careening down the tunnel at full speed.

SIXTY-SIX

AS MARY emerged from the end of the placard-filled tunnel, her curiosity to see what was going on beneath her began to get the better of her. She dared not stop the car to get out and peer directly over the edge as she'd done before, but she did bring the vehicle as close to the edge of the rail as her nerve would allow, slowing down just a little and straining to see what she could over the edge.

She couldn't see with any significant detail what was happening now. Dust and chunks of debris from the pulverized eggshell had spread by now until they choked out most of the light. Amorphous shapes drifted through the murk, appendages of uncertain nature and function. Some of the "pillars" had detached themselves from the inner surface of the Tantalus shell and stretched their waving, lightning-filled tendrils in the direction of the open portion of the shell. Toward her . . .

She gunned the engine once more and took the car all the way into Grand Central Station, parking it on the elevator disk and allowing it to bring her into the vaulted chamber above. As the disk reached its destination, a tremor struck so heavily it sent her and the car a full foot into the air. *It's trying to break through now . . .*

Mary clambered out of the car and stumbled toward the titanic staircase, beginning the torturous task of mounting each oversized step. Another sharp impact sent her airborne again, accompanied by a rumbling sound of tearing metal deep below. Once again, fear-fueled adrenaline pumped her exhausted muscles into overdrive, and she climbed the remaining stairs on all fours at a near gallop.

At last, she staggered to her feet at the top of the staircase, nearly falling right back down it as another resonant tremor rocked the floor beneath her. Struggling to keep her exhausted legs under her, Mary set her eyes on that horrid black pit in the far wall and stumbled toward it. Then, to her heart's agonized despair, a form emerged from behind one of the spider-walrus statues.

It was SCARAB's last drone.

SIXTY-SEVEN

THE MACHINE charged her at full speed, and in her weakened state, Mary didn't have the slightest chance to evade it. The drone struck her full on, sending her flying backwards, stumbling back down the top two steps. As she lay there crumpled in pain, the drone wheeled to the top of the staircase and loomed over her. Then, SCARAB screamed.

"YOU WILL NOT HARM THE CHILD!" SCARAB shrieked. There was no doubt about it. Mary was not projecting an emotion onto the machine, it was not merely amplifying its voice. SCARAB screamed, with unmistakable fury. The carefully modulated veneer of gentility its voice had always carried had absolutely shattered. The grinding sound SCARAB used to make each time it lied now seeped into each word, layering every syllable with a surge of electronic indignation.

The panic, the desperation in SCARAB's voice was not entirely its own. Before, the Hatchling had lent SCARAB its own mind power to enhance its intellect. Now, it was lending its emotions as well.

Mary backed away as the drone swiveled its eight arms forward and downward to pull itself onto the lower step. *Its treads . . . It can't handle the stairs . . .*

As the drone clumsily pulled itself the rest of the way down the stair and began descending the next one, Mary clawed her way back to her feet and vaulted the last two steps once more. Not sparing a second to look over her shoulder to see how the drone managed, she stumbled toward the hole once again, passing the first row of statues.

"YOU WILL NOT HARM THE CHILD!" SCARAB screamed once more, its voice a grinding plurality of demented electronic fury as all the cacophonous emotions of a planet-sized newborn raged through its artificial mind. The whirring of the drone's treads behind her signaled it had climbed back up the steps and was charging her again. Mary dove between the legs of the giant jellyshroom statue, and SCARAB slammed into its rigid, low-hanging tentacles, clawing at her with all eight arms in desperate fury.

"It doesn't belong in this universe, SCARAB!" she shouted. "If it gets free, it'll destroy Earth and everything else!"

"THE UNIVERSE IS ITS BIRTHRIGHT!" SCARAB screeched with fanatical conviction. "THE CHILD IS PERFECTION! THE CHILD IS LIFE! YOU WILL NOT HARM THE CHILD!"

SCARAB used its metal shearing claw to slice off the arm bearing its reciprocating saw at the shoulder joint, then grabbed the severed end with its heavy manipulator claw. It swung its severed arm like a saw-tipped club, desperate to reach Mary where she hid.

She was no longer safe. SCARAB would pursue her the second she left her cover, but with its crudely increased reach, it would soon skewer her on the tip of the blade.

Another thunderous tremor knocked both Mary and SCARAB off the floor once again, but this time she had been waiting for it. The instant her feet hit the ground, Mary bolted from cover, taking advantage of SCARAB's momentary instability. It didn't last, as SCARAB immediately discarded the severed arm and swiveled its treads to pursue her.

Mary made it to the wall a fraction of a second before SCARAB got there. She knew what she had to do to kill the Hatchling, but she equally knew SCARAB would not give her the time to do it, and as weakened as she was, she had no chance in a fight with the frenzied machine. She had exactly one opportunity to defeat SCARAB once and for all, and very little reason to believe it would work.

The drone barreled toward her, its seven remaining arms flailing and shuddering with psychotic mechanical rage. "I PERCEIVE A NEED!" it shrieked, its words so filled with electrical distortion she could barely understand them. It leveled its lit plasma torch at her skull, flaring it wildly.

Mary summoned every last ounce of her strength into a desperate dive away from SCARAB at the last possible second. SCARAB came so close, she felt a blast of heat as the torch carved a gash in the side of her helmet. She tumbled away, turning back to watch it slam into the wall so hard it rocked forward off its own treads. Its head and three of its arms plunged into the black abyss in the wall.

A flash of lightning coursed through the walls, illuminating brilliant shifting shapes behind the solid, textured surface. A deep rumble of machinery slowly wound up, then gradually wound back down again. SCARAB's drone spasmed sharply once, rocking back on its treads, its head facing Mary with malevolence smoldering in its four black eyes. Then, a cloudy haze of white ice crystals coalesced over its entire surface, coating SCARAB's shiny platinum finish in a frosty white. Another mighty seismic impact struck, sending Mary and the frozen SCARAB airborne. As the drone landed, the top half of its body shattered into a dozen pieces, scattering across the floor.

Mary allowed a grin of triumphant satisfaction to spread across her trembling lips.

"Did you perceive that?"

SIXTY-EIGHT

MARY'S ADRENALINE rush depleted quickly. When the next ground-jostling tremor hit, it knocked Mary's feet from under her and sent her sprawling on the floor. With a groan of effort, pain, and exhaustion, she tried pushing herself to her feet, but her arms gave out beneath her and she collapsed back to the ground.

"It is only a baby, Mary." SCARAB's voice had taken on a new emotional characteristic: sorrow. The underlying electronic spooling noise no longer distorted its words. It was just SCARAB now. Suddenly, the AI sounded very small, very helpless. It had lost, and it knew it.

Mary stumbled to her feet, steadying herself against the wall. She reached into her satchel and removed the heavy Pompeii Coconut that Rook had given her. The code was still active on its input screen; it merely awaited activation.

"Please, Mary . . . it is only a baby." SCARAB's voice was pleading now, with a mournful desperation Mary's heart knew all too well. "It is alone in all the universe. It only wants to live. Please . . . give it a chance."

Mary stared blankly into the void of the hole in the wall. She felt it again . . . that morbid call, that seductive oblivion. Even now, it would be so easy to give up . . .

She looked down at the nuke in her hand, then back at the hole.

"Everything dies, SCARAB," Mary whispered, tears trickling down her face. "The universe goes on."

Mary reached at the side of her helmet and ripped off her comm receiver, throwing it to the ground. She then set the timer on the nuke for its lowest setting of five minutes, activated it, and tossed it into the open hole.

Her task was done. Whatever the machinery connected to that hole did, in five minutes, it was going to have a megaton and a half of energy to do it. Hopefully, it would wipe both the creature and SCARAB out of existence forever. She would have preferred not to go with them, but at this point, she'd run out of moves. All that was left was to find the best seat for the end of the world.

SIXTY-NINE

MARY EASED herself down the treacherous staircase, step by step. It felt good to move slowly for a change. She was free at last. No one depended on her for anything, she had no responsibilities to uphold. Even death was no longer a concern to her at this point. It would come, and come soon. She knew this, and somehow the certainty of death was more reassuring than the possibility of life. She was so tired of fighting, so tired of surviving.

She had saved humanity, or at least done as much to save humanity as anyone could have in her position. She'd likely saved hundreds, thousands, perhaps millions of other civilizations humankind would never even know of. This creature, this last of the world-eaters, would never inherit that "birthright" SCARAB had raved about. It would die here, before it could properly be born.

Die before it could be born . . .

"Emily, my love," Mary whispered as she continued working her way down the vast stairway. "I'm coming to meet you soon."

For a flickering moment, she felt a tinge of embarrassment for speaking those personal thoughts out loud. Only for a moment, though. She almost laughed at the absurdity of that sheepish thought; here she was, the only living human for millions of miles, in the middle of an apocalyptic event, moments away from her own death, and there was still a part of her that was afraid to give voice to her feelings.

A thundering crash knocked Mary off her feet and sent her tumbling down the next few steps. Groaning with a hundred different pains, Mary pulled herself back to her feet. Not yet. She wouldn't give up here. She was going to return to that rail. She would watch the end.

"I wish we could have met in life, baby," Mary spoke softly as she continued to ease her way down the stairs. "I had such big plans for our family. We would have had such a life together . . . you, your father, and I."

Suddenly, the walls flashed brilliantly around her. The floor vibrated as the machines rumbled to life once more. This time, the flaring lights and mechanical noises remained constant, showing no signs of fading away. The nuke had detonated, and its power had been fully absorbed by the mechanisms of Tantalus.

Mary smiled faintly. It had worked. Whatever would happen was happening now.

"It wasn't fair that you never got the chance to live. It wasn't fair that we never got to meet, or live together as the family we should have been. But, my darling girl . . . I have turned my love for you into something that's been killing me . . ."

At last, she reached the bottom of the staircase, and she limped slowly to the car. She stepped in and started the engine.

"Maybe it's too late now, but . . . I'm letting go, Emily. I love you. I can't forget you. But it's time to let go."

Mary smoothly drove onto the elevator disk, waiting for it to take her down to Grand Central Station once more, so she could bear witness to whatever cataclysm was about to unfold.

But it did not descend.

The entire vaulted chamber began to rise, quickly leaving the four computer alcoves and the monumental stairway behind. Warm lights pulsed upward as the chamber rose through the smooth-walled shaft around it.

Mary sat at the wheel, watching in silent awe as the chamber rose mile after mile. After several minutes of uninterrupted ascent, a deep shuddering shook the platform, accompanied by the sound of thousands of tons of cascading dirt and stone. At last, the chamber ceased its motion, and the vaulted ceiling split above her, peeling away like a great five-petaled flower, showing the clear starfield of a Tantalan night, gently colored by a green aurora.

The walls folded until they rested on the ground on five sides. A light but frigid breeze sent a flurry of snowflakes across the hood of Mary's vehicle. She was sitting atop Tantalus's south pole.

The experience was so beautiful, so spiritual, so surreal, it took a few minutes for Mary to appreciate what it really meant. She was out. She was on Tantalus's surface. Once again, she had a chance.

She sat there for a moment, her hands resting on the wheel, her foot poised over the accelerator, yet frozen with indecision. Just a few moments ago, her death had been certain. Inevitable. She'd been ready for it, almost eager for it. No, she *had* been eager for it. She'd been looking for it.

Looking for an excuse . . .

It would be a challenge to get back to the ship. The Hatchling would try to stop her, and it would pull out all the stops this time. The six-month flight to Earth in an empty ship would be hell, and what waited for her there might be even worse. There was nothing but bumpy road for her ahead, no guarantees but suffering and pain. No promise of anything good at the other end of the line . . .

It's time to move on.

Mary shook her head and smiled. She revved the engine and pointed her car toward the *Diamelen*. All six tires squealed as she tore off the platform and slid across the hardpacked polar snow.

It's time to live.

SEVENTY

WHAT HAD been a twenty-mile drive along the rail five miles below proved to be significantly longer on the surface above. Still, Mary didn't care. Nothing could stop her now, not SCARAB, not the Hatchling. Nothing short of the ground opening up beneath her would keep her from her goal.

Though, that was an actual possibility . . .

She tore across the polar tundra until ice and packed snow gave way to stone and permafrost, then to the crater-pocked gray dirt she'd grown used to. The ground rumbled constantly now, and it was increasingly difficult to keep the car under her control, but through sheer iron willpower she did it. She could see the stones on the ground vibrating and hopping around from the seismic phenomenon. In the far distance, mountains crumbled and split, colossal fissures opened and widened as the surface of Tantalus 13 began to break apart. Mary didn't know if it was the Hatchling or the machines inside Tantalus doing it at this point, but either way, time was growing short.

At last, she came to the lip of the vast asteroid crater SCARAB had built its base in. Without a second thought, Mary drove off the edge, soaring into the open air above the cavernous expanse. The car slammed into the ground hard enough to snap its central wheel axle, but the shock absorbers were strong enough to save her from the effects of the impact. The car slowed only briefly as the broken axle separated into two pieces and tumbled away behind her.

Though damaged, the car continued to make good progress. However, now there was a new and wholly alien obstacle. The crater basin was infested with the Hatchling's neural tendrils. They no longer lay innocuously on the ground; now they stood on end, waving in the windless air like a savanna of electrified, transparent grass.

Mary plowed through them, feeling them whip against the undercarriage of the car. They stretched out toward her as she drove, zapping the vehicle's hull, groping for purchase. She could feel them tangling in the remaining axles below. Still, she dared not stop. Slowed only as much as the tendrils forced her to, she pressed onward.

At last, the familiar shape of SCARAB's base appeared, and, more importantly, the *Diamelen*, still sitting lopsided on a crippled landing strut. The closer she came to the ship, the bigger and stronger the tendrils grew, and soon they had reduced her speed to a lurching crawl. At last, just a few yards away from the ship, the tendrils immobilized her car.

"Not now!" she hissed. "No way do you stop me now!"

Mary reached into the back seat, pulled out a plasma torch, and ignited it, setting its arc to its full foot-long maximum reach. She mercilessly carved into the writhing tendrils, ignoring their attempts to shock through her suit. As she severed them, the cauterized stumps went dim and shriveled away back underground. She grabbed a second plasma torch and jumped out of the car, burning a path through the tendrils with both hands.

A dust storm grew on the horizon beyond the crater's lip as Mary scorched her way toward the *Diamelen*. In between glances at the impeding tendrils surrounding her, Mary saw a crack the size of a fault line rapidly descend the far crater wall, splitting the basin in half. The previously seamless sheet of exposed platinum at the center of the crater split neatly in two. The ground shook constantly beneath her feet, making it even harder for her to keep her footing amid the ensnaring tendrils, and the horizon itself began to warp and flex unnaturally.

She pressed on through the last of the Hatchling's vile appendages, giving the nearest ones one last spiteful singe before she threw the torches aside and leapt into the *Diamelen*'s still-open boarding ramp, sealing it behind her. She ran up the precariously slanted floor to the cockpit, rushed through the preflight checklist of only the most critical systems, and fired up the engines. It took a few moments for them to activate from a cold start, but she breathed a sigh of relief when they ran without a hitch. Mary opened up the throttle, firing the engines for takeoff.

For a few horrifying seconds, the ship remained stationary. The tendrils had wound themselves around the landing gear, and were attempting to anchor the *Diamelen* in place. Mary jostled the navigational thrusters rapidly from side to side, rocking the ship and crunching the tendrils beneath it. At last, they broke free with a satisfying ripping sound, and the *Diamelen* blasted jerkily into the sky.

She wasn't sure if the electric field that had nearly downed the *Diamelen* when they had landed would still be there. It might be gone now, or it might be even stronger. She didn't care. She activated the mass de-simulator to slip smoothly past it and allowed herself a howl of triumph as the vibrations in the hull and the sounds of the wind outside disappeared as the *Diamelen* sheathed itself once again in a null-mass field, separating it entirely from the chaos of the unraveling world behind her. The ship swiftly gained altitude, leaving the wretched false planet of Tantalus 13 forever.

SEVENTY-ONE

AS THE comforting blackness of space filled the cockpit canopy, Mary finally felt courageous enough to look back. She opened one of her console's display screens to show the rear camera's view.

Tantalus 13 no longer resembled a planet even from orbit. The surface of the world had split in half along the equator, and huge radial cracks had opened along its longitudinal lines. Continent-sized panels of Tantalus separated outward, breaking into segments, showing brief glimpses of the gargantuan creature stirring within. Then, with glacial speed, the segments reconfigured themselves, reorienting and closing back inward again. Like many-fingered hands on two hemispheric fists, Tantalus squeezed inward. Soon, the creature was once again obscured by the rapidly imploding shell of Tantalus. Tantalus squeezed tighter and tighter, compacting into an ever smaller world. The Hatchling was being crushed alive.

Mary shut the camera off. As much as she'd hated that creature, and as much as she'd dreaded what it could have become, something about its fate unexpectedly saddened her. It had to die, there was no question of that. If it hadn't, humankind would have fallen to it swiftly, followed eventually by any other living races that might be out there beyond explored space. The creature had been a threat to the very concept of civilization. But had it really been evil? It couldn't help being what it was, even if it was a devourer of worlds.

But then, it had driven SCARAB insane. It had killed off her crew one by one. It had forced itself on her mind. No, this thing had had to die. She would lose no sleep over that.

There was no shortage of things over which she would lose sleep, though. She already missed her crew. Flying the *Diamelen* didn't seem right without Gorrister breathing down her neck quoting protocols, or Rook and Yancy goofing off in the hab-mod. These next six months would be the loneliest time of her life.

Mary completed a full systems check. The landing gear had been damaged badly, and the atmospheric engines had been overstrained, but there was no damage worse than that. If she could keep going after the damage she'd taken, the *Diamelen* could, too.

"Steady, girl," she whispered, caressing the console lovingly. "Remember who really owns these stars."

She gently brought the superluminal drive online, and the ship began building up to light-speed travel. "The universe is our birthright."

End

BONUS PREVIEW:
PROTEUS

EVAN GRAHAM

ONE

IN THE purgatorial slumber of cold stasis, Jacob Sicarius dreamed of war.

He shouldn't have. His brain was supposed to experience virtually no activity in stasis. Blood did not flow through his veins. His nerves did not signal each other. Until revived from stasis, his inert state was indistinguishable from death. And yet, he dreamed. Or remembered.

Flames licked out the windows of a half-submerged Atlantic City high-rise as he and the other Razorbacks lobbed incendiary grenades at the pirates holed up within. Smoke billowed and debris flew as an armor-piercing shell blew apart a Coalition D-23 Pangolin armored transport on Samrat. Blood flecked his face as the butt of his assault rifle concaved an Aftothysian terrorist's face on Showalter.

The barrage of flashbacks ripped through his mind with merciless intensity. Conflict after conflict from every tour of duty erupted from the depths of his subconscious. Earth, Mars, Samrat, Showalter, Buyan . . . what felt like a hundred other worlds and a thousand other battles joined the infernal procession in his brain's war zone. Fire, smoke, and blood, fire, smoke, and blood; Jacob's ravaged psyche tumbled without relent through a burning, shrieking, rending conflagration.

It wasn't until he'd succumbed to the hope that immanent madness would grant him a reprieve from his tormented senses that the veil began to lift. The smoke from his crashed troop transport on Buyan obscured the pale red sky, then the jagged, irradiated desert rocks. Soon, smoke concealed everything, leaving him once again in darkness. The heat of the inferno dropped away, leaving him deathly cold. The explosions and screams of dying soldiers melted into oblivion, leaving him with no sound but the distant wail of a Klaxon.

Finally, Jacob opened his eyes.

He was still in his stasis pod on the *Somnambule*. No lights were on in the cramped cylinder, and the hallway outside the transparent window was dim as well, lit only by a strobing yellow warning light.

Wrong . . . something's gone wrong.

Jacob attempted to move, but succeeded only in slumping forward, banging his head against the window, and finding himself too weak to lift it again. His muscles felt like gelatin beneath his skin, refusing to respond to the commands of his fevered brain. The impact of his head against the window sounded like it should have hurt, but it didn't. He felt nothing at all.

It shouldn't be like this . . . I shouldn't be awake . . .

Once again, he tried to move, to free himself from his technological sarcophagus. His bones may as well have been lead plated. Fortunately, not all of his limbs bore the limitations of bone and muscle.

As if a separate living entity, Jacob's prosthetic left forearm probed the inside of the chamber for the emergency latch. Its black metal fingers moved deftly about the pod with the elegance of an orb weaver, even as the rest of the limb from elbow to shoulder hung with a cadaver's limpness. Finally, his talon-tipped metal digits found the mechanism and pulled.

The pod's cover popped open, folding outward like a newly opened parcel. Warm, metallic-smelling air washed over Jacob's clammy body, and for the first time he could smell himself. He had a sickly, fetid odor, something akin to gangrene. His entire body smelled like a limb that would need to be amputated.

Jacob barely had time to register the sensation before he began sliding forward out of the pod. It was still mounted with the other stasis pods in the gallery, locked against the wall at an eighty-degree angle to the floor. That was *definitely* wrong. There were designated revivification centers on the ship that held the necessary equipment for bringing people out of stasis.

Jacob tried to stop himself but couldn't support his own weight. He slumped forward and watched helplessly as the floor raced toward his face. He crumpled in a heap at the foot of his stasis pod.

Once again, it seemed like the fall should have been painful, but once again he felt nothing. He lay in a pile where he landed, face helplessly pressed against the floor grating. He watched as his human hand twitched and curled weakly, failing to comply to the simplest of commands from his nervous system. A slimy film of condensation and dead cells coated his pale skin.

I'm dying . . . I must be . . .

The thought sickened him. It would have enraged him if he'd had the energy for anger. He had lived his life on the battlefield, defending big ideals and opposing worthy threats. He had survived countless bloodbaths through perseverance, skill, and luck. For him to die here, alone, naked, lying in a crumpled pile unable to move a muscle, was an insult above any other.

Get up.

Jacob's mechanical hand, the only part of him that seemed functional at the moment, clutched the floor grating with the scritching sound of metal against metal. The arm tried to push Jacob off the ground, bracing his elbow against his side and pushing down against the floor. The effort only succeeded in rolling him onto his back. He stared blankly at the ducts and tubing of the ceiling, flickering yellow from the warning lights that still throbbed on in the distance.

Jacob lifted his hand and passed it in front of his face, watching the frost-covered metal fingers curl into a fist. He slammed the robotic appendage against the side of his open stasis pod three times and attempted to call out for help. The only sound that escaped his throat was a faint, hollow-sounding wheeze. He noticed for the first time that there was a subtle but distinct ratcheting sensation in his chest that accompanied each inhalation and exhalation. He wasn't even breathing on his own: his implants were doing it for him.

Get up.

Jacob slammed the pod door, clutching the open doorframe tightly and attempted to pull himself upward. It was an awkward gesture, as he had no strength at all in his shoulder and only limited strength at his elbow. His fingers slowly crept up the side of the doorframe, carrying the dead weight of his body with them as they slowly brought him to his knees.

Get up.

His hand now clutched the top of the pod's doorframe and could climb no farther. He attempted once again to move his feeble muscles, managing only a slight arching of his back and a faint flexing of his thigh. It was barely enough.

Jacob's right leg unfolded from beneath him, and more frost-covered black metal came into his view. Hooklike talons unsheathed from his two-toed boot-like prosthesis and anchored firmly into the grate of the floor. The universal joint that replaced his knee and anchored his prosthesis to the reinforced bone of his femur slowly raised him higher. As soon as he was elevated enough, he dragged his other leg forward, and the claws of that artificial foot anchored him to the floor as well.

With agonizing slowness, Jacob's limp body rose. Supported only by the strength of the mechanisms in his robotic forearm and lower legs, his body hung in a withered stoop. Finally, after a torturous eternity, Jacob managed to hold steady in a position that could almost be considered standing.

Get help.

Walking was out of the question. Perhaps he could crawl along the walls, staggering from one handgrip to another as his mechanical hand lunged from stasis pod to stasis pod. But to what end? The *Somnambule* was a colossal starship with hundreds of levels. At the rate he was moving, it could take him days to encounter a member of the crew.

Unless some were already nearby . . .

Jacob twisted his grip so that his limply hanging head could get a better view at the warning lights. *Yellow . . . code yellow . . . engineering emergency . . . mechanical failure.* That much was self-evident by the fact that he was awake at all. Of course a code yellow would go off if a colonist's pod failed. Especially his pod. An engineering team should be on the way, as well as a medical team.

So where were they? How long had it been since his pod failed? The frost had already melted off his prosthetics and the mucus-like film on his skin was drying. It must have been several minutes already. Someone should have arrived by now. Something else was wrong . . .

Jacob's vision swirled and darkened. He shut his eyes tightly to try to refocus. The distant throbbing of the Klaxon grew clearer for a moment, and he realized something he hadn't picked up before.

Not the alarm for code yellow . . . that's the alarm for code black.

The lights signaled an engineering emergency, but the Klaxons signaled an attack.

A new sound joined the wail of the alarm: gunfire. Three short staccato bursts echoed from some hallway adjacent to his pod bay, answered by two more bursts not far off.

Combatants. At least three . . . four. Rivali V-780 SMGs, modified muzzle-brakes. Low-penetration hardstopper rounds.

Every instinct in Jacob's body felt a need to answer that call, in the same way that a dog feels the instinctual need to answer a howl. Ghost images tracked into his vision; phantom targeting reticules, range markers, and environmental prompts. His CE 1500 *Erymanthos* combat implant was fully alert now, pumping tactical information directly into his occipital lobe and getting ready for a fight.

For the first time since Jacob left active duty, Proteus was awake.

He wanted a gun. He wanted armor. He wanted a knife, grenades, a rocket launcher, anything. What he had was a 90 percent nonfunctional body that would be dead in the next few minutes whether it took a bullet or not.

Get. Help.

Jacob dragged himself forward, pulling his body from one stasis pod to another, his lolling head offering him an occasional glimpse at the serene faces of the colonists contained inside each one.

Another short barrage of gunfire, accompanied by indiscernible shouting this time.

Seven combatants . . . two on five. One down; kill shot. Two on four. One female, three males on defending side . . .

Lunging for another pod, Jacob failed to get enough forward momentum and his hand fell short of its intended handhold, sending him to his knees. A faint groan of frustration escaped his lips as he slowly pulled himself back up and continued forward.

Another one down; kill shot. Two on three . . .

At last, as he neared an apparent intersection between stasis blocks, three figures stormed around the corner toward him, glancing backwards at unseen attackers. His implants immediately locked onto them, evaluating them for every possible piece of relevant data. As predicted, they were two men and one woman. One man appeared to be in his late twenties, another in his mid-thirties. Both were physically fit, of average height and weight, but lacking the toned musculature typically expected in a career soldier. The woman, or perhaps "girl" was a more appropriate term, couldn't be any older than her late teens, and was more likely only fifteen or sixteen. She was also physically fit, but very slight of build. Although none of these people seemed suited for combat, they all wore the standard security officer's uniform, and were all armed.

The three individuals halted in their tracks as soon as they set eyes on Jacob, looks of shock on their faces. The girl shouted something to the older man that Jacob couldn't quite make out, and he moved to a defensive position at the corner of the wall, blindly firing his weapon in the direction they'd come from.

Jacob slipped and once more fell to his knees. The girl quickly holstered her weapon and rushed to Jacob, placing her hand on his useless biological arm. His combat instincts warned him of danger, and he thought for a second about seizing her by the neck and ripping out her throat with his mechanical hand. Helpless though he might otherwise be, that was something he knew he could do. However, he didn't have enough combat data. He knew two groups of combatants were in a shoot-out with each other, but had no information about the nature of the conflict.

Jacob scanned the girl's face in more thorough detail. Brown eyes, brown hair, mixed Hispanic features. Softness of the skin and lack of age-related blemishes confirmed a mid-teens age range. *Dimples . . . a soldier with dimples, of all things . . .*

He didn't know her: Proteus cross-referenced her image with every known member of the *Somnambule*'s crew, and there was no plausible match. He didn't have an ID for either of the other crewmen, either, which suggested he must have spent enough time in stasis for at least one new generation to be born among the crew.

The girl began speaking to him softly but urgently, scanning him with a piece of medical equipment from a satchel at her side. For some reason, Jacob couldn't quite parse her words. Certain sounds and cadences were clearly standard Coalition English, but they seemed to run over each other in indiscernible ways, as if he were suffering from some kind of auditory dyslexia.

The younger man shouted something at the girl, who snapped urgently back at him. The older man, peeking around the corner for another volley of suppressing fire, took a head shot directly between his eyes and slumped to the deck.

Kill shot . . . two on two.

The girl gave an insistent command, and the remaining man hurried to her side. The two of them lifted Jacob to his feet, and he was once again struck with the distressing realization that although he should be able to feel them touching his skin, he could not.

The male security officer managed to sling Jacob over his shoulders in a fireman's carry, and they began to rush down the corridor in the direction Jacob had come from. His head lolled aimlessly, and his vision blurred and darkened again.

Too slow . . . no cover . . . shouldn't have stopped for me . . . be dead in seconds . . .

Jacob's vision tunneled as his targeting images distorted and drifted aimlessly in his failing optic centers. The girl was speaking again, and although he could almost make out the words "be alright," it sounded like they came from a hundred yards away, ten feet under water. He could feel his consciousness fading as his eyelids grew heavy and his breathing shallow.

Through the fevered haze, he watched two indiscernible figures charge around the corner, weapons raised and ready to fire.

Jacob's mechanical arm darted to his rescuer's holstered weapon, seized it, spun it around in his hand, leveled it at the two assailants, and fired two short spurts. The men stopped in place, dropped their firearms, and fell to the deck with pieces of their heads missing.

Jacob dropped the gun and let his prosthetic arm hang limp with the rest of him. He managed a weak smile as his eyes rolled back in his head, everything around him fading into silent blackness.

Kill shot . . .

ACKNOWLEDGEMENTS

I would like to give thanks to my loving and supportive family: Mom, Dad, Bethany and Jonathan, David, Felicity, and Ira. You all give my life a wonderful depth of meaning and warmth, and without you at the foundations of my world, I would be forever adrift. I love you all very much.

I must also offer the utmost gratitude to the hundreds of people who supported me during my grueling preorder campaign. You backed this wild project of mine on nothing but a distant promise, and all your patience, camaraderie, encouragement, and belief in me changed my life forever. Without you, this would still be nothing but an ambitious dream, hidden away forever in obscurity.

Lastly, I must single out the inimitable Dr. Noelle Bowles, who dragged this story kicking and screaming out of my head and forced it to exist on the page. Without your teaching and guidance, I never would have written a page of this, so I'm blaming you if nobody likes it.

GRAND PATRONS

INKSHARES